HEART'S
A NOVEL
JOURNEY

HEART'S

A NOVEL

JOURNEY

Kristen McKendry

Covenant Communications, Inc.

Cover image © Covenant Communications, Inc.

Cover design copyright © 2015 by Covenant Communications, Inc.

Published by Covenant Communications, Inc.
American Fork, Utah

Printed in the United States of America
First Printing: September 2015

21 20 19 18 17 16 15   10 9 8 7 6 5 4 3 2 1

ISBN 978-1-68047-126-7

Gold rushes in general attract some fascinating and intriguing people who each deserve books of their own. I would like to dedicate this story to all those with a pioneering spirit, who dare to imagine that life can be different and reach beyond themselves to achieve it.

Author's Note

When you choose to set a story amid actual historical events, it's a difficult line to walk between remaining true to fact and allowing creative freedom. I find it easier to avoid the whole debate by writing whatever I want and then gently reminding my readers that this is a work of fiction. Any real names of people or places in this story are used fictitiously, and most place names have been changed to suit my purposes. I hope the real Mr. McMicking doesn't mind that I hijacked his company. It was convenient at the time. Mrs. Catherine Schubert was the only woman to join the actual McMicking Overlander Company that left Fort Garry in 1862.

Rupert's Land is the name given to the large drainage basin of the Hudson Bay, comprising a great deal of what later became Canada. Eventually the part of it that encompassed the Red River Valley was renamed Manitoba. British Columbia joined the Canadian Confederation in 1871, but the area now called Alberta, where much of this story takes place, did not join until 1905.

During the American Civil War, nationality was not a barrier, and many men from both Canada and the States either went to join or fled from the turmoil, flowing in both directions across the border. That part of the book is true. After the war was over, others went looking for respite or new adventure in the wilderness of the northwest.

I have tried to use the terminology of the times when referring to the Native people of North America.

Chapter One

1862

"Doesn't like the rocking motion, does he?"

Rachel turned from the window. The elderly woman on the wooden seat opposite her was smiling. She had a face like a friendly pudding, and her clothes were cut with an eye more toward comfort than fashion. Her hat was tied tightly to her head with a big bow under her chin, like a Christmas package, to keep the wind from blowing it off.

Rachel stroked Geordie reassuringly. His claws were digging through her skirt into her thighs.

"I'm afraid not. He isn't fond of boats," Rachel told the woman. Nor had the cat been thrilled with the coach or the train before that.

"What kind is he?" the woman asked.

"I'm not sure. A little of everything, I think." Rachel smoothed Geordie's long gray fur. His claws continued to puncture her leg.

"Very finicky, cats. May I? He seems to be shredding your dress." The woman leaned across the narrow aisle and scooped the heavy cat into her arms. She made kissy noises into his flat face, and Geordie blinked at her a moment, then settled into the woman's lap with a docile stretch.

Disbelieving, Rachel shook her head, brushed the cat hair from her skirt, and stretched her arms. "Thank you," she told the woman. "You have no idea how heavy he can be. But he doesn't like to ride in his basket. I've had to carry him most of the way."

"How far have you come then, child?"

"From Toronto, in Upper Canada."

The woman's eyes widened in astonishment. "All by yourself? So far?"

"Oh, yes." It was easier to be casual about it now that the nightmarish weeks of travel were behind her. Never before had Rachel lived in such close, smelly, dusty quarters with total strangers, and she had feared constantly that someone would steal her trunk or that Geordie would run off or fall overboard. She had come by rail, steamer, and coach, and now she was on a steamer again. But they were nearly to Fort Garry in Rupert's Land, and she was feeling pleased with herself for having traveled this far. She had never journeyed on her own before, but she had read extensively about the adventures of the men of the Hudson Bay Company, which controlled Rupert's Land, and was looking forward to seeing the Red River Valley for herself.

"I'm Agnes Willoughby," the woman said as she stroked the cat. "My husband and I are on our way to see our first grandchild."

"That's exciting for you."

"My husband and I travel quite often," Mrs. Willoughby went on cheerfully. "He sells European imports. It's stay at home by myself, or go with him. I prefer to go with him. Not that I don't trust my Wilberforce, you understand. He's a saintly man. It's all those women out there who may have designs on him that I don't trust."

Rachel slid a glance at Mr. Willoughby, who was snoring gently on the other side of his wife, his beaky nose tilting toward his chest. With his halo of fly-away white hair, he resembled a roosting chicken. He had to be older than God.

"I understand your concerns completely," she told Mrs. Willoughby politely.

"Are you going to Fort Garry to stay with family?" The woman was mindlessly rubbing Geordie's head, making the hair stand up with static. Geordie had begun to purr like a swarm of bees.

"I'm going to the Colony of British Columbia," Rachel replied and watched Mrs. Willoughby's jaw go slack. The middle-aged couple sitting in the next row perked up and listened with undisguised interest.

"All that way? Surely not alone!"

Rachel tried not to sound smug as she answered. "Yes. Well, but I have Geordie, of course. So I'm not completely alone."

"But . . ." The elderly woman screwed up her face, trying to make sense of this. "You can't cross an entire continent by yourself, my dear. Do you have anyone joining you?"

"I'm planning to join a company of settlers heading west. I'm going to meet my father in Bellefontaine," she added. "He went prospecting there five years ago, in 1857."

"Well! I suppose there are plenty of people going out to the gold fields. But that's quite a journey for you to undertake," Mrs. Willoughby said. "I couldn't face such a thing, let me tell you. And so much to worry about! All the arrangements! Do you have a particular company in mind? Are you going to purchase a wagon and team and find a driver?"

"I suppose I'll figure that out when I come to it," Rachel said. She gave a smile that was pluckier than she felt. She'd been fairly confident about her journey as far as Fort Garry. After that, her plans turned rather vague. She knew about the gold-mad crowds heading west in a steady stream. There had been stories in the *Globe* in Toronto, with inch-tall type declaring how all a man had to do was bend over and pick up the nuggets that lay in the rivers beyond the Dunant Mountains and his fortune was secured. The gold rush had been drawing people away for several years, so no doubt there was an established road of some sort. She had no reliable map, but she had a general understanding of the series of trails and rivers one had to follow to cross the continent. She was sure she could find a group to travel with.

As to the particulars of that group, she hadn't given them much thought. She hoped to find a company of settlers that included women and children and not just a band of uncouth prospectors. But whatever the makeup of the group, it didn't matter so long as they could get her to Bellefontaine. Undoubtedly that was a large town, but surely someone there could help her locate the Happy Scot claim. That was the name her father had written in his last letter, and he had given directions of a sort too. It was on a tributary of the Henderson River called Washed-Out Creek. Rachel wasn't sure she approved of that name—it didn't sound very optimistic to her—but once she found it, she would find her father.

She pictured herself having a very happy reunion with him, and in her mind, Hamish Hamilton hadn't aged at all. He was still the same hearty, booming-voiced man who'd slipped her mints from his trouser pockets in church. The same twinkle-eyed man who'd introduced her proudly to all the factory workers on his rounds . . . and then had left her five years ago.

Mrs. Willoughby looked disapproving. "I see. Perhaps I can help you. I have a friend, Mrs. Banting, who lets out her spare room. I'll direct you to her, and no doubt she'll know whom you can contact about going west."

"That's very kind of you," Rachel said with relief. "I appreciate your assistance."

"I'm delighted if I can help." She hesitated, then leaned closer to speak in quieter tones so the couple behind her couldn't hear. Rachel leaned over too. Close up, Mrs. Willoughby smelled of camphor.

"You aren't by chance in some kind of trouble, are you, my dear? Escaping from a cruel husband or fleeing the law or something? Because if you are, I can help. My son-in-law is a very good lawyer."

Rachel laughed in spite of herself. "No, no, nothing like that, but thank you all the same for the offer," she assured the older lady. "I've just never traveled so far alone before, so I'm not sure exactly what to do. But I really am all right, thank you."

Mrs. Willoughby's pudgy face relaxed, and she returned to petting the cat with a practiced hand. "All right, then. I didn't want to pry, but you understand I had to ask."

"Of course. And it was very nice of you."

"Mind, don't let yourself get caught up in all this gold-fever foolishness either."

"Of course not," Rachel said. "I'm just going to meet my father, that's all."

"But he went out there prospecting." Mrs. Willoughby raised a disapproving eyebrow.

"Well, yes. But he isn't like the others," Rachel said. "He's been to the Henderson River many times. When he was younger, he was a messenger for the Hudson Bay Company's York Factory Express, so he knows the land very well. It isn't such a gamble for him as it might be for more inexperienced miners."

Mrs. Willoughby nodded. "Oh, yes, I've heard of that. Running messages back and forth across the continent. Well, that's good, then, that he knows his way around."

"Yes."

"When we reach Fort Garry, I'll take you to see my friend Mrs. Banting and fix everything up for you."

Mrs. Willoughby lapsed into drowsy silence after a while, and Rachel turned and gazed out the window at the unfamiliar countryside along the river. There were trees, but the land was fairly flat, and the warm June sun gave everything a wilted look. It was far different from the streets and shops of Toronto.

For her first trip alone, it had been uncomfortable but uneventful. Once, the rain had been so heavy that her train had had to stop due to floods covering the tracks, but other than that, travel had gone smoothly. However, the whole adventure had cost her more than she had expected, and her purse was dangerously light. She couldn't touch the money her aunt had left her until she was twenty-one, but she had saved her allowance from her brother, Richard, for months in preparation.

Now she suspected she had woefully underestimated what this enterprise would cost and wished she had managed to bring more with her. It irritated her to discover she had not prepared as well as she'd thought she had. But she was well out of reach of her brother now, and Rachel found if she didn't think too much about what lay ahead—or what lay behind—she could quite enjoy herself. She thought it good fortune that she had met Mrs. Willoughby, who could help her find a place to stay in Fort Garry. Perhaps if she met such helpful strangers all along her journey, she would arrive all right at Washed-Out Creek, after all. She could do this. It wasn't so hard. She felt slightly proud of herself.

At last they reached Fort Garry. The fort itself was a boxy structure with a round tower at one corner that reminded Rachel of a salt can, and a settlement had grown around it like a fungus ringing a tree stump. Altogether it wasn't the most beautiful place she had seen, but it felt good to get off the steamer and finally stop moving for a while. She could hardly believe she had been traveling for over a month already. And there was still such a long way to go.

She didn't let herself feel depressed about it though. She focused instead on collecting her things and getting herself settled at Mrs. Willoughby's friend's crumbling wooden boarding house.

Mrs. Banting, who put Rachel in mind of a cross poodle, was a frizzy-haired, sharp-tongued woman who interspersed everything she said with remarks about how foolish it was for a young girl to travel alone, how Rachel mustn't venture out after dusk, and that she shouldn't speak to strange men. Since there were few women to be found in the settlement, Rachel gathered that she shouldn't talk to nearly everyone. Mrs. Banting made Rachel feel young and inexperienced, a feeling she greatly disliked. She knew immediately that she would sorely miss Mrs. Willoughby and was sorry to say good-bye to her.

"I think you're foolish to go west," Mrs. Banting pronounced as she set a bowl of stew in front of Rachel that evening. She stood over it, hands tightly clasped in front of her as if she was prepared to stand there all night if necessary in order to supervise the eating of the meal. "It isn't smart for a girl your age to be running around the country by herself."

"That is why I need to find a company to join," Rachel replied. She took a spoonful of the stew and found it watery and bland, and there was a bitter aftertaste she couldn't identify.

"Well, if you're determined to do it, you should talk to Mr. McMicking. The older one, not his brother. He's taking a company of men to the Dunant. If anyone can help you get organized, he can."

"That's wonderful! I'll find him and speak with him tomorrow, first thing."

"Mind you, he won't let you go with his group. They're all prospectors. No women allowed in the group. It isn't proper."

"Well, I'll just have to convince him otherwise."

"I hear he's from your neck of the woods. Welland or some such."

"Oh! That isn't far from my home in Toronto." This was a good omen. Surely Mr. McMicking would allow her to join his party when he learned she was a neighbor. Well, close enough, anyway.

* * *

She located Mr. McMicking by asking several people on the road as she went, being sure to ask for the older brother, not the younger, and finally ran him to earth at the blacksmith's, where he was getting a horse shod. Mr. McMicking was a dark-haired, rather fierce-looking man, and he wore only a sweat-stained shirt with no coat or hat. He was much younger than Rachel had expected. He couldn't be over thirty-five. He listened to her request but was shaking his head before she'd finished speaking.

"I'm sorry, but I won't allow women in our group," he said. "Even one as pretty as you. *Especially* one as pretty as you," he added without a trace of a grin. "It will only cause problems."

"I'll stick to myself," Rachel promised. "I won't mix with the men. I could be helpful with the cooking and campfires and . . . things." She unconsciously lifted her chin a little as she said this. She had never cooked over a fire in her life and few enough times over a proper stove. But surely it couldn't be that difficult, and she would be able to do it with a little practice.

"I'm sorry, the answer is no. It's rough, unsettled country and very isolated. Sometimes you run into some unsavory characters."

"Indians, do you mean?" She had read a lot about the Natives in preparation for her trip and was a bit anxious about meeting one.

He scowled. "No. I've never met an unsavory Native. It's the gold hunters you need to worry about. It isn't right for you to travel unaccompanied."

"But I'm *trying* to be accompanied. That's the whole point," Rachel said in frustration.

"You know what I mean. Accompanied in *particular*. You're not married?"

"No. I'm only eighteen."

"You a runaway?"

"Certainly not!" Rachel felt the heat rise in her cheeks and knew her ears were glowing red. She wasn't accustomed to lying. "I told you I'm trying to join my father. He's in Bellefontaine on the Henderson River."

"And he approves of this crazy scheme of yours?"

"I've come this far by myself," she said evasively.

"Trains and ships aren't anything. You'd be going by Red River cart, by canoe, on horseback, on foot. There's nothing soft or easy about this journey."

"I can manage anything you can." She hoped she looked more certain than she felt. "And I have some money for supplies. Just tell me what I need to bring."

"There's hardly time. We're leaving next week. It's late in the season as it is. But it doesn't matter because you aren't going."

"If you don't agree to take me, I will get my own cart and just follow along behind you. You can't stop me from doing that!"

"You don't have any conception of what the trail is like!"

The blacksmith, who had been thoughtfully rubbing the neck of McMicking's horse, gave a low cough. "Thomas, think for a moment. She could travel with . . . um."

McMicking paused, looking at the other man, and a thoughtful expression came over his angular face. "You think?" he asked the blacksmith.

The big man nodded. His neck was so short and thick that the movement was almost imperceptible. "Might be safer that way, even. It would support the story. Make it more believable . . ."

McMicking sighed. "All right," he said, turning back to Rachel. "It's against my better judgment, but you can go. But this is the thing—you'll be traveling as Mrs. Cameron."

"Oh. I—why?" Rachel asked in confusion.

"Because *Mr.* Cameron needs someone to accompany him and help him with driving his cart," McMicking said.

"Is he elderly?"

"No, he's not much older than you are. But you'll share a tent and a cart, and you'll refrain from conversation with anyone else. It's good that you have spunk, but on this trip you must be as inconspicuous as possible and do what I say. Pretend you are shy and retiring, if that's possible for someone of your impetuous nature and hot temper. Is that understood?"

"I can't share a tent with a—with Mr. Cameron. It isn't proper."

"*Now* you're concerned with being proper?" McMicking snorted. "Listen, you do it that way or not at all."

"Couldn't she just do the same—" the blacksmith began, but McMicking cut him off.

"There's no way it would work with her," he said, jabbing his thumb toward Rachel.

Rachel saw the blacksmith skim his eyes down her body, taking in her hourglass figure and expensive though travel-stained dress. His eyes returned to her face, where they lingered.

"You're right. Nobody would believe it."

"I know I'm right. That's why she's *Mrs.* Cameron," McMicking said cryptically.

"I don't understand," Rachel said, wanting to stamp her foot with frustration. "What are you talking about?"

The blacksmith leaned close, overwhelming her with a scent of smoke and sweat and metal she could almost taste on her tongue.

"The only thing you need to understand," he whispered, "is that *Mr.* Cameron's first name is Lucy."

* * *

It took most of the week and nearly all of her remaining money to outfit herself for the journey. She purchased new boots and clothing better suited to the physical exertion ahead. She had slipped away from home in such a way that taking a large number of supplies with her had been impossible, and she was glad to see that Fort Garry could supply everything she needed. When the shopkeeper heard that she was going west, he suggested a traveling skirt that did not require a crinoline under it, in anticipation of riding a horse.

Rachel felt a bit awkward discussing such personal items as crinolines with this gentleman, but she agreed that the usual bone or wire contraption she wore to hold out her voluminous skirts would be a hindrance on the trail.

"But do women really go without them?" she asked in embarrassment.

He scratched his head, looking around the store as if seeking the right words. "Well, now, not many women have come through here," he finally said. "But the few who did bought these new-fangled traveling skirts, and you had best do the same."

Rachel selected one in a sky blue and watched him wrap it in paper. She thought she probably needed two or more, but she simply didn't have the money, so she told herself one would suffice. It looked a bit daring to her, since she was used to the full, bell-shaped skirts that were the current fashion in Toronto, but she could see the practicality.

The shopkeeper suggested she also buy a small woman's pistol to keep on her person.

Rachel rebelled at the idea. "I couldn't possibly carry a gun!" she said with a gasp. "What are you thinking?"

He spread his hands wide. "I'm only thinking of your safety. You're heading into the heart of gold fever and Indian territory. Not only that, there are men heading northwest to get out of the American war. I see them go through here all the time."

"What do you mean? Deserters?" She knew about the war between the States. Her brother had talked of little else. At times she had wondered if *he* wanted to run away from home too and join up to fight for the Union. Would they let a Canadian fight in their war? She didn't know.

"It's turned everybody in the country a bit mad," the shopkeeper said. "Between that and the gold rush, people are looking out only for themselves. Don't trust their neighbors. Keep their cards close to their chests, you know what I mean. I wouldn't want a woman of mine going out there on her own."

"Well, I won't be on my own. I'll be with a group of a hundred forty armed men who can protect me," Rachel said.

"It's the armed men I'm afraid of," he muttered, but he dropped the subject and wrapped the rest of her purchases for her.

His words brought her anxieties to the forefront. She didn't know any of these people she would be traveling with. She had no idea what life on the trail would be like. And most frighteningly, she didn't know what she would find at the end of her journey. She hadn't heard from her father after the first two years he had been away. Was he still alive? Or was Richard right and their father was dead? After all this effort, surely things would turn out all right. They *had* to.

"Another thing," the shopkeeper added as she turned to leave. "I would advise you to stay close to your company and never go wandering out of the camp on your own."

"The Natives," she said, nodding knowingly.

"No, not so much that. Most of them are quite friendly these days. But it's easy to lose your sense of direction in the tall prairie grass. It grows above your head so you can't see any distance at all, and the land is flat and virtually featureless."

Rachel was quite skeptical about this. Grass taller than her head? It was unimaginable! "Thank you for the warning, sir, but I suspect you are exaggerating. You can't frighten me into not going, you know. My mind is quite made up about it." She gave him a pretty smile and left the shop.

When she returned to Mrs. Banting's house, her hostess was standing at the head of the stairs, arms folded across her chest, her sharp eyes narrow. Rachel stopped short at the older woman's expression. Mrs. Banting's hair was positively bristling, enhancing the poodle image.

"What's wrong, Mrs. Banting?" she asked politely.

"Perhaps you can explain this."

Mrs. Banting held out a scrap of paper, and Rachel took it and moved to the window to read it. It was a small square, roughly scribbled on in a hand she didn't recognize.

Missing: Miss Rachel Hamilton of Toronto, aged 18. Left home May 14. Five-foot-four, blonde hair, blue eyes, assumed to be heading west. Anxious family offering reward $500. Contact Richard Hamilton, 921 Acton, Toronto. Family not responsible for any debts Miss Hamilton incurs.

Rachel stared at it in disbelief, then looked up to see Mrs. Banting scowling at her. "How?" was the only word she could force from lips suddenly gone numb.

"That is you. You can't argue with plain facts. It's you to a T," Mrs. Banting said.

"But how—?"

"My brother works at the telegraph office. That message came in over three weeks ago, and he copied it out to put on the wall in case anyone ever heard word of you. When I told him I had a female boarder staying with me from Toronto named Rachel Hamilton, he copied it down and brought it with him to lunch today. It is you, isn't it? I can see I'm right."

"But why would Richard telegraph Fort Garry?"

"It says right here your family suspected you were heading west. This is the only non-Native settlement on the prairies. Anyone wanting to go west usually comes through here." Mrs. Banting took the paper back and pushed it into her apron pocket. "How could you go off and leave your poor family worrying themselves half sick to death?" she demanded.

"I had no idea he'd be this concerned," Rachel said. "I'm not entirely convinced it's sincere."

"What were you thinking, girl? I don't like being lied to."

"I didn't lie. I'm going to join my father. But if I'd told my brother, he would have stopped me. I had to run away."

"Why would your brother stop you from going to your father? The dangers of the journey, I guess?"

"He doesn't want me to find him," Rachel said miserably, feeling the tears threaten at the back of her eyes. "He wants my father to be dead."

Mrs. Banting's mouth fell open. This clearly wasn't the answer she'd expected.

Rachel sat on the top stair and tucked her hands into her armpits and hugged herself. Her crinoline billowed around her awkwardly, and she thought fleetingly of her new skirt wrapped in paper at her feet. She had been leery about donning it, but now she wondered if she would even get a chance to. Was her journey over before it had properly begun?

Mrs. Banting studied her a moment, then sighed and sat on the step beside her. "Tell me," she ordered.

Rachel sniffed. "My father left my brother and me five years ago and went to look for gold on the Henderson River."

"He and thousands of other foolish men," Mrs. Banting said glumly. "I can't believe he left you alone."

"He was responsible about it," Rachel said defensively. "My brother, Richard, is eleven years older than I. We lived with my aunt, but Richard was technically left in charge of me. The board looked after Father's factory."

"Yes, yes," Mrs. Banting said impatiently.

"Father wrote a few times from British Columbia. He said he hadn't found a lot of gold, but other men were leaving the Henderson Canyon and striking it rich all over the colony. Father left too and went to a place called Washed-Out Creek off the Henderson River, near Bellefontaine, where he found gold. He said the area was rough and he didn't want me to come yet but that once he'd gotten comfortably established, he would send for me to join him. But then the letters just stopped three years ago."

"What happened?"

"I don't know. That's just it, you see. He could be alive or—well, not. My brother wants to have him declared legally dead so he can take full charge of my father's affairs. He's been talking about probating Father's will, taking over management of the factory and everything. It's horrible. You don't know Richard. He'll ruin Father's business and make my life miserable. So I'm going to find my father and prove he's alive. Or, at least, I'll know one way or the other," she added sadly.

Mrs. Bunting was silent for a moment, then took the slip of paper from her pocket and looked at it.

"What are you going to do?" Rachel asked, wiping her eyes with the back of her hand.

"Nothing," Mrs. Banting barked irritably. "Go and find your father, then, if that's what you've a mind to do. But just remember I'm not the only person who will hear of this bulletin, and there are some who would find that reward money a powerful lure." She sniffed self-righteously to show that she, for one, was above such temptation.

Rachel gripped the woman's hands in both of hers. "You are so kind, Mrs. Banting. I can't thank you enough."

"All right, none of that."

"You know," Rachel said, standing and straightening her dress, "$500 doesn't seem like very much for the return of a person. I could find it insulting."

Mrs. Banting laughed and went downstairs, shaking her head. Rachel took her packages into her room and closed the door, but her relief was short-lived. Mrs. Banting was right. If Richard was sending out telegrams to all major towns, it was only a matter of time before someone else heard about it and matched her with the description. She hadn't been cautious enough, traveling under her real name and making no secret of where she was headed. At least she would soon be on her way into territory where there was no telegraph, and her name would no longer be Hamilton but Cameron.

Chapter Two

THE MORNING WAS CLEAR AND warm, the sky a cloudless blue when Rachel arrived at the stable where the company was gathering. She had her supplies packed in her trunk, Geordie tucked into his carpet bag, and her new stout boots on her feet. She was also self-consciously wearing the travel skirt. Even though it was cut in a full circle, it didn't bell out in the way she was used to but instead hung straight from her hips to the ground. You could almost sense the shape of her legs beneath the blue cotton when she walked, and she felt as if every male eye in the fort was on her. Richard would never approve of this. He would accuse her of dressing like a harlot, if he were to see her.

Well, she thought, lifting her chin and stiffening her gait defiantly, he *wasn't* going to see her. She was heading west this very hour, and there was nothing he could do to stop her.

She tried to ignore the fluttering in her stomach and sought out McMicking. The crowd seemed to consist of all types of men, some dressed in long coats and top hats, as if they were on their way to a Sunday church social, and some in canvas trousers and buckskin jackets. And there were the Red River carts, those odd wagons that looked to her like fruit baskets on wheels, hitched to horses and oxen, crowding the road. Sure enough, there were no women or children among them. At least . . . not visibly. But *somewhere*, she knew . . .

She located McMicking speaking with a knot of men, set her heavy trunk down, and planted herself by his elbow. When there was a lull in the conversation, she cleared her throat.

"Good morning, Mr. McMicking," she said. "I'm here."

He turned to her with a serious face and gave a polite half bow. His glance took in her attire but seemed to find nothing notable about it. The men with him gaped at her.

"Good morning, Mrs. Cameron. All settled?"

She looked around the crowd. There were about a hundred thirty, maybe a hundred forty men in the gathering, she'd been told, but it seemed like more to her. "I am having difficulty finding my . . . er . . . husband," she told him.

"Ah. I think I saw him preparing his cart over by the dry-goods store. I'll help you find him, shall I?"

He took her trunk and strode off, and she hurried after him.

When they were out of earshot, she muttered, "I assume Mr. Cameron knows I'm coming?"

"Yes, he's been told. He agrees it's a good arrangement. It will lend credibility to his disguise."

"Isn't it a bit—well, I mean, I think society would see it as quite scandalous for her to masquerade as a man," Rachel said primly. "I'm surprised you would allow her to do it."

"She is my cousin, the only child of my favorite uncle, and it is expedient for her to leave her—erm—current situation as far behind as possible, and quickly. Disguising her as a man in a company of men seemed the best solution at the time, and for practical reasons, it is the only viable way to transport her west. And you must remember to refer to her as 'him.'"

"But I don't completely understand. If I'm posing as a wife, why couldn't sh—I mean he?"

He lowered his voice, slowing his step to speak almost in her ear. "Because to do that would entail having her—er, him—dash it all! This is a difficult conversation! Lucy would have to live with one of the men on the trail if she were posing as his wife. I'm sure you can see how inappropriate that would be, and it would entail finding a man willing to carry out the ruse while leaving her honor intact. That would be difficult, especially among a ragtag collection of fortune-seekers such as this. A woman traveling alone is walking into danger, as I'm sure you yourself must agree, so this little subterfuge was to keep Lucy safe."

Rachel frowned. "Then why are you allowing me to travel as a female? Why am I not in disguise as well?"

His eyes flicked over her, and he picked up his pace again. "Impossible. There is no amount of clothing or makeup that would disguise the fact that you are female, Mrs. Cameron."

They drew to a stop before a Red River cart piled with burlap sacks and wooden crates. A skinny brown mare stood in the traces, her head hanging, looking tired already. If Rachel hadn't known Mr. Cameron was a woman in disguise, she would have sworn the person turning cheerfully toward her was a young man. She—*he*, she corrected herself—was slightly taller than Rachel, with intelligent brown eyes and a floppy-brimmed hat pulled low on his forehead. His clothes were new but inexpensively cut, his coat slightly loose fitting, and his voice a mellow (and surprising) tenor as he said, "Hello there."

"Pleased to meet you." Rachel reached to shake his hand and found his grip strong and firm. She glanced down. Lucy's nails were trimmed short, and the knuckles on her hands looked rough, as if accustomed to work.

"Of course you've met," McMicking said irritably. "You're married."

"Yes, of course," Rachel said quickly, pulling her hand back and hoping no one had seen the exchange. "Sorry."

"If this is going to work, you need to play the part consistently from this point on," McMicking said in a low hiss. "The safety of you both depends on it."

"I won't forget again."

"We're off in fifteen minutes," he said. "Be ready to move out." He strode away, and the two looked at each other appraisingly.

Lucy's eyes glinted. "He's always bossy."

"What am I to call you? I can't very well call you Mr. Cameron."

"I'm going by Lucas."

"Oh, that's easy. Thank you. And I'm Rachel."

"Is that all you've brought? Let's tie your trunk on the back, then. Give me your bag."

"Oh, I'll carry it on my lap, thank you." Rachel looked uncertainly at the cart. "I am riding, right? Not walking?"

"Of course. Let me help you." Lucas took her elbow and half lifted her as she scrambled awkwardly up onto the cart. There was a board at the front where she could sit with her feet dangling down above the horse. Rachel instantly knew this was going to be a long and uncomfortable journey. There was no padding, no back to lean against, and only a thin rail to rest her heels on. She gripped the bag on her lap, Geordie curled inside it, and felt a surge of anxiety. Did she really want to do this? Would it be better to go back to Toronto with her tail between her legs to face Richard's anger?

No, it was too late. Lucas was swinging up beside her, picking up the reins, and expertly chirping to the horse. The cart gave a creak and began to roll to join the others. The carts had begun to form a haphazard line down the road. Some of the men had brought small cattle herds with them, intending to settle before reaching the Dunant Mountains rather than prospect. Horses neighed, men called out to each other, and McMicking was in the midst of it all on a piebald horse, barking instructions. Somehow the chaos began to sort itself out, and the line of men and animals began to move noisily out of town. Rachel and her unlikely companion were drawn along with it.

At first there was too much to pay attention to, and Rachel and Lucas didn't speak to each other as they made their way out of town and the carts strung out on the trail with space between them. In no time at all, they were coated with a fine film of dust churned up by the animals' hooves. Finally, Rachel glanced sideways at her "husband" and tried to suppress a nervous giggle.

She felt as if she was back in school, pulling an elaborate prank on the teacher. Lucas held the reins with easy experience, squinting in the light at the trail ahead. He sat with his knees apart, elbow on one knee, looking exactly like all the other men around them.

"Thank you for allowing me to come with you," Rachel said, keeping her voice low. "I know you weren't expecting me, and your food supplies probably can't accommodate . . . I mean . . . well, I explained to Mr. McMicking that I have some money, and I am happy to reimburse you for whatever I eat."

"Of course. There will be places along the way where we can take on more supplies. I will expect you to contribute to their purchase."

"Of course." Rachel felt Lucas was being a little brusque, but she supposed there was no more polite way to phrase it. Perhaps being blunt was best. As long as they were being forthright with each other, she decided to ask the question she had been pondering. "Can I ask you . . . ?"

Lucas glanced before and behind to judge whether anyone could hear them, then nodded. "You want to know why I'm doing this?"

"Yes."

"Why are *you*?"

"I'm going to join my father. He's prospecting off the Henderson River."

Lucas considered this and nodded.

"And you?" Rachel asked.

"Why should men get all the fun?" Lucas replied.

Rachel wasn't satisfied with Lucas's answer, but she could tell he didn't want to talk about it, and it probably wasn't safe to speak very much when others were nearby anyway. She was glad she hadn't pressed the conversation when a man suddenly approached on a bay mare that fell into step beside their horse.

He was a rough-looking character, his hair straggly on the collar of his sweat-dampened coat, his jaw covered in three days' worth of whiskers. Rachel felt a natural repugnance at his appearance and an instinctual distrust of the speculative look in his gray eyes. He tipped his hat to Rachel.

"Morning, folks. Adam Marshall, from Chicago."

"Lucas Cameron. Toronto." Lucas's voice was suddenly slightly deeper, rougher.

"And this must be your missus?" Those hard eyes slid assessingly over Rachel, and she straightened her spine and looked away.

"Yes." Lucas's tone didn't invite further conversation, but Marshall didn't pick up on it.

"It's a difficult trail for a female."

"I can manage," Rachel said.

"Your cart looks a bit overburdened, don't you think?" he suggested. "What's in the big crate?"

Lucas shot him a cool look. "Why do you ask?"

"Just being neighborly."

"We're not your neighbors," Lucas replied calmly. "We're your competitors. If you're headed for the gold fields, that is."

Marshall gave a brassy laugh. "Well, I guess that's true enough. You're right. We're all headed west to make our fortunes, and the more one makes, the less the other does. But until we get there, we're all in the same boat, helping each other across the country."

"True enough," Lucas replied.

Marshall tipped his hat again. "Pleased to make your acquaintance," he said and moved away.

When Marshall was out of earshot, Rachel slumped in her uncomfortable seat. "Why did you talk to him that way? Now you've made an enemy."

"No, I haven't. But I wanted to make sure I didn't make a friend either, or next thing you know, he'd be inviting me to have a whiskey with the boys around the campfire tonight," Lucas said.

"Oh," Rachel said. "I hadn't thought of that possibility."

"Our safety depends on our keeping as much to ourselves as possible."

"I understand." Rachel glanced behind her at the crates and bags lashed in the wagon. "What *is* in the big crate, anyway?"

"A stove," Lucas said.

Rachel hadn't expected that. "A *stove*? You're hauling a big hunk of iron all the way across the country?"

"It's small," Lucas said, sounding defensive. "I have to be able to make a living once I reach Fort Reilly, don't I? That's where I'm headed."

"But . . . I thought you were a prospector. Aren't you?"

Lucas glanced at Rachel and smiled, his face dimpling and suddenly looking very unmasculine. Rachel thought it would be wise if he didn't smile often.

"I'm not going after gold myself," he replied. "I'm going after the gold other people find. There's more money to be made in running a cookhouse than there is in mining."

Rachel thought about it and decided Lucas was probably right. A miner might search all his life for gold and never find it, but he would always need to eat. There would always be money in supplying the miners. And there would be a steady stream of men flowing through Fort Reilly to reach the gold fields of British Columbia.

"You're pretty smart," she said.

The cart gave a lurch just then, and Rachel clutched at the bag on her lap to keep it from falling. Lucas eyed it curiously.

"What do you have in there? Why don't you just toss it in the back of the cart?"

Rachel opened the top of the carpetbag, and Geordie's furry, flat-faced head popped out with a yawn that exposed his needle-like teeth.

Lucas gave a shout of astonishment. "A *cat*? You think you're going to take a *cat* across the country? In a *bag*? You're crazy!"

"No more crazy than you taking a cookstove," Rachel said. She rubbed Geordie's ears fondly. "He's traveled with me for the past weeks all the way from Toronto, and he can make it to Bellefontaine."

"I'm not coddling a cat on this trip."

"You don't have to. I'll take care of him."

"He won't make it. It's too dangerous."

"He'll be fine. I'll look after him, I said."

Lucas shook his head grimly and turned his attention back to his driving. "What a messed-up pair of lunatics we are, you and me."

Rachel was so busy laughing she almost forgot her fear.

CHAPTER THREE

THE DAYS FELL INTO A pattern. The company started off early in the morning, trying to make as much distance as they could before the heat of the day. At noon they stopped in a large circle to cook lunch and rest. Then they continued on until dusk, when they pulled into another circle and had supper. Most of them had canvas tents they pitched to sleep in, though some of the men slept under the stars or, if it was drizzling, under their carts, and the horses and oxen were hobbled in the center of the circle to keep them from wandering.

It took some time for Rachel to get used to having so many men around her, their low voices, their rough laughter. She often felt their eyes on her when she walked through the camp or helped haul water in the evening. For the most part, though, they treated her politely and left her alone, and she would have thought McMicking's worries had been unfounded if it hadn't been for Marshall. Of all the men, he made her uncomfortable, persistently seeking out excuses to talk to her. She kept close to Lucas and did her best to ignore him.

Rachel found it unpleasant trying to dodge the smoke of the cook fire, and it was a lot of work setting up their tent each evening and taking it down again each morning. The ground was hard to sleep on, food never cooked properly over the fire, it was difficult to dress in the small confines of the tent, even with Lucas to help her, and, worst of all, there was no privy. She was amazed to learn she was expected to go in the bushes and make do as best she could. This was something she had somehow never anticipated in all her dreaming and scheming about running west, and she found it terribly crude. Long skirts and petticoats were inconvenient when it came to answering nature's call. She thanked her lucky stars every day that she had listened to the man at the store and abandoned the crinoline, which really would have been too impossible, but she found herself envying Lucas, who had far fewer layers of clothing to deal with, though admittedly, Lucas had to go fairly far afield from the company so he wouldn't be seen inadvertently and give the game away.

It wasn't long before they left behind any semblance of civilization and struck out across open prairie. Rachel's first view of the untamed land astonished her. It was true what the shopkeeper had said! The green-gray grass was tall—head-high in some places—and dotted with only a few broadleaf trees. From her high perch on the cart, Rachel could see that the earth stretched out on all sides, with no sign of houses or buildings. Unaccustomed to un-settled territory, she found such a vast expanse nerve-racking. Her ears missed the constant thrum of noise back in Toronto, and her eyes sought in vain for any tall thing to break up the spread of flatness around her.

However, the more she figured out where to look, the more her eyes were opened. Rather than being the desolate barren she had first thought, the land was filled with grouse and small birds she couldn't identify, foxes, rabbits, and even an occasional mule deer. She hoped to see bison, but Lucas told her rather scornfully that they would be unlikely to meet such creatures here, especially this deep into summer. They were not so plentiful as they had once been, he told Rachel, and the ones that were left would be far north, grazing, and wouldn't come this far south until winter.

Rachel gradually grew used to the rocking cart, the glare of the sun on the flatland, the constant breeze on her face. She couldn't see ahead unless she was up on the cart, where she could view the land from above. When she was on the cart, she felt like she was on a boat trudging across a sea of blue-green, and when she was on the ground, she felt she was drowning in grass. She grew accustomed to spending her days in silence because Lucas hardly spoke. She even reconciled herself to sleeping in the tent on the hard ground alongside Lucas, who usually dropped into sleep like a stone at the end of the day. But Rachel never could quite reconcile herself to having to do with a clump of tall grass rather than a nice privy.

Rachel also learned to manage Geordie's needs on the trail. The cat had behaved admirably on the journey so far, other than occasional forays into the grass after rodents he never caught, but he always came straight back to her. He seemed to prefer the carpetbag over the vast, alien expanse of countryside, and whenever he walked on the ground, he lifted his paws exaggeratedly high, his face drawn up in an unmistakable look of finicky disapproval. Lucas softened toward him, and occasionally he would reach over to fondle the cat's ears where he rode on Rachel's lap.

Finally, one day, a low line of hills appeared on the horizon, indicating the beginning of the Saskatchewan Plain.

"Don't get too excited," McMicking told her when she pointed the hills out to him. "That isn't the edge of the prairie. It's really the true beginning of it."

She had never heard anything so disheartening.

* * *

They camped one night beside a small river, where willows grew in shady elegance. There were muskrats and wild geese, with which the men quickly enhanced their dinner, and McMicking quietly slipped part of his catch to Lucas so the two women could eat well that night. Full and content, Rachel slept well, her dreams filled with images of sun-dappled grass.

The next morning, Rachel got up early, when few others were stirring, and left the camp, walking down the river a short distance until she was out of view behind a rise of ground. She and Lucas had made do with sponge baths in the tent, but she wasn't going to forego this opportunity to wash herself entirely. She stripped to her camisole and one petticoat and quickly washed herself in the cold, shallow water, teeth chattering, muttering to herself. She hated the feel of cold water on her skin. She hated the slippery rocks underfoot. She squeaked whenever an insect hovered too close. *I miss my bath at home*, she thought, gritting her teeth. *And my maid to draw the water*. The memory brought back an unexpected wave of homesickness. Toronto seemed impossibly far away.

Impatiently, Rachel pushed away the longing and unbraided her long gold hair to wash it. She turned to pick up the soap and stopped dead. Marshall was watching her from the rise of ground above her.

He smiled and waved cheerfully at her. Rachel screeched, scrambled back up on the bank, and reached for her dress. Her underclothes covered the essentials but still left her shoulders and legs bare to his gaze.

"I didn't know you were there." She clutched the dress in front of her.

"Don't mind me. I was just admiring the view."

Rachel stared at him, her mouth open, and felt her shame give way to anger. She thrust her dress over her head and fought the buttons with trembling fingers.

"Don't interrupt your bath on my account," he called down, still grinning.

Rachel jammed her feet into her shoes and gathered her other clothing.

"You ought to be ashamed of yourself," she snapped. "My husband will hear of this!"

He only laughed. Rachel marched back to camp, her chin in the air. Men were awake, moving quietly about, making breakfast and rolling up tents. Lucas was building a cook fire, hunkered down awkwardly on his heels. Ordinarily Rachel would have stopped to help, but this morning she stomped past him into the tent, where she sat on her blanket and rebraided her hair in a fury.

A moment later, Lucas came into the tent and stood with hands on hips, looking at Rachel's bare feet crammed into her shoes. Then his eyes lifted to meet Rachel's. "What happened?" he asked quietly.

"That Adam Marshall person—the one I told you keeps finding excuses to talk to me—I was bathing in the river outside of camp, and he . . . he watched me. I didn't know he was there. I don't trust him. I don't like the way he looks at me."

Lucas thought a moment, then sat down on the blanket beside Rachel and wrapped his arms around his drawn-up knees.

"If I were really your husband, I'd call him out and fight him for his rude behavior," he said in a low voice. "But you and I both know I can't do that. You'll just have to be careful from now on and not go anywhere alone. Stay close to me or McMicking. Promise me."

Rachel nodded.

"You finish getting properly dressed, and I'll have breakfast ready in a minute," Lucas said and left the tent.

* * *

After that morning, it seemed as if Marshall was always there when Rachel turned around. She would look up from her task, and his cold, gray eyes would be on her. He rode his horse just behind their cart, out of speaking range but within eyesight if she turned around. The look on his face made Rachel uncomfortable. Vulnerable. She hated the feeling. Marshall never did anything that could be labeled as outright inappropriate, so if she ran whining to McMicking, she knew he would only roll his eyes and say this was what came of letting a female come with them, and she wasn't about to give him the chance to say that. So she said nothing and sat closer to Lucas on the hard plank seat.

After several days, they reached St. Cloud, arriving in a light rain. Rachel had heard some of the company talking about the settlement as they grew nearer. She had been hoping to find shelter in a cabin in the village, somewhere with a real hearth and beds, but Lucas informed her the company would sleep in tents as usual.

"Even if anyone was willing to put us up, there are no cabins in St. Cloud," he pointed out. "Only soddies."

"What are soddies?"

"Shelters made of stacked layers of earth cut out of the prairie. The grass grows right over the roofs."

"They're made of mud?"

"Well, they don't have forests around here to build out of wood, now, do they?" Lucas asked with some irritation. "The soddies keep the weather out fair enough, but I hear they are dark. My cousin has told me about them."

"They still have to be drier than tents in the rain," Rachel pouted.

"You can't expect a small village to accommodate a hundred forty men. I anticipate they will be willing to trade with us, but that will be as far as their hospitality goes. You can't expect them to treat white men with any great love, despite our friendly relations."

"White men? You mean the people in St. Cloud are Indians?" Rachel's voice rose an octave.

"There certainly aren't any white settlements this far out on the prairie," Lucas said, staring at her. "The occasional fort or Hudson Bay outpost, yes. But no towns or villages. You've left white civilization behind, Mrs. Cameron; hadn't it occurred to you yet?"

Rachel spent a sleepless night in her tent, squirming to avoid damp patches and bumps in the ground. Her imagination, alive with images and stories of the Natives from her books back home, kept her skin prickling and her ears alert for the sound of any footsteps approaching over the sound of the rain pattering on the canvas above her. She simply couldn't believe there were Natives this close, a whole village of them—and she couldn't picture them living in mud huts instead of tepees. The idea that perhaps reality was not exactly as her books had portrayed it made her uneasy. She was glad when dawn rose over the prairie, murky and gray in the rain, and she refused to go anywhere near St. Cloud when Lucas went with some of the other men to barter. When Lucas returned, Rachel had the tent stowed in the wagon and everything packed and ready to leave.

The next landmark they reached was Snow Goose Lake, a shimmering stretch of silver that Rachel thought very pretty, nestled under the lowered clouds like a spill of mercury in the grass. The sun glinted from its surface as if off a mirror. A few trees grew along its banks, and its water was clean and cold. It was a refreshing change from flat, featureless land.

She helped Lucas fill their canteens and containers in anticipation of the long stretch of dry grass yet to come and wondered how Lucas could heft the heavy water so effortlessly when she, herself, struggled to lift the containers into the wagon. But when she remarked on it, Lucas only muttered, "Used to work in a laundry," and carried on.

This short but surprising phrase gave Rachel much to think about as they continued their journey. She really knew nothing about this person riding beside her, even after weeks of traveling together. But she suspected Lucas's life had not been an easy one if it had toughened her—him—so. The remark about the laundry gave her a new perspective on his background, which obviously wasn't one of privilege. Lucas hadn't gained those work-roughened hands just as a disguise for this journey. The thought made Rachel look down at her own pale hands, now dry from the summer heat but uncalloused and undamaged, and she felt a vague sort of shame.

The contrast between them was suddenly more visible to Rachel. She envied Lucas's confidence with the horse, his strength, his apparently unflappable demeanor. He wasn't afraid of the mosquitoes that sent Rachel into squealing dances when they descended with the dusk. His skin didn't even seem to toast in the sun as badly as Rachel's did. Rachel felt rather limp and ineffective in comparison and wondered if the life she had lived back home had been a pampered one. She hadn't considered it so at the time, but something had to account for the difference between them. While Lucas had apparently been building muscles in a laundry, Rachel had been . . . what? Lying on a goose-down pillow, strolling in the lakeside park, buying satin shoes, playing the pianoforte at musical soirées, embroidering cushions. Lucas had turned out capable and strong, and she had turned out soft. Would she willingly have traded her own gentle upbringing with whatever had been Lucas's life in order to turn out as strong as he? She suspected not and wondered if that revealed something weak about her character.

The company made its way through the Saskatchewan Plain to Fort Carlton, where the group replenished their supplies before moving on. Rachel, mindful of the possibility of a telegraph reaching the fort before her, stayed with the wagon while Lucas went into the stores.

McMicking declared himself satisfied with the pace of their progress. Other than the occasional broken axle or lame horse, they had encountered little difficulty. Twice it had rained, but usually the weather was relentlessly hot and dry, and they could make good time.

Rachel watched the grasshoppers spurt away from their path as the wagons crushed their way through the endless prairie. She felt a stupor descend over her, and she felt she had been wandering into oblivion for months and that the rest of her life would be spent in grass.

Three days outside of Fort Parker, the company settled for the night in a mercifully shady hollow sheltered by broadleafed trees. The weather was warm but not baking, the night sky was clear and bright with stars, and some of the men pulled out the whiskey and cider bottles they'd carefully hauled with them. After a while, someone started to play the fiddle, and before long some of the men were dancing around a bonfire. Lucas went over to talk to McMicking, who was rubbing down his horse outside the ring of firelight. Rachel stayed well back from the rowdy crowd, seated on the ground and dangling a string for Geordie to bat at.

Rachel felt a shadow fall across her, and she looked up to see Marshall standing over her. He had lost his hat somewhere, and he held a half-empty whiskey bottle in his hand. He grinned down at her, his teeth sharp and stained yellow from tobacco.

"Care to dance with me, Mrs. Cameron?"

Rachel shook her head, but he suddenly bent down, seized her wrist, and pulled her to her feet with a rough strength she hadn't anticipated. Geordie tensed and then ducked into his bag, where he blinked dolefully out at them.

"Can't hold out on us," Marshall slurred. "You're the only girl we got to dance with."

"No," Rachel said, trying to free her wrist from his grip. "I'm not dancing with you, Mr. Marshall."

But he was dragging her out into the center of the circle, closer to the bonfire. She looked anxiously around, trying to catch McMicking's eye, but he was deep in conversation with Lucas, and neither of them seemed to be aware of her predicament.

"Give us another tune!" Marshall commanded, waving the bottle and making its contents splash. The fiddler obligingly launched into a reel, and Rachel had no time to react before Marshall pulled her to him with an arm around her waist and began to spin her across the trampled grass.

"Stop!" she shouted, trying to plant her feet. "You're drunk! Leave me alone!"

He yanked her along, whipping her around so she collided with the other men who were dancing. They laughed and pressed around her, clapping to the rhythm, cheering Marshall on. Some formed a ragged line, and Marshall spun her and flung her to the next man, who grabbed her around the waist, spun her in a circle, then passed her down the line in a sloppy version of a reel. Rachel couldn't catch her breath as she tried to fight her way away from their grasping hands.

At the end of the line, the last man flattened one broad hand against the small of her back, his other hand crushing hers and his alcohol-laden breath bathing her face.

"Well, hello there," he said with a grin. The fiddler merged into a waltz, and the man struck off across the circle, pulling Rachel with him.

"Let me go!" she demanded.

The line of men dissolved, turning back to their bottles and companions, but Marshall was there once again, disengaging her from the other man's grip and pulling her against him.

"I believe I was dancing with the lady," he said.

The other fellow looked as if he wanted to argue, but he said nothing as Marshall waltzed Rachel back across the crushed grass. She could feel his hand sliding lower on her back, and she dug her nails into his shoulder.

"Stop it, Adam Marshall! I mean it. Right now! I'll call my husband."

"He's not here," Marshall replied, and he pressed her against his chest with one arm while he tipped his bottle to his lips with the other.

Rachel looked around desperately. She couldn't see McMicking or Lucas now in the darkness outside the circle. Where were they? Would no one help her? Surely they could see she didn't welcome Marshall's attention.

"Can't keep you all to himself anyway," Marshall said thickly. "Not good sportsmanship." He laughed and released her so suddenly she nearly fell backward. Then he caught her hand in his free one and headed toward the thicket of trees. "C'mon, let's go find us a bit of privacy."

"Not on your life!"

"Don't you like me, Rachel? Even a little bit? I think you do. I've seen you watching me," Marshall said with a chuckle. He pulled her into the shadows, and she felt a surge of panic as he tossed aside his empty bottle and grasped the back of her neck in his rough hand.

Rachel did the only thing she could think of: she stamped on his foot as hard as she could and yanked herself backward. She nearly got away from him, but before she could whirl around, he caught her arms in hands the size of hams and propelled her farther into the darkness.

"Leave me alone!" Rachel shrieked, struggling against his hold.

"Now, don't fight me, Mrs. Cameron. Your scrawny little man isn't here to save you, and even if he was, I could finish him with one punch. In fact, if you don't oblige me, I'll make sure your loving husband doesn't make the next river crossing. He might have a sad accident and drown. Are we clear on that?"

Rachel froze, her breath stopping in her throat.

"Don't know what you see in him anyway when you could have a strapping big fellow instead. He's milk toast," Marshall went on. He was starting to sound drowsy, and she thought his grip was weakening a little.

"Don't you threaten Lucas," she hissed.

"If you don't want any harm to come to him, seems to me we could come to a little arrangement," he said, nodding his head.

She could just see the movement in the blackness under the trees, and she felt his hands fumble at her neck, his foul breath hot on her cheek. He gave the fabric of her dress a sudden yank, and the top three buttons of her dress flew off and were lost in the dark grass. With a desperate twist, Rachel turned her head and sank her teeth into his wrist. Marshall yelled, and Rachel broke free of his powerful embrace and started to run.

She couldn't see very well, but pure fright made her feet light, and she ducked through the trees without stumbling over the rough ground. She didn't stop to think which direction to run; her only thought was to get away from him. The salty taste of his blood filled her mouth, nauseating her. Far behind her, she could hear him crashing through the brush, cursing and shouting, and the last thing she heard him shout was, "If I ever see you again, you'll be stone dead!"

Rachel burst out the other side of the thicket into open ground, where she hiked up her skirt and put on a burst of speed. She didn't know how long she ran, but she pushed her way through the tall grass with one hand in front of her to keep it from whipping her face and concentrated on not letting it trip her up as it tore at her legs. After a while, she realized the only sound she could hear was her own breathing. The terrible cramp in her side and the metallic taste in her mouth became too much for her, and she fell to her knees, retching until she thought she'd bring up her very stomach. When at last the heaving stopped, she sank back on her heels, her skirt billowing around her as she gulped the cool air.

She had no idea where she was. Shakily, she stood and looked around. There was no light but the distant stars and no sound at all. Completely disoriented, she searched the blackness around her for the glow of the campfires, but she thought the swell of the ground must be hiding them from her. She couldn't even tell where the trees were that she had come through. Where was she?

Chapter Four

Rachel awoke and found herself lying on her side in the grass, her arms wrapped around her for warmth. She was stiff and damp from dew, and there was a nasty taste in her mouth. She struggled to her feet and looked around. The sky was starting to brighten in front of her, pearl pink, and she guessed that that way was east. She stood on tiptoe to see over the grass, but she wasn't tall enough. Feeling ludicrous, she gave a few little jumps, trying to get a better look. The empty, rolling land around her gave her no clue, no landmark. She winced with mortification when she remembered her flippant disregard when the shopkeeper had warned her back at Fort Garry not to leave her company. The idea of being alone on the prairie now terrified her.

Rachel jumped again, but she couldn't see the camp or trees or campfire smoke or any sort of trail. The prairie grass spread all around her in a great green-blue wave spattered with blotches of color where there were flowers. Ordinarily she would have thought it beautiful, but today it frightened her. She told herself fiercely not to cry.

"It won't do a bit of good," she scolded herself as the tears rolled hotly down her cheeks anyway. "You just have to keep your back to the sunrise and head west, that's all you have to do. And you keep doing it until you reach British Columbia."

But her words sounded ridiculous to her own ears. How could she survive alone, with no gun, no way of finding food, no shelter, no fire? She had to find the company. She didn't relish the thought of seeing Marshall again. The thought of his leering face and grasping hands made her stomach lurch again, but McMicking and Lucas would protect her. She wished she'd known where she'd been last night so she could have run to the center of camp where there was help to be had, but she hadn't had her wits about her, and she'd only known she had to run. She desperately felt the loss now. All her belongings were in Lucas's cart, including her coat and last fifty dollars and—good heavens!—Geordie. She couldn't leave her cat behind. With a wail, she turned her back on the sunrise and started walking. She thought she saw a faint trail thrashed into the grass where she had run through it, and she followed this now with a hopeful heart.

It was difficult going. The grass grew thickly, and the tough stems were rough and didn't give way easily. She pushed through them, feeling like an explorer in the deepest jungle, and wished she had a machete to slash her way through. Her arms quickly tired from pushing the grass from before her face, and she walked until her legs ached, but she couldn't find the camp or the trees where they had stopped. Surely the carts wouldn't have gone on without her. Wouldn't they be out looking for her? Lucas would surely say something to McMicking. Even if they'd gone ahead without her, she should find the remains of the camp from last night. Doubts and anxieties plagued her as she fought through the grass. When she came upon a stubby tree, she felt panic threaten to close her throat. She didn't recall ever seeing a tree after she'd left the camp. What if she was going in the wrong direction entirely? What if she was ahead of the company instead of behind it? Why wasn't there a trail?

When the sun began to descend, Rachel began looking for a place to spend the night. She found a low hollow in the ground, something McMicking had once pointed out to her as an old buffalo wallow, and made herself a bed, pulling up handfuls of the sharp, tough grass to make a pile, with more to cover her where she lay.

She awoke several times in the night, starting in nameless terror, shivering, feeling ferociously thirsty and hungry. Each time she awoke, she peered anxiously around her hiding place, but the tall grass around her revealed nothing. She'd grown accustomed to the bellowing of the oxen and rattling of the carts over the past weeks, and now the world seemed huge and empty and silent but for the chirping of bugs. The stars were faint and cold overhead. She had never felt so alone or helpless in her life. She fell into a undisturbed sleep at last just before dawn, her arms wrapped around her drawn-up knees and her cheeks wet with tears of self-pity and homesickness.

The next day dawned warm and incongruously cheerful. The sky was blue, without clouds, and the sun turned the waving grass a beautiful dusty green. The night's terrors fading behind her, Rachel pulled herself together, rebraided her straggling gold hair, picked the grass seeds out of her stockings, and set off determinedly with her back to the sunrise. The brisk exercise took the edge off her hunger, but her mind, unoccupied, was free to wander over her predicament. She hoped Lucas was watching after Geordie. She wondered what was happening back in Toronto, if Richard was terribly angry with her. She had never defied him before. And Philip Wycott would be flabbergasted.

It had been a long time since she'd even thought of Philip. Richard had already made noises about marrying her off to him. Philip's father owned a shipping company in Montreal. *Such a good match for you*, Richard had said, but she knew he was thinking all the while of the advantages to his own pocket. A textile manufacturer needed to move his product, and what better connection to have in the family than the heir to a shipping company? Rachel was surprised her brother hadn't suggested marrying her off to Philip's decrepit father himself to speed up the process.

Not that she overly objected to Philip. He was no better or worse than any of the other few men of her acquaintance. He was quiet and solicitous, but he had definite opinions about what he liked and thought Rachel should naturally share the same interests. He was tall and had thick blond hair and a kind smile. She thought he would be as good a match as any. But somehow he just wasn't . . . well, he wasn't very exciting, if truth be told. He sparked nothing in her imagination, and there was nothing about him that really stood out—which was probably why she hadn't really thought of him lately.

He worked in his father's Toronto-branch shipping office doing something with numbers; she wasn't sure exactly what. There were times she grew impatient with his politeness and properness and inaction, and she had to resist a constant urge to do or say something outrageous just to see if she could get a reaction out of him. While she supposed she would marry him, a part of her felt she was betraying her own youthful fantasies of marrying someone with a bit of dash and color to him, someone a bit outrageous himself. She imagined Philip Wycott at thirty was much as he would be at seventy—patient, quiet, and dull. He'd certainly never understand her running off to British Columbia, missing father or no. She doubted he had ever skipped a meal, much less several.

As the day wore on, her hunger became more and more pressing. She was so weak she had a hard time staying on her feet and plodding forward. She kept her eyes open for any animals, even though she knew she couldn't very well kill, cook, and eat one without tools or a fire, even if she'd had the stomach for it. She saw birds high up, which did her no good at all, but they gave her hope that there must be water nearby, for didn't all living things require water?

She finally had to admit she wasn't going to find the company today either. When the sun slipped down the sky's hot surface to the flat horizon, Rachel had to give in and look for a place to spend the night. She didn't want to spend another chilled night like the previous ones. The handfuls of tough grass she'd pulled to pile over herself had done little against the cold that always settled over the prairie when darkness fell. She was shaky with hunger, but there wasn't much point in thinking about it. She hadn't seen so much as a rabbit all day. The only sign of life had been the occasional hawk overhead and the hum of insects in the grass. She tried not to think about the insects either.

She'd given up picking the grass seeds out of her snagged stockings. She wondered vaguely what Philip would think if he could see her now, striding across the uneven ground with no bonnet, the sun bringing out freckles on her nose. Before this journey, the farthest Rachel had ever walked was around the park or along the shops by Toronto's waterfront. She'd never slept anywhere but a regular featherbed, and the only time she had ever gone so long without food was the time she'd had a terrible stomach flu two years ago, when she'd refused the weak broth her maid had tried to coax her to eat. The memory made her smile, and she felt her dry lips crack. She suspected she was no longer the same person who had taken the spoon the maid had proffered and flung it across the room.

Had she come all this way just to die of exposure and starvation on the prairie? Rachel plucked a long blade of grass with fingers grown thick and clumsy from dangling at her sides all day. She chewed its white root, but it did nothing to assuage her thirst.

As the last crimson and lavender light drained from the sky, she found the first reason for hope when she stumbled across the remains of a campfire.

It wasn't a company site. There was no sign of cart tracks, no crushed trail in the grass, and only one small mound of ashes, but they were recent ashes and still smelled acrid. She poked hopefully through the remains but found nothing edible. Whoever had camped there had been tidy. They had also left no sign of which direction they had gone. If they had left any trail, the long prairie grasses had fallen closed and obscured it.

A few feet from the fire, Rachel found a spot where the grass was matted as if someone had lain there, and farther on was a pile of horse droppings. She took courage, thinking surely she couldn't be too far off the trail. Someone had traveled this way.

Of course, they could be as lost as she was.

Fastidiously avoiding the manure, Rachel lay down for the night in the same spot the unknown traveler had slept in and somehow felt less lonely.

The next day commenced as hard and hot as the one before, and Rachel lay on her back and stared up at the cloudless sky. No hope of rain. No breeze. She sat up and looked around, brushing wisps of hair from her face. The prairie stretched unbroken in every direction. She searched for any sign of a river, trees, life, but none had magically popped up while she slept. There was just the same bleak, bare expanse.

She walked until the sun was directly overhead, and then she could go no farther. She had been walking in a blind daze, not watching where she was going or caring in which direction she was headed, and at last she allowed herself to slump to her knees and sit back on her heels. She bowed her forehead slowly to the earth and remained in that position. She would just huddle here and wait for death. There was nothing else to do.

"Aren't you supposed to face east when you pray?" a voice above her asked.

* * *

Rachel started and lifted her head in disbelief, squinting up at the sun. "Pardon?" Her voice came out as a croak.

"Oh, sorry, I thought from your position that you must be a Mohammedan."

Rachel's eyes came into focus, and she saw a pair of trousers a few inches from her nose. Her eyes traveled down and saw worn boots. Hands took her under the arms and pulled her to a sitting position, then a pair of very blue eyes frowned down into hers.

"What in the world are you doing out here all alone?"

Rachel tried to speak, but her dry tongue wouldn't move. The man seemed to understand and fumbled with something behind him, then pressed a canteen to her parched lips. Rachel's eyes popped fully open, and she gulped at the tepid water.

"Slow down. That will do," the man said, pulling the canteen away again. Rachel gave an animal wail of frustration, but the man just as quickly pushed something into her hands and told her to eat it. She sank her teeth into it and tore off a chunk like a wild dog. It was dried meat, jerked beef, salty and sharp. Lucas had given her some before, and she'd detested it at the time, but now it tasted better than any tender roast. She wolfed the entire strip down, followed by the chunk of dry bread he gave her, and only then did she really look to see who'd rescued her.

He knelt a few feet from her, his hands resting on his lean thighs. His hat was pushed far back on his head, and he watched her with a look that mixed concern with annoyance. He looked to be about thirty and had a few days' growth of beard that was darker than the shaggy brown hair showing below his hat. He wore no coat, and the sleeves of his peasant shirt were rolled to the elbow to expose bronze, muscular forearms. His face above the beard was tanned the same color. A short distance behind him, she saw a large bay mare cropping at the grass and swinging her black tail. A little boy of about five sat on the mare's back, staring at her from under a thatch of black hair that seemed to mimic the mare's mane.

Rachel swallowed the last of the food and waited expectantly to see if the man would offer any more, but he made no move. She wiped the crumbs from her mouth with the back of her hand—a most unladylike gesture, she realized, reddening—and muttered, "Thank you."

"How long has it been since you've eaten?" he asked.

She could hardly remember. "Three days, I think."

He shook his head and handed her the canteen again, letting her have only a few swallows before taking it back.

"What are you doing out here by yourself? Where's your family?"

Rachel hesitated only a moment before saying flatly, "Back in Toronto. I was traveling with a company of overlanders—Thomas McMicking's company, from Fort Garry. But I got separated from them and haven't been able to find them."

The man stood and slung the canteen strap over his shoulder. He seemed so tall from her position on the ground. He looked around the landscape as if expecting a wagon train to materialize on the horizon. "How can you lose a whole company?" he muttered.

"It was night," Rachel said lamely.

He eyed her a moment, then shrugged one shoulder. "Serves you right for wandering off. Anyone with any experience with the prairie would know better. What's your name?"

"Rachel. Cameron," she added, keeping her eyes on his. She had learned her lesson about traveling under her own name; this man might know about Richard's telegram.

"I haven't seen any company along this way. Where were you headed?"

"Fort Parker, and then Fort something else that I think starts with a *K*, and then—Oh, I remember the name: Fort Reilly."

"Reilly!"

"I—I'm heading for Bellefontaine ultimately, on the Henderson River."

He shook his head, removed his hat, and ran a hand through his hair. "Well, you're off to a discouraging start to such a long journey. Come with me; maybe we can find your group. If not, I'll take you to Fort Parker, and you can wait for them there. You could send a telegram to your family from there. I understand there's a line now."

"Oh!" She stopped in confusion. If there was a telegraph line in Fort Parker, then word of her might have reached there already. She had thought she'd left that possibility far behind in Fort Carlton. How thorough had Richard been in sending out notice of her disappearance? She cleared her throat, thinking hard. She couldn't very well say she was going to Fort Parker and then object to him taking her there. What would he think? She knelt, staring at the hand he held out to her, feeling sick and bewildered.

The blue eyes came level with hers again as he replaced his hat and squatted to peer into her face. "Are you all right?"

She shook her head, unable to speak, and felt hot tears come to her eyes. She had the urgent desire to lie down in the grass again, but his hands were gripping her shoulders, shaking her slightly.

"You're in sad shape, girl," he said finally, and picking her up around the waist, he hoisted her over his shoulder like a rolled-up carpet. Rachel was too stunned to struggle. She let him carry her in long, steady strides to the grazing mare and thrust her into the saddle as if she weighed nothing. The child, who had skittered backward, perched on the mare's rump and put his arms around Rachel's waist to hold her up. The young arms were surprisingly strong. The man gathered a hank of black mane and curled Rachel's fingers around it.

"Can you hang on to that? Shorty, don't let her fall off," he ordered.

Rachel nodded, clinging to the mane tightly. The man gathered the reins and started walking through the grass with the horse in tow. He didn't ask Rachel which direction to go, and she couldn't have told him if he had. She sat with her eyes half closed, feeling the child's arms steady around her, and concentrated on not falling off.

Her last coherent thought was that it was a good thing she had abandoned her crinoline, or she couldn't have straddled the mare.

CHAPTER FIVE

SHE DIDN'T REALIZE SHE'D FALLEN asleep until the man roused her by seizing her waist and lifting her abruptly to the ground. She put her hands out to steady herself, startled, and blinked around. The sky was fading into grayish purple, and clouds were gathering overhead. It was somewhat cooler, and a light breeze caught the tendrils of hair around her face, blowing them across her eyes.

"Fall asleep?" the man asked.

Rachel realized her hands were resting on this stranger's hard chest, and she snatched them hastily away. "I think so. I'm still awfully thirsty."

"I'm low on water," he said briefly, but he dug in the saddlebags and produced another chunk of food, this time a dried apple ring. "Suck on that."

"Thank you. I am grateful to you for helping me." Rachel forced herself to chew the apple slowly to make it last longer.

The little boy had jumped off the horse behind her, and now the man unsaddled the mare, hobbled her, and turned her loose to graze. Rachel discovered her legs were wobbly, and her rear end was sore from riding. She sat in the grass to watch while the man built a small fire using twisted bunches of grass for kindling. All around the fire, he pulled up the grass to leave a ring of dirt around the flames for safety. He fished in the saddlebags and emerged with some dry twigs, which he added to the smoking fire that eventually grew to handle dry wood, and the smoke ceased. Without wasting time or motion, the man set up a small tin pot of water over the fire to heat before the small flames could die down. He fished out another chunk of dry bread and broke it in half, then offered her a piece.

"Thank you," she said, trying to nibble it nicely instead of swallowing it whole. The ache in her stomach had dulled to a grumpy growl, but her hands still felt shaky. She wished for the dining table back home, spread with china platters of beef and roast mutton and steamed potatoes dripping with golden butter.

She watched the man break the remaining bread in half and give the child a piece before polishing off his own, the muscles working in his temples. The little boy crouched on his heels across the fire from her, absorbed in his minuscule meal. Rachel glanced from him to the man and noticed for the first time the look of hunger on both faces. The fine bones of the man's face showed sharply, his tanned skin stretching over them. He had a straight nose and thin lips drawn now into a grim line. She examined the little boy's tanned face and saw the same expression. How much of their rations had she just gobbled down?

"I don't know your names," she said suddenly. "You saved my life, and I don't even know who you are."

The man put another grass twist on the fire and the smoke rose in gray billows. "He's called Shorty. I'm Peter," he said.

"Peter what?"

"It doesn't matter. Just Peter." His words were abrupt, irritated.

And no wonder. He'd suddenly been burdened with a helpless female who'd eaten half of his food and taken over his horse. She resolved to walk the next day and let him ride.

"Are you trying to catch up with my company?" she asked. "Or are you heading straight for Fort Parker?"

"What do you mean, catch up? Do you think they went on without you?" He stared at her.

"Well, yes, probably. I don't imagine they'd wait, would they?"

"Wouldn't anyone notice you were missing?"

"Well, yes, my—" She choked on the word *husband*. She felt entirely too exhausted to try to explain Lucas. "The person I was traveling with would have noticed. But it was made very clear to me that my coming along was an imposition. They didn't want to let a female travel with them in the first place."

"Meaning they would have said 'good riddance' and kept moving."

"It's likely."

"With me on foot, they may get too far ahead of us. We may reach Fort Parker to find they've already come and gone again."

"What if we don't catch up to them at the fort?" Rachel asked.

Peter shrugged. "Then you stay at Fort Parker until another company comes through. There may not be one headed west, but you may find one going east that will take you back home, or at least as far as Fort Garry."

"How far is it to Fort Parker?" Rachel asked, not certain she liked this idea. She did not want to return east. Who knew when another west-bound group might come along and especially one that would be willing to take her? McMicking had remarked that it was already late in the season to be setting out.

"About four days away on horseback." He shot her a dark look. "Longer on foot."

"I don't suppose your horse could carry all three of us?" Rachel asked hesitantly, knowing it was a foolish remark before she'd even finished saying it.

He thrust his bearded chin at the figure of the mare, now nearly invisible in the falling darkness. "Sure, if I don't mind her collapsing in a few hours. She's fourteen years old. Any other brilliant questions?"

Rachel winced. She pressed her lips shut and watched him fuss with the fire a while longer. Then he stood and picked up the canteen and walked into the darkness without another word. Rachel huddled next to the small fire, feeling its flames pushing away the dark night around her. She felt too tired to think about her plight tonight. She couldn't blame Peter for being resentful of her. She was an unwelcome burden because he wanted to travel fast. He probably didn't want to go clear to Fort Parker either, and it was only gentlemanly consideration that had made him say he'd take her there. Then again, where *was* he headed?

She glanced at the child, who had curled up on his side on a blanket without a sound and fallen asleep. Was it Peter and Shorty's fire she'd found last night? Perhaps the crushed hollow where she'd slept had been formed by their bodies, and it was the bay mare's manure she'd found. What were they doing so far from the trail, all alone? And why didn't he tell her their last name? She was suddenly wide awake as ideas swam into her head. He might be an outlaw fleeing the Mounties. A fugitive deserter from the U.S. army—but from which side? North, most likely. He didn't sound like a Southerner. Maybe he'd turned coward and abandoned the battlefield. Maybe he had a reward on his head.

Like she did.

But she hadn't broken the law, Rachel reminded herself self-righteously. Besides, what outlaw would have his little boy with him? She was being ridiculous.

Peter came back then and dropped the canteen to the ground beside the saddle. He unlashed another blanket and shook it out, standing over her. The fire cast his dancing shadow long on the ground.

"I don't want to wake Shorty. I only have one other blanket," he said brusquely. "And I don't intend to be noble and let you have it all to yourself while I freeze. We'll share it."

"Oh!" She was panicked at the thought of lying near this man all night. "I'm fine, thank you. I'm really not cold. You take it."

"It gets cold on the prairie once the sun goes down," he warned.

"I know. But, really, thank you. I don't need it."

He shrugged and slung the blanket about his shoulders, then lay on the ground by the dying fire. Rachel, who was slightly miffed that he *hadn't* been noble, pulled her knees to her chest and tucked her dusty travel skirt around her feet. She sat staring into the fire, listening to it spit and hiss. It gave more smoke than heat, and she realized it *was* cold, and she wished she'd had her shawl at the dance. Within half an hour, her rear was numb from sitting on the ground, and her arms were dotted with goose bumps in spite of her long sleeves. It was uncomfortable sitting, but she rebelled at the thought of lying in the dark night with this strange man only feet away. Who knew what he would do if she closed her eyes?

Peter's back remained firmly toward her, but she saw Shorty stir and raise his head to look at her across the firelight. Then the little boy crawled toward her, dragging his blanket with him. He snuggled right up against her side and pulled the blanket over both of them. Almost instantly, Rachel felt bathed in warmth radiating from the little body pressed against her. She slid her arm around him and held him close, touched by his kindness. She looked down, trying to catch his eye, but he was already falling back to sleep, his dark lashes long on his cheeks. She could feel the bones of his shoulder blades under his shirt, and in the flickering firelight, his skin looked like smooth mahogany. She could smell his scent, a not unpleasant mixture of horse and prairie grass. He was beautiful but quite thin and not talkative or playful like most little boys his age. Probably too hungry to feel like playing. Where was his mother? What was Peter thinking, dragging this poor child around the prairie? He should be at home, going to school, sleeping in a proper bed.

Comforted by his presence, and believing Peter would do her no harm while she was holding his little boy, she finally allowed herself to relax and fall into sleep.

* * *

Rachel slept well that night. Although the ground was uneven and the grass was prickly, close proximity to another body kept her deliciously warm through the night. The blanket fended off the dew, and she was so grateful for this little comfort that she forgot the awkwardness and unfamiliarity of sleeping so close to another person. In fact, when Shorty slipped out from under the blanket sometime before dawn, she heard herself give a sleepy moan of protest. She awoke feeling a hundred times better. She looked around at the sun already rising, the fire crackling . . . and Peter and Shorty gone.

Rachel sat up, blinking stupidly around. The horse grazed nearby, and the saddle and things were still there, but she didn't see Peter and Shorty anywhere. Then, suddenly, Peter was rising out of the prairie like a groundhog emerging from his hole. He carried a laughing Shorty on his shoulder, and as he approached and grew ever taller, she realized it wasn't magic after all. He had been down in a hollow, hidden from her by the prairie itself. She squinted closer. Both of them had wet hair slicked back against their heads like chocolate caps on strawberries, and Peter's face was clean shaven. He was surprisingly nice looking, almost aristocratic, with so smooth a jaw.

Rachel sprang to her feet and felt herself start to black out as the blood tried to reach her head. She steadied herself and waited until it cleared. Then she jogged toward them, scowling.

"There's a stream down in that hollow, isn't there?" she demanded. "Why didn't you tell me?"

Peter caught her by the arm as she tried to pass him, balancing Shorty on his shoulder with the other hand. A leather case hung from a strap at his wrist, probably his razor.

"I didn't tell you precisely because I knew you would throw yourself in it head first," he said. "In your half-dried-out condition, the last thing your body needs is a sudden intake of water. It'll make you sick."

"I won't. But at least let me wash my face and hands."

He released her, and she hurried past him to the hollow that opened up at her feet. A thin, clear stream of water wound along the bottom of it, half overgrown with grasses. The delicious smell of damp earth tickled her nose as she slid down into the hollow and joyfully scooped up water to bathe her parched skin. She obediently allowed herself to drink only a little, and nothing had ever tasted so good.

She looked up, dripping, to see Peter standing above her.

"If you've finished drowning yourself, breakfast is ready," he said.

Rachel clambered up from the hollow, feeling reborn. Water dripped coolly down her neck, trickling over her sternum and between her breasts. She stopped short, and her hand went to her throat. She'd forgotten the missing buttons at her collar, the buttons Marshall had ripped away. What must Peter think of her, running around with half her neck exposed? But if he'd noticed, he'd given no indication. He preceded her back to the fire and gave her, without a word or even a glance, her breakfast.

Rachel sat looking down at the tin plate in her hand, with its small mound of boiled oats and slice of salt pork, and a keen sense of dismay ran through her. She hadn't expected anything more (he was being generous to give her this much, really), but somehow the word *breakfast* had unintentionally conjured up visions of muffins and marmalade, strawberries and cream, and sausages and griddle scones.

She looked up to see him watching her narrowly.

"Something wrong with it?"

She forced herself to smile. "No. Thank you. I . . . I don't mean to take up so much of your food supply."

He only nodded and downed his own breakfast in a few brief mouthfuls, then stamped out the fire. Shorty, who had polished his plate in silence, took it down to the stream to rinse it, and Rachel followed his example. She was still hungry, and this time she allowed herself a good long drink of the clear water, deciding it was probably safe now that she had some food in her stomach. When she climbed back up the rise, the horse was saddled, and Peter was waiting with his customary annoyed expression. She and Shorty handed him their plates, which he shoved into one of the saddlebags, but when Peter reached to lift her onto the horse, Rachel backed away.

"I'm perfectly all right walking," she said. "You can ride today."

He gave a sound suspiciously like a snort and seized her around the waist, hoisting her roughly into the saddle.

"I said—"

"You're riding," he barked. "I don't have the time or the patience for you to walk, especially in those skirts. The last thing I need is whining about blisters and muddy hems."

Rachel bit her lips tightly together and swung her legs to the other side of the horse, letting herself drop to the ground. Thankfully, she landed more or less gracefully on her feet, and her skirt followed modestly. Without waiting for his protest, she took off walking in the approximate direction she thought he meant to go. There was silence behind her, and then a moment later the horse moved up beside her, with Peter riding and Shorty sitting behind him. He kept the horse at a slow walk, his boot level with her shoulder, and did not look down at her or speak for some time, other than to say "Mind the prairie dog hole" from time to time.

CHAPTER SIX

IT WASN'T LONG BEFORE RACHEL began to regret her pride and stubbornness. The sun was hot overhead, and though the grass was only waist deep here, it kept catching at her feet and snagging her skirt and trying to trip her. She grew extremely thirsty from the exertion of trudging over the uneven ground, but she refused to let herself slow her pace. She wouldn't be a burden to him. She knew he thought she was a hot-house flower that had to be coddled. She had caught him eying her expensive dress and new boots. Well, she would prove his impression of her wrong. She kept her head up, looking forward, craning to see over the grass and watching for any sign of a trail or other travelers moving like themselves across the vast expanse. She saw nothing but grass and blue sky.

When the sun was high, Peter reined the horse to a halt and slid to the ground. Shorty dropped to the grass behind him and wandered away, soon lost to sight. Peter unfastened the canteen and took a long drink, and Rachel watched with fascination as his Adam's apple bobbed in his lean throat. Richard's Adam's apple didn't do that. You couldn't see his because of the fleshy folds of his neck.

Peter resettled his hat and handed the canteen to Rachel. She was desperately thirsty, but she fastidiously wiped the rim of the canteen with her skirt before drinking. The water was still somewhat cool, and she made herself stop before she felt she'd had enough so there would be some for Shorty.

The little boy reappeared, adjusting his pants, and accepted the parched corn and thin strip of jerked beef Peter doled out to each of them for lunch. Rachel didn't like the expression on Peter's face.

"Are we terribly low on food?" she asked quietly, accepting her share.

"We'll manage."

Rachel took herself off to "visit the prairie dogs," not daring to go too far away for fear of becoming lost again. When she returned, Peter climbed onto the horse without another word and moved forward once more, with Shorty hanging on to his waist. Rachel forced her sore legs to follow, but it took all her efforts not to lag behind. She kept her shoulders back and her head up, determined not to let Peter see her fatigue. Her feet hurt inside her boots. And who had invented corsets anyway? Some man, probably.

That evening they came suddenly and unexpectedly upon the trail.

It opened out before them, a wide swath of beaten earth ploughed through the grass, stretching endlessly away to the left and right like a great, dry river. It seemed to Rachel that it was running entirely in the wrong direction, but Peter nodded in satisfaction and pushed his hat back on his damp forehead.

"We should make better time now," he said. "Those tracks are fairly fresh. Your group can't be more than two or three days ahead of us."

Rachel wasn't sure if she was glad to hear this or alarmed. She desperately wanted to ride in the rattling cart again, eat decently cooked food, and hear human voices laughing and chattering around her . . . and get away from Peter's grim silence. She

wanted to laugh with Lucy in their tent over their adventures—
she found she was thinking of Lucas as Lucy now, as she missed
female companionship—and hug Geordie to her. She would feel
safer surrounded by people and not alone on the trail with this
solitary man and his child.

But, no, catching up to the company meant facing Marshall
again. His leering face appeared unbidden in her mind, and the
feel of his grasping hands on her body made her shudder, and
all idea of safety faded. She closed her eyes and shook her head,
pushing the thoughts away. She didn't doubt he'd meant his
threat to kill her at the time, but he'd spoken out of pain and
frustration. Surely he wouldn't still be so upset, with several
days' distance between them and the dance.

On top of all that, meeting up with the company also meant
that soon she would be in Fort Parker . . . where there was a
telegraph. And if people like Marshall got word that there was a
$500 reward out for her, she had no doubt she'd be sent straight
back to Toronto in humiliation and they'd collect the money.

Then again, meeting up with the company also meant getting
her trunk back and her fifty dollars. Her cat. And a fresh change
of clothing, glory be! She glanced at Peter, who had moved ahead
of her on the trail, and hurried to catch up.

They camped that night a few yards from the trail. Peter
didn't say anything but took his rifle and walked off into the
night. Rachel didn't want to think about what he was doing.
She knew, of course, that salt pork and roasted grouse didn't just
appear magically on the spit over the fire, but it still made her
uncomfortable to think about the process by which the meat
was obtained. Back in Toronto, she had never questioned where
her meals had come from. Life on the trail was forcing her to
acknowledge some of her own naiveté, she supposed, and it wasn't
comfortable. She remembered Lucy's laughter the first time she'd
gutted a bird in front of her and Rachel had had to cover her face.

She busied herself pulling up a ring of grass to expose the
earth in preparation for a fire, wanting to be useful in some way.

The tough grass slit her palms like thin wire. Gritting her teeth, she gathered the loose piles and twisted them awkwardly into approximations of the bundles Peter had made the night before. But she had no way to light them, so she sat beside them with her arms around her knees to wait for his return. She looked up to see Shorty watching her. When their eyes met, he gave a solemn nod of approval, and Rachel felt ridiculously pleased.

It occurred to her that she hadn't heard him speak in all the time she'd been traveling with him. She wondered if he was mute. But she'd heard his voice in laughter, so she knew he had one, and his face was intelligent. She gave him a friendly smile.

"Shorty, what's your last name? You and your father's."

He continued to watch her in silence, his eyes on hers. They were a different shape from Peter's and as deep a brown as Peter's eyes were blue. Rachel supposed he must take after his mother. His shirt had once been white but was now a dirty gray, and the trousers he wore looked several sizes too big for him, bound around his waist with a leather strip. His dark hair was in dire need of a cut, hanging long on the back of his neck, which, when he bent his head over the fire, she saw was an alarming shade of brown that made Rachel wonder how long it had been since he'd seen soap.

She must have fallen asleep because when the sound of a shot came through the dusk, she jerked her head up, disoriented and frightened out of her wits. For a moment, she had no idea what had awakened her or where she was. Then she saw Shorty grinning at her, his white teeth shining in the firelight. The familiar outline of the horse stood nearby as it tore noisily at the grass. Rachel rubbed her cheeks vigorously, and by the time Peter reappeared, she was more or less composed.

He carried his rifle in one hand and a long, gray object in the other. When he drew closer, she saw that it was a rabbit he held by the scruff of the neck. The long legs dangled limply, and there was a dark stain on one side. Peter tossed the rabbit down and pulled a knife from the saddlebag. Rachel averted her eyes, pleased that at least this time she didn't feel the nausea Lucy had teased her about. After a few minutes and some indescribable sounds, the rabbit was skinned, cleaned, and skewered. Peter looked over her fire preparations with a brief nod of approval and lit it. Encouraged, Rachel moved closer to feed the grass bundles slowly into the flames. Peter dropped to the ground beside her and propped the rabbit over the fire, rotating it from time to time. He had wiped his hands on the grass, but his long fingers were still darkly stained with the rabbit's blood. Rachel kept her gaze away from them. The rabbit roasted slowly, dripping and spitting, and gradually it began to smell recognizable. A moment ago, Rachel had thought never to eat meat again. Now her traitorous stomach constricted in anticipation. She caught Shorty's eye, and they both wiggled their eyebrows at each other.

When Rachel thought she couldn't bear to wait any longer, Peter lowered the rabbit onto the tin plate and began to saw chunks of meat away from the bones with his knife. Rachel forgot to be repelled and moved closer. Peter looked down at her, and she caught the first glimmer of a smile on his face. The lines at the corners of his blue eyes deepened.

"Hungry, I take it?"

"Famished," she admitted.

He handed her some of the scraps, and all thoughts of blood and death fled. She popped the hot meat into her mouth and smiled with pleasure.

"Good?" he asked.

"Marvellous!"

He divided the meat between the three of them, then put a morsel in his mouth more delicately than she had done and chewed. "It's all right," he agreed.

Rachel laughed suddenly for the first time in a long time. Shorty looked up at her in surprise.

"What's so funny?" Peter asked.

"I am," she told him. "A few weeks ago, if you'd told me I'd be sitting on the ground, eating a half-raw rabbit with my fingers, I'd have said you were insane."

"I take it this isn't what you do back home?" he murmured.

"My brother would fall down dead with astonishment," she replied, reaching for another piece. "But, you know, it really is quite good."

"Everything's good cooked outdoors," he replied with his mouth full.

They smiled at each other with real smiles for the first time.

That night was less awkward. She realized she had begun to trust Peter a little more, and she no longer felt quite as strange about sharing his camp. She wasn't surprised to see Shorty come over to her with his blanket. Her stomach was full at last, and her mind—for the moment, at least—was at rest. With the coarse blanket around her shoulders, her feet toward the fire, and Shorty's back against hers, she felt positively cozy. She had the distinct feeling that if they could see her at this moment, Richard and Philip would most decidedly not approve. This only heightened her sense of comfort.

She dreamt that night of her father. She couldn't remember the details of the dream when she awoke, but his bearded face still hovered before her eyes as she sat up, yawning, and a feeling of peace and contentment still enveloped her. Peter was already up brewing coffee in his battered pot over the fire. The smell reminded her of waking up at home, with Dorothy, her maid, coming into the room with her breakfast tray. Dorothy would have been amused at how Rachel looked this morning. Rachel shook out her hair and rebraided it tightly before standing, straightening her clothes, and rolling up the blanket. Her corset felt molded to her ribs. Though she had purposely purchased one that could be laced from the front so she didn't require assistance with it, she had not removed it since the night she had run from Marshall, and there hardly seemed to be an opportunity now that she was traveling with Peter and his son. It felt as if the confining stays had left imprints in her skin, and she longed to be rid of it.

This time when Peter wordlessly held out his hands, she let him lift her effortlessly into the saddle without protest. She told herself that they would make better time if Peter was the one on foot. He hoisted Shorty up behind her, then, taking the reins in one hand, he struck off down the trail, his long, easy strides covering the rutted ground twice as swiftly as she could have managed in her hampering skirts. Rachel held on to the horse's mane and watched the countryside move slowly past. She refused to think about what lay ahead. If Marshall meant to do her harm, she would appeal to McMicking. It was all she could do. After all, she couldn't very well expect Peter to take her all the way to the Henderson River. He was being kind enough already taking her this far. She had to rejoin her company sooner or later.

Where was Peter going, and why had he and Shorty been traveling off the beaten path? She glanced down at him. Something in the set of his shoulders kept her from asking.

Travel was much smoother along the track, and visibility was greatly expanded. The way was rutted from the passage of the carts and wagons and was relatively clear of the long grass that caught at and tripped travelers on foot. The sun beat down, and sweat trickled over her ribs under the corset. Never before in her life had Rachel questioned the wearing of corsets, but she couldn't get the impracticality of them out of her mind now. It was difficult to think of anything else. Surely comfort was more important than a flatteringly slim waist. Musing, she let her head nod forward, drowsing in the heat. Her mouth was dry with dust, but she didn't dare ask for a drink. The canteen had felt light the last time she'd lifted it, and she didn't know how long it would be before they'd reach the next stream. Besides, if Shorty could go without asking for water, so could she. She glanced at Peter, who was walking slightly ahead of her, his head and back straight, his stride not slowing as the hours passed. He didn't even look sweaty. Irrationally, she resented him for it.

When the sun was high overhead, Rachel began to shift uncomfortably in the saddle and wonder when they would stop for lunch. Her rear end ached, unaccustomed to riding, and her throat was closing over with thirst. She was about to inform

Peter of this when something shiny at the side of the trail caught her eye. She let out a hoarse squeal.

Peter jerked to a stop and glared up at her. She pointed an excited finger.

"That's my trunk!"

He frowned in the direction she was pointing, dropped the reins, and went to investigate the object. Rachel squirmed down from the saddle, settled her skirts, and hurried over. The trunk was badly battered, the catch broken, the lid ripped from one hinge. The calico-lined interior had been slashed in several places, and the only survivor of her belongings was a bedraggled petticoat, which was spilled out onto the dirt and torn. There was nothing else.

Peter reached down and gingerly held up the undergarment between two fingers. "Yours?"

Rachel flushed crimson and snatched it away from him. "Yes. But where are the rest of my things? My dresses, my comb, my atlas. I had over fifty dollars in this trunk!"

"You don't now," Peter said calmly.

"But that was all the money I had left!"

"I guess they discovered you were missing, figured you weren't coming back, and helped themselves."

Rachel couldn't imagine Lucy doing such a thing. They hadn't known each other long, but they were guardians of each other. They had shared a tent and a cart. She knew Lucy's secret. And she couldn't imagine, frankly, that one woman could do such a thing to another. But what if it was Marshall who had taken his revenge on her belongings? Had he stolen them? How would he have known which was her trunk? She felt a chill go over her, and she wondered if Marshall had accosted Lucy in some way. She dearly hoped nothing had happened to her friend. Surely McMicking wouldn't have tolerated that.

"Can't be helped," Peter said now. "You can have a reckoning when we catch up to them."

Rachel stamped back to the horse, crammed the ruined petticoat into one of the saddlebags, and tugged the laces on the bag tight. She didn't know who had done it or how it had come about, but this had been no mere theft. Her trunk had been broken open, robbed, and viciously thrown from the cart. No doubt the money was safe and deep in Marshall's pocket. Sheer anger made her hands tremble, and she gripped the saddle and tried to pull herself into it. She couldn't make it all the way up and hopped awkwardly on one foot, the other heel caught in the stirrup. She knew her petticoat and likely half her leg was showing, but she was stuck, one foot up and one foot down, unable to move in either direction. She was furious with herself now too.

With what sounded like a sigh, Peter walked around behind her, put both hands on her rear end, and shoved. With a squawk, Rachel landed in the saddle, face flaming, her skirt hiked up to her knees. She tugged the fabric sharply into place. Peter said nothing, only picked up the reins and resumed walking. After a moment, Shorty tentatively slid his hands around Rachel's waist.

They left the battered trunk where it was at the side of the trail and went on for about fifteen minutes in silence. Then Rachel let out another cry, this one of dismay. All thoughts of her lost belongings flew out of her head. She didn't wait for the horse to stop walking before she slid to the ground and ran. She fell to her knees beside the gray matted bundle lying like a discarded rug a few feet from the road. The wagon wheels and horses' hooves had left few features, but Rachel instantly knew it was Geordie.

She knelt, staring in horror, and a feeling of terrible loneliness came over her. Her last link to home had been taken from her. And she suddenly knew Marshall had done this maliciously. He knew she would be following behind them, and he had purposely left her cat for her to find. Unreasonably, with dead certainty, she knew it.

Chapter Seven

Rachel ignored the wetness on her cheeks. She had nothing to dig with, no stones to pile over Geordie, so she plucked at the long grass, yanking up thick handfuls and spreading them gently over the cat's body. Her mind seemed numb, far removed from what her hands were doing. The razor-sharp grass slit her fingers, and she saw thin lines of blood appear, but she didn't feel any pain. She built a great pile over Geordie. And then Peter was kneeling in the dirt beside her, catching her wrists, forcing her hands to hold still. She stared up at him in vague astonishment. She'd forgotten he was there.

"It's enough," Peter said, and his usually abrupt voice was gentle. "It's all right."

"It's not all right," Rachel said flatly. "He killed Geordie on purpose, to get back at me."

She pulled her hands away and lurched to her feet, but the world spun around her, and her dry throat constricted. She staggered away a few feet, gripped her knees, and began to retch. They were only dry heaves; her stomach was too empty to produce anything. She kept seeing her poor cat's body behind her eyelids.

Hands gripped her shoulders, then arms were going around her, turning her. Her cheek came in contact with the front of

Peter's shirt, and she let it rest there. His chin rested on top of her head as if she'd been made just the right height for him to hold. For a moment, he stood pressing her against him, until her trembling stilled. Then he picked her up in one fluid motion, one arm under her shoulders and the other under her knees, and carried her farther down the trail. When they were well away from the site, he lowered her carefully to the ground, fetched a blanket, and wrapped it around her. In spite of the hot day, she clung to it, shivering.

Peter crouched in front of her, peering into her face. His eyes burned with a blue intensity, like the center of a gas flame. "You said someone wanted to get back at you. What did you mean?"

Rachel shook her head, unable to speak. After a moment, Peter sighed and reached out to take her cold hands in his. He turned her palms up and inspected them, then took the canteen and poured the last of their water over them, washing away the thin trails of blood. The tiny cuts began to sting, but Rachel watched silently as Peter wrapped her palms tightly with strips of cloth torn from the ragged petticoat they'd found. It wasn't clean, but it was cleaner than any other fabric they had at the moment. When he'd knotted the rags securely, he tipped his head to look into her face again, assessing her thoughtfully.

"Thank you," Rachel murmured.

Shorty, who had been watching quietly, now came to sit with her, a comforting warmth at her side. Rachel felt his small hand on her arm and had to struggle not to cry. He was so sweet, and Peter was so kind.

Peter went to the horse again, but instead of fishing their lunch from the bags, he unsaddled the mare and let her wander away to graze. Then he came back and dropped the saddle and bags beside Rachel.

"What are you doing? It's only noon," Rachel said, surprised.

"We're stopping for the day. The mare could use the rest," Peter said. He went quickly through the routine of preparing a fire ring and fried up salt pork for their lunch, along with, he reported, the last of their bread. Rachel ate without really tasting it, but her aching stomach felt better afterward. There was no water to wash up with, and Peter rubbed the frying pan with dry grass to clean it before repacking it. When he finished, he came to sit beside Rachel, his elbows on his knees and his back resting against the saddle.

"We won't catch up to the company," Rachel said, gazing over the empty plain. "They'll get too far ahead of us."

"You don't want to catch up to them," Peter replied. She looked at him, startled, but he only shook his head and said, "Why don't you tell me what's going on?"

Rachel hesitated, not sure how much to say and how to say it. He took her hesitation as reluctance. "All right, then, I'll begin, and you just tell me if I get it wrong. You didn't get lost. You left your company, and you left all your possessions behind when you went. You were running away from something, or rather, from someone. My guess it's the someone who ripped your dress." He gestured toward Rachel's missing buttons, and she cringed. He had noticed.

"Whoever he is, he's very angry with you," Peter went on. "Angry enough to destroy your belongings and kill your pet. You were plumb foolish to try to bring a cat on the trail in the first place, but that's beside the point. It doesn't seem to me, if I were in your shoes, that I'd be overly anxious to rejoin this person. Who is it, your husband?"

Rachel pushed away the blanket, suddenly too hot. "I don't think I want to talk about it."

"Don't you think you owe me some sort of explanation?" His tone grew harsh. "I need to know what I'm walking into. If I'm going to have a jealous, violent husband waiting for me up the trail, I'd like some advance warning."

"He's not my husband," Rachel muttered.

"Ah well, at least you concede *someone is* after you."

Rachel sighed. "There are two people after me, and no doubt there will soon be more as soon as we reach Fort Parker."

Peter took off his hat and ran his fingers through his sweat-dampened hair. "Are you going to explain that one to me?"

"No."

"Are you running from the law?"

"No."

"And you swear your husband isn't in that company up ahead of us?"

"No. Well, yes, sort of. He's—he's not my husband. She's—" Rachel stopped in confusion.

Peter's eyebrows shot up, disappearing beneath his shaggy hair, and Rachel realized she sounded idiotic. She didn't want to say anything that might jeopardize Lucy's position.

"It's hard to explain," she said. "I needed to get to British Columbia. The captain of the company didn't want to take a female along. In the end, he agreed on the condition that I'd pose as someone's wife, so he . . . he'd be responsible for me and so the other men would be more inclined to leave me alone. It was a ruse but for my safety."

"And this fellow decided to carry the ruse too far, and you refused. Is that it?" Peter blew out an impatient breath. "All this was because you were defending your honor?"

"No, not . . . well, yes. But it was someone else in the company, not my pretend husband." Rachel felt her cheeks grow warm. All her life she had hated her tendency to blush. It made her feel like a beacon, shining for all to see her discomfort.

"Right. So if this other fellow was bothering you, why didn't you run to your pretend husband? After all, that was what he was there for—to protect you."

"I know that," Rachel said hotly. "I looked for him, but I didn't see him, and frankly, I was rather busy at the time trying to get away from the man. I didn't really have time to think. I just started running. I didn't intend to get lost." There was no way to explain to him that she was in fact there to protect Lucy as much as Lucy was there to protect her. And she knew she couldn't have appealed to Lucy in the end anyway. As Lucy had pointed out, if she fought the man, her own secret would soon come out. And if it came right down to it, whose side would McMicking have taken? The inconvenient female's or the seasoned trail man's?

Peter wiped a hand over his rough jaw, making the whiskers rasp. "Do you want to rejoin your company?"

"No. Not now." Rachel looked back toward the spot where Geordie lay hidden beneath the grass. "I knew he was angry, but I didn't know he was *that* angry. I—I admit I'm afraid of him."

"What do you want me to do with you, then?" Peter asked.

"I don't know. What are the alternatives?"

"My first impulse is to leave you out here to fend for yourself," he said bluntly. "I'd be on my merry way. But you're so useless, you'd starve to death in a week."

Rachel didn't think he was serious—at least not very.

"Second choice is what I said before. I can take you to Fort Parker, but we can take our time and make sure your company has left again before we go in so you don't run into them."

"Where were you going before you found me?" she asked. "Were you intending to go to Fort Parker?"

"I hadn't planned to."

"But you're low on provisions. Don't you need to restock?"

"Yes, but I deal with the Natives along the way or the occasional white settler if I can find one. I prefer not to do my business at the forts, for reasons of my own," he replied, replacing his hat.

"Natives! Are there Indians around here too?"

"Yes, of course. Mostly Cree in this area."

Rachel couldn't help shivering. "Aren't you afraid to deal with them?"

"Why would I be?"

"Well, aren't they . . . well . . . they're not civilized, are they?"

Peter scowled. "They have their own civilization, and it's older and probably more advanced than ours."

"Advanced! Whatever do you mean?"

"They have a very sophisticated culture. Practical rules for dealing with each other. Very detailed laws around leadership and self-governance. A wise approach to living on the earth."

Rachel eyed him narrowly. "You sound as if you admire them."

"I do, a great deal. I've had a lot of dealings with them over the years, and I've always found them to be kind and fair."

Rachel shook her head. "Well, I for one hope I don't cross paths with any. I wouldn't mind seeing one from a distance, of course, because I *am* curious about them. Who wouldn't be? But I wouldn't deal with them or trust one. I've heard too many stories."

Peter put his hands on his hips, exasperated. "Then you've been told some falsehoods. You sound as if you think you're better than they are."

"Well, I wouldn't put it so rudely," Rachel told him. "I'm sure they're fine in their own way. All I'm saying is I hope we don't have to run into any."

"This is their land," Peter said gruffly. "Of course we're going to run into them."

"Theirs! It's called Rupert's Land, is it not? The Hudson Bay Company owns it. Or at least, governs it." She wasn't clear on the exact particulars of the arrangement.

"White men can write up all the deeds and charters they want and pass them amongst themselves and *think* they control the land, but it doesn't make it so. Furthermore, if you plan to cross this land, you're going to have to enlist the Natives' help."

"Their help!"

"If you're set on crossing the Rockies and reaching the Dunant and the Henderson River alive, you're eventually going to have to get help from the people who know the trail."

"There has to be another way. Surely I won't need the help of any old savage."

"That's a fine thing to say! You'd best watch your tongue. Shorty understands most of what you say, you know."

Rachel glanced at the little boy, who was watching them with open curiosity, looking from one to the other.

"Well, I don't mean to sound *judgmental*," Rachel said. She wasn't sure exactly what she had said to anger Peter so much, but she acknowledged she probably shouldn't have spoken so freely in front of such a young child.

Peter appeared to pull himself together with effort and rein in his temper.

"So," he said firmly, returning to the subject, "I can drop you off at Fort Parker and let you find another company to join. Not that you'll likely find one this late in the season. You'll probably have to spend the winter at the fort and find another group next spring."

Rachel hesitated, and he eyed her narrowly. "What? I can see from your face that you don't like that idea either," he said.

"I think I'd go crazy waiting around until spring," Rachel declared. "I need to get to the Henderson River."

"Well, you will, but maybe not on your timetable."

"Is there another route that bypasses Fort Parker? If we could swing around it and get to the next stop at Fort whatever-it-is-with-a-*K*—"

"Fort Kiaayo?"

"That was it. How do you say it again?"

"Kiaayo," he said. "It's a Blackfoot word meaning 'bear.'"

"Well, if we could reach it before my company arrives there, and I could find another company ahead of them that I could join . . ."

"Fort Kiaayo is over a month's hard travel from here."

"Oh. Well, what do you suggest?" Rachel asked. "I've never been this way before, and you obviously have."

Peter went to stamp out the remnants of the fire, then crammed his hands into his pockets and began to pace back and forth in front of her.

"You don't want to go back to your company. You don't want to stay at Fort Parker. You're a spoiled brat, you know that? Waiting one winter there wouldn't kill you."

"I want to avoid Fort Parker altogether if I can. For reasons of my own," she added pointedly.

"But your company will have moved on by then. I told you—"

"The person who . . . who attacked me—Adam Marshall—isn't the only reason I want to avoid the fort," she said.

He stopped and looked at her. "That's right, you said earlier that more people would be after you once you reached the fort. What did you mean?"

She pinched her lips shut and fiddled with a blade of grass growing beside her knee.

Peter sighed. "Am I correct to assume that word of some sort about you will have preceded you west, and people at the fort will be on the lookout for you? Is that why you don't want to go there?"

"Yes," Rachel said with some relief. "That's it exactly. I don't know if word has reached them yet, but you say they have a telegraph line."

"And yet you say you're not running from the law."

"No. I'm running away but not . . . rather, I'm running *to*."

Peter held up his hands. "Just tell me who is after you. Besides this fellow in your company."

"My brother, Richard."

This obviously wasn't the answer he had been expecting. His eyebrows shot up again. "Why is your brother after you?"

"Because I ran away from home."

"And he's sending out telegrams, trying to find you and have you returned home?"

"Yes."

"Frankly, I don't see what the fuss is about," Peter said. "So you get sent back home. Maybe get a sound thrashing. So you run away again."

"I'd never get the opportunity to run away again," Rachel said gloomily. "He'd ensure I was kept well reined in after that by cutting off my access to money. I was fortunate to get the chance to leave the first time. And I've made it so far already. I couldn't bear to be taken back."

"Was life at home so unbearable? Were they beating you or something?"

"Well, no. I wasn't happy there, but they didn't mistreat me," Rachel said. She felt exhausted and wished he would leave her alone. "I told you, I'm running *to*, not *from*."

"To Bellefontaine. You're one of these gold-digging hopefuls."

"Not at all."

"Then what's in Bellefontaine? Your lover?"

She shot him a nasty look. "My father."

Peter sat down on the grass beside her and shook his head. "Your father."

"Yes. *He's* a gold-digging hopeful, as you put it."

"And your brother objects to your going to see your own father?"

"Yes. It's complicated."

"I imagine so. Try to explain it to me."

Rachel took a deep breath. "Are you for the North or South?"

"What?"

"In the American War. Which side are you on?"

"I'm not on any side. I'm not from that country, and what they do doesn't have any bearing on me. "

This answered one question. "Which side would you support, though, if you had to choose? North or South?" Rachel persisted.

"Neither. I'm for the human race. Why?"

Rachel shook her head in irritation and tried to find the words to explain. "My father went west to look for gold. My brother has plans to take over my father's business in his absence. Richard has no scruples and, frankly, little business sense. I believe he wants to take advantage of the opportunity in my father's absence to make a deal with the Union Army. If my father ever heard of it, Richard would be ousted faster than he could blink, and all his plans for wealth would go with him. My father is a peace-loving man, and I'm sure he would be against trying to profit from war. Like you, he thought we should stay out of it if the States went to war."

"It doesn't make much business sense, but he and I would agree on that. So write and tell your father about your brother's plans," Peter said, shrugging. "Let him deal with it."

"There's more to it than that. Richard wants to control everything—not just the business but my life. He'll ruin both, I'm sure of it."

"Well, I still don't see what all the fuss is about," Peter said. "Odds are, no one in Fort Parker cares a hoot whether you're a runaway or not. Even if your brother has sent a telegram, people will probably just shrug and say, 'So what?' They're not going to bother sending you back home all that way."

"Yes, they will," Rachel said in a low voice. "My brother is offering a reward for me."

She immediately wished she hadn't said it. Peter's face brightened with interest, and he asked, "Oh? How much?"

"Substantial!" she barked. "Shall I give you his name and address so you can rush off and collect it?"

Peter scowled again. "I'm not the world's most perfect man, but I would like to think I'm not as low as all that."

"I don't mean to offend you, but I don't know how much I can trust you," Rachel replied. "For all I know, you're not any more trustworthy than Adam Marshall."

"If I wanted to harm you, I would have by now," Peter said tersely. He hadn't moved. His position hadn't changed, but suddenly he seemed bigger, menacing. "I've never blackmailed a female or forced my attentions on one. And I'm not about to save your life and haul you clear to . . . to wherever we're going at great inconvenience to myself just so I can collect your brother's stinking reward money."

What could she say to this? Rachel shrank back, chastised, and remained silent. After a moment, Peter sighed and lowered his voice.

"It seems to me you've got no choice but to trust me," he said.

Rachel bit her lips together a moment, then nodded. "We'll have to trust each other," she said. "It can't be one-sided. You have something to hold over my head. Now you give me something to hold over yours. That way we're both protected."

There was a brief silence. Then Peter began to laugh in real amusement, his head thrown back so she could see all his white teeth. It was a pleasant, infectious sound, and his smile transformed his face.

"You're a conniving little thing, aren't you? Why should I give you anything at all?"

"To prove you're trustworthy."

"You'll get your proof when I don't turn you in at Fort Parker," he replied.

"Not good enough."

"It will have to be," he said. "I see no reason to make myself vulnerable just to ease your worried little mind." And he wouldn't discuss it further.

Chapter Eight

Rachel slept that afternoon, glad to have the chance to let her aching bones rest. She wasn't used to riding a horse, and her hands and feet were as sore as her backside. She awoke long enough to eat supper and take herself off to "visit the prairie dogs," as they still euphemistically referred to it, and then lay down again. She was only dimly aware of night falling and Shorty's little body stretching out beside her under the blanket. She slipped her arms around him and smelled the dusty warm scent of him as she drifted back to sleep.

She dreamt of Geordie, of running her hands through his luxurious fur, but he turned into the rabbit, legs dangling, blood dripping, Peter swinging him by the scruff of his neck. Then Peter tossed him onto the road like a discarded cloth, and no matter how fast Rachel ran, she couldn't reach him in time. The wagon wheels rolled over the cat, obliterating him. Rachel awoke screaming.

"What on earth?" Peter fumbled toward her in the dark. Shorty gave a yell and scrambled away, dragging the blanket off of her. Rachel couldn't stop screaming. Then Peter found her head and delivered a resounding slap across her face. Rachel's screams ended on a sudden intake of air. She sat up, holding her cheek.

"What did you do that for?" she shouted furiously.

"That's what you're supposed to do with hysterical people," he shouted back.

"I'm not hysterical!" Rachel retorted and burst into tears.

"What's the matter with you?" he bellowed. "You nearly stopped my heart. I've heard women scream less when they're having their scalps lifted."

Rachel started to form a retort, then froze. "You have? Seen women scalped, I mean?"

"Twice, in fact, and neither one sounded as bad as that," he replied. He wiped a hand over his face. "What was it? A grass snake crawl into your hair?"

"No. Are there snakes around here?" Rachel cried in fresh terror.

"Oh, here we go," Peter muttered. He took her by the shoulders and tried to speak calmly. She could feel the warmth of his breath on her face. "What happened to make you scream like that?"

"Oh. I had a dream," she said meekly. "About my cat."

He again wiped his hand slowly down his face, as if scraping off the impatient reply he had been about to form, and instead said in clipped, careful tones, "It was a dream. It's over now. You're all right."

"Geordie isn't."

"Geordie?"

"My cat."

There was a pause. Then Peter sighed and pressed her gently back down, tucking his own blanket around her chin as if she were a child. Then he lay down close beside her, one arm slipping under her head to cushion it and the other going around her middle in a comforting hold. His mouth was an inch from her ear. His breath stirred her hair.

"Go to sleep," he murmured. "It's all right."

Rachel lay still, stiff with surprise. His embrace was warm, his nearness reassuring and alarming at the same time. She closed her eyes and concentrated on calming her pounding heart, matching her breaths with his. The dream receded quickly, and her pulse slowed. She had to admit she hadn't been so physically comfortable since leaving her featherbed back in Toronto. Richard and Philip would never have approved of this either, but she suddenly didn't care. To her own vague surprise, she managed to fall asleep again, and this time she did not dream.

* * *

When Rachel awoke, the fire was out, her head rested on the hard ground, and Peter was gone. She sat up and blinked around. The sun was well up. Tiny birds flicked through the grass, singing. The saddlebags, Shorty, and the horse were gone too.

Rachel started to her feet in horror. He'd left her after all. She had tried his patience, used up his supplies, slowed him down, and disturbed his sleep, and now he'd gone without her. She ran into the track and looked wildly up and down. She couldn't see him.

For a while, she stamped and raged and waved her arms about, addressing no one. She voiced what she thought of the villainy of men in general and Richard and Marshall and Peter in particular. When her rage was spent, she dropped to the ground and sat with her knees drawn up to her chest. She wrapped her arms about them, pressed her forehead into her knees, and tried to force her mind to think rationally. She was still several days from Fort Parker and a month or more from Fort Kiaayo, and she didn't know in what direction Kiaayo lay. Peter had left her the blanket, at least, but that was all. She didn't have a prayer.

She was still sitting glumly, not moving, her head on her knees, when Peter came back.

He returned, not by the road but from across the prairie, riding the horse with Shorty behind him, his hat pushed back from his forehead. He reined to a stop and sat looking down at her with a smile playing on his lips.

"Waiting for a coach?" he asked.

Rachel's voice came out as a croak. "I thought you'd left me like you said."

His mouth dropped open. For a moment, he just stared at her. Then he let go of the reins, kicked his leg over the horse's neck, and dropped to the ground. Reaching down, he took her wrapped hands in his and pulled her to her feet. He looked down into her tear-swollen eyes. "I wouldn't do that," he said firmly. "I could kick myself for scaring you. I didn't mean to."

"Where did you go?" she demanded, the anger starting to return.

"I thought I'd be back before you woke up." He turned to the horse, lifted Shorty down, and pulled open the saddlebags. "Look. I've got food—apples, corn dodgers, beans, biscuits, potatoes, even another plate."

She shook her head in confusion. "But where did it come from?"

"Some German homesteaders. I've traded with them before. They settled a couple of miles north of here. They even had spare ammunition for the gun. I'm sorry, next time I'll tell you what I'm planning to do. I thought if I stocked up now, we wouldn't have to go anywhere near Fort Parker."

The hard little knot in her stomach started to unwind. "You aren't going to leave me at the fort, then?"

"Do you want me to?"

She shook her head. "No, I don't."

"Then I figure we can go on tolerating each other's company a while longer, at least as far as Fort Kiaayo," Peter said. "They don't have the telegraph. You start slicing strips off this ham, and I'll build the fire. There's cheese too that won't keep, so we'll eat that today."

"Marvellous," Rachel said.

And the sun was bright again.

* * *

At breakfast, Shorty refused to sit near Rachel or accept food from her. He squatted on the opposite side of the fire like a dark little owl staring at her balefully.

"What's the matter?" Rachel asked. "Why is he looking at me like that?"

"How would you feel if someone woke you up in the night the way you did him? You plumb terrified him. I doubt he'll share his blanket with you again for a while."

Rachel felt a pang of regret. "I'm so sorry," she told Shorty. "I didn't mean to. I had a bad dream. It's all right now, really." But Shorty wouldn't move any closer.

After they'd eaten and cleaned up camp, they made a late start, moving at an easier pace now that they'd decided they weren't trying to catch up to McMicking's company. Rachel rode for a while, with Shorty behind her but pointedly not holding her waist as before. Rachel's rear end was complaining by midmorning, and she opted to walk instead. Peter didn't mount in her place but walked along beside her, the horse following amiably, and Shorty slid into the center of the saddle with a distinctly satisfied smirk at having it all to himself.

The mare had had a good long drink at the Germans' homestead's well, Peter told Rachel, and was much better tempered for it. Peter had filled the canteen and an extra leather water bag for good measure. Rachel had allowed herself just a little of it that morning to wash out her stockings, and now she walked with bare feet pushed into her boots and her stockings dangling discretely from the saddle to dry. It had been longer than she cared to think about since she'd last had a real bath.

In the early afternoon, they found a hollow, another old buffalo wallow now overgrown with grass and thick with tiny white flowers. It provided shade of a sort, and Peter suggested they stop to rest there for a while. Rachel sank gratefully into the sweet-smelling grass and watched the grasshoppers leap away like drops thrown into the air by a rock lobbed into a pond. Peter hobbled the horse and turned her loose to graze. Shorty lay a small distance away, spread-eagled on the ground and looking up at the cloudless sky. Rachel put her stockings back on, set her boots to one side, and sat with her legs stretched out, enjoying the cool shade and chewing on the last of the cheese. There was plenty of water in the bulging water bag. A soft breeze had risen, bringing with it the peaceful sound of the tiny birds and the lazy buzz of bees. Really, did life require any more than this? She lay with her eyes closed and let the tense, sore muscles of her legs and back melt contentedly into the earth. She was surprised to realize she felt happy.

"I really should find you a sun bonnet."

She opened her eyes. Peter was lying on his side near her, his head propped on his hand, watching her.

"Why?"

"You don't have a mirror, or you would know why," he replied, smiling.

Rachel put a hand to her face. "I know I'm burnt to a crisp, and the sun always brings out terrible freckles. I'm—I *was*—very fair."

Peter reached out a finger and lightly traced the bridge of her nose. "The freckles are charming, but I'm sure that burn hurts."

"No one has called me charming since I was five," Rachel replied, closing her eyes again, but she was smiling.

"Which was what, ten years ago?" Peter asked.

"Thank you for the compliment—I think. But since you obviously want to know, I'm eighteen. Soon to be nineteen, I guess."

"So old."

She opened her eyes enough to give him a glare. "What about you? I told you; now you have to tell me."

"I'm thirty-one," Peter said.

"Practically ancient." She chuckled. "Where are you from, Peter? Who *are* you?"

He didn't answer. She opened her eyes fully and found him studying a wisp of flower he twiddled in his fingers. "What do you think?" he finally asked lightly.

"Oh, I know this game," she cried happily. "I get twenty questions, and you have to answer yes or no. Question number one . . ."

"Two," he corrected. "You already asked my age."

"But that was before the game started," she said. "And it wasn't a yes or no question. So question number one is, are you from back east?"

"Yes."

"Your accent isn't from around my part of the country," she said. "And you say you aren't American. I'd guess maybe Lower Canada. Montreal?"

"No, but close."

"Ottawa, then."

"Yes."

Rachel sat up with a cheer. "I now know something about you. And I can tell from the way you talk you were well educated."

"Yes, you could say that. Reasonably so."

"I thought so. Do you have any other family?"

She thought she saw the briefest hesitation in his eyes. He looked over at Shorty and said, "No."

"None at all?"

"None."

"Not even distantly?"

"No," he repeated. "And that's your seventh question."

She thought for a moment before asking, "What do you do for a living?"

"That's not a fair question."

"All right. Are you a traveling teacher?"

"No." The thought seemed to amuse him. A smile played about his lips and made his sky-colored eyes dance. He was close enough that she could see the fine spray of lines radiating from the corners of his eyes. At one time, he had laughed often, she thought.

"An itinerant preacher?"

He laughed aloud. "Not likely."

"I can't think why else you'd be traveling alone across the prairie. Do you hunt furs for the Hudson Bay Company? Are you a military scout carrying messages for the government?"

"No and no."

"A surveyor?"

"No."

"Are you running from the law?"

His head jerked, and he stared at her. "Is that what you think?"

"You asked me the same thing," she pointed out. "Please answer the question."

"No," he said. "I'm not running from the law."

"Are you the law yourself? A policeman?"

"Heavens no."

"You aren't American, but did you go down to fight in the war, and now you've deserted?"

"No. I've never been near the war."

"Why not? A lot of Canadian men have gone down."

"Not a yes or no question."

"I do want to know though," Rachel said. "If I were a man, I'd go fight."

"Heaven help both sides if you did." He lay back in the long grass with his hands behind his head, his lips curled in a lazy smile.

"Why didn't you go sign up?" she persisted.

"Because, like I told you, I'm for the human race. Of both sides."

"That seems like a rather wishy-washy sort of answer." Her opinion of him slipped a notch. A bee buzzed past, close to Rachel's head, and she fanned at it absently.

Peter nudged her foot with his. "Don't judge. Someday you'll understand my position," he said.

It was the sort of statement that irritated her, older people telling her she'd understand things when she was their age. She was almost nineteen, for pity's sake. She was old enough to understand anything. She studied Peter's face a moment, its freshly shaven planes, the deep brown tan against the whiter rim where his hat usually sat. Her irritation faded, and she suddenly had the oddest urge to touch that smooth jaw with her fingers, push away the curl of dark hair on his forehead. She made a fist in her lap.

"You're not running from anyone," she said suddenly. "You're running *to*. Like me."

"Is that a question?" he asked quietly.

"Yes. Are you?"

"In a way," he said. "Aren't you out of questions yet?"

"Four left. Are you going to look for gold?"

"No."

"Are you going west though?"

"Yes. I am on my way to Fort Reilly myself."

"Same as me! Are you going to return east someday?"

"Presumably."

Rachel considered her last question for a little while. She might not get another opportunity like this again. He watched her, still smiling, surrounded by the sweet-smelling white flowers.

"Why are you helping me?" she asked.

"Unfair question. Yes or no."

"Will you take me all the way to Bellefontaine?" she asked quietly.

Peter jerked. "Are you daft? Do you know how far that is?"

"It's a fair question. Yes or no," Rachel said.

"You don't know what you're asking. You're talking about months of hard travel."

"I know. You're going west anyway. You just said so. Fort Reilly is more than halfway there, isn't it?"

"My horse is on her last legs now. She can't carry you over the mountains."

"I'll walk. Answer the question, please."

"Hasn't it occurred to you that I might have a life of my own? Plans of my own?"

"I wouldn't interfere with them. I'm just, as they say, tagging along."

"Tagging along! For months. Across the continent," he muttered, rolling his eyes at the sky.

She waited, watching him.

"I thought you didn't trust me," he said.

"You said I'd have to," she replied. "I've thought it over, and I know you're right. I figure I can trust you about as much as I can trust anyone at this point. You're the only one I *have* at this point. So will you take me?"

"It's insane." He groaned.

"Yes or no?"

"Yes," he growled. He rolled to his feet and strode away to catch the horse.

Chapter Nine

Across the campsite, Rachel combed her hair with her fingers and watched Peter yanking at the grass, twisting it viciously into bundles for the evening's fire. He hadn't spoken to her very much all day; he'd only barked orders. She could see he was seething, even from here. His hands moved in sharp, jerky gestures, lighting the fire, setting the pot of beans over it. His jaw was set like granite. Their easy camaraderie of the afternoon had disappeared, and Shorty sensed it too and kept a distance from the two adults, watching them warily like a small, feral animal.

Rachel couldn't believe she'd asked such a thing of Peter. It was a ridiculous imposition she was pressing on him, she knew. No matter that he was going west already. He hadn't planned to go as far as the Colony of British Columbia, and certainly he hadn't planned on the burden of her company. But she could think of no other alternative. She didn't want to rejoin her company. She didn't want to wait in hope of finding another one and risk having to stay in a settlement all winter. And she didn't want to risk going anywhere where there was telegraph service, and Peter knew how to help her do that. She had no chance of making it on her own, and turning back now was unthinkable.

If she traveled with a seasoned guide who knew the terrain and could live off the land and his wits, she had a fighting chance.

And she would get to spend another three or four months with him.

Rachel started guiltily at this thought and glanced at Peter. The idea had been shocking enough to her; if he'd heard it, he'd have been astounded. But he went on doling out the mess of beans without looking up. He couldn't read her mind, then.

Rachel tied off her braid and went to busy herself slicing the wedge of farm ham, fumbling with the knife in her bandaged hands. She was appalled at herself. She'd met him only days ago, and not in the most auspicious of circumstances. She couldn't possibly be attracted to him. He was cold and snappish with her, and she had no idea who he really was, not even his last name. For all she knew, Shorty's mother was still in the picture, waiting patiently at home for her husband and son to join her. She hadn't used one of her questions to find out about Shorty's mother. She wished she had.

Then again, he'd said he had no other family. Perhaps his wife had died.

She glanced at Peter again, watching the sure movements of his hands, the way his shirt stretched over his back when he bent over the fire. His dark hair was plastered to his temples where the hat had sat. Mentally she compared him to Philip back in Toronto, who probably hadn't sweated in his life. Peter was black sulphur molasses to Philip's honey.

She was a fool. Peter wasn't interested in her, she told herself fiercely. She was baggage he had been coerced into dragging westward by his own courtesy. He'd made it abundantly clear she was just an aggravation to him. He thought she was fifteen and silly. *Useless*, he'd called her.

But compared to molasses, honey was just, well, ordinary, tame, old honey.

Rachel hacked at the ham. If she had any brains at all, she would get herself and her thoughts tightly under control. There was no room for flights of fancy on this journey. She was on a mission to find her father, with months of hard work ahead of her, and she couldn't let anything else distract her. She would let Peter help her a while longer, out of his own generosity, to Bellefontaine, and then she would take herself off and let him get on with his own life. It was shameful to think anything more would come of it than that.

Peter must have been watching her vigorously attacking the ham, her face lost in dark thought, because he came over and took the knife from her. "It's already dead," he said sharply. "You're going to lose a finger doing it like that."

He took away the wedge of ham and the uneven slices she had cut and carried them to the fire, where he took over the slicing. Adding some of it to the beans on her new tin plate, he handed it across to her. She accepted it with a resentful thank you.

Peter leaned back against the saddle lying behind him and ate his own beans with relish. Shorty, perched on his heels, picked up the ham and tore at it with his teeth, ignoring his knife and fork, and Peter said nothing to correct his son's atrocious manners.

"I get awfully tired of jerked beef, I have to admit," Peter said. "A little variety is welcome about now."

"How long have you been traveling like this?" Rachel asked, poking at the meal and remembering her great-aunt's rare roast beef with longing.

"Unfair question. Yes or no."

"We're not playing now." Rachel's tone was sharper than she'd meant it to be.

He raised his eyebrows but answered her question. "I've been traveling on and off for about three years. I guess it's been a year or more since I was last home."

"To Ottawa?"

"Yes."

"That's a long time to be traveling. Do you ever get to where you're going?"

He glanced at her and returned to his beans. "Usually, yes."

"At some point, won't Shorty have to settle down and go to school?"

He blinked at her, and Shorty, hearing his name, shot her a dark look.

"School?"

"Yes. He's what, five years old now? Six?"

"I don't know. How old are you now, Shorty?" Peter asked.

Rachel felt he was making fun of her and frowned. "I'm just suggesting life on the trail might not always be possible with a small child. There are certain responsibilities . . ." She realized she had probably pushed her limits and forced herself to stop talking. Peter rose and went to wash his plate without replying.

That night Shorty pointedly wrapped his blanket around himself and lay down across the fire from Rachel, his back turned to her. She felt the heat climb to her cheeks.

"I can't help having a nightmare," she said to his back. "It's not as if I planned to wake you."

Peter gave a low chuckle and, pulling out the other blanket, walked over to Rachel. "Give him time to come around," he said. "He likes you. In a day or two, he'll remember that. Meanwhile, you'll have to share mine."

Rachel shook her head. "Thank you, but I'm fine."

"Now, we've had this conversation before," Peter said, dropping to the ground beside her and flinging the blanket over both of them. "I'm not going to have it again."

Rachel lay still, careful not to bump into him, but the protest that rose to her lips died as Peter turned his back on her with a groan and pulled the blanket around his ears. She supposed there was no better alternative, and after all, they'd shared a blanket before. She couldn't very well argue about it now. She turned her back on him too and stretched her feet toward the last of the fire's coals.

* * *

She wasn't cut out for this kind of life.

Rachel viewed the hole in her stocking ruefully. At home she would have tossed it out without a thought. But here she had no replacement. No maid to darn it. No needle to darn it herself, even if she'd known how. She felt like crying. Brushing angrily at her eyes, she thrust the stocking back on her foot and folded the end underneath to keep her toe from sticking out of the hole. Feeling very sorry for herself, she began picking the grass-seed stickers from the other stocking.

They'd been traveling for days across the endless country, until the days blurred together in her mind. Sometimes she'd ridden the horse; sometimes she'd walked. The landscape never varied, only stretched forever before her. She'd never reach the Henderson River. She was doomed to walk straight ahead across vast nothingness until she was an old woman. She'd been an idiot to try. She had severely underestimated the vastness of this continent. She had half a mind to write to the publisher of her atlas and berate them for misrepresentation . . . if she lived long enough to ever reach a post office.

Peter gave her no time to sit and sulk but announced it was time to move on.

Rachel couldn't suppress a wail. "We only just stopped!" she protested. "My feet are killing me. Don't you ever get tired?"

"You have no one to blame but yourself," he replied curtly. "Those city boots are useless out here."

"I bought them in Fort Garry especially for this trip."

"They're city shoes for a city girl," he said. "And a city girl shouldn't have come out here in the first place."

"I can do it!" she shouted back. "I just need to rest a minute. I swear, you're a machine. You don't have a heart!"

"If I didn't have a heart, I would have left you where I first found you. I took one look at you kneeling there and said to myself, 'Peter, my boy, this one's nothing but trouble!' I should have listened to myself. I'm not too proud to admit I've bitten off more than I can chew this time." He flung his arms wide. "Burdened with women and children! All I need is an injured horse and a stray dog tagging along, and the picture would be complete!"

Rachel stood up, stomped over to the canteen, and picked it up. "I'm soaking my feet at that little stream down there. You can jolly well wait for five minutes."

"Why don't you strip down and wash your clothes too while you're at it?" he snarled back. "I don't mind standing here and waiting for an hour or two."

"I just might," Rachel snapped, provoked to rage by his crassness. "It's not as if we're on a timetable. It wouldn't hurt you to wash either, you know. It's been weeks since your clothes saw any soap or water." She turned her back on him and walked down to the stream—a trickle of tepid water snaking through the grass—took off her stockings, and, no longer caring if he saw or not, hiked her skirts to her knees and waded in. The water was a pleasant shock to her hot feet. It was shallow, barely coming midcalf, and the bottom was rather squishy. Too squishy, really. Clouds of mud swirled up when she stepped. She was going to end up muddy rather than refreshed, and she began to regret coming in at all, but her stubbornness wouldn't let her retreat yet. She stood with teeth gritted and held her skirts up out of the water. She'd said five minutes, and five minutes she was going to stay.

"Watch the water snake," Peter said cheerfully.

"Oh, very funny. Ha ha," she replied and looked down. Something smooth and slippery was gliding around her ankle. She frog-hopped across the grass to the horse and climbed nimbly into the saddle. Shorty laughed so hard he had to sit down.

"Sure that was five minutes? It didn't seem so to me. Sure you don't want to stay longer?" Peter asked.

"Oh, shut up and hand me my shoes," she said.

* * *

The next day Peter pointed out dust rising in the distance. They were overtaking the company. Without comment or question, he veered the horse off the trail and detoured across the prairie, parallel to the track, until the grass swells hid them from view. He dismounted and lay in the grass, and Rachel and Shorty flopped down beside him until the company had moved well ahead.

"Should be all right to go back to the trail," Peter said finally, sitting up to peer after the slow-moving carts.

"Let them get a good distance ahead of us," Rachel said. "Are those trees over there? Those little smudges?"

"Look to be. Might be a spring or stream there. Maybe even the same one we crossed yesterday. Why? Do you want to go snake hunting again?"

"Not particularly, but since we have to wait a bit anyway, it's a good opportunity to wash our clothes. They really do need it."

Peter looked down at his shirt, startled. "*Our* clothes?"

"You suggested it yourself. Look, you can keep the outer ones on because they'll just be dirty again in a few minutes. But both of you give me your underthings, and I'll wash them out for you," she offered.

Shorty, who still had not forgiven her, pouted sullenly.

Peter gripped the front of his shirt, looking stricken. "I'll do no such thing," he said.

Rachel stood and faced him with hands on hips. "The sun will dry them in no time at all, and we can be on our way again. But ever since you mentioned washing clothes yesterday, I can't help noticing you're beginning to smell like an overripe cheese. I'm no better myself. And Shorty needs a good scrub too. Come on, both of you hand them over."

Peter turned away. "If I let you do it, you'll probably beat them to rags. I'll wash them myself, thank you. Come on, Shorty."

Chapter Ten

Some distance downstream and out of sight, Rachel draped her newly washed underclothes and stockings on the grass to dry and, dressed only in her outer dress, stretched out beside her clothes, hands behind her head, and gazed at the fiercely blue sky. The air was hazy with heat, and tiny bugs flicked through the grass with soft whispers. As always, she vacillated between irritation and utter contentment. The feeling of being free of her hated corset was delicious. The weather was flawless, the grass smelled sweet in the sunshine, and the water had been lovely. But the bugs were an annoyance. Much of life was an annoyance. She was tired of sponge baths and cold water. She hated smoky fires. Her skin was parched and chapped. She missed her soft bed and a clean china plate at mealtime. Goodness, she would be happy just to have her own blanket and not have to share with Peter. She hated sleeping on the ground, sitting on the ground, never being tall enough to see far over the grass unless she was seated on the horse. She would give a lot to have a different dress to change into. She found Shorty's continual silence a bit unnerving, though she supposed she was growing used to it. But she especially hated the annoyance she saw in Peter's eyes when he looked at her.

At the same time, she had never experienced a freedom like this before, far from home, away from Richard's critical eye and Philip's possessive gaze. No one made demands of her; there was no one to boss her about, no servants to watch her every move. And she did have to admit that when Peter wasn't being surly, he was a good traveling companion. He knew how to live out in this empty nothingness of the prairie. He provided food and fire, which she couldn't have done herself. The fact that he spoke little could be seen as a blessing too because she was free to talk or to keep silent, whichever she liked. Over the past few days, she had babbled about nothing and everything, saying whatever had come into her mind, making observations of the countryside through which they were passing. She didn't know what Peter thought of her comments because he rarely offered an opinion of his own or tried to keep up his side of the conversation. He never offered information about himself, and he never asked her anything, but, then, he never contradicted her or interrupted her either. After years of competitive conversation with Richard, it made for a welcome change. Peter made few demands of her, clearly had no high expectations of her, and didn't need her to agree with anything he said. It was oddly comforting even while it was insulting. And when heat or weariness overcame them and they fell silent, the silence was comforting too. Yes, she could have fared a lot worse in a road mate. If he would just be a little more civil. If he would just *like* her a little . . .

* * *

She opened her eyes to find Peter lying in the grass beside her, his head propped on his hand, his eyes on her face. She gave a jump of surprise and sat upright, heart pounding as if he had shouted at her. "Peter! My word, you nearly gave me a fit."

"You were gone for hours. I thought I'd better come find you."

"I must have fallen asleep." She rubbed at her cheeks. "How long have you been here? You should have woken me." She found it slightly unsettling to think he had been lying there watching her sleep . . . for how long?

"You looked so peaceful and relaxed, stretched out in the sun like a cat; I didn't want to disturb you."

"I'm sorry. What time is it?" She tried to rake her loose hair into place with her fingers, then gave a squeal and struggled to her knees.

"What is it?" he asked.

"Bugs! There are bugs in my hair! Eeew!" She began flapping her hands in panicked revulsion.

Peter rolled his eyes but got to his knees and took her head in both hands. "Hold still. I'll get them out for you."

It was all she could do to force herself to remain still when she wanted to jump and shake and scream. She imagined fleas could be no worse. She closed her eyes tightly and felt him comb through her hair again and again with his fingers. Her unwanted little stowaways fled into her ears and over her face, and she squirmed and whimpered. Peter held her firmly still, working through the tangled locks, brushing over her ears, her scalp, the back of her neck until finally she couldn't feel the flitting bugs anymore. Still, his hands moved repeatedly, carefully combing her long hair, spreading it on her shoulders until it crackled with static and fell in a smooth gold veil. Cautiously Rachel opened her eyes.

"Have you got them all?"

"I think so," he murmured and spread his long fingers through her hair once again, letting it slip through them like silk. The setting sun turned the strands a burnished amber. For an instant, he paused, one wisp curling gold against his palm, and slowly his thumb stroked it. Rachel hardly breathed, transfixed as she watched. Then he let it fall and rose to his feet, tall against the crimson sky. He clasped his hands behind him. "You're all right. Let's get back to Shorty. He'll be wondering what's happened to us. We may as well stop here for the night. I'll go start the campfire while you get dressed."

Dressed! With horror Rachel remembered her underclothes spread out on the grass for all the world to see, her corset like a gray helmet, her stockings fluttering like banners. She scrambled to her feet—her bare feet—and snatched up her things. They had dried nicely to the consistency of boards. Peter grinned and coughed and moved off with his long, easy strides.

Embarrassed beyond words, Rachel beat her clothes into something approaching flexibility, shook them once more for good measure to make sure there were no stowaways, and quickly glanced around to make sure Peter couldn't see her. She yanked her dress off over her head and scrambled into her underclothes. The fabric scratched against her skin, but when it came to the corset, she couldn't bear to put it on again. It was just too civilized to deal with. She left it sitting on the ground like an odd-looking birdcage, abandoning it with a sense of triumphant daring. Then, muttering, she put on her outer dress and hurried after Peter.

When he went to lift her onto the mare, grasping her about the ribs as usual, he paused, and his eyes met hers briefly, then he looked away and said nothing. But she knew he had noticed the corset missing beneath his hands. She fought the embarrassed flush that rose to her cheeks and felt she should defend herself. Would he think her indecent for discarding it? Yet how could a decent woman even bring up such a subject? She squirmed and looked sideways at him, and he suddenly smiled.

"Much more practical. I was wondering how long it would take you to realize that," he said simply and strode off.

* * *

They neared Fort Kiaayo the third week of July. Peter explained to her the next stop would be Fort Reilly, well to the northwest, and he really ought to stop here for supplies.

"After Fort Reilly, we'll be going up the Amiskwayan River," he said. "Then to Rupert, over the mountains through Sugarloaf Pass to Arch Station, then Fort Loyal and then—"

"All right, never mind." Rachel sighed. She didn't have the energy to sort out the names in her mind; it all sounded hopelessly long, but she trusted him to know what he was talking about. And if he thought they needed to stop for more supplies, then it was probably a good idea. But going into the fort made her nervous. "Do they have telegraphs there?" she asked.

"I doubt it, and even if they do, no one is going to escort you back all that distance to Toronto for whatever measly reward," Peter told her. "You're safe enough. But if it makes you feel better, I'll go in first to make sure your old company isn't there right now. I doubt they'd linger long. They'll want to get over the Rockies before snowfall."

"Snowfall! It's July."

"We'll reach Sugarloaf Pass in mid-September," he said. "I've seen snow fall that early. In fact, it might be better, considering how inexperienced you are—if you'll pardon my saying so—if we wait out the winter at Fort Reilly and push on in the spring."

"I notice you only worry about my inexperience and say nothing about Shorty's tender age," she said sourly.

Peter shrugged. "Shorty can manage. I'm not worried about him. He's been over this land before."

"But I can't manage as well as a five-year-old boy? Thank you very much."

"It was just a suggestion," Peter said.

"We will stop for supplies," Rachel agreed, "but I'm not staying anywhere for the winter. We're going on."

"When we reach the river, we'll have to find another company to join. We won't have a choice. We'll need the help with the portages," Peter added. "Two adults by themselves—it would be impossible. I'm just letting you know."

"At least you counted me as an adult and not a child," she said, but he had already turned aside, and she didn't know if he'd heard her.

* * *

Rachel had grown oddly used to lying beside Peter at night until she no longer even really thought about it. She was used to his mannerisms and moods. But she never learned any more about him than what he'd told her at the very first. However, one morning she learned something about him that she never would have dreamt. That was the morning she woke and found their little camp surrounded by Indians.

At first she thought she was dreaming, and then she sat up with a jolt and realized she was not. They stood in a silent ring around her and Peter and Shorty. She counted eight of them, all tall and sinewy, with white shirts and leather leggings. Their skin was the color of coffee, and they had long, greased-looking hair pulled into loose tails with strips of leather. A couple of them had feathers randomly trailing from the leather strips. Their regal faces bore no expression; they stood in unearthly stillness, arms folded or hands on hips, apparently just waiting for them to wake up. Even in Rachel's panic, a part of her brain took time to be surprised that the Indians were so handsome. She had read about them so much, but as far as she could recall, none of the books had mentioned that.

Rachel slowly reached out a shaking hand and tugged at Peter's shoulder. He muttered something, still asleep. The sun was just rising, and the blanket was wet with dew. Rachel hissed his name between clenched teeth.

He caught the tension in her voice and sat up, squinting.

"Oh," he said.

"What now?" Rachel whispered. She was afraid to move or make any sudden noise. Would they attack? She had read stories . . . Her eyes slid from one man to the other, assessing the rigid muscles in their forearms, the solid strength of their stances, their swift-looking, lean legs. Their narrowed eyes. She and Peter were hopelessly outnumbered, and she desperately wished she'd never left Toronto. Without thinking about it, she reached out and tucked Shorty's blanket over the boy's head in a vain attempt to hide him.

"What do they want?" she whimpered. Her heart was beating so hard she thought she might be ill.

"Let's find out," Peter said, pushing back his blanket. He stood up slowly, almost casually, and his face was calm as he opened his mouth and said something unintelligible. Rachel blinked up at him. But of course! He'd said he had picked up some of their language. She looked at the Indians anxiously to watch their reaction.

The Indians apparently understood him. They glanced at each other. Then one of them, who looked slightly older than the rest, with gray streaking his hair, frowned and made a sound back. He pointed a long finger toward Shorty, who lay still sleeping, hidden under his blanket.

Peter responded, and the two grumbled and clucked at each other back and forth for some time. Rachel thought she would go insane with impatience.

"They say there's a large river half a day's journey to the north," Peter said at last, turning to her. "With fish, where large game come to drink. We can replenish our meat supply there. If we follow the river, we'll reach Fort Kiaayo in two days."

"You understand them?" Rachel asked foolishly. Her voice was an octave too high. "I mean, I knew you picked up some of their words, but that didn't even sound like it meant anything!"

"I speak four different Indian languages," Peter replied. "This one is Cree." He turned back to the men and made more noises, gesturing toward Rachel. She saw the dark faces break into white-toothed smiles.

"What did you say?"

"That the foolish white squaw does not understand plain speak," Peter said.

"I do if it's English," Rachel replied, injured. "And a little French and German."

"Which will do you little good here." Peter returned to the conversation, and the Indian pointed again toward Shorty, frowning and shaking his head. At that moment, the little boy emerged from his sleep, rubbing his face, and saw the Indians. For a moment, his face went slack with surprise, and then he jumped to his feet. Peter put a protective arm around the boy's shoulders and said something earnest-sounding to the Indian. They seemed to debate back and forth for a while, Peter's face growing more and more cloudy with anger, their voices rising in pitch, and then finally the Indian gave a dismissive sort of wave and shook his head in clear disgust.

Whatever he said seemed to please Peter, who visibly relaxed and pushed Shorty toward Rachel. The little boy stood pressed close to her side and said nothing, but his eyes were large.

The Indian looked around the camp, looking dissatisfied, and said something more.

Peter turned to her. "He wants either the horse or my rifle," he said. "We can choose."

"Why should we give them anything?"

"It's that or they take Shorty. I've been trying to convince them they don't want him."

"Oh! Which is the most difficult to replace?" Rachel asked, wondering edgily whether, if they gave the gun to the Indians, they would use it on them.

"Probably the gun. The mare is old, and we were going to get another horse anyway."

"Then give them the horse. We can walk. Fort Kiaayo isn't that far away, you said."

Peter sighed and spoke to the Indian again. He nodded, and without further ado, the ring of men turned away. They took the mare but good-naturedly left the saddle and saddlebags. They also gave Peter a wickedly sharp-looking hatchet, which he accepted with solemn thanks. Rachel and Peter stood and watched them walk to where their own sturdy horses were waiting.

When the Indians had ridden away, they gathered their belongings. Peter slung the heavy saddle over one shoulder and the saddlebags and rifle over the other. Shorty carried as big a bundle as he could, but Rachel had to carry the rest, and it was slow and tiring after that.

They walked for a while in silence, and then Rachel asked, "How did you learn to speak their language, anyway?"

"I picked it up. It doesn't matter." He glanced sideways at her. "I have to say, you didn't scream or faint or any of the other things I figured you'd do when you met your first Natives."

"They didn't look the way I thought they would. Their shirts looked like store-bought cotton."

"Probably were."

"And they didn't have big feathered headdresses on."

"This wasn't exactly a ceremonial occasion," Peter said with a wry grin. "I'm sure if they'd known they were going to meet a pretty young lady, they'd have dressed up a little better."

She scowled at his banter and ignored the comment. Pretty lady, indeed. She felt far from pretty, with her teeth fuzzy from sleep and her dress a wrinkled mess, baggy from the absence of her corset.

Peter, on the other hand, strode vigorously along, looking fresh as May. Wrinkled clothing actually looked *good* on him, and if his hair was mussed, his hat hid it. It was unjust, Rachel thought resentfully, that he could look so energetic and clear-eyed after their rude awakening. Her own feet were lumps of iron, and her eyes felt gritty.

It was slow, hard work without the horse. Peter began to flag after an hour of carrying the saddle and rifle. Rachel was finding the iron frying pan terribly heavy, and before long she felt as if her arms had been pulled from their sockets. She kept her mouth closed, though, and said nothing as she struggled to keep up with Peter's long strides. She couldn't very well complain when Shorty, walking along beside her, hadn't made any protest.

A half hour later, Peter reached over and took the frying pan from her.

"I can carry my share," Rachel protested. "You already have so much."

He said nothing, only kept walking, but he shortened his pace a little so she wouldn't have to jog.

At about ten o'clock, they reached a slow-moving river with scraggly trees growing beside it. Rachel dropped to the ground at the foot of one of them and groaned in exhaustion. Shorty followed suit.

Peter dumped his burden to the ground and sank to the earth beside them. "We'll have to lighten our load," he said. "If I have to carry that much weight every day, we won't make more than a few miles." She thought he was probably saying it for her benefit; he certainly didn't look as worn out as she felt. Only the sweat darkening his shirt spoke of the strain.

Rachel flapped the loose collar of her dress to cool her throat. "Can we get by without the frying pan?"

"Probably. We can roast meat on sticks," Peter said regretfully. He began to burrow through the saddlebags. "The salt pork we can finish off now. The scraps from your—er—petticoat can go. This can too." He pulled out a thick, tattered book and gently set it aside on a rock.

"A Bible?" Somehow Rachel was surprised that he had one. It seemed too domestic, and Peter Whoever-He-Was was not what she would consider domesticated.

He tipped his head to one side. "I can replace it someday. And this." He set aside a length of rope and an iron horseshoe pick. "Won't be needing those right now."

"I'm sorry you lost your horse."

"Couldn't be helped. We'll get another when we can. At least they gave me the hatchet in return. That was a gesture they didn't have to make, but they felt it was fair."

"It's heavy though. Can you carry it?"

"I think so. It would be rude to leave it behind."

They threw out everything they dared. Rachel joyfully added the frying pan to the small pile.

"That will do until we get to the fort," Peter said. "I don't want to throw out more, or I won't be able to afford to replace it."

They made better time with the lightened load, but when they stopped at dusk, they were still too tired to bother lighting a fire or cooking. They ate dried beef strips and parched corn and curled up in their blankets. In spite of her exhaustion, Rachel lay awake long into the night, trying to find a comfortable spot for her aching muscles on the lumpy ground.

The next morning, she woke first. Her shoulder muscles were stiff from yesterday's exertions, but she felt a little more optimistic by daylight. The sun was just coming over the long grass in a molten splash of light. Small birds made repetitive conversation through the cool air. As Peter and Shorty slept on, she lay a moment, enjoying the golden spray of sunshine in the leaves of the tree overhead, and then she got up and went down to the river. It was shallow and sluggish at the edges, with muck at the bottom rather than stones, but the water was clear and cool and tasted sweet. Rachel followed it downstream a short distance to where it cut into a slight knoll that hid her from view of the camp. She didn't know when she would get a better chance for a decent wash. Quickly, shivering, she stripped off her clothing and waded in. She felt faintly heathen, being completely bare in full view of God and sky. The water was too cold to allow much soaking, so she splashed quickly, wishing for soap, then dowsed her head and scurried out again onto the dry bank. She had no towel to dry herself with either, so she stood shaking and dripping until the morning breeze dried her somewhat. She pulled her clothes back on—how blessed, without the corset!—with fingers that were swiftly turning blue, and squeezed the water from her hair. She left it loose on her shoulders and tipped her head back, breathing in great pulls of air, enjoying the feeling of her ribs expanding unrestrained and the joy of being fully clean at last. Refreshed and cheerful, she hurried back to camp.

Peter was sitting on his heels beside a bright crackling fire while Shorty gathered sticks along the bank.

"I wondered where you'd got to," Peter said.

"I wanted to have a thorough wash. The water is freezing!"

"Coffee's hot." He held out a tin mug, and she took it gratefully. Her fingers brushed his as she did so, and he wiggled his eyebrows at her. "You *are* cold. Sit by the fire." He rose and, taking one of the blankets, draped it about her shoulders and snugged it under her chin. It was a simple, considerate gesture, and it warmed her to her depths. She tipped her head back and smiled up at him.

"Thank you."

He looked down at her and seemed to hesitate, still holding the blanket closed. She couldn't quite read the look in his eyes as he studied her, and he looked about to say something, but then he only nodded and returned to his place across the fire.

* * *

They made slightly better progress the next three days. With lighter loads they were able to swing along at a good pace, and Rachel was secretly smug that she was able to keep up with Peter with less effort. She should keep a journal of her adventures, she thought. She could get it published in Toronto. She could call it *Rachel Hamilton: Woman of the Trail*. She glanced down at her dirty skirt and disreputable stockings. *Wild Woman of the West* was more like it. She was so busy entertaining herself with this idea that she didn't notice the gray smudge on the horizon until it broadened into small, distinct hills.

"What's that?" she asked, pointing.

Peter squinted against the sun and then turned to her with his rare broad smile, the smile that made her forget her sore feet and sunburnt nose, that made Philip recede into distant history. "The end of the prairie," he announced.

Rachel had never heard anything so encouraging. She'd spent weeks trudging through flat, featureless grass until she despaired of ever reaching the end of it. And now, unexpectedly, here it was.

The population of the land rose as they neared Fort Kiaayo. They met a few other travelers on the trail and saw a few of the low sod houses cut out of the prairie that Lucy had told her about. They looked positively snug to her now, with dusty-looking vegetable gardens sprawled around them and grass waving on their roofs. Fat, sleek cows stared at them without interest as they passed.

It was no use trying to avoid all contact with other people now. Rachel kept her face averted when they met someone on the trail and let Peter do all the talking that common courtesy demanded. When one inquisitive fellow asked who they were and where they were headed, Peter replied promptly that they were William and Mary Mitchell on their way west. Rachel peered out of the corner of her eye at him, but he kept looking straight ahead, ignoring her. The man didn't push for more information but only nodded in a friendly fashion and went his own way.

Rachel cleared her throat. "William and Mary Mitchell?"

"Well, what was I to say? You obviously don't want your identity known. Neither do I, for reasons of my own. And a couple traveling together will raise questions unless they're married."

"You could say I'm your sister," Rachel suggested.

"There's too big a gap in our ages, and we don't look a thing alike. So I'm William Mitchell, and you're my wife, Mary. We're from the Red River Settlement, and we're coming out here to prospect for gold."

"And Shorty is our son?" Rachel asked, smiling.

Peter glanced at her, frowning. "Don't be daft. We'll say he's our ward. There's no way you look old enough to be anyone's mother. And no one would believe it anyway. We'll say we've only been married a year, so we have no children yet."

A funny sensation shivered up Rachel's arms, and she felt herself grin stupidly. "All right."

The hills turned into rolling countryside, and the trail became a proper road, pounded flat from use. Water was no longer hard to come by; no one objected to tired strangers taking a drink from their well. That night Peter stopped at a shack not far from the road and asked the farmer for permission to camp in his barn.

"I don't see why not," the old man said, rubbing his whiskers and glancing from Peter to Rachel. "It's not the most comfortable place . . ."

"I'm sure it's better than where we've been sleeping," Peter said with a nod of thanks.

"All right, then. Help yourself to feed and water for your horses."

"Thank you, but we're on foot."

The man stared at him, eyebrows raised. "On foot?"

"We're planning to buy some pack animals."

"Oh, well, that's all right, then. I'll send my wife down later with a bite of something for you."

"You're very kind."

The elderly man's wife turned out to be as plump as one of her own hens and at least thirty years younger than her husband. She arrived with a basket crammed with chicken pie, mashed potatoes, brown beans, and apple tart. She hardly spoke, only gave Rachel the basket and apologized that the food wasn't very hot. She cast an almost nervous glance at Shorty, a shy look at Peter, then retreated.

"Now, this is living." Rachel sighed half an hour later, her mouth full of warm apple tart. She leaned back against a sack of grain, with her legs stuck out in front of her. She didn't suppose it was very ladylike, but at this point, she didn't care. The floor was cool, packed earth swept clean. Half of the structure was filled by a curious horse tethered to one side, and various leather straps and bits of tack hung neatly from pegs on the wall. The air smelled strongly of horse and hay, and dust motes drifted lazily in the last of the sunset's light coming through the chinks in the walls. The cool dimness soaked into Rachel's bones, relaxing her aching muscles. She hadn't realized just how long it had been since she'd had a roof overhead.

Shorty finished his meal and contentedly wiped his hand across his mouth. Peter observed him and then grinned and wiped his own mouth on his sleeve. "Not bad," he agreed. "If nothing else, Mrs. Farmer can cook."

"She can indeed."

"A vital quality in a wife."

Rachel cocked an eyebrow at him. "I don't know if I'd call it vital."

His grin spread lazily across his face. "I take it you can't cook?"

"Well, we had Maria to do that sort of thing," she said a touch defensively. "And Anna came on Thursdays for the baking. I never had much practice at it. I can make a decent fried egg though."

"I suppose that's something," he said. "A useful skill. Right up there with embroidering and playing the pianoforte." He stood and stretched, and she heard his spine crack. He pulled an armful of hay from the stack and spread it thickly on the floor, then flung their blankets flat over it. He sank onto one of them and stretched out with a groan.

"I'll have you know, my embroidery won first place at the church bazaar." Rachel sniffed.

"I'm sure it did."

"And I can play the piano as well as anyone in Upper Canada."

"I'm sure you can."

"Some people think those are good attributes in a wife."

"I'm sure some people do." She heard him yawn. The light had faded to gray, and she could hardly see him.

"I don't expect a wild frontiersman with one suit of clothes to his name could judge the matter," she added under her breath.

If he heard her, he ignored the comment. "First thing I do when we reach the fort is try to find a couple of horses," he said. "All this walking is tedious."

"Feet hurt?" Rachel inquired. She crawled awkwardly to stretch out on her own blanket with Shorty between them. The air was thick with dust from the hay, making her want to cough.

"These boots wore thin a hundred miles ago," he replied, but there was a chuckle in his voice.

"Maybe we should try to get you new boots instead of a horse." Rachel squirmed. The hay was itchy, poking through the blanket.

"If I had a horse, I wouldn't need boots."

They lay quietly a while as the gray turned to black and then back to gray as the moon came up. The horse sagged on one hip, making comfortable, sleepy sounds.

"I feel rather responsible for your horse," Rachel confessed after a moment. "I mean, if you didn't have me slowing you down, you may have avoided those Indians all together."

"It would have happened sooner or later."

She rolled onto her side to face Peter across Shorty, who was breathing deeply in sleep. Peter was just a dark shape, darker than the air around them. "Do you meet them frequently in your travels?"

"Yes. This time I didn't have to look for them; they found us. But I would know where to look if I needed to. They're friendly, nothing to worry about, if that's bothering you. The men looking for gold often hire the Indians to help them over portages."

"You've mentioned that word before. What is a portage?"

"When you reach a waterfall or rough rapids on the river, you have to stop and carry your boat and belongings along the river until you reach more peaceful waters again. If you don't have someone to help you, you may have to make several trips back and forth to move all of your things. And two people can't very well carry a raft or boat. Traveling alone, you'd have to use a canoe, and that poses its own problems on rivers like these."

"Oh." Rachel didn't like the sound of this. "So we have to go on a river?"

"Several of them."

"There's no way to avoid them?"

"They're the best way to travel. We'll build a raft. Easy doings now, with this fine hatchet the Cree gave me."

"What about the horses we're supposedly getting?"

"We'll sell them on the trail. There are places where people switching to boats leave their horses, and people who are heading the other way and just getting off of boats pick up horses."

"I see. It sounds very organized."

He chuckled. "Not really. But that's the general idea."

"Still, this adventure is costing you," Rachel said. "The new horses, the supplies we'll need . . . When this is over, I'll see that you're reimbursed for your food and—and everything." Even as she said it, she knew there was no way she could possibly repay him for all he'd shared with her, the help he'd given her and would yet give. It went beyond monetary things.

There was a pause, and then his hand moved in the darkness to touch her arm. "I'm not keeping track," he said quietly.

For a while, they lay contemplating the invisible ceiling above them and listening to the soft sounds of the horse's breath mingled with Shorty's. Somewhere a dog barked. After a moment, Peter's hand moved away, and he rolled onto his side, away from her. His breathing deepened.

Rachel propped her head on her hands, a contented drowsiness settling over her, stomach pleasantly full, warmth radiating from the spot where he'd touched her. It was different lying near him under a roof—rickety as it may be—instead of the vast sky. She supposed she should feel awkward about it, but she didn't. She lay smiling to herself in the slivers of moonlight until she too fell asleep.

CHAPTER ELEVEN

Two days later, they reached Fort Kiaayo.

The fort looked to Rachel like a medieval fortress—a wall of wood perched above the North Rupert River like something out of a fairy tale, with towers built at the corners. It was a place of trade more than a place of defense, Peter told her, since the Natives in the area were not hostile, but it still looked imposing enough to Rachel, especially after seeing virtually no man-made structures for so long. They dusted themselves off and tidied their hair as much as possible and stepped back into society—of a sort—for the first time in weeks.

It was tiny compared to Toronto, but Rachel was as excited as a child to be back in the midst of people. There was, to her surprise, a church and shops and blacksmiths and cobblers and bakers and any number of other trades, fueled by the Hudson Bay Company and the gold rush.

Peter found her a sort of rooming house where she could take a real bath in genuine hot water, with actual soap, and she felt she'd died and gone to heaven as she soaked in the sudsy water and let the steam curl the hair at her temples. She slid the cotton washcloth over her sunburnt skin and breathed in the delicious scent of lavender from the soap. Utter bliss, though the water was cold and positively black by the time she finally stepped out of it.

The cheerful woman running the house scrubbed most of the travel stains from Rachel's dress for her, then let her sit toasting by the fire in the kitchen, wrapped in a wool blanket, while her clothes dried. If the woman thought anything of Rachel appearing without corset or crinoline, she kept her thoughts to herself and set a tea tray at Rachel's elbow. No doubt she saw all sorts pass through this place. The woman kept up a steady stream of light chatter, happy to have a new person to talk to, but after a while, Rachel—grown so used to Peter's silence on the trail—felt overwhelmed by the flow of talk. She soon lost track of the conversation and slumped into a doze, and the woman tiptoed away to let her sleep.

When she awoke, dinner was on the table, her dress was nearly dry, and Peter and Shorty were back.

"I've got work," he announced without preamble when she came into the dining room dressed in her clean clothes.

"What?" Rachel stopped in the doorway, startled. "I thought we were going to Bellefontaine."

"We are," he replied, giving their hostess a smile of thanks as she set a plate of stew before him. He picked up his spoon and dug in without formality. "But we can't go anywhere without supplies and at least a couple of horses, and I don't have the money for them up front. I found a fellow homesteading just up the river. We can stay in their hayloft for a month, and his wife will provide meals for us. You'll help her in the dairy, and I'll work with him in the fields in exchange for a four-year-old mare. With the money I have left, we'll have enough for the additional horse and the supplies we'll need. You can't ask for a better arrangement."

Rachel could think of several better arrangements, including her comfortable home back in Toronto where a maid did her bidding and no one expected her to do anything, but Peter looked so pleased with their luck that she couldn't spoil it. Besides, he was right; neither of them had enough money, and he was doing this to help her, so she forced herself to smile and say, "That sounds good."

He reached across the table suddenly and surprised her by running a finger lightly down her cheek.

"I know it's not what you had in mind, but it's only for a month, and then we'll be off again. We really can't attempt to go farther without good horses."

She nodded. "I'll try to be as useful as I can."

He smiled and returned to his stew, adding with his mouth full, "You slick up nice."

Rachel couldn't help laughing. "Thanks. A little soap does wonders. You should try it yourself." When he glanced at her, she added earnestly, "No, really. You should try it. As soon as possible. Both of you."

"Point taken. We'll bathe after dinner," Peter said and laughed. It was the first full-throated laugh she'd heard from him, and it entranced her. His voice was a rich baritone, and his laugh filled the room. Even their hostess straightened from the stove and looked at him in wonder. Rachel picked up her spoon and bent over her own stew.

When Peter sobered again, Rachel asked in a low tone, "Have you heard anything about . . . about me? Is there a telegraph here?"

"No need to worry about that," Peter said. "I haven't heard anything about a missing girl, and besides, you aren't Rachel Cameron anymore, you are Mary Mitchell, remember? A respectable married woman, not traveling alone. And whatever you were like when you left Toronto, I doubt you still fit that description, anyway."

Well, that was true enough, Rachel thought. Richard and Philip probably wouldn't recognize this skinny, sunburnt creature as Rachel Hamilton if they were to meet her face-to-face. Her anxiety lessened a little. She had come so far; surely no one and nothing could stop her now from reaching her father. She did feel a little guilty, though, that Peter didn't know her real name was Hamilton, not Cameron. Then again, she didn't know his last name at all, did she?

"What's more," Peter added, reaching for the battered coffee pot, "the people we will be staying with are basically illiterate; they haven't got access to telegraphs or newspapers, and they don't seem the type to gossip with the neighbors, even if they had any." He eyed her a moment, then turned back to his plate. "I stuck with the story about being husband and wife. I figured they'd object to our traveling together if they knew we weren't married. I told them we lost all our supplies and wagon in a fire a few weeks ago, and we're on our way to join your family. Shorty is the son of an acquaintance we're transporting to his family. I didn't get more detailed than that. The more facts to remember, the more likely we are to make a mistake."

"That's good," Rachel agreed.

* * *

The farmer and his wife, Edward and Joanna Hunsaker, were both short, white-haired, and as round as twin muffins. He was German, she was from Minnesota, and they had only one son, a giant, yellow-haired man of about thirty named Karl, who helped run the farm. They had twenty-five acres in the river bottoms, ten of it in corn, and kept a small herd of dairy cows.

They had a two-room house, a luxurious place by that area's standards, with one room serving as kitchen and the other as a bedroom. Karl slept on a straw tick on the planks in the attic. The house had wood floors and a window covered in oiled paper. The fireplace was enormous, built of river rock, and their furniture was hand-built from rough wood, other than a scuffed rocking chair Joanna said she'd brought from her grandmother's house in Minnesota. The whole place would have fit in Rachel's sitting room back home. But after her experiences on the prairie, it seemed like a palace to her.

"Ed won't admit it, but we're starting to slow down in our old age," Joanna said confidentially as she dished up baked beans that evening. "We're glad to have your help."

"Who's getting old?" Ed retorted, eyes sparkling at his wife. "Speak for yourself, old woman."

"All right," she said amiably. "*I'm* getting too old to manage the dairy by myself anymore. Karl here needs to find himself a wife to help me."

Karl, who had the build and face of a patient ox, and probably the intelligence of one as well, grinned bashfully and turned as pink as his mother's broadcloth dress.

"I just wish I could put you somewhere better than the hayloft," Joanna fussed, pouring out the first milk Rachel had seen since leaving the company of overlanders.

"That's all right," Peter assured her happily. "We're used to roughing it. So long as it doesn't rain on me, I'm happy."

Joanna bent to Shorty's level and asked, "What do you think, little man? Are you all right with sleeping in the barn?"

"Oh, he doesn't speak," Rachel told her.

"No?" Joanna straightened. "Why not?"

Rachel opened her mouth, then closed it again and looked at Peter. Why not indeed?

Peter just smiled. "He's a deep thinker. Just doesn't have that much to say."

"Can he hear all right?"

"Yes. Just keeps his cards close to his chest."

Joanna pondered this and then accepted it. She gave Shorty a cup of the milk and touched him lightly on the top of his head in a motherly caress as she moved around the table.

* * *

Rachel hadn't expected dairy work to be all that tiring. Joanna was probably about sixty and hardly a muscular sort of woman, and she managed alone, didn't she? But the first day showed Rachel how wrong she had been. There were buckets to haul, heavy wooden cheese molds to lift and wash and pack and stack. The hard earthen floor of the dairy room had to be swept and cleaned.

Rows of thick round cheeses had to be wiped and turned. But worst of all, there were the cows. Not only was Rachel expected to milk them, but she was also expected to wash them off first.

She discovered very quickly that she was terrified of them, something she hadn't considered before. She stood staring at the ponderous, bony-hipped, large-eyed creature before her and hadn't a clue how to begin.

"There's a bucket of warm water and a rag," Joanna prompted. "Make sure you get all the mud off, or it will get in the milk."

Rachel bit her lips together and picked up the dripping rag. Cautiously she approached the cow and crouched down. She didn't want Joanna to see her fear, but she couldn't help wincing when her fingers touched the bulging udder. The rubbery skin felt indecent, obscene as she dabbed tentatively at the splatters of mud. The cow stared round at her a moment, then whipped its tail forward and swatted her in the face. If it had been human, Rachel would have sworn it had done it deliberately.

"Stop that!" she ordered, affronted. The cow replied by stomping one huge, dirty hoof dangerously close to Rachel's foot. She jumped back, squealing, and Joanna straightened from sweeping.

"What's the matter?"

"It tried to crush my foot!"

Joanna's lips twitched. "Butternut is the gentlest cow I've ever laid eyes on. Don't be afraid of her."

Rachel approached again, screwing her face up with disgust as she scrubbed the muddy teats. The cow rolled its eyes at her but made no more murderous attempts. Still, Rachel feared for her life every minute she sat next to it on the tippy stool.

Her first attempt at milking brought a honk of protest from Butternut and a burst of laughter from Joanna.

"I'm sorry!" Rachel cried, her nerves strained to the breaking point. "I've never done this before. I thought I'd learn quicker—"

"I don't believe it! How can you grow up not knowing how to milk a cow?" Joanna laughed.

Rachel shrugged miserably. "My father was a shoemaker," she lied. "We bought our milk."

"Well, you should have said so. It's easy enough to learn. Just don't squeeze hard. Let me show you."

It was tiring work. When Rachel thought she was finished and moved away with a relieved sigh, Joanna sat down and stripped another half a bucket from the same cow.

"You have to get it all," she warned gently. "Otherwise the cow is uncomfortable and will start to produce less. Your muscles will get used to it. You'll see."

"I'm sorry I'm no good at this."

Joanna shot her a look. "Why should you be good at it? It's your first day. Don't be so hard on yourself, Mary."

Rachel crawled into the hayloft groaning after her first day in the dairy. She'd learned all she'd ever want to know about cows and butter and cheese. She could think of nothing but sleep. Peter had smoothed a section in the hay and spread one of the blankets over the prickly strands. Shorty crawled into this and squirmed around, settling himself in a little ball like a puppy. Peter chuckled as Rachel collapsed beside the boy, moaning.

"I see you earned your keep today."

"That woman is a slave driver. A fiend from the fiery pit," she mumbled, then rolled her eyes at him. "How dare you look so fresh and cheerful! What did you do all day?"

"Hoed row after endless row of baby corn." He displayed a couple of fresh blisters on his palms. "Cheer up. It's only for one month, and we're being well fed and housed while we're here."

"I'll never make it. I don't want to stay. We're late in the season already; you said so yourself."

"We don't have much choice. The things we're going to need will cost more than I anticipated and more than either of us has."

She knew it was true, and there was no point in arguing, but she still felt close to tears. She busied herself covering Shorty with the other blanket and fiercely told herself not to cry.

Peter pried off his boots and tossed his hat aside. He hesitated; then, turning his back, he unbuttoned his shirt and slung it across the jutting handle of a pitchfork in the hay. He turned back toward Rachel with his chin raised, a challenging look in his eye.

She saw how gray his union suit was, how it stretched too small over his chest and gaped between the buttons. She kept her face carefully expressionless and met his gaze.

"We're going to be living in close quarters for a month," he said, his voice sounding a little high. He cleared his throat. "I mean, we have been already, but this isn't like camping outdoors. It's warm and dry here. I don't know about you, but I've hardly been out of my clothes in weeks, and . . . I mean, we're getting filthy working like this, and . . . that is, I hope it's all right with you." He glanced down at his disreputable union suit morosely.

Rachel decided he was right, and she pulled off her own boots and stockings before she could change her mind. She wiggled her bare toes in the cool air. It was exquisite. She undid her hair and let it fall to her shoulders as she rubbed her scalp.

"That's better," she admitted, turning back to Peter. "It's a bit close in this loft. I'm sorry if I smell of Butternut and her sisters."

She expected him to chuckle again, but he didn't. The loft had grown nearly dark, the last rays coming in through the small window at each end, and she couldn't see his face, lost in shadow, but his voice was quiet as he said, "You are one beautiful girl, Mary Mitchell."

A horrified silence fell over the hayloft.

"Sorry, did I say that out loud?" he muttered.

"You did."

"I take it back."

Rachel started to laugh. "You can't retract something like that."

"It's pitch black in here now. Anyone looks pretty in the dark," he retorted, and she heard him stretch out with a sigh on the blanket on the other side of Shorty. "I feel like I've been trampled by a bull," he said. The hay rustled below him, a homey sort of sound.

"Smell like one too," Rachel remarked pertly and tucked herself into her nest again. She could feel her bones settling into the hay. "Now that we're in semicivilization, we can have a regular laundry day." She smiled dreamily, breathing in the comforting smell of hay and horses, three of which stamped in their rough stalls below her. It was an honest smell, with earth and sunshine mingled with it. Rachel closed her eyes. Her aching muscles began to ease.

"I've never felt so wrung out," she remarked drowsily. "My shoulders are screaming. I had no idea it took so much work to produce butter."

"No?"

"I'll never take it for granted again. You know, my brother would die of shock if he could see me now."

"Why is that?" His voice came to her low and amused out of the dark. He was a few feet away, but he sounded closer under the low rafters.

Rachel laughed and held out her hands, barely visible in the air above her. "Look at me. I have dirt under my nails. I'm sunburnt to a crisp. I smell like a cow. I'm sleeping in a hayloft."

With you, she added to herself.

"I take it this isn't ordinary fare for you back home." He chuckled.

"Hardly. Back home, I'd lie in bed until late in the morning, and my maid would bring my breakfast on a silver tray and then draw my water for my bath . . . with soft French soap . . . and lay out my clothes. Clean clothes, closets of them, in the latest fashions. I must have had twenty dresses." She was growing boneless, her voice dropping lower as she grew sleepy. "And I don't think," she added, "that it's usual fare for you either, no matter what you act like."

There was a pause. "No?"

"No. You're much too educated-sounding. I can't imagine how you ended up here, like this—" She broke off in an enormous yawn.

"Go to sleep, Mrs. Mitchell," he said and turned his back.

He didn't have to tell her twice.

Chapter Twelve

RACHEL CAME TO HATE WAKING up in the morning. Joanna was a jolly, benign-looking woman, and her cooking was wonderful after weeks on the trail, but she was a firm commander in the dairy. She kept Rachel running all day long, hoisting things that were too heavy for her, scrubbing until her hands were chapped and raw, rocking the great barrel butter churn, and combing the vats of cheese curd until her arms dropped with fatigue. She slopped milk pails and dropped cheese molds. She was still afraid of the cows but soon grew too tired to care about the fear anymore.

To give Joanna her due, she slaved right alongside Rachel, doing more than another woman her age could probably manage, and in spite of Rachel's blunders, Joanna was unfailingly cheerful to the point that Rachel felt like screaming at her in irritation. She told herself that no horse could be worth this much work, that she didn't want to go to Bellefontaine after all, that she didn't care if she never saw her father again. She only wanted to go home. But she couldn't very well slack off if Joanna was still going, so Rachel kept working, her hair straggling from its knot, her arms and legs moving automatically while her mind numbed itself. She didn't want to complain, so she kept her lips pressed tightly together most of the time, causing her to grow increasingly drawn and silent. Her soft body grew trim and toned with the work until her dress hung on her like a sack and a new hardness came to the muscles in her limbs.

Ed remarked on the changes in her one evening at supper. He had asked for the soup pot, and Rachel had handed it to him one-handed without thinking about it. He had blinked at the heaviness of it as he took it, and his kind face broke into a grin. "You have built some muscles," he declared, setting the pot on the table with both hands. "You aren't the same person who came to us."

Rachel felt herself blush. "It's all the lifting I do in the dairy."

"You are holding up better than I expected," Joanna admitted, giving her an approving nod. "When you first came here, I admit I had my doubts. But you have done everything I've asked of you, and you have more grit than most men I know."

"You'd have to, to survive Mother," Karl added unexpectedly, and everyone laughed.

"What do you think, William?" Ed asked Peter, giving him a poke in the shoulder as he sat at the table. "What do you think of all the changes in your wife? Isn't she healthy-looking?"

Rachel looked at him across the table, and Peter's lips twitched with amusement. But she thought she saw a spark of admiration in his gaze. She watched his eyes slide lazily over her trim frame. "She's very pretty and healthy-looking," he finally said. "In a mud-stained, frizzy-haired sort of way."

"William!" Joanna scolded, but she was smiling.

"She's especially pretty when she's tramping after the cows with her skirts in the mud, swearing in French because she thinks we won't understand her," Peter added.

"Oh, you!" Rachel cried, but everyone laughed again, even silent Shorty.

She didn't think much about what Peter had said, but after that night, Rachel became aware of little things Peter was doing for her every day. Just small, quiet things, insignificant really, but now she was suddenly aware of them in a way she hadn't been before. He carried the basket of heavy washing out to the line for her. He got up a few minutes earlier than she in order to scare off the mice that lurked on the barn floor below so they were gone when she came down the ladder. Each night he smoothed out her nest of hay for her so when she dragged up the ladder she could fall into bed like a sack of wet wheat without having to make up her bed first. Small things. But they made her wonder.

* * *

One afternoon as Rachel and Shorty were helping drive the cows into the corral for milking, Rachel saw three men approaching up the lane on horseback. Joanna saw them at the same time, and Rachel saw fear flicker briefly over the woman's round face. Rachel studied the men more closely, noting their dusty clothing and half-grown beards. They didn't look much older than she was. They were unwashed and disreputable looking but no more frightening than any of the other people she had seen going to and from the fort—or than she, herself, had been at times, for that matter. But Joanna pressed her hand and whispered urgently, "Go get the men."

Wondering, Rachel flew around the barn and out into the corn field, waving her arms above her head to draw their attention without calling to them. They were working clear down by the river, and it took her a few minutes to get their attention. Peter saw her first and jogged to meet her, still carrying his hoe. Karl followed close behind him.

"What's the matter?" Peter asked.

Rachel tugged on Peter's sleeve. "Joanna said to come get you. There are three men out front. I don't know why, but she seemed frightened of them."

Peter exchanged looks with Ed, who had followed more slowly. There was a tight look to Ed's face that Rachel didn't know how to interpret, but it spurred Peter and Karl into a run. Rachel wanted to go with them, but she didn't want to leave Ed on his own. Taking his arm, she followed the others at a walk.

"Who is it?" she asked in a low voice as they rounded the barn.

"I don't know. But it takes a lot to rattle Joanna," he replied. "She doesn't mind about the miners, the con men, the quack doctors. You see all types here. The only time I've seen her scared of a man is when deserters come through."

"Deserters?"

"From the war between the States. They come through here sometimes, more often than you'd think, causing trouble—rousing up people's tempers, stealing food and horses. I've heard some have . . . er . . . interfered with women." He was panting with exertion, and Rachel forced herself to slow her steps.

"Have they caused you trouble too?" she asked.

"Last time some came through, they wanted our pig, and when Joanna wouldn't give it to them, they set fire to our woodshed. Luckily it was late spring, and there wasn't much wood left in it."

The three men had stopped in the yard, still mounted on their horses. Karl hovered near his mother protectively, but Peter stood apart, hoe in hand, eyes squinting speculatively. He didn't move, but Rachel could see the tension in his shoulders and the muscles like coiled springs that left him ready to move in a hurry if necessary. As she and Ed drew closer, Rachel could see the hardness of the men's faces, the grim set to their jaws, and the emptiness of their eyes. She'd never seen such a bleak look on any man. One of them wore boots with the toes worn out of them. One had something wrong with one of his eyes; it drooped sideways, and a reddish substance oozed from it. She stopped in her tracks, gripping Ed's arm. The torn and dirty trousers they wore beneath their coats were blue, not gray.

"I have only corn bread and rabbit stew," Joanna was saying in a high voice not quite her own. "But you're welcome to it."

"Thank you kindly," one of the men said. He nodded at the others, and they all dismounted. Their horses looked no healthier or cleaner than they. Peter lowered the hoe to the ground, and without a word, he held his hand out for the reins. The men eyed him.

"Your horses are in good hands," Ed said in his careful English. "He'll feed and water them. They need care."

The men glanced at each other and then handed the horses over to Peter, who led them away toward the barn.

Ed stirred himself and detached his arm from Rachel's grip. "Please, come sit down."

The men scarcely fit in the small house, but as they dropped into seats around the table, Joanna and Rachel busied themselves getting a meal together. There was only a bit of the stew left from lunch, but there was plenty of corn bread. Joanna cut hunks of bacon to fry and sent Rachel into the root cellar for potatoes and onions and to the dairy for a round of cheese. These she sliced and fried with the bacon, the strong smell mercifully covering the stench coming from their guests.

"Where are you boys headed?" Ed asked as Joanna took plates from the cupboard.

They exchanged looks once again, and then the one who seemed to be their leader replied, "Dunant Mountains seem a good place."

"Yes, they are. I've heard a man can do well there if he's willing to work. You'll want to rest up a while, maybe, before you go that far," Ed said.

Joanna gave a start and glared at her husband, but he ignored her peacefully. No one asked the men where they'd come from or their names.

When the food was ready, Joanna cleared her throat. "Pump's out back if you want to get washed up for dinner," she said firmly.

The men broke into grins. Their teeth were yellowed from tobacco, and Rachel doubted they ever cleaned them.

"Yes, ma'am, I imagine we're a bit rank by now," the leader said, and they all slouched good-naturedly out to the pump.

As soon as the door closed behind them, Joanna rounded on Ed. "What are you thinking, inviting them to stay?"

Ed spread his hands. "They need rest. That one with the eye . . . It's the Christian thing to do."

"Twenty-six years I've been after you to go to church," Joanna hissed, "and *now* you decide to become a Christian?"

When the men returned, they looked damper but not much cleaner. Joanna poked Rachel in the ribs, sending her into motion, and they served plates around.

"This looks delicious, ma'am," the one with the worn-out boots said. "It's been a long time since I had such good-smellin' food."

"I imagine so," Joanna replied a bit sourly, pouring milk into tin cups.

Rachel watched them fall on the food like starving dogs, scooping up potatoes and onions with their spoons, pushing great wedges of corn bread and butter into their mouths. She kept their tin cups full and gave them as wide a berth as she could in the confined space as she moved around them. She had a hard time not staring at the one's drooping eye. She wished Peter would come back from the barn because she felt safer with him around. It occurred to her that she had come to think of Peter as being able to handle any and all situations.

Shorty, with his own bowl and spoon, sat to one side of the stove, out of the way. While he watched the newcomers carefully, the men took little notice of him, and after a while, the child began to eat. Rachel noticed that Shorty seemed to tense, though, whenever she moved near one of the men to serve them, and only relaxed when she had moved away again.

Ed hesitated, then leaned forward on his elbows and addressed the leader.

"You can speak to us as friends here," he said. "Tell us, what's the news? We don't hear much out this way, and I have family in Pennsylvania."

The man drained his cup and drew his hand across his mouth before answering. "It hasn't reached Pennsylvania last I heard. We've been . . . gone a couple of months."

"But what way was it going when you last heard?"

"The boys have their work cut out for them," the man said reluctantly. "It doesn't look good." He looked away, and Joanna turned abruptly to the stove and began to scrape at the bacon grease congealing in the pan. Rachel felt somehow off balance. The North wasn't in danger of *losing*, surely.

One of the men glanced at Karl sharply. "Big, strong son like that—you should be glad you live well out of it. They'd snap him up in a minute."

"Wouldn't be much left of him when they were through either," another muttered with his mouth full.

"We could have used someone your size in our outfit," the one with the bad eye agreed.

"Are you all from the same outfit, then?" Ed asked, looking from one to the other.

"Yessir. Knew each other before that too. We're all from the same town in Virginia."

"Virginia!" Rachel couldn't stop herself from blurting. "But that's a Southern state. Weren't you with the Union?"

The leader stared at her with the coldest blue eyes she'd ever seen, and they chilled her bones. He pushed away his plate and addressed her directly. "I had no love for the North at the first, ma'am, that's certain. But if you'd seen what the Confederate Army did to our town, you wouldn't ask why we're wearing blue. They burned our houses, stole our grain and horses, assaulted my mama and Jake's little sister. Sam here lost his pa. Didn't matter to them one way or the other what side we were on. They just took what they wanted. So we joined up with the Union Army to take our own back. But turns out they weren't much different neither."

Rachel pinched her lips shut and said nothing more. Peter came in as the men were finishing their meal, and she caught his eye across the crowded room, then looked away. He propped himself against the wall near the stove and folded his arms across his chest, casual, watchful.

"You boys are welcome to say in our loft tonight," Ed said, glancing at Peter. Rachel tensed in protest, but Peter only nodded. Joanna cleared her throat.

"Karl can go out in the loft too, and Mary and William and the boy can have the attic."

The men's leader rubbed his jaw, scratching at his straggly whiskers. "Well, now, that's kind of you, thank you. I'm sure we won't object."

So the men trooped out to spend the night in the loft, and Rachel went up to the attic. Shorty seemed unconcerned at the change in arrangements and dropped off to sleep quickly, but Rachel tossed on her pallet, expecting the barn to go up in flames at any moment.

Peter joined her much later, after the Hunsakers had retired themselves and the little house had fallen silent. He crawled up through the trap door in the floor and slid his boots off, setting them down quietly. Rachel rolled over and looked at him in the light of the moon coming through the tiny window. She had thrown the shutter open to let out the lingering smell of the men and the onions.

"I'm awake," she told him.

"Still?"

"Who can sleep with them here?"

"Karl's with them. It's all right."

She heard him undressing in the dark, feeling his way to a spot two feet from her, where she lay on Karl's straw tick, and stretching out on a blanket with a groan.

"I don't understand how Ed can have them in his home," Rachel said in a whisper, shuddering. "I thought Joanna was going to faint when he said they could stay and rest up a while."

"Ed has a good heart."

"So does Joanna, but I don't blame her for not wanting them here. So rough and unrefined! They exude danger."

"They exude a lot more than that. Did you see how firm Joanna was about having them wash? I don't doubt she'll be doing their laundry in the morning!"

"This isn't a laughing matter, Peter. They frighten me."

He sobered. "It would be wise to be careful around them, yes, but you needn't be frightened. I don't think they'll harm us at this point; they know we are trying to help them."

"But that's just it! We're helping them! They were with the *Union*, for heaven's sake, and they're from Virginia!"

"What? Can't Southern boys choose sides?"

"Well, of course, that's not what I mean. I hope I am fair enough to acknowledge that every man must choose for himself what his beliefs and stance will be. I personally favor the Union, but I grant that those on the opposing side have their own reasons for supporting the South."

"Noble of you," Peter said wryly.

"But that's my objection, don't you see? They're *deserters*, Peter. They left the South to support the North, and then they abandoned even that. I believe once a person has a conviction strong enough to fight for, he should remain committed to it. To abandon it when things prove difficult or not to his liking displays a paltry sort of character."

Peter made a dismissive sound. "Can't they be afraid? Can't they be human? They can't be more than nineteen or twenty years old."

"They've abandoned their fellow soldiers, and they've ignored orders. If they go back to the States, they could be hanged for treason."

"Yes, they could. Which explains why they're here in the northern wild. I don't understand your tone, Rachel. Do you *want* them to be caught and hanged?"

She cringed. "Oh, I don't know. I suppose not. They may be cowards, but they probably don't deserve to die. At least they *tried* to fight."

There was absolute silence in the attic, and then she heard Peter sit up. A gleam of moonlight struck his brown hair, turning it silver, but his face was in shadow.

"Is that what you think? That they're cowards?" His voice was suddenly quiet.

"What else would they be? You said it yourself; they were afraid."

"Girl, you are so young and stupid it's scary. You have no idea what those boys have been through. You can't begin to understand it. You shouldn't be so hard on other people. Don't you have an ounce of compassion? You're so quick to judge!"

Stunned, Rachel remained silent as hot tears spilled over her temples and into her ears. She rubbed them away, furious and mortified. After a moment, she heard Peter let out a long, hard breath. Something rustled, and then she felt his hand on her arm.

"I'm sorry. I shouldn't have called you stupid," he muttered. "You *can't* understand it. It's not your fault, and I've no call hammering you for it."

She sniffed loudly. His hand slid up her arm and found her cheek.

"Are you crying?" he asked, sounding disbelieving.

"No," she snapped, knocking his hand away and scrubbing at her face.

"Aw, girl, I'm sorry." He moved closer and put one arm around her. "In all we've gone through together, I've never known you to cry. Not since we found the cat."

She didn't want to think about that. "I'm not crying," she said.

"I'm sorry I was the cause of it."

"I'm not crying!"

"All right." He paused. "I know you believe what you said. You exemplify it in your own character; you haven't turned away from your commitment to reaching your father, no matter the difficulty. You make your mind up, and you adhere to it. Someone with your stubborn resolution perhaps can't understand people who aren't as resolved and firm in their own convictions or who weaken in the face of hardship."

She wasn't sure if this was meant as a compliment or a slight. Still, Rachel was glad for his arm, heavy and comforting around her shoulders, and for the darkness that hid her face. When he made no move to return to his blanket, she slid over, and he sat on the pallet beside her.

"Were you ever in the war, Peter?" she asked softly. She waited, wondering if she had overstepped her bounds, not expecting him to reply. But after a moment, he cleared his throat.

"No, I haven't been. I've stayed out of what's going on in the States."

"But you are a Union supporter, aren't you?"

He sighed. "I told you I'm for the human race. I'm not on one side or the other. Those divisions are just contrived political concepts."

"Fancy words. What do they mean?"

"They mean there is no North or South to me. That distinction means nothing."

"Hmm. Well, it means something where I come from. It was a fiercely debated topic at my house, let me tell you, years before the war even started. Father and Richard would go at it hammer and tongs, predicting what would happen, fighting about who was in the right. Father left us before the war began, but I often heard them arguing. Father believed in peace and fairness, and Richard believed in making money. I know Father wouldn't want Richard profiting from this war. They never saw eye to eye about it."

"It's amusing to me that your father wanted peace, yet he fought about it with your brother."

"Yes, well, the theory was always easier than the practice. They both had hot tempers," Rachel said wryly.

His chuckle was low and soft in her ear. "I'm sure they did if they're anything like you. Good night, Mary Mitchell."

"Rachel," she murmured. She lay down again, and he moved to his blanket, but he reached across the space between them and gently took her hand. She fell asleep with his hand still holding hers.

Chapter Thirteen

In the morning, the barn still stood intact across the yard. Karl came in, and Joanna gave him, Ed, Shorty, and Peter their breakfast, but they made no move to go out to the fields to work. Instead, they sat about the house, poking at the fire, examining their fingernails with great interest, not looking at each other. Shorty lounged by Peter's elbow, looking bored, and much to Rachel's astonishment, Karl took out knitting needles and a ball of red wool and worked away at a long scarf, his thick fingers surprisingly nimble. The clacking provided a gentle rhythm against the snapping of the fire. No one would say so aloud, but there was a silent acknowledgment that the women wouldn't be left alone in the house until the visitors were well on their way.

When the sun had been up for a while, Joanna got impatient and sent Rachel out to call the men to breakfast. There were cows waiting to be milked, and Joanna insisted she wasn't about to go do it with three strangers sleeping above her. Rachel went reluctantly, entering the barn cautiously and looking around, not knowing what she expected to see. All looked perfectly ordinary, and the horses whickered cheerfully in their stalls.

A sound above her made her spin around. One of the men was coming down the ladder from the loft. His suspenders dangled from his waist, and he wore no shirt, only a filthy union suit. It was the one named Jake, whose little sister had been attacked. Rachel swallowed at the memory and tried to fix a smile on her face. The result didn't feel convincing. At the bottom of the ladder, he paused.

"Good morning." She spoke first. "I'm meant to tell you breakfast is waiting."

He nodded. "Matthew and I will be in directly. Sam is doing poorly this morning."

"What's wrong with him? Is he the one with the eye . . . ?"

"It's bad. Got gunpowder in it."

Rachel felt her jaw drop. "What battle did it happen in?" she asked in a whisper.

Jake gave her a funny look and then broke into a wry grin. "He was shooting at a rabbit a few days ago, and his gun malfunctioned."

"Oh." She felt her cheeks grow hot.

"Last battle we saw was McDowell back in May."

"I see."

"Anyway, he's all fevered up this morning and talking funny."

Rachel's manner turned brisk to cover her embarrassment. "Let me have a look at him."

She hiked her skirt and climbed the ladder to the loft, and her eyes went immediately to the man lying on the blanket in the hay. His skin was glazed with sweat, and his head rolled back and forth as if seeking a comfortable position. His eye was swollen almost shut. Under the dry, dusty smell of the hay a sickening smell of sweat and something else putrid festered.

"Yes, he has a fever," Rachel agreed, not needing to go any closer to tell.

"But the sweating's good, right?" Matthew, the leader, said, coming to stand close behind her. Like Jake, he wore his suspenders dangling behind him, and although he wore a shirt, it was only half buttoned. Neither seemed concerned about being half dressed in front of a female. She moved imperceptibly away.

"Well, I don't know. He doesn't look good, does he?"

"You know how to help him?"

"There might be a doctor at Fort Kiaayo. I can ask Karl to go."

"Doctor's no good. Doctor at Kernstown tried to set my brother's leg, and he died."

Rachel turned to stare at him. "I'm sure this is an entirely different case. If he doesn't get medical attention, he might die." She went back down the ladder and jogged to the house. When she reported the news, Joanna's face fell.

"It's a sure bet they won't be moving on in a hurry. Probably be laid up here for weeks."

Ed made soothing sounds and nodded at Karl. "Go see if Dr. Ralston will come. Tell him who we've got in the loft; he deserves to know. If he won't come, don't press him. It's sticky business, getting mixed up with Americans and deserters."

"And who's going to pay for the doctor?" Joanna wanted to know.

Ed spread his hands. "What else can we do, Joanna? Let him die in our barn? It isn't Christian."

"You on again about being Christian?" She sniffed. "Is what those boys did Christian?"

"What did they do?" Rachel asked, but Peter shot her a dark look that made her fall silent again.

"Doctor may not choose to come anyway," Joanna added.

But the doctor did come, arriving an hour later on a weary-looking black horse. He was a square-jawed man, with a heavy Irish accent and completely bald but for a fringe of red hair around his ears. He spoke for a moment with Ed, then followed him out to the barn. A little while later, he returned to the house and washed under the back pump.

"That man should have had his eye seen to days ago. It's awfully poisoned," he reported, patting his face and hands fastidiously with the cloth Joanna gave him. "I wouldn't be surprised if it's made its way through his bloodstream, throughout his whole body."

"Can you do anything for him?" Peter asked.

"I've given him what I can. My main concern is to keep the fever under control. Someone will need to bathe him with cool water—forehead, neck, trunk. Try to get him to drink water. After that, we can only wait and see if he pulls through. I think he'll lose the eye though. I'll come back tonight. If the swelling has gone down, maybe I can remove the eye then. I can't get at it the way it is now." He paused beside his horse, one hand on its nose. "Ed, I have a lot of respect for you, you know that. But I don't think you're doing your family any favors harboring these men. I have to tell you honestly, I think you'd be foolish not to inform the authorities at the fort."

Ed spread his hands again, his lined face troubled. "They haven't broken any laws here. And they're guests in my home."

"It's best to stay out of the American problem."

"I'm not in it. I'm just offering hospitality to three travelers."

The doctor shook his head. "Whatever you think is best; I won't stand in your way. But I admit I don't understand it." He mounted his horse and rode away.

Joanna looked at her husband. "I'm not sure I understand it either," she said and went back in the house.

Ed drew his hand across his lips and looked at Peter. "Do you understand it, William? They came to me for help. They're just young boys, younger than my Karl. They have families somewhere. If Karl was in trouble and ill and hungry and far from home, I would want someone to care for him."

Peter ran his fingers through his hair and replaced his hat. Rachel waited, wondering what he would say.

"If you ask me what I think," he said at last, "they're doing less harm in your loft than they would be on the battlefield. Maybe if they were *all* on the run, this fool war would be over."

Ed stared at him, watery eyes wide in astonishment, and then his face collapsed into a hundred wrinkles, and he began to laugh. He clapped Peter on the shoulder and walked away, still laughing.

Rachel was horrified. Of course she wanted the war to end too. She didn't like to think of all those men—mere boys, many of them—dying. She knew having to choose sides was tearing families apart, including her own, but surely Peter didn't condone desertion! Had he heard nothing she had said to him in the attic? Had he been truthful when he had told her he wasn't a deserter himself? She felt a little ill as she watched him walk away to the barn, and once again it struck her how little she really knew about him and his background.

For all her bluster, Joanna herself spent the day caring for the ill man. They brought him into the house and bedded him down on a pallet before the fire. Rachel took over the older woman's duties in the dairy while Joanna bathed Sam over and over with cool water, soothing his tense muscles, wiping away the poison that drained from his bad eye. She moved carefully, as if afraid Sam would suddenly rear up and bite her, but he lay limp and mostly unresponsive. By evening Joanna was exhausted. Rachel could see her motions growing slower and slower, and her face was haggard. Guiltily Rachel thought she should take over for her, but she wasn't sure she could bring herself to do it.

She was properly ashamed of herself when Peter came in for supper. He took one look at Joanna and went to take the washcloth from her.

"I'll take a turn," he said softly. Joanna looked startled a moment and then thanked him and moved stiffly away. Peter settled himself on the stool beside Sam and wrung the cloth out in the bowl of cool water. Rachel, who was setting the table, lingered and watched Peter's hands move the cloth slowly but confidently over the man's fevered skin. For a moment, he placed his palm on Sam's forehead, not so much to measure the fever as to give comfort. It was the gentle touch of a parent for a child. The gesture went straight to Rachel's heart. No matter how Peter's beliefs about desertion differed from her own, whatever his convictions about the right or wrong of war, she knew his undiscriminating compassion for people was deep and sincere. Seeing him demonstrating this in this simple way both touched her and left her feeling shaken. She turned back to her work in silence.

The doctor came and went with a worried look on his face but did not feel he could operate on Sam's eye just yet. The two other soldiers sat around the house, keenly watchful, silent, alert. Rachel found their presence unnerving, but she could see the frustration in their faces. They were men of action, and they truly cared about this man before the hearth, but they could do nothing to help him, and their impotence grated at them. She was glad to keep busy in the dairy and away from the house. Ordinarily Shorty had the run of the farm, going wherever he liked and, more often than not, shadowing Peter, but today Rachel kept him with her so she could keep her eye on him. When she finally finished her last chore and climbed onto her pallet in the attic, she found it difficult to fall asleep, knowing the men were right below her. And that Peter was down there among them.

When she went down the next morning, Peter was still sitting beside the pallet. He looked as fresh as he had the night before, other than a slight redness to his eyes. He greeted her with a nod and stood up, easing the small of his back. "Morning, Mary."

"Morning. You sat here all night?" Rachel asked.

"Someone had to, and Joanna wasn't up to it. And if one of the other men had done it, I doubt I'd have been able to sleep." He took up a fresh washcloth, wrung it out in the water, reached for Rachel's hand, and plopped the rag into it. "Your turn," he said cheerfully and went out of the house.

Rachel stood looking at the cloth in her hand, then looked at Sam. He appeared unconscious, his mouth open, his arms and legs limp. Cautiously she sat beside him, spread the cloth open, and laid it on his bare chest. He didn't move. Pushing away the awkwardness, she began to move the wet cloth carefully back and forth.

Ed and Joanna entered, and Joanna began rattling kitchen things, getting breakfast ready and supervising as Shorty set the table. Ed came to stand beside Rachel and looked down at the sleeping man.

"Thank William for us," he said quietly, "for taking a turn all night. Joanna surely needed the rest."

"I will," Rachel said. "He's just gone outside."

"It's a good man you've got there, Mary," Ed said. He turned to his wife. "I'll take Jake and Matthew into the fields to work with me today. Better to keep their hands and minds busy. They can do nothing for their friend here, and you don't need them underfoot."

When breakfast was over, Joanna went out to the dairy while all the men traipsed out to the fields. Peter went with them, ignoring Rachel's murmured suggestion that he get some sleep instead. Rachel was left to tend Sam.

She'd never nursed anyone before. It felt foreign, placing wet cloths on a stranger's body, lifting his head to turn his pillow, touching and soothing as she had seen Joanna and Peter do. After a while, though, it didn't seem so intimate, and by noon she no longer thought much about it. She would have enjoyed it, actually, feeling useful and needed, if she wasn't so worried he would die.

At one o'clock, Rachel went to put a pot of soup together for the men's lunch. When she returned to the fire, Sam's good eye was open, watching her. She was struck by the clear blue depths of it and the long dark lashes. If it wasn't for the poisoned eye and the half-grown beard, he'd be quite handsome.

"Sorry to be so much trouble," Sam murmured as Rachel knelt beside him.

"You can't help it," Rachel said, wringing out the cloth to wipe his face. She pushed a stray lock of dark hair from his forehead. "I think your fever has broken. You look better. Are you feeling any better?"

"Some. That man who was here—he the doctor?"

"Yes. Dr. Ralston, I think his name is. He's coming back again tomorrow."

He shifted anxiously on the pallet. "Don't let him take my eye. He wants to remove it, doesn't he?"

"He said he couldn't yet, with the swelling—"

"Don't let him do it." His good eye bored into hers.

Rachel looked away. "He'll do what he thinks is best to save you."

"I don't want to live with only one eye. Better to let me die."

"How can you say that?" Rachel was genuinely shocked.

"I've seen plenty of people die. It's not good, but it's over pretty quick, and I would rather that than fifty years of . . . of . . ."

"Of what?"

"Blindness. Pity. Women afraid to look at me."

"Don't be silly. You'll look just fine. And you're not going to be completely blind. Plenty of people live with one eye."

"I'm telling you, I don't want it. I've seen men with half a face, half a body—"

Rachel hushed him, seeing he was growing agitated. "It won't be like that," she tried to assure him. Then the full horror of what he had said sank into her, and she whispered, "You have seen that?"

"Lots. Yorktown. Williamsburg. McDowell. McDowell was the last straw. We'd been in plenty of fights before, but somehow it was nothing but confusion that time. Stonewall Jackson—you know who he is?—we couldn't hold against him. We lost that one." He turned restlessly on the makeshift bed. "Al died," he muttered. "My best friend, Al Harrison. Got his leg blown off. Bled to death before I could drag him off the field." His voice croaked into silence.

Rachel sat staring at the rag in her hand, not knowing what to say.

"Well, I couldn't take any more of it after that," Sam said quietly. "I told Matthew and Jake I couldn't do it anymore. I was going, and they could go with me or stay and die. They came with me. But even though that was over two months ago, I . . . I can't stop thinking about it. Al and the others. *So* many others. The ones who lived will go home to whatever's left of home with broken bodies and injured souls. What kind of a future are those men going to have? I've seen the damage done to them, and

I don't know how they lived or how they even wanted to. I'm telling you, I don't want to go through life like that. Better to die than that."

Rachel tried to think of what to say to comfort him, but she felt out of her depth. She tried to make her tone lighter as she said, "But you got through it. It's done. Your life can be whatever you want it to be from here on out. You don't have to be injured and broken. You can be healthy and strong. Isn't that worth saving, even if it means giving up your eye? It's making you ill. If you don't fight off this infection now, what will be the good of having survived all those battles?"

He was silent a moment, and then his lips quirked in an ironic smile. "Yeah, I got through all that fighting, and then I nearly blew my own head off trying to shoot a rabbit."

Rachel set the bowl of water on the floor and put a hand on his arm. "Does it help to talk about it?" she asked gently.

It was as if those words, her invitation, opened a floodgate. Story after story poured out of the young man: horrific accounts of his family destroyed, his father gunned down in his own barn, rain and mud and starvation rations. It had been so cold the previous winter that the damp blankets froze in a shell around the soldiers' bodies at night, and they had to cut their way out in the morning. Insects in the food. Feet in soaked boots for so long that when at last the boots were removed, a layer of skin went with them. Cutting open fallen horses so the heat from their bodies warmed the men. The most terrible thing about Sam's stories was the flat, matter-of-fact way in which he told them. They might have been sitting on a porch chatting about memories of a school foot race. Rachel listened with growing distress and disbelief. Was it really like this? Was this what had turned this ordinary young man into hollow-eyed stone? It was as if the spirit had been sucked right out of him. Fear and disgust and even bitterness had faded, leaving him only empty. Rachel held tightly to the damp rag in order to keep from slapping her hands over her ears.

At last he broke off, and his good eye slid toward her. There was a fine sheen of sweat on his face from the effort of talking. "I imagine you think I'm a coward for running away," he said.

"No," she said instantly and meant it. "I don't. You're better off away from it. No one should have to see such things."

The door creaked, and Rachel looked over her shoulder to see Peter coming in. She didn't know how long he had been listening. Their eyes met, and he must have read the trauma in her face because he came to sit beside her and slid his hand into hers to lace his fingers between her own.

"How are you feeling, Sam?" he asked.

"Better, thank you."

"Sam's been telling me about the war," Rachel said quietly.

Peter's eyes half closed, and he nodded. "I imagine that's been difficult to talk about," he said to Sam. "But you'll feel lighter now for having spoken."

"I do," Sam said, nodding. "Like there's been a big sack of grain on my chest and now I've put it down. Now maybe the nightmares will go away."

"I'm sure they'll ease," Peter agreed. "That's the way of these things. Memories can poison you as sure as your injured eye poisoned you. But those kind of memories can't stand the fresh air, Sam, so the more you put them out there in the sunlight, the less power they'll have. The less they can poison you."

Rachel had never heard such soothing things come from a man before. But she had had all the stories she could take. She climbed to her feet and picked up the bowl of water. "You should rest a while, Sam. I'll go tell the others the soup is ready." And she fled from the house.

Chapter Fourteen

She called the others to come for lunch, but she herself couldn't face the thought of eating, not after what she had heard. She went instead to the dairy, where she sat on the hard dirt floor with her back to the wall. Closing her eyes, she inhaled deeply the smell of cows and hay and curing cheese. The once distasteful scents were now comforting, grounding, and she leaned her head back and let her muscles relax.

Life had to allow for change, she decided. Just as the sickening smell of souring milk was now associated in her mind with succulent, tangy cheese so that it no longer turned her stomach, her disdain and contempt for weakness in others was now crumpling and shifting within her. It was like watching a wadded-up tablecloth unfold to reveal new patterns within. And one of the things she feared it was revealing was her *own* weakness: that of intolerance and arrogance. Believe what she might about desertion, she could not help but wince at how judgmental she had been about Sam and his companions. She had forgotten simple compassion and humanity. She was young and foolish and knew nothing at all. She hoped Peter didn't have such a disparaging opinion of her as she had of herself at this moment.

She didn't know how long she sat there thinking, tears dripping quietly down her face unchecked, before she heard the door creak and opened her eyes. Jake stood looking down at her, hands resting lightly on his hips. Mud clung to his worn-out boots, and she saw that the knees of his trousers, at her eye level, were wearing thin too.

"What are you doing?" He sounded amused.

"Just thinking," she replied, tipping her head back to look into his face. There was something in his face that she hadn't seen there before: a glint in his eye, a thoughtfulness to the set of his mouth. It made her uncomfortable, though she couldn't say why.

"Are you coming in for lunch?"

She shook her head. "Later. I'm not hungry right now. But you go ahead."

He didn't move, just stood gazing down at her. After a moment, he said conversationally, "You're a right pretty woman, Mary, even sitting there on the floor with dirt on your face."

"Is there?" she asked, distracted, and rubbed haphazardly at her damp cheeks.

He chuckled. While Peter's laugh always warmed her, this man's laugh made goose bumps stand out on her arms. She started to her feet, but he suddenly knelt on her skirt so she couldn't rise and caught her shoulders in his hands. His smile never slipped, but his grip was hard. "Now, don't run off, Mary. I'm not going to hurt you."

"Let go of me."

"Don't be like that. I just want to thank you. Seeing how you're being so nice taking care of my friend Sam and all."

"Pet—I mean William has taken care of him too, and Joanna. Go thank them." Rachel tried again to get up, but she was effectively pinned. It had occurred to her that female fashion was just plain cumbersome and poorly designed, but now she realized it could also be dangerous. Jake's eyes were level with hers, so close she could see their long lashes and how the gray-blue was lit from inside with a cold intensity. Her stomach tightened, and she wondered if she was going to be sick.

"Be nice, Mary," he whispered. "Only be nice to me." The childish phrase coming from this man made the hair on her head prickle. Rachel felt a surge of fury and began to struggle in earnest. Jake only laughed, holding her against the wall without effort as if she were a fly in a bottle.

"Here now, why fight it? I'm only trying to be friendly. It's not like it's anything new for you. I'm sure you've romped plenty of times with William."

Rachel filled her lungs and let out a scream, high and piercing, a sound she hadn't known she was capable of making. It sounded more enraged than terrified to her ears, and the notion gave her courage. She dug her nails into the skin of his neck and clung. As she drew breath to scream again, Jake reared back with a yell and raised his fist. Rachel ducked instinctively, waiting for the blow, but it didn't come. His neck was ripped from her grasp, his hands left her shoulders, and she sprawled on the floor while he magically flew backward away from her through the air. He landed with a sharp thud against the great wooden cheese vat. Rachel brushed her hair out of her eyes and saw Matthew standing over her. For a long breathless second, he gazed down at her, breathing hard, his hands poised at his sides, tensed and ready. She couldn't read the expression on his face, but she knew suddenly what a Confederate soldier would have felt facing this man in battle. Then he took a step backward, and the charge in the air dissipated as quickly as it had come.

"Are you all right?" he asked.

"I think so. Thank you."

Rachel got to her knees, but before she could stand, the door flew open and slammed against the wall. Peter froze for only an instant, and Rachel imagined what he was seeing—her on the floor and Matthew standing over her. But Peter didn't go for Matthew first. He came straight to her, dropping to his knees beside her.

"Are you hurt? Are you all right?" He ran his hands quickly over her face, her hair, her arms, back to her face as if checking for damage on a piece of dropped pottery.

She shook her head. "I'm fine."

Peter sprang to his feet and was about to confront Matthew when he saw Jake lying on the floor, his legs sprawled in the dirt. Matthew lifted both hands, palms out. "I didn't touch her, I swear."

"That's true," Rachel said, scrambling to her feet. She reached out to steady herself against the wall. "Matthew only stopped Jake. Don't hit him."

All three turned to glare at Jake, who half sat and half lay, one hand holding his ribs. The angry claw marks were vivid red streaks on his throat. He glared at Rachel and Peter, but when he met Matthew's eye, he winced and looked away.

"You're a guest in the Hunsakers' house," Peter growled in a voice Rachel had never heard him use before. It made shivers scamper up her spine like mice. "They've fed you and given you a dry place to sleep, and right now Joanna's in there fighting to save your friend's life. Is this how you repay their generosity? By attacking a member of their household?"

Matthew reached down and hauled Jake to his feet by the back of his shirt. "You have my word he won't try anything like it again," he said, and Rachel could hear his teeth snap. "He'll answer to me if he does."

Peter seemed to accept this. Slowly he lowered his fists. Matthew shoved Jake out the dairy door, slamming it behind them. There was a pause, and then Peter startled her by laughing.

"I'd hate to get on *his* bad side."

"I'm glad you think it's funny," Rachel replied, shaking out her skirt.

Peter instantly sobered. He caught her hand and held it in both of his against his chest. She could feel his heart hammering as hard as her own. "It isn't funny. I was coming out to see what was keeping all of you. When I heard your scream, I thought—I don't even know what I thought. All thought just stopped, and I was running before I knew it. Who knows what could have happened to you?"

"I know exactly what could have happened to me," Rachel replied sharply.

Peter tugged her toward him, looking intently into her face.

"But it didn't happen," he said gently. "And I'm very, very grateful."

For a breathless moment, Rachel waited, willing him to pull her into his arms, to soothe her, hold her, still her jangling nerves. But he made no movement, only stood looking at her with an odd expression on his face, as if he wasn't sure exactly who she was or how she'd come to be here. She was shaken by the depth of her disappointment.

"I'm grateful too," she said and added, "to Matthew. He came just in time."

Peter gave a stiff nod. "You shouldn't go wandering alone while those men are here, Ra—I mean, Mary."

"Oh, so now it's my fault?"

"I didn't say—"

"This is the dairy. It's where I *work*. I'm here all day."

"I just suggested—"

"Besides, I thought everyone else was going in to eat."

"You should have been in the house with us."

Rachel pulled her hand away and marched to the door.

"What? Why are you acting angry?" Peter called after her.

"I'm not angry!"

"She cries at the top of her lungs," Peter said, lips quirking.

"Ooh, you're so infuriating!" Rachel spat, spinning back around to face him.

Peter gave a sage nod. "I know what this is. This is just the after-effects of the confrontation," he said. "All the leftover energy you didn't get to use up—"

"That's not it," Rachel said, walking up to thrust her finger in his face.

"It's a perfectly normal reaction to an upsetting event."

"I'm not upset!"

He tipped his head to one side and quirked an eyebrow at her.

She felt her hands form into fists. "All right, so I *am*. But it's not about Jake or what happened. I'm upset with *you*."

Peter's eyes widened. "Me? Why?"

"Because what I *want* from you is some sympathy, some comfort, maybe a hug, and instead I get a lecture and a—a scientific analysis!"

For a moment they stood staring at each other, and then Peter moistened his lips and looked down at his feet. Rachel felt a sudden embarrassment at what she'd said, and she turned back toward the door. Peter's voice came low behind her and stopped her in her tracks.

"I wanted to hold you," he muttered. "It was my first impulse when I saw you kneeling on the floor. It's *still* all I can think about. Wrapping my arms around you and not letting go."

"Then why didn't you?" Rachel asked, her voice nearly a whisper.

"I didn't want to spook you off. The last thing you needed so soon after being attacked by one man was to be attacked by another."

Rachel drew in a sharp breath, and suddenly she could see the absurdity of the whole situation. She only just managed not to giggle, afraid he would pass it off as leftover hysteria. "And is that what you would have done?" she asked lightly. "Attacked me?"

Peter shot her a dark look. "Still might," he said. "Come on, let's get out of this dairy and go eat your confounded soup."

* * *

No one said anything to the Hunsakers about the incident, and whatever threats Matthew made seemed to have penetrated Jake's brain. He didn't so much as make eye contact with Rachel after that.

That night, back in the attic with Peter and Shorty, Rachel couldn't sleep. She lay thinking about the three deserters and the things Sam had said to her that afternoon. They were all so young, her own age. It was selfish of her, really, to be running off to Bellefontaine on her own quest while the world was in such turmoil. So many people were in pain right at that moment. She should go to the States, become a nurse, and *help* somehow. What if the unthinkable happened and the North lost? She'd never considered the possibility before. She'd never considered a lot of things. She wondered what would happen to her father's fortune if Richard entered into a contract with the Union Army as he wanted and then the Union lost.

"Can't sleep?" Peter's voice was a low rumble in the dark.

"No. My head's too full."

"Mine too."

"I used to wish I was a man," she confessed.

"What? Why?" He sounded amused.

"So I could go join the army and fight. Contribute somehow. I guess I was glamorizing the whole thing in my mind. I had this insane idea that if I were to go, I could have the whole war wrapped up in a few weeks."

He chuckled, and she squirmed.

"I know. It sounds pretty silly now. After what Sam told me."

"It isn't that simple, is it?" he murmured.

"No. And it's far from glamorous. I still believe there are things worth fighting for. I just wish people didn't have to get hurt doing it."

"I know."

"How could I ever have thought Sam and the others were cowards?"

"I told you you would understand my position one day," he said.

"Now I know what you mean. War is just death. No side wins."

"The human race loses."

"I'm thinking now that maybe the best way to contribute is to help the people who are hurt, whose lives have been ruined by all this. By being a nurse or something."

"That's a good thought."

"Maybe I'll do it if I go back to Toronto." She rolled onto her side, trying to see him in the faint moonlight coming through the half-open shutters. "Why can't they just stop the war, Peter? I mean, William. Let the leaders work it out themselves without involving all those innocent lives . . ."

"What, like playing a game of poker? Winner takes all?"

She scowled. "Don't make fun of me. I know it isn't that easy. I just wish it were."

After a moment, he said quietly, "I do too."

"And I also want to say I'm glad you're not in it. I'm glad you didn't go down and join up and that you're safe."

There was a pause, and then she heard him shift on his blanket. "Thank you. But I don't know how safe any of us really are. We may not be at war here, but there are always things facing us . . . not the least of which is the land itself. We have a long way to go over mountains and rivers."

For a while, the darkness grew silent as they thought this over. It was sobering, the idea of leaving this comfortable home and welcoming family and moving on into the wilderness. Rachel tried to imagine herself in a canoe and couldn't quite do it. She squirmed irritably, the straw of her pallet poking through the blanket beneath her. She couldn't remember the last time she hadn't felt itchy. She stretched to scratch a spot between her shoulder blades. "I'd never have made a good soldier anyway," she said. "I miss my featherbed too much."

"Turn your back."

Rachel rolled over to her other side, and Peter obligingly reached over and scratched the spot for her. Then, in a smooth movement, he slid closer, slipped his arm around her middle, and gathered her back against him. She lay still, caught off guard, torn between comfort and alarm at his closeness. His mouth was warm against the back of her neck as he murmured, "For what it's worth, I'm glad you're not a man, Rachel Mary."

She began to laugh. He gave her a little squeeze and slid away again to his own blanket, but the warmth of his gesture lingered. After a while she heard his breath come long and deep, and he slept. It was a long time before she followed him.

* * *

The next day Sam was back on his feet. His eye wasn't completely healed, but the inflammation had receded significantly, and it had ceased to ooze. He was able to partially open it and announced to them with relief that he could see out of it. Rachel was glad for him, happy that the doctor hadn't been quick to remove the eye. As soon as Sam was able to walk to the privy by himself, he announced he was fit to ride.

"You're not going anywhere in your condition," Joanna told him flatly. "Don't talk nonsense. You have a long way to heal yet."

"But we're aiming to get to the Dunant before winter," Sam said. He was sitting at the table with a blanket around his shoulders. "We're riding hard. I've slowed my friends down enough already." He looked at his companions, and they averted their eyes and shifted their shoulders.

"If you're not well, you're not going anywhere," Ed agreed with Joanna.

Sam shook his head. "We've caused you enough trouble, Mr. Hunsaker. I'm fit to hit the road first thing tomorrow."

"Tomorrow's Sunday," Joanna replied. "Nobody's departing this house on the Sabbath. You're staying put until Monday." And she shot such a ferocious look around the table that no one argued with her.

Later, Rachel remarked to Peter how funny it was that Joanna had been so set against the three men staying, and now here she was refusing to let them leave.

"It's because she got to know Sam," Peter told her. "You can't care for someone that intimately without, well, coming to *care* for them."

"I think I understand that," Rachel said. "And you can't make quick judgments about people as a group based on prejudiced stories you've heard. You have to become personally acquainted with them. And then you generally find out your preconceived notions were wrong."

Peter regarded her thoughtfully. "You've learned something on this crazy journey of yours."

"I've learned more than that," Rachel said. "You were right. I'm too hard on people. Sam has shown me that too. And Joanna is helping me see I don't have to be hard on myself either. I can be patient and let myself learn and grow at my own pace."

Peter began to laugh. "You really *have* been doing some thinking, Mary."

"Well," she said, shrugging, "there's not much else to do while you're sitting and milking a cow."

Chapter Fifteen

Monday morning they all gathered in the yard to see the men off. Their saddlebags were filled with foodstuff Ed had pressed on them, and Karl had put a new leather strap on Matthew's horse's bridle to replace a worn one. Peter held the horses' heads, rubbing their noses speculatively.

"You won't get far on these mounts. They're worn out and stringy. They need more meat on them."

"They've got enough in them yet," Matthew replied.

"You're pushing your luck wearing the blue," Ed said. "Someone down your path will surely recognize those trousers for what they are, as we did, and they may not be as sympathetic. Karl has three pair of good broadcloth. Why don't you trade him, and you'll be safer?"

The three men looked at each other and then at Karl, who nodded.

"You'd do that for us?" There was a new respect in Matthew's voice.

"It isn't much, but it might make your journey easier," Ed said.

"What do you say, boys?" Matthew looked at Jake and Sam.

"I can't get out of these fast enough," Sam said bluntly. "But they're worn thin. It isn't a fair trade."

"It's all right," Karl said.

Jake hesitated. "I don't know. I think I want to hang on to mine. Maybe I could buy yours off you and keep mine rolled up in my pack where no one will see them."

"All right."

The women waited on the porch while the others trooped inside to make the exchange. They reemerged with the legs of their trousers rolled up in cuffs because Karl was so much taller than they. Rachel kept her smile under control as the three men mounted again and touched their greasy hat brims to Joanna and Ed.

"You're good folks," Matthew said. "Thank you for all you've done."

Ed patted Matthew's mare on the neck. "You're good folks too. God bless."

Matthew tossed his head, his eyes narrow below his hat. "God lost track of us months ago."

Ed considered. "Don't be so sure," he said and reached up to shake hands.

The three horses moved away down the road. Matthew rode in front, his back straight, his eyes staring ahead. Jake gave a brief glance backward at Rachel, tipped his hat, then didn't look behind him again. But Sam grinned and waved and called his farewells and thanks until they were out of view.

Karl stood with his hands on his hips in his acquired blue trousers, which were too short and straining at the seams. There was a pause, and then Joanna sniffed. "Waste of good broadcloth. I suppose I'll have to make you more trousers now." She sniffed again, then went inside. But Rachel caught sight of the woman's red-rimmed eyes as she went.

* * *

Rachel woke the next morning in the loft, filled with the pleas-
antness of having had good dreams, though she couldn't remember
them. She lay with her eyes half-closed, the sunlight filtering
through chinks in the barn wall, turning the hay to gold. She
supposed it was silly, but she'd missed the loft while they'd stayed
in the Hunsakers' attic.

She suddenly registered something heavy lying across her
stomach—Peter's arm. She craned her neck to look behind her.
His eyes were still closed, his lashes long on his cheeks. He looked
softer, somehow, when he wasn't awake. The tense lines around
his mouth and the corners of his eyes were smoothed out, the
bristly plane of his jaw slack in sleep.

As she watched, he stirred, and his breathing changed. She
knew he was waking, and she thought he would be embarrassed
if he woke to find his arm around her and her watching him.
Reluctant to break the peaceful spell of the quiet loft, Rachel
quickly closed her eyes and pretended she was still sleeping.
She felt him shift slightly. Then the hand encircling her ribs
lifted. She felt a light touch, his finger slowly tracing the curve
of her cheek, her profile, brushing so gently that she scarcely
felt it. Then his hand moved away, and she heard the hay rustle
as he crawled toward the ladder. Below, a horse stamped and
whickered, and the spell was broken.

For a while longer, she lay, a hollow feeling in her chest,
longing for she didn't know what.

* * *

It occurred to Rachel that afternoon as she chased the cows
through the dairy door that she wasn't as tired anymore and her
body no longer ached. She realized that tasks that had once made
her strain with effort didn't even give her second thoughts now.
She no longer tumbled in brainless exhaustion into the nest in the
loft. After milking, she went inside and studied with new interest
her reflection in Joanna's shiny soup pot. She hardly recognized

the lean, tan face gazing back at her. She was toasted nearly as brown as Shorty, and she was pleased with what she saw. Philip Wycott wouldn't even recognize her.

Philip. Her life in Toronto seemed very far away, almost as if it had happened to someone else. She'd nearly forgotten what she was doing here. Somehow it seemed perfectly natural to be here living like this, working like this, as if her life had no other object. It seemed she'd always been Mary Mitchell, that she'd always smelled of the curing room, and that she'd always been with Peter and his little boy. But she realized with a shock that their month with the Hunsakers was nearly over.

When she mentioned it at supper, Joanna began making a fuss about them staying on, but Rachel was firm. "We need to go on if we're to arrive in British Columbia before winter," she said and glanced at Peter. "Don't we, William?"

"Afraid so. We're pushing the season already."

"Why don't you stay the winter here and start out fresh in the spring?" Ed suggested, and Joanna nodded vigorously.

For a small moment, Rachel was tempted, but she thought of her father and shook her head. "Thank you, but we can't. My . . . my family is waiting for us. It's time to go. But we're so grateful you've let us stay with you."

"You've worked as hard as three women," Joanna said. "You've more than earned your keep."

"And your horse," Ed added.

Joanna arched an eyebrow at Karl, who sat eating at the other end of the table.

"You'll just have to hurry and marry, son, so I have someone to help me in the dairy after Mary goes."

And as before, Karl turned pink and hunched over his plate, and the others laughed.

* * *

The horse Ed gave them in return for their labor was a sturdy four-year-old mare, green-broke and eager. Peter had been working

with her periodically over the past month and declared himself
well satisfied with the trade.

"She should be able to carry both of us," he said. "I think
we'll only need to get one more pack horse from Fort Kiaayo
before we go, and Shorty can ride on top of our goods."

"And what's after that?" Rachel asked.

"From here we go to Fort Reilly, which is on the Amiskwayan
River. There we trade the horses for a boat. We want to get to
Rupert. From there it's by horse again through the mountains
to Arch Station, and we'll be on the Henderson River. Then it's
Fort Loyal and then Bellefontaine."

"Bellefontaine!" Rachel's heart leaped. "We're nearly there!"

Peter laughed. "There's a lot of mountain and river between
here and there. A lot of companies hire Indian guides to get
over the Rockies. You—are you all right with that? It's best to
hire the people who know the land the best."

"Yes. That makes perfect sense." She hoped she sounded
more unconcerned than she felt. Her experience with Natives
so far had not been wonderful, after all. She was still afraid of
them, but she trusted Peter's judgment.

"We need to move fast," he said. "Staying with the Hunsakers
has slowed us down. Couldn't be helped, but all the same, I'll feel
better once we're on the other side of the mountains before snow
flies."

Rachel watched Peter's limber hands caressing the mare's
deep bay coat and felt she and the mare were both in good
hands. Only a few more weeks of hard travel, and she would
be in Bellefontaine. Somewhere downriver from there was
Washed-Out Creek, and her father's mine was somewhere along
that. She felt hope and excitement return as she imagined the
surprise on her father's face when she turned up. She looked up
with shining eyes to see Peter watching her pensively.

"This month has been good for you," he said. "You look
much healthier. Not so weak and pale as when I first found you
praying on the prairie."

"Thank you," she said, surprised, and added, "At least you can't say I'm useless anymore."

"I've never said that."

"Yes, you have. When we first met, you said I was so useless I'd starve to death if you left me alone."

"I would never have said such a thing!" Peter said indignantly.

"You would, and you did."

"Well, you have to admit—if I did—I was right at the time."

Rachel fought against a smile and then gave in to it. "All right, I admit it. I was a sorry excuse for a person, and I couldn't have gotten along without your help."

"You're welcome," he said lightly.

"But I'm not so weak anymore," she added.

"No, not so much," he replied.

They smiled at each other a moment until it became awkward, and then she said, to change the subject, "You're looking pretty fit yourself. All this farm work has been good for you too."

"I've sometimes tried to envision myself as a farmer," Peter said, giving the mare a last affectionate pat. He stood aside to let Rachel climb to the loft first and followed after her. The last rays of the sunset filled the loft with a golden glow.

"Do you want to farm?" Rachel asked.

"I don't know. I can't quite see it. But it is a satisfactory way of life, isn't it?"

Rachel thought of the tubs of butter, the rows of cheeses aging on the shelves in the cold cellar. There *was* a certain satisfaction in knowing she'd helped put them there, to have something to show for her efforts. It pleased her to imagine the Hunsakers eating this winter what she had helped to make.

Peter went through his usual brief bedtime preparations, prying off his boots and removing his stockings, hat, and shirt. He'd lost a button on his union suit, and Joanna had replaced it with a pink coral one, an incongruous little bright spot in the center of his chest.

Rachel thought nothing of the situation anymore. She rebraided her hair, then peeled off her shoes and stockings without any of the qualms she'd felt at the beginning of the month. It was funny how she'd grown used to things and didn't think about them anymore. Her eyes slid to where Peter lay stretched out on his blanket.

Well, hardly thought about them, she amended.

Shorty was already near sleep, sprawled in his nest, and Rachel didn't want to disturb him, so she stretched out in the available space between him and Peter. The rustling died away as they settled themselves. Below them, their new mare stamped and blew air through her nose. It was a comfortable, happy sort of sound.

"It will be hard getting used to being on the road again." Rachel sighed, hugging her blanket around her. "I'll miss the Hunsakers' privy. I've learned to appreciate the value of a proper outhouse." She giggled.

"Yes, I have to admit that's been nice. If I stayed here any longer, I'd grow soft."

"You know, I lived in Toronto for nearly nineteen years," she mused, "and I can't honestly say I have anything to show for it."

"What do you mean?"

The light had faded to dusk, and Rachel turned on her side to see him better. "The Hunsakers will be eating my cheese for months to come. They'll know I was here. Oh, I can't explain it very well."

"I understand what you mean."

"Do you? What about you, Peter? Have you left anything behind that marks that you've been here? I mean, will people remember you?"

As soon as the words left her mouth, she felt she'd said something stupid. There was his son, of course. Peter's legacy was lying right here beside her. She leaned over, slid her arm lightly around the little boy, and breathed in his warm, salty smell as she placed a light kiss on his forehead. Then, when Peter remained silent, she rolled the other way on an impulse, reached out, and put her hand over his. "I'll remember you," she said.

It was quiet for a moment, and then Peter leaned up on his elbow and pulled his hand from hers to put his arm around her. Before she could anticipate it, he pressed his lips to hers in a brief, firm kiss. Rachel couldn't suppress a little squeak of surprise.

Immediately Peter drew back, releasing her. They both lay on their backs on their blankets, looking up at the ceiling. The loft was silent but for their breathing.

"I'm sorry," Rachel stammered, not sure what she was apologizing for.

"No, I'm sorry," he muttered in an unfamiliar voice. "I had no right to do that. I meant it to be . . . I just shouldn't have. I'm sorry."

She could feel him moving away from her, retreating, and found herself following after him. "Peter, wait. We should talk about it."

"No, we shouldn't."

"But I—"

"Forget it happened. Go to sleep, Mary Mitchell."

Rachel waited, but he said nothing more. Troubled, she lay down again and turned her back to his.

CHAPTER SIXTEEN

EVERYTHING WAS READY FOR THEIR departure. The horse stood patiently bearing on its back full saddlebags, freshly laundered blankets, a new frying pan and newly knitted socks for Rachel and Shorty (gifts from Joanna), a week's worth of food, and a hunting knife (a gift from Ed). Even hulking Karl had contributed a pair of soft rabbit-fur mittens in Rachel's size, for, as he explained, he'd heard it got very cold in the Dunant Mountains on the other side of the Rockies. It was far more than they had earned by their labor and, Rachel reflected, probably more than they deserved. She wished she could at least have told these good people her real name.

Joanna gave Shorty a strong hug, and Rachel was touched to see the child return the gesture. Then Peter lifted Shorty up onto the pack and ensured he had a good grip on the horse's mane. Rachel hugged Joanna tightly too, shook Ed's hand, and stood on tiptoe to kiss Karl's cheek. Karl grinned and kissed her cheek in return, then headed into the house. With many good wishes and waves, the Mitchells took their leave.

They walked the first part of the way, the horse ambling between them. Peter walked with his face a perfect blank; if he thought of the awkward moment in the hayloft, he showed no indication. Whenever Rachel thought of it, her face grew hot. She wanted to reach out to him, touch his hand, ask if they were still friends because the thought of jeopardizing their friendship made her stomach feel awful, but she didn't dare broach it.

Peter also didn't show what he thought of their departure and the journey ahead of them. But Rachel found herself near tears over leaving the Hunsakers. She had become used to civilized life, and the thought of more weeks on the trail was daunting. Her father was ahead of her, though, and Richard and Philip were behind her, and all she could do was keep going. They would go to Fort Kiaayo, pick up the second horse, and then ride overland to Fort Reilly. She remembered at that point they would take to the Amiskwayan River, but she didn't look any farther ahead than that. That was enough to tackle.

They were a mile from the Hunsakers' house when Peter said suddenly, "They were good people."

Rachel nodded glumly. "I don't feel right not even telling them our real names."

Peter glanced at her but said nothing. She felt the familiar discomfort knowing they had never told each other their real names either. They continued in silence a moment, leading the horse at a contented plodding pace.

"They were very kind to us," Rachel said. Her voice seemed higher to her ears, and she wondered if he could sense her reluctance to take to the trail once more.

"Yes."

"Edward reminded me of my father a little. All smiling and crinkle-eyed."

"Not mine," Peter said. "Mine was very thin, with a sharp goatee, and if he'd ever smiled, his face would have shattered. Strict New England, my father."

"I thought you were from Ottawa."

"I am. My mother was French. But Father was from New Hampshire, and a more rigid man you will never find."

"You sound as if you don't have very good memories of him."

He shrugged. "Not warm ones. But I respected him very much."

"Has he passed on?"

"Yes."

"Your mother too?"

"Everyone."

"Did you have any brothers or sisters?" Rachel held her breath, wondering how long he would go on answering questions before he caught himself and stopped.

"One sister. She died of scarlet fever when she was eleven. I was a year older." He shifted the reins to his other hand so he was walking beside her instead of with the mare between them. She thought it was an encouraging sign. "What about you? I assume there's only your brother and father . . . ?"

"Yes. My mother died years ago, and Father raised us by himself. We stayed with an aunt when he left for British Columbia, but she's passed on now too, last summer."

"And now your father's prospecting."

"Yes. Isn't that why everybody's there? He owns the Happy Scot Mine. Maybe you've heard of it," she added hopefully. But she wasn't surprised when he shook his head.

They were descending a low hill into a valley where two men labored behind mules in a field of wheat. Peter gestured toward them with a smile.

"Yesterday that was me."

"Will you miss it?"

"I guess," he admitted. "It was back-breaking work, but you felt good at the end of the day."

"I know what you mean. I enjoyed the cheese-making part, but all in all, I don't think I'll miss milking cows."

He reached out and gave a stray wisp of her hair a gentle tug. "I thought you made a fetching milkmaid. Look at the healthy bloom in your cheeks."

"Stop it." She laughed.

"And the muscles you've developed! By the end, you were pitchforking manure around just as well as Joanna."

She rolled her eyes. "That's one thing I'm not going to miss: going to bed every night smelling like a barn."

"I don't know. Some fellows like that good, earthy scent." He wiggled his eyebrows at her exaggeratedly, and she felt the scarlet climb up her cheeks. When he saw it, he grinned.

But to her relief, he moved on to a different topic, discussing their plans for the next stage of their journey. His manner was easier now. Their friendship was intact after all, and the thought lightened her heart.

They stuck to the main trail leading to the fort, passing through countryside peppered with settlements and even fences here and there. People came and went past them, but no one seemed overly interested in who they were or where they were headed. They camped beside the road that night, and even though passersby hardly spared them a glance, Rachel felt she was sleeping in the middle of Toronto's Dundas Street. They slept wrapped in blankets that still smelled comfortingly of Joanna's soap. Rachel and Peter lay on opposite sides of the fire from each other, and Rachel felt disturbingly exposed without the loft roof close above her. She felt triumphantly happy, though, when Shorty, given the choice, quietly chose to sleep beside her.

The next day they purchased the second horse and the supplies they needed from Fort Kiaayo and resumed their journey. It was a hundred eighty miles to Fort Reilly, but the horses were both willing and strong little mares, fresh for the trail. Rachel named them Bess and Tess, which made Peter roll his eyes. It was easier traveling now, with all of them mounted and the land flat. The tall grass prairie had given way gradually to short grass mixed with some scrub and a few trees, which also made travel faster. The trail was beaten nearly into a road, reflecting the frequent passage between Forts Kiaayo and Reilly. Though settlements were sparse, there was some indication of farming efforts underway along the trail. Here and there the countryside had been tamed into submissive, square patches by plow and ox, and once they even passed a rough windmill lazily spinning. From time to time, they met others on the way, sometimes local settlers and sometimes gold seekers with pack mules. There was less game to hunt, but they managed to stretch out their stores to last. Once, Peter helped a man stack freshly mown hay in exchange for a great wedge of bread and all the milk they could drink. Sometimes they were allowed to refresh themselves and the horses at people's wells. All in all, it was the easiest part of their journey so far.

The routine of each day became so familiar to her that it was difficult for her, when she stopped to think about it, to fathom how far she had come. She no longer shied away from buzzing insects or the quickly disappearing snakes that fled from the horses' hooves. She no longer thought about sleeping on the hard ground in the open air. She even reconciled herself to visiting the prairie dogs. She was, she grimly told herself one day as she washed her and Shorty's stockings in an icy stream, an experienced traveler now.

She grinned suddenly. A wild woman indeed. She hadn't worn a corset or crinoline in weeks. Her hair hadn't seen a comb since she'd left Joanna's home, and her shoes were worn to scraps. She'd put on the same poor, much-mended and laundered dress day in and day out for three months or more.

That night, great billowing gray clouds rose up from the horizon and blotted out the dusk-lit sky. They were the darkest clouds Rachel had ever seen, and they rolled across the expanse faster than she believed possible. Peter took one look at them and started packing up their things, even though they'd only just set up camp for the night.

"What? Where are you going?" Rachel asked, tired and cross.

"We're too exposed out here on the flatlands. We shouldn't be the tallest things out here. We need to find a valley or—no, no time. Head for the river!"

"It will only be a little rain," Rachel complained. "We've managed that before."

"This will be more than a little. No, wait. Don't head for the river. There could be flash flooding coming out of the hills."

"Surely not. Why not just wait under the trees over there? They'll block most of the rain."

"Not trees. We don't want to be by anything tall."

Peter had crammed everything back into the packs and now flung the saddles onto the horses, not taking time to cinch them properly. Shorty hurried to help, and Rachel, finally catching the fear sparking off of Peter, stopped complaining and grabbed the reins of one of the horses. Shorty gripped Peter's hand and pulled, pointing to the north.

"You think?" Peter asked the child but then struck off in that direction without waiting for a reply—not that Shorty ever spoke. But the boy nodded vigorously, hurrying after him, obviously approving.

A moment later, they found what Shorty must have discovered while visiting the prairie dogs: the ground swelled upward a few feet and then dipped deep on the other side. The little dell was perhaps eight feet lower than the surrounding landscape and was filled with pretty white flowers and fescue, like a bowl in the middle of the prairie. They tumbled into it, kneeling in the grass to stay as low as possible, and Peter pulled the loose saddles from the horses and forced them to lie down. They did so, groaning and blowing unhappily.

Then the sky opened.

Rachel had read that phrase before in various books back in Toronto, but until that moment, she hadn't understood what it really meant. This wasn't rain—separate, individual drops of water. It was as if someone had turned over a massive bucket and the water was pouring in sheets, unstopping. In thirty seconds, they were soaked to the skin. Rachel couldn't call to the others but only huddled with her knees drawn up and her hands over her head to try to soften the pelting of the rain on the back of her neck. In ten minutes, the rain began to slacken, but the wind rose rushing over the open ground and flinging itself over the lip of their sheltering bowl, making the flying drops feel like pellets. Peter pressed Shorty up against one of the horses and huddled over him, trying in vain to give him some protection.

There was a stab of light and a simultaneous cracking sound, like a whip, and Rachel thought she could detect a funny smell in the air. A strange creeping feeling ran over her arms and scalp, and she knew suddenly that if her hair hadn't been soaking wet it would have been standing on end. There was another stab of lightning, and Shorty gave a cry of fear.

The rain and wind dropped slightly, then, and the lightning took over. Stab after blinding stab, it struck the prairie repeatedly with only a few seconds between bolts until Rachel felt her retinas were burnt. She kept her eyes shut tight and tried to keep her whimpering quiet so Peter wouldn't hear.

And then it stopped. Just like that, the wind dropped completely, the rain slackened to a gentle drizzle, and the lightning storm was over. The clouds rolled through, revealing early stars and a graceful silver half-moon.

Rachel dared to lift her head and ease herself to the top of the slope, expecting to see great burnt spots all over the grass where the lightning had struck. But the grass looked as it had before, though now flattened. The trees though . . . The shade tree she had suggested they rest under was now a black, bony snag sticking up, smoking damply, its leaves and branches completely gone.

Peter fished his hat, which had blown off, out of the pool of water gathered in the bottom of their shelter, shook it off, and put it on his slicked-down hair. He smiled broadly at Shorty and said something Rachel couldn't hear. The little boy lowered his arms he had flung over his head and laughed.

"That," Peter told Rachel, "was a real prairie storm."

"Which is why I live in Toronto," Rachel replied shakily.

* * *

Late one afternoon, they reached Fort Reilly.

It was a smaller place than Rachel had imagined, perched in the narrow stretch between the wide, swift river and the encroaching granite cliffs. It didn't remind her of fairy castles the way Fort Kiaayo had, but it was surrounded by dark pine forest, which gave the fresh, cool air a tangy scent, and the sound of the rushing brown river provided beautiful background music. The granite ranged from gray to rust-colored to green, shimmering in the sunlight, and made up for whatever beauty the fort itself lacked.

They stopped at a log-framed supply store, which, compared to Kiaayo's, was quite crude and desolate but which, after weeks on the trail, seemed lively and bustling to Rachel. The sight of barrels of grain, bolts of fabric, and piles of apples made her feel giddy with contemplation of such riches.

But Peter didn't seem to notice the abundance around them. He went to the counter and the gentleman serving there and greeted him. "I'm looking for my friend Walking Pine," he said, making Rachel turn to stare at him in puzzlement. What had he said?

"He was in here this afternoon," the storekeeper replied. "I assume he's gone back to camp by now. It's near suppertime."

"Can you tell me where his family is staying?" Peter asked.

"Bend in the river about a mile north. At the foot of Saamissapi Hill."

"Hunter's Lookout? Where the granite makes a natural shelf over the river?"

"That's the place. You know it?"

Peter nodded. "I do. Thank you."

He turned and walked toward the door, and Rachel, astonished, hurried after him. "Aren't we going to purchase supplies? We need some things. And we need to find a place to stay tonight."

"In due time," Peter replied. "Right now I need to find Walking Pine's camp. If you want to wait here, you can. It's a fairly difficult walk upriver. I'll leave the horses here; it's too rough a trail for horses."

"I can come with you," Rachel said. "But who is this person? I assume from the name he's Native."

"Yes."

"Why do you need to find him?"

"I'm taking Shorty to him." Peter looked down at the little boy tagging alongside, and a sad look washed over his face. It was gone a moment later, and he straightened and turned north out of the fort. He walked quickly, as if he had made his mind up about something difficult, and Rachel nearly had to jog to keep up. She saved her breath for the strain and didn't bother asking more questions, though her brain was jumping with them. She knew from the stony look on Peter's face that he wouldn't answer them anyway.

The trail was as rough as he had warned her it would be; she was out of breath from scrambling over loose scree and fallen logs behind Peter, and she was out of sorts that Shorty seemed able to keep up without effort while she struggled. She concentrated on her footing, trying not to twist an ankle, and didn't look up often. Then, suddenly, Peter stopped, and she ran into his back. Catching her balance, she peered over his shoulder and grew still.

A group of Indians were camped beside the river a few yards ahead of them, sheltered under a gray thrust of rock in the cliff. A campfire burned cheerfully in the growing dusk, reminding Rachel that it was indeed past suppertime and they still had a long walk back to the fort, where they had yet to find a place to spend the night. What was so important that Peter felt they had to come to this place tonight before even getting settled?

A figure rose from his bedroll and came toward them. He was elderly, taller than Peter, with long gray hair pulled into a loose tail, and he had narrowed dark eyes. As Peter, Rachel, and Shorty drew closer, the broad, weathered face took on a look of astonishment, and he said something in his language and gave a shout of what sounded like welcome and recognition.

Peter replied in kind, and the two men embraced, pounding each other on the back. Rachel relaxed slightly, glad to know Peter knew this man well and clearly considered him a friend. She turned to look at the rest of the group, several men and women in their midthirties and a handful of children. They were all standing now and were edging closer, looking interested in what was happening. Rachel stopped herself from stepping back, not wanting to appear rude, but she kept her legs tensed, ready to run the way they'd come if need be.

Rachel looked at Peter, who was speaking urgently to the man. She watched the Native man's cheerful face grow still and then solemn, a sorrowful look coming into his eyes. He looked back at the group of people near the fire and called something to them in a rough voice. Immediately two of the women set up a wail and threw their arms around each other in distress.

And then an astonishing thing happened. The Indian stooped and held out his arms, and Shorty ran into them, shouting, "Naaahsa!" For a moment, the old Indian rocked the child, his eyes closed and tears escaping and running down his face.

The little boy pulled back from the embrace then and started talking rapidly. Rachel felt her mouth fall open, and her breath caught. Shorty was speaking! But she couldn't understand what he was saying, and slowly it dawned on her that he must be speaking the same language as the old man, who was nodding and talking back. But how had he learned such a thing? Well, she supposed Peter must have taught him, but, then, why had she not heard them speak it together?

Peter said something more, then dove into a long and seemingly impassioned speech.

The older man replied, gesturing toward the fire and the dinner waiting there.

"We're being invited to share their meal," Peter told Rachel.

Rachel felt panic rise in her throat. Seeing the group from afar was much different from being surrounded by them. And it would be dark soon. She didn't trust them, and in spite of the fact that Peter was on such friendly terms with them, she was afraid. But it didn't appear to be an option to decline. Peter was already following the old Indian, who had placed his hand in a friendly fashion on Shorty's shoulder.

The other men in the camp welcomed Peter in a similar fashion, with embraces and smiles. The women, still wiping their eyes from whatever outburst had overtaken them, hurried to set out the food and serve their guests. The women struck Rachel as elegant—slender, graceful, in long brown skirts with long-sleeved tunics over them and soft leather shoes that came to their ankles. Each wore her black hair in two long braids down to her back. One woman in particular seemed enamoured of Shorty. She crouched down to hug him, then took his hand in both of hers and pressed it to her lips. Shorty gave her a shy smile and said something that dispelled the last of her tears and brought an answering smile to her face.

As Rachel nervously watched them, she couldn't help drawing the comparison between the women and her aunt laying out a nice dinner for guests. She couldn't understand what the women were saying to each other in low, urgent voices, but she could guess immediately what they were discussing. She had seen her aunt dither just so at the realization that she didn't have enough plates for everyone.

One young woman of about twenty marched to the trunk of a nearby fallen tree with a knife and deftly sliced away several strips of thick bark to solve the problem. The women cheerfully ladled food onto them and handed them around. When Rachel received hers, she gave a jerky nod of thanks, and the woman serving her nodded back.

Rachel found herself seated on the same fallen tree between the old Indian and a boy of about thirteen. Shorty was on the old Indian's other side, and Peter was across the fire, being fussed over by some of the women, so Rachel didn't have him to translate anything for her. She smiled tentatively at the young man, who met her gaze frankly and smiled to reveal two missing front teeth. He wore trousers and a cotton shirt any boy in Toronto might wear, but his hair was long and neatly braided, with bits of feathers and strings and she-couldn't-tell-what-else woven in. She thought he smelled strange, a combination of smoky fire and something unidentifiable but that put her in mind of horses and rain.

Rachel poked at her food with some temerity. It appeared to be boiled rice, but it was blackish and longer, like spruce needles and not like the short white rice she was used to. Mixed in it were chunks of some sort of greasy meat, some greens she didn't recognize, and red berries that had been boiled to a gluey consistency. Bits of the crumbly bark "plate" had joined the berries. There was no fork. Her stomach began to rebel.

In consternation, she looked at Peter for help, but he was scooping his own serving of the concoction into his mouth with two fingers of his right hand, his lack of fork appearing to concern him not at all. Shorty, she saw when she craned to look, was doing the same. Rachel supposed it would be very rude of her to refuse it. The last thing she wanted to do was anger the Indians when she was surrounded by them. Resigning herself, she took a fingerful of the goop and raised it slowly to her mouth.

The flavors were strong and smoky, a wild mingling of sweet and nutty, and the rice gave the mixture substance. Her eyes widened, and she took another scoop. Delicious! She thought the meat might be venison but couldn't tell. She forgot about manners and decorum and simply ate, cleaning the last morsels out of her flaky plate.

When she finally looked up, replete, she saw several of the women watching her with approving smiles. Rachel lifted her plate a little in salute and nodded her appreciation, smiling back.

She was afraid the evening would drag on with the dances and songs she had read about going on around the fire until the wee hours of morning, but to her relief, Peter stood, set down his plate, and began to make what sounded like a farewell speech. He gestured toward the darkening sky and pointed back toward the fort several times.

There was some discussion back and forth, and then the old Indian rose and called something to one of the women. She came quickly, bringing something in her hands. Rachel saw that it was a fine hunting knife in a leather scabbard. The Indian took the knife, crossed the circle to where Peter was standing, and placed the knife gently in Peter's hands. Peter thanked him and put the knife in his belt. The two men shook hands, and the Indian said something in a low voice.

Rachel stood and brushed down her skirt. She went to join Peter, and Shorty followed. But then Peter surprised Rachel by scooping Shorty up in a strong hug. The two looked at each other solemnly for a moment, and then Peter ruffled Shorty's hair fondly, set him down, took Rachel's elbow in his hand, and walked away from camp.

Confused, Rachel looked back and saw Shorty going to stand beside the old Indian, who looked down at him and put his hand on the boy's head. The woman who had kissed Shorty earlier came to stand on Shorty's other side and took his hand in hers. She smiled and waved to Rachel in farewell.

"But . . . but wait!" Rachel cried, her blood turning to ice. "Peter, what are you doing? Wait for Shorty!"

"He's staying here. That's the idea," Peter said as if it should be perfectly clear to anyone.

"What? Wait. You can't leave him." Rachel stopped short and pulled her elbow free of his grasp. She turned back, tripping over her skirts and nearly falling, but Peter caught her by the wrists and held her. Rachel struggled, and when he wouldn't release her, she began to beat on his chest with her fists. "What's the matter with you? Why are you letting them take him? Stop them!"

"I can't, Rachel. He has to go with them. I understand; I really do. I like the boy too. But it's best all around."

"I can't believe you!" Rachel felt the tears flowing freely down her cheeks. She freed one hand from his grasp and aimed a punch at his face, but he deflected it, startled. "How could you? How could you trade your son for a knife?" she demanded.

Peter stared at her, his mouth open, letting her fists rain down against him. Then he spluttered and stepped back so suddenly she nearly fell over. "Trade my *son*? What are you talking about?"

"You gave Shorty to those savages."

Peter gave a whooshing noise, half laughter and half shout. "Shorty *is* one of those so-called savages. Don't you understand? They're his family."

Rachel stopped, stunned, uncomprehending. "They are?"

"He's half Blackfoot, Rachel. That man is his grandfather, and the woman holding his hand is his aunt. I'm delivering him to them."

"He—Shorty's an Indian?"

Peter's eyes widened in amazement. "Couldn't you tell? My word, girl. What have you been thinking all these weeks? You thought he was my *son*?"

"Well, yes. Of course!" she replied. She felt rather weak and wished she could sit down. "What else was I to think? I just assumed."

"Did you not look at him in all that time? Did you not wonder why he was brown as the earth and hardly spoke?"

"Well, I thought he was mute. And I thought him rather dark, but I thought it was just a combination of being sunburned and unwashed."

A grin had slowly started to spread across Peter's face as she replied. At her last word, he gave a loud whoop of laughter. "Unwashed!"

"And I assumed perhaps his mother had been dark."

"Well, yes, she was! She was indeed!" Peter bent over to hang on to his knees, he was laughing so hard. "Unwashed!" He straightened and wiped his eyes. Rachel could see the Indians behind them staring in their direction, no doubt wondering what all the fuss was about, and she wished Peter wouldn't speak so loudly.

"Girl, no wonder—I couldn't figure out how you could feel so against the Natives, talking the way you did about them and yet being happy to share your blanket with one all that time."

"I didn't know!" Rachel wanted to sink into the ground with mortification. "I wouldn't have spoken that way if I'd known."

"You shouldn't have spoken that way at all," Peter reminded her, growing sober but still dabbing at his eyes with his sleeve. "You *wouldn't* speak that way about the Indians if you really knew them. I mean, you knew Shorty. Was he a savage?"

"Of course not. He's entirely sweet." Rachel wanted to cry all over again at the thought of leaving the little boy. "I don't want to leave him."

"Neither do I. But it had to happen eventually. He belongs with his family. Go and say good-bye more thoroughly if you want to. I can wait."

Rachel hesitated, looking back, wondering if it would anger them if she ran back into their camp. She didn't know if she had the nerve to do it. But Shorty had been watching, and now he moved away from his grandfather's hand and walked toward her and Peter. He looked entirely calm and dignified, as if he was the patient adult and she the inconsolable child. Rachel felt a catch in her throat and, picking up her skirts, hurried to meet him. When he drew close, she dropped to her knees and put her arms around the boy. "Shorty, I don't know if you can understand me. I . . . I didn't know you spoke Blackfoot. But . . . well, I'm going to miss you."

Shorty squeezed her neck with his brown little arms and then drew back to look at her before breaking into a sunny smile. He put his palms on her cheeks and said very distinctly, "You a nice lady."

Rachel felt tears sliding down her face. She ignored whoever was watching and planted a firm kiss on the little boy's cheek. He smelled of dust and sweat and little boy, and Rachel felt a sudden, terrible loss. She didn't want to let go, but Shorty pulled away and walked confidently back toward the camp, where his grandfather stood waiting.

CHAPTER SEVENTEEN

RACHEL COULDN'T SPEAK FOR A while as they walked back along the rough trail toward the fort. Her mind spun with confusion and sorrow. It seemed entirely wrong to be walking along without her small, black-haired shadow. Those people couldn't have him! He belonged to her and Peter!

"You should have told me," she finally said when she trusted her voice not to tremble.

"I assumed you could tell for yourself. I guess I was wrong," Peter said, still sounding amused.

"I mean, you should have warned me you were going to Fort Reilly to return him to his family."

He hesitated, then said, "Would it have changed anything?"

"I could have prepared myself. I wouldn't have let myself become so attached to him," Rachel said.

He eyed her a moment, then looked away. "You've always known from the beginning that you would have to part from him one day."

This hit her with a shock, but she saw clearly that he was right. She wasn't Shorty's mother. She was merely traveling with him and Peter for a while. She would have had to say good-bye eventually . . . as she would have to say good-bye to Peter one day too. She swallowed hard and pushed the thought away. "All right," she conceded. "I would have become attached to him anyway, even if I'd known right from the start what you intended."

"I apologize for not preparing you. But perhaps it was best this way. It gave you less time to be sorrowful. If I'd told you sooner, you just would have rehearsed saying good-bye to him over and over again in your mind instead of having to do it just the once."

"Well, I suppose so," she said, unconvinced.

Peter took her elbow to help her over a large log in their path. "Truth be told, I didn't realize you had grown so fond of him. From the comments you have sometimes made about the Indians, I didn't think you would let yourself grow to love one."

Rachel winced. "I didn't know he *was* one. But that's no excuse. I shouldn't have had such an attitude. I hope he didn't understand me." She glanced back over her shoulder, but the camp was out of view. "I think you were probably right not to warn me what you were going to do, after all. I *would* have spent this whole journey dreading this."

"Sometimes the anticipation is worse than the actuality. Better to have a swift cut than a slow, lingering burn," Peter said.

Rachel wasn't sure about that, but it seemed pointless to argue. There was nothing to be done about it now. She pictured Shorty's round little face and felt a hollowness in her chest.

"How on earth did he come to be with you?" she asked. "I want to know his story."

Peter let out a long, tired-sounding breath. "His mother was Walking Pine's daughter. She ran away and married a Cree and had Shorty. A couple of years ago, they went to live with her husband's family in the Red River area. I knew them when I was at Fort Garry. She and the whole family died last spring of the red measles, but Shorty survived."

"How awful!"

"I hated having to tell Walking Pine his daughter had died," Peter said, his voice dropping. "*I've* been dreading *that* this whole journey."

Rachel suddenly understood the sorrow on the family's faces. She swallowed her own tears and asked, "But how did Shorty come into your care?"

"The Anglican minister at Fort Garry wanted to raise him like a white boy, put him into a church school, but I thought he belonged with his mother's people. When the minister objected, I . . . well, I sort of liberated Shorty, and we took off west."

"You kidnapped him."

"It was what Shorty wanted. That's not his real name, by the way. It's Sooyaisiihtsi. It means 'Prairie Smoke.' It's a kind of plant."

"I see why you call him Shorty. And no wonder you wanted to avoid the forts," Rachel said, shaking her head. "You took that little boy without permission."

"I had *his* permission," Peter replied. "And now he's reunited with the Blackfoot. It's where he belongs and where he wants to be."

"I can't stand leaving him."

"I know. Don't worry. They'll take good care of him. And it will give his grandfather great consolation to have him. He'll be treated well." He glanced down at her. "So I guess you've revised your opinion of the Natives?"

"I don't know that I can say that about all of them," Rachel said, gazing back in the direction of the camp and feeling bereft. "But I loved Shorty. I'll miss him."

"Me too. Come on, let's go. It's getting dark."

They stayed in a hastily made camp just outside the fort, and Rachel spent the night alternating between dozing and crying. She thought about Shorty's grandfather and the joy he would feel to have his grandchild with him and his sorrow at hearing of the death of his daughter. She thought about Shorty's aunt pressing the child's hand to her lips, the love plain on her pretty face. Somehow Rachel had never stopped to think about Indians' family structures or home life. It felt surprising somehow that they would value family relationships as much as she did . . . and then she was surprised at her surprise. Of course they would. Why wouldn't they?

Not for the first time, she had the sneaking suspicion that she had led a narrow-viewed life back in Toronto and may have formed her assumptions about other people too hastily.

* * *

The next day, Peter went off to negotiate for a boat and the remainder of the supplies they would need. This was the last opportunity to lay in supplies before crossing the mountains. Rachel reluctantly said good-bye to Bess and Tess, sorry to let the horses go so soon.

She felt less tough suddenly and more vulnerable and fearful of what lay ahead in this next leg of the journey. She took the opportunity to wash what laundry she could in the river, wanting to keep busy so she didn't have time to think. More than that, she missed Shorty's warm little presence near her. She missed even his silence. Thank goodness she could always rely on there being laundry to do to occupy herself.

When she had scrubbed her dress as best she could, she wrung it out and draped it over some bushes to dry in the sun. In the interest of practicality, she had given up her mortification at being under the wide open sky in the daylight in only her underclothes. There was no other way to manage because they each owned only one set of clothes, and the summer had grown far too hot to sit around swathed in blankets while their clothes dried.

When Peter came back, she was dressed once again, her hair was neatly braided, and she had a pot of beans boiling on the fire for lunch. She looked up hopefully when she heard him returning and was surprised to see he wasn't alone. She stood and wiped her hands on her skirt. The Native man with Peter appeared to be about fifty years old, she supposed, though his face was so weathered and lined he could have been younger than he looked. He wore leather leggings and a red-checked shirt, with a black felt hat low on his forehead. His hair hung down in two dark braids over his shoulders.

"Rachel, this is Frank."

Rachel nodded at the man, who gazed rather disinterestedly back at her. Then his gaze shifted to the fire, and he sniffed.

Peter gestured toward the pot and dug out his own plate and fork, which he handed to the visitor. Frank stooped over the fire to poke at the beans.

"Frank's a local Blackfoot," Peter told Rachel. "I've hired him to help us."

"Did you manage to get a boat?" It seemed odd not to see their horses tethered nearby. One more thing to let go of, she told herself sadly.

"I did. It's tied down by the river. You can see it after we eat," he added as she turned in that direction. "Sit down, and let's serve our guest."

"How do I say 'good morning' in Blackfoot?" she murmured to Peter.

"*I'taamikskanaotonni*," he replied easily.

She blinked at him. "Surely not."

"I'm afraid so. It's easier just to say hello. That's *oki*."

Rachel recited this in her mind a few times and then said carefully to Frank, "*Oki*."

Frank had helped himself to exactly one third of the beans and was now sitting comfortably with his legs stretched before him on the ground, crossed at the ankles. He looked at her for a moment without expression, then said calmly, "I grew up speaking English."

"Oh! Well, that makes things easier," Rachel muttered, shooting Peter a nasty look.

Peter just smiled benignly.

Rachel took out their one remaining plate and fork and looked at the pot. Peter took the beans and dumped the whole thing on the plate.

"Looks like we're sharing the fork," he said matter-of-factly and sat down opposite Frank.

Rachel sat beside him on the ground. Peter held the plate between them, and they shared the fork back and forth. After a while it ceased to be awkward, and Rachel was struck once again by how adaptable people could be when they had to.

They spent the afternoon settling their goods in the boat, balancing the weight to ensure the best stability. The boat, Rachel thought, had seen better days, its outside scarred and unpainted, but it was large enough to hold everything yet small enough to portage easily.

Fortunately Frank had brought some of his own supplies, including a blanket. In camp that night, they each rolled up in their own to sleep, circling the smoldering fire. Rachel lay gazing up at the stars and the flickering orange firelight on the surrounding trees and listened to the crackling of the dying flames. It was sad to have the blanket to herself, with no Shorty to share it with. But as she lay waiting for sleep, a pervasive feeling of peace gradually overtook her. It wouldn't be long now. With these two knowledgeable and capable men to help her, she was sure to reach Bellefontaine and find her father.

The next morning, Peter built the fire while Frank disappeared toward the river. After a few minutes he walked nonchalantly back into camp and held out a large fish by the gills.

"What kind of fish is that?" Rachel asked, going to examine it delightedly. "Is it a trout?" She was far less squeamish about gutting fish than she was about gutting rabbits.

"Maybe a whitefish," Frank said. "Who knows? Not my area of expertise. Whatever you call it, it's edible, and you can cook it for breakfast."

Rachel was about to remark in astonishment when Peter said behind her, "Frank is a scout in the summer for extra money, but in the winter, he's a bookkeeper at the fort. He grew up in Victoria." Then he added with a low chuckle, "Not fitting the image you had of the exotic Native river guide?"

"I'll cook it, thank you," Rachel said, ignoring Peter's comment. "And I could do up some griddle scones to go with it." They were one of the few things she had learned how to cook over a fire. Most of her attempts at other dishes had been singularly unsuccessful.

Peter had been heroically silent about her failures, but with Frank joining them for their first breakfast together, she wanted to show herself competent.

"I can clean it," Peter offered, holding out his hand for the fish, but she shook her head.

"I want to be useful," she said.

His blue eyes grew serious. She was suddenly aware of how long his lashes were and how they gave his eyes a pensive look.

"You *have* been useful," he said. "I've never had it so easy, with you hauling the water and doing the laundry and building the fires and gathering fuel and rubbing down the horses and . . ."

She laughed. "All right. At least your statement isn't true now."

"I've never—"

"We're not going to argue over that again, are we?"

She made quick work of gutting the fish. Peter watched, and then he said quietly, "I've been on the road off and on for four years. But I think I like it better not traveling alone."

There was something in his face and voice that made her smile fade. She put a hand out to touch his arm, then thought better of it and pulled her hand back, wiping it on the grass. She looked around, but Frank was busy down by the river and couldn't overhear them. "Why have you traveled so much?" she asked softly. "Why has it been so long since you were home?"

He hesitated, and she thought he wasn't going to answer. He'd always put off her questions before or else ignored them completely. He took the fish from her and turned toward the fire. As he skewered the fish on a stick and set it over the fire, he spoke, his voice low. "You almost guessed it once. I was a teacher—not a traveling one but at a college in Montreal. I taught languages— French, German—but Indian languages were a special interest of mine, and I received permission from my college to do field research. I was given a financial grant, and I started compiling material for a book. A dictionary of four of the Algonquian Indian languages: Cree, Ojibwa, Innu, and Blackfoot. Each year I spent several months living among the Natives, studying their languages."

Whatever she might have imagined about him, this wasn't it. She stared at him in wonder. It was as if he'd shed his familiar skin and become someone completely new.

"You said you thought I was well educated," he reminded her with a wry quirk to his lips.

"I had no idea how well," she said.

He turned the stick, revolving the fish, watching it begin to drip and sputter. "After my last journey, I went home and married a girl from Ottawa. Her name was Angelina. I planned to stay home after that, not travel so far again. We'd been married eight months when she died of cholera. She was all I had in the world." He looked up and gave Rachel a crooked, self-conscious smile. The expression in his eyes made her throat grow tight. "So, you see, there wasn't really a reason to stay home after that. Or a reason to go back."

Rachel felt tears burn her eyes and swiped them away with the back of her hand. Frank was walking back toward camp, and she didn't want him to see her crying. "I'm sorry. I never knew," she muttered.

"How could you have? I never told you," Peter replied. He lifted the fish from the fire and began deboning it.

She watched him a moment, then asked, "What is your full name, Peter?"

He finished the fish and scraped some onto one of the tin plates for Frank, who took it and walked a little ways away from the fire to sit and eat. The rest of the fish Peter slid onto the other plate for them to share, then he paused for a moment and said slowly, "It's not Peter. It's Jacob. Sinclair."

Rachel stared at him, aware that her mouth hung open stupidly. "I've heard of you."

He glanced at her and turned away to wipe his hands dry.

The pieces fell into place with a click. "Jacob Sinclair, well-known anthropologist and Indian interpreter, disappeared without a word over a year ago. It was in all the newspapers. Everyone thinks you were killed by the Indians. You never came back."

"No, I never did," he replied with a note of wariness in his voice.

Rachel touched his arm softly. "I won't say anything to anyone if you don't want me to."

He glanced down at her hand. "I know."

She picked up the plate and busied herself with her portion of the fish, eating delicately with her fingers. "I've read your book on the French explorers," she said with her mouth full. "My father had a copy in his library. He had another one too, something about the French and immigration, but I haven't read it, I'm afraid."

"You haven't missed anything," he said shortly, his eyes sparkling, and reached for the water bag. He took a long swallow, his Adam's apple moving in his long, bronzed throat, and then took the plate she offered him with his half of the meal. "It was the first book I ever wrote, and it wasn't my best by any means. I was twenty-three years old and thought I knew everything."

Rachel took the water bag he had set down and drank deeply, then recorked the bag. She wiped her chin with the back of her hand, licked the last of the fish oil from her fingers, and looked up to see Peter—Jacob—smiling at her. She reddened.

"I'm sorry. I seem to be forgetting my manners," she said. "But you know, using your fingers is much more practical than using a fork, and . . . well, it's not as if I have a serviette or anything. What am I to call you?" she added suddenly. "I've known you as Peter for months, and then with the Hunsakers I called you William, and now I find out you're Jacob . . ."

"Peter. I've been Peter for a year now."

She stood and took the empty plate from him. "Peter, then. I promise to regain my manners once we're back in civilization. My goodness, my father would love to meet you when we get to British Columbia. Would it be possible to—I mean, could I tell him who you are? And nobody else?"

Peter shrugged. "I suppose you can tell him. It's not exactly a great secret. I just needed solitude. I didn't want people hounding me, consoling me. I know they were well meaning, but I couldn't take it so soon after . . . Anyway, it's been a year now, and I suppose . . ." He looked up at her soberly. "I suppose I don't need solitude so much anymore. I've been thinking maybe it's time I rejoined civilization myself."

"As yourself?" Rachel asked quietly, returning his gaze. "Or as Peter?"

He made a wry face. "Maybe as William Mitchell. He seemed to do very well for himself."

Rachel laughed. "Yes. Mary Mitchell wasn't a bad milkmaid either, you know."

"No, she seemed to do all right too," he agreed. As she returned to sit beside him, he leaned over and gave her shoulder a nudge. "We were a good team."

"Yes, we were." She didn't like the taste of that past tense in her mouth.

"But you seem to do all right as Rachel Cameron too," he added.

She squirmed a moment, then shook her head. "Fair is fair. You were truthful with me and deserve only the same in return."

"Let me guess. You're not Rachel Cameron?" A smile played on his lips as he watched her.

"Rachel Hamilton."

"And your brother? Is he real? Or your father in Bellefontaine?"

"All the rest I told you is true," she said.

"Well," he said after a small pause, "I don't blame you for giving me a false name. When we first met, you didn't know if I would turn you in for the reward money. But I'm glad you feel you can trust me now."

"Likewise," she replied.

For a moment, they just looked at each other, considering this alteration in their relationship. Then Peter slapped his knees and got to his feet. "I'm going to stretch my legs for a bit."

"Why would you need to stretch your legs?" Rachel laughed. "You've been walking for days."

"I'll bury the fish guts away from camp so the wolves don't come sniffing after them."

"Wolves?" Rachel froze.

Peter just made a face at her, turned, and walked into the woods. Rachel glanced at Frank, who was watching her without expression. She smiled at him, and he smiled back. Satisfied, Rachel set about cleaning up from the meal.

Chapter Eighteen

The next few days ran together in her mind when Rachel looked back on them later. She had discovered several things during that time, the uppermost being that she was afraid of water. She had never been before, but, then, she had never experienced it in quite this way before. She hated the tippy feel of the boat, the sound of water rushing around her, the rock and jolt as the current carried them along, and the fear of moving in case she fell overboard. Granted, she appreciated the speed with which they moved through the countryside, but the river carried them so quickly at times that she didn't have a chance to look around her, and then at other times, the river spread out and moved so slowly that she felt time had stopped and the riverbanks were slipping lazily past them while they held still. It was disorienting. She also didn't like sitting in the center of the boat while Peter and Frank did all the labor.

She found herself wishing they were alone on the trail, just Peter and her together. She was not sure she liked having Frank there all the time, not talking much or apparently listening either but always within sight. It was like having a nanny again. She had to concede he was extremely useful when they came upon strong rapids they had to portage around. There was no way she could have carried one end of the boat herself. She did help carry the supplies though, hurrying back and forth along the riverbank to shuttle armload after armload until all was shifted downriver. But as always, she adapted, and as the days passed, she grew used to Frank's polite, quiet presence. In a way, it almost felt like having Shorty back.

One morning as they slipped along the water, Peter called to her and pointed toward the far bank of the river. Rachel looked up and at first did not see what he was pointing at. Then she saw one of the granite boulders move.

A large hairy animal stood up on its hind legs, its front paws dangling in front of its massive chest, watching them in open curiosity. It had a broad head but tiny eyes and a muzzle like a dog. The morning sun struck its fur, turning it silvery gold.

"A bear!" Rachel cried, thrilled. She had seen pictures, of course, but had never thought she might actually see one in person.

"A grizzly," Peter added. "Usually you see black bears. A grizzly isn't so common."

The river carried them past, and Rachel turned around to keep the bear in her sight. The animal lost interest in them and, dropping to all fours, lumbered down into the water, its back hunched, where it stood turning its large head from side to side as if scanning for something.

"What's it doing?"

"Fishing," Frank replied, his tone implying he didn't think much of Rachel's intelligence.

"She's eating all she can before she starts her winter sleep," Peter added, shooting a grin at Frank. He had caught the disgusted tone. "Bears put on extra weight in the summer and fall to carry them through their hibernation. That bear can go for a hundred days without eating and drinking once winter's snow comes."

"That's amazing," Rachel remarked. "I wish we could have had a better look."

"It's best not to linger when bears are around," Peter told her. "They may look beautiful and sedate, but you need to stay as far from them as possible. Especially in the spring when they're waking up hungry and have cubs to protect. If you ever encounter a cub in the bush, get away as fast as possible because the mother will be somewhere nearby."

* * *

Rachel's mind was occupied with bears the rest of the day, and she kept a close eye on the rocks and pine trees lining the river, hoping to see another one. But she saw nothing more than a few birds and a muskrat before they finally stopped to make camp.

Rachel dreamt of bears that night, and when she awoke, the sky was a faint gray, the temperature had dropped, and there was something warm and unfamiliar curled against her stomach. Rachel jerked fully awake, stretching out her hand, and touched soft fur. The object moved, and Rachel gave a scream and rose out of her bedroll like a duck lifting off the water in a flap.

"It's a bear cub!" she screeched, scuttling backward. She tripped over a log and fell hard on her backside, then flipped onto all fours and crawled fast, fighting to get away, waiting for the mother bear to emerge from the trees and rip her to shreds at any moment. She felt her skirt rip away from the waistband. A foul ammonia smell nearly knocked the air from her chest and made her eyes burn, and her screams cut off in a choking gasp.

"Wooee! That's no bear cub," Frank cried, scrambling away half in and half out of his blanket. Peter followed suit, coughing and yelling.

Rachel looked back and saw a black-and-white catlike animal waddling quickly away from her tangled blanket. It disappeared into the forest, leaving the lingering stench behind. The horses stamped and tossed their heads, and Peter laughed in airless gasps.

"That was no bear cub," he agreed, fanning the air limply with his hand. "And you, my girl, are going into the river before you come anywhere near our boat."

A harsh scrub in the freezing water did not reduce the skunk smell sufficiently, and even though Peter beat the blanket for half an hour in the river, the horrible smell lingered in the fiber. Frank luckily produced a needle and black thread with which she could fumblingly mend her torn dress. When they resumed their journey, Rachel sat in the very back of the boat, downwind from the men, and refused to speak about it. Frank wisely said nothing further, but Peter commented gaily, "Shorty is sorry he missed that."

* * *

The smell faded after three days, and Rachel, humiliated, was allowed to return to her place in the center of the boat. There was a distinct autumn chill in the air when at last they reached Rupert and exchanged their boat—to Rachel's relief—for three sturdy horses for the next leg of their journey through the mountains.

The Rockies were like nothing she had seen before—great, rolling, brown hills, bald like bread loaves, leading up to jagged gray rock forested with pines. The sky seemed higher here, the clouds distant and wispy, not fat and rolling like the clouds back east. Even the air had a different taste to it, of heated rock and citrusy pine, with a cold, fresh dampness underlying it. Looking at the rising, tough terrain before them and the cluster of small dwellings huddled in the mountains' shadow, Rachel felt very small and insignificant. It felt as if the mountains would fall on her at any moment, and she marvelled that anyone could live in their shadow without fear.

To Rachel's surprise, Frank did not leave them at the river. He was going to accompany them through the mountains, Peter explained, because they would need help getting their load of supplies over the difficult landscape.

"And," he warned, "there's the Henderson River to contend with on the other side."

Rachel didn't want to think about it.

They were to cross the mountains through Sugarloaf Pass. Peter made inquiries and found a group of settlers going the

same route, trying to make it through the mountains before
winter weather descended. The leader of the company, Jonas
Peabody, had passed through this route several times, which
made Rachel feel better when she heard of it. There were fifty
in the Peabody Company, including three women and their
children, on their way to Briarton, British Columbia, to farm.

The women were Mrs. Julia Barker, Mrs. Amelia Glade,
and Mrs. Lizzie Myers. Mrs. Barker was a capable-looking and
cheerful woman. She was a midwife from New York and the only
medical person in the group. Mrs. Glade was a shrewish person
with a thin, stern face and a pointed nose like a woodchip, and
her husband was equally crusty. They were from Minnesota and
had four children under the age of seven, all of sour disposition
and red cheeks that looked scrubbed raw. Mrs. Myers, however,
was short, pudgy, and friendly as a puppy but not overly
inquisitive, and she gladly accepted William and Mary Mitchell
into her family without many questions. She was happy to have
an able-bodied man to help because she was, she explained, on
her way to join her husband, who had already forged northwest
that spring to prepare a home for them. She had traveled up
from the Utah Territory with her two amiable young sons, who
were tall and thin and as red-headed as their mother. She told
Peter she would welcome the help getting over the mountains
and would be pleased to share her tents in exchange for their
muscle. And she didn't bat an eye when Peter informed her that
Frank the Blackfoot would be accompanying them.

"The more the merrier, and the lighter the load," she replied
simply. And she astonished both Rachel and Frank when she
reached out and gave Frank's hand a vigorous shake. "You four
males take the larger tent, and Mary and I can share the other."

Rachel enjoyed Lizzie's company and her cheerful conversation,
but she was surprised to learn as they chatted that Lizzie was
originally from New York and her family back home had disowned
her because of her Mormon religious beliefs. She had made her
way across the continent with a company of others of her faith

to the Salt Lake Valley, trekking all that way by wagon and, when that broke down, on foot. And then she had married Davey Myers and trekked again to a hardscrabble farm in the northern part of Utah Territory. But her husband had dreamt of the lush farmland he had heard about in British Columbia and wanted to help colonize the wilderness, so she had agreed to uproot once more. It had taken her husband and her a long time to get together enough money and supplies to make the journey north, and she had been separated from him now for five months.

Rachel couldn't understand how Lizzie could remain so optimistic in the face of such trials, but Lizzie just shrugged and waved a hand. "It's in the past. One can only keep going," she said lightly. "I have my weak moments, same as anyone, but my husband, now, he's the truly strong one. He lost his first wife and all three of his children on the ship coming from England. Without Davey, I wouldn't be here now." Her gesture encompassed the entire group of ragtag people, the roiling dust, and the noisy horses as if there was nowhere on earth she'd rather be.

"I'm sure you'll be glad to be with him again," Rachel said.

"He's building us a house on a hundred acres," Lizzie said. "It will be a good place for our children to grow up." She nodded to where her two sons, David Jr. and Walter, were loading the saddlebags with Peter in preparation for the next morning's departure. They were both quiet and friendly boys and had taken to Peter within five minutes of meeting him.

"I can't complain," Lizzie added, watching her boys lovingly. "I'm blessed. Two good sons and a good husband, and each of us has a horse so we can all ride. It's more than anyone could ask for."

"I'd settle for the one good husband," Rachel joked without thinking and then caught herself. She was meant to be Mary Mitchell again, and Peter—for all anyone knew—*was* her husband. She watched Lizzie's eyes flick to Peter, who hoisted the heavy bags into place as if they were pillows. Dust coated his clothes, his sleeves rolled to bare his forearms, turning him a pale tan, and even from here, they could see the sweat glazing his face. He had lost his hat somewhere, and a shock of chocolate hair fell over his forehead. He looked splendid.

"Oh, I think you've got that," Lizzie mused. "No, I don't think you can complain either."

* * *

The company set out the next morning at dawn, the horses churning the earth to powder. Some of the men in the group were attempting to bring a small herd of cattle over the mountains, and Peter, Frank, and the two boys rode with them to help move the slow beasts. Rachel felt slightly put out that Peter didn't intend to ride beside her and then told herself not to be selfish. These settlers needed cattle when they arrived in their new home, and they would need all the help they could get to drive the animals there. Personally she thought it would have been smarter to bring the cattle up from California by boat through Victoria instead of trying to cross the Rockies with them. But perhaps she didn't understand these things.

Lizzie, shocking in a pair of leather Indian trousers and a large sun hat, looked vaguely ridiculous balanced atop her skinny mare, surrounded by her load of supplies, like a mushroom perched on a fence. But she turned out to be adept at riding. Before they'd gone a mile, Rachel could feel herself grow stiff and gritty with the dust. It got into everything—her hair, the food, her blanket. The heat and stench and noise didn't seem to distress Lizzie at all. She was a great talker, and when she wasn't chatting, she was singing. It took a little getting used to after Peter's customary silence on the trail, but Rachel liked her. It was fun to have a woman to talk to, especially an entertaining one. It helped the time pass, the sun seem less intense, and the journey seem less tedious.

An un-looked-for additional bit of light was Harry. He was Walter and David Jr.'s dog, and Lizzie confessed that to herself she referred to him as Hairy rather than Harry. Rachel had always preferred cats and had thought dogs rather uncivilized and smelly, all hair and drool, so she was surprised to find she genuinely loved Harry's company. He was a great, black thing with white splotches on his face and feet. He was of uncertain parentage but was devoted to the boys and greeted Rachel with such joy, assuming a warm welcome, that she couldn't help but fall in love with his grinning face. He spent the days running beside Walter and David Jr.'s horses, staying out of the way with uncanny intelligence and pure nerve, but he spent the nights flopped across the flap door of Lizzie's tent like a guard, and Rachel felt comforted knowing he was out there in the dark, alert to wolves and anything else that might try to molest the camp. Rachel slipped him treats at dinner, ran her fingers through his long hair to dislodge burrs and dirt, and felt her heart warm in his company.

But in the quiet of the night, she couldn't ignore the great part of her that wished she was alone on the trail with Peter, just the two of them. She missed the quiet evening campfires, when the only sound was the popping of the green wood in the flames. She missed having him beside her instead of out riding amongst the other men. She missed the Hunsakers' golden loft and their nest in the rustling hay. Even though Shorty had been with them, it had felt at times as if the world had contained only them alone. Sometimes she would look up from the crowd around the supper campfire and Peter's eyes would meet hers, and in those brief moments, she suspected he missed their former companionship too. There was an intensity in his eyes at those times and a question too, and she didn't know how to respond to either. There was no opportunity to respond anyway, with all these people about. She understood the necessity of joining with a company to cross the mountains, but she resented it too.

The mountains were the best and the worst things Rachel had ever encountered. Their beauty was breathtaking. The granite peaks already topped with white towered over her magnificently until she felt her eyes strain with gazing. But she found it difficult to breathe the thinner air, and her muscles didn't seem to keep up as well as they should. The air at night plunged toward freezing, leaving a rime of frost on Rachel's blanket. Rachel found herself longing for home and a down-filled duvet, and the thought of it brought her to tears. The horses sank back on their heels to go down steep inclines, which unnerved her, and several times the group passed so close to the edge of a sharp drop that she felt the slightest imbalance would send her and her horse toppling over. Rachel would grit her teeth and squint her eyes and hold her breath until it was safe again. She never quite trusted her horse not to leap out over the edge.

One afternoon after an especially intense ascent, she confided to Lizzie that the mountains frightened her a little.

"They're nothing to be afraid of; you just need to respect them, and you'll be all right," Lizzie told her.

"But whenever I'm at the top of a steep cliff, I feel this awful desire to lean out over it, to . . . to throw myself off," she whispered. "I don't understand it. I don't *want* to die."

She had expected Lizzie to be alarmed at this confession, but Lizzie surprised her by laughing. "Well, that's easily explained," she said. "That's just mathematics."

"It is?"

"Of course. You just spent how many weeks walking across a flat prairie?"

"More than I want to think about," Rachel replied.

"So you're used to the horizon being a straight horizontal line in front of you, and you're used to being perpendicular to it. So if you look down the sheer face of a cliff, *that* becomes your horizon. And you have the strong need to lean forward so that you will be perpendicular to it. That's why you feel the desire to fall forward off the cliff."

Rachel pondered this a moment, and she felt a great heaviness lift from her heart. "Is that all it is?"

"Yes."

"How did you figure that out? How do you know so much?"

Lizzie hitched her shoulders in a shrug. "I attended a girls' school in New York, and they taught geometry. Just makes sense to me. And, you know, you're not alone." She shot Rachel a grin. "There've been plenty of times in my life I've thought about throwing myself off a cliff because of mathematics."

* * *

The mountain trek taxed Rachel's muscles and willpower more than any other part of her journey so far. In spite of the freezing nights, the sun would dawn with such brilliant intensity over the crags, illuminating like fire every twig of the pines and larches, that Rachel would be lost in wonder at the soul-wrenching beauty of it, and she would be ashamed of her weakness. She wanted to be wild and strong like the wilderness around her. She felt the eastern land where she had grown up was too tame and mild in comparison, almost bland. Then as the day progressed, it would grow uncomfortably hot, and the scent of the horses permeated her clothing, and dust got into everything, and she was grumpy again.

Every morning before starting off, Lizzie would call her boys together to pray. She just assumed the Mitchells would join them, though she said nothing when Frank excused himself every morning and made himself scarce. Rachel stood with Peter and listened to Lizzie's simple request for a safe journey and health for her family, and covertly peeked at the three bowed red heads. She wondered at the stubbornness, the sheer faith that drove Lizzie forward. Compared to Lizzie's, Rachel felt her own troubles were rather insignificant. She said as much to Peter once, and he only nodded and touched her shoulder briefly before turning away. She guessed he'd been thinking the same thing.

She rarely got a chance to talk with him, but one afternoon as the company stopped to eat and rest in a sheltered little valley, Peter sought her out. "Walk with me," he said simply, and Rachel dropped the kettle she had been holding and followed him. Harry dropped happily in line behind them.

They walked uphill away from the group, just far enough that they wouldn't be overheard, and Peter took her hand in his.

They stopped at a low ledge of rock, and he sat down, drawing her to sit beside him. He kept hold of her hand. Harry pressed himself against Rachel's other side, his tongue lolling out in a dog grin. Rachel put her free hand on his silky head, and he rolled his golden eyes at her. For a moment, they all three sat watching the birds wheeling above them against the sun and listening to the clanking and lowing of the company and cattle below them.

"Was there something you wanted to tell me?" Rachel asked, wondering if she ought to be worried. The expression on Peter's tanned face was serious.

"No, no. I just feel as if I haven't talked to you in a while," he replied. "Every time I look for you, you're busy building a fire or hauling buckets of water or talking with Lizzie or burning the supper . . ."

"I only burned it the once!" Rachel protested, but secretly she felt happiness bubble up inside her. He had missed being alone together as much as she had.

Peter nudged her shoulder with his. "You're plucky, I'll give you that. You always smile and try again. You might slosh half the bucket away, but you won't let anyone take over your burden."

"Why would I?"

"You're good with the children too," Peter went on. "Even those surly Glade children. I saw you playing with them yesterday. I didn't know you could throw a ball like a boy. Well, it was a rotten potato, not a ball, but you lobbed it right over the trees into the brush."

"I did grow up with a brother," Rachel reminded him, keeping her eyes on the dog's fur as she smoothed it so Peter wouldn't see her pleased smile.

"Well, anyway, it's been a new experience, watching you from a distance when you didn't know I was watching," he said.

"You have been?"

"And I guess what I'm trying to say is I like what I've seen. You're a nuisance of a female, and you tripped up my plans and took over my life, but you're spunky. And fun. And pretty, to boot."

Rachel didn't know what to say to this, but she didn't have to say anything because Peter reluctantly let go of her hand and stood. "I'm starved. Let's go eat."

Harry leapt up, sensing the promise of food, and Rachel followed, musing.

* * *

The temperature dropped steadily the higher into the mountains the company climbed. Lizzie told Rachel she should be grateful for this because the cold kept the mosquitoes down. Rachel, who felt a person could carry the virtue of positive thinking too far, nonetheless wrapped her shoulders in her blanket as if it was a shawl and tried not to complain. Besides, despite the bitter temperatures and the constant exhaustion, this leg of the journey was too beautiful for her to allow her spirits to sink. She had never imagined rocks such as these, jagged and fierce above her. Where the bare peaks descended into scalloped valleys, early snow collected, bringing the textures and ridges into relief. The lower slopes were covered in undergrowth and scrubby trees that blocked the trail and made going slow, but she thought the bare, pale granite at the top of the mountains was breathtaking.

One afternoon she managed, with Walter's help, to catch a fish in a high mountain lake, a rainbow trout that was nearly as long as her arm and glittered silver and pink in the sunlight. Rachel felt she had dredged up a priceless jewel from the depths, as if somehow she had broken off a piece of the beauty of the mountain itself.

"I guess I'm not useless now, right enough!" she chortled to herself, and she was so eager to show Peter her catch that she nearly forgot to call him William when she found him and only caught herself just in time.

Lizzie baked the trout in the coals with a little salt and pepper, and Rachel thought it was the most delicious thing she had ever eaten. She sat back, replete, and looked up at the shining stars above them and the sparks flying upward from their fire to join them.

"What amazing things there are in the world!" she exclaimed to Lizzie. "And how little of the world I saw before this!"

After that evening, Frank seemed to decide she was worth the effort to teach a little because he began to show her how to forage along the trail, pointing out what roots and plants were edible and which to avoid. He showed her how to locate the best pool in the stream, where fish would lie waiting. He introduced her to squawberries, like wild cherries, and taught her to identify the deep purple bearberries that grew on the slopes, first teaching her how to scout the area for bears, who also liked to forage.

"Not," he added with a twinkle in his eye, "the little black-and-white cat-shaped smelly bears."

Rachel chose to ignore the comment.

"You can infuse the leaves of the bearberry and use them medicinally," he explained. "But don't eat too many of the berries themselves. They can cause stomach problems."

"That's good to know," she said, hoping she could remember everything he was teaching her.

He also pointed out where wild strawberries would grow next summer and showed her the serviceberry trees that had finished yielding. He showed her the Rocky Mountain junipers that had edible berries too, though she found them mostly unpalatable.

"You know, the things you have taught me make me feel the mountains are more friendly somehow. They provide so much of what we need," she told him. "They're not so scary to me now."

"The earth is kind," Frank replied. "You just have to know how to approach it respectfully."

One evening as they were making camp, there was a deep, muffled booming sound, followed by another farther away. Rachel straightened and looked around, confused. It sounded as if someone had set off a volley of distant cannons.

"What is that?" she asked Lizzie.

Lizzie had paused with her mouth hanging open, one hand to her throat. "I have no idea. It sounds like giants on a bowling green."

Rachel heard someone chuckle and turned to see one of the men of the company watching them.

"Never heard that before, have you?" he said cheerfully.

"What is it?"

"Thunder up in the canyons. It gets caught up there, rumbling and bouncing back and forth against the canyon walls until it dies out."

Rachel stared up at the looming peaks. "Thunder! Is there a storm going on up there?"

"I suppose so. Which means it will be storming down here in a little while. Best take cover."

Mr. Peabody confirmed this prediction a few minutes later, riding his horse up and down the spreading line of the company to warn them not to pitch their tents anywhere near gullies or streams.

"If it's storming up the mountain, the streams can swell within minutes," he explained. "Flash flooding is always a possibility. Stick to high ground."

Lizzie laughed and pushed her blowing hair out of her face. "Good advice for any time," she said. "Let's put the tents farther along the hillside, shall we?"

The rain didn't come until later that night, and by the time it reached them, the storm had lost some of its energy. There was hardly any wind, blocked as it was by the rocks around them, and Rachel was able to squat in the doorway of their tent and peer out at the drizzle without getting wet. Far off down the lower valleys, she could see the jolt and blink of lightning, but here where they were camped, there was none.

"The clouds dump their load of water when they hit the mountains," Peter told her the next morning. "If they're coming from the west, by the time they reach here, they've dropped most of their load."

"I wish I could drop *my* load," young Walter declared, rubbing his sore feet despondently.

"We're nearly there," Lizzie told him with fond encouragement. "Not much farther to go, and you'll see Father."

"It can't come too soon for me," her son replied. "I feel I've been traveling forever."

Rachel knew just how he felt.

Chapter Nineteen

The company finally reached the Henderson River, which flowed down through the valley between rocky cliffs, on a day that had been filled with harsh wind and snow flurries. The river wasn't terribly wide, but it was deep and swift, the water tumbling white and icy over boulders as big as horses. The noise was tremendous. Already disheartened by the cold and wet weather, Rachel gazed at the expanse in despair.

"We can't possibly cross that," she said.

"We're not crossing it, we're going down it," Jonas Peabody said grimly. "There isn't usually this much water this time of year, but no difference. We'll have to do it."

One of the other men in the company, standing nearby, shook his head. "The current's awfully swift. We'll be smashed to bits on those rocks."

"This is the way to Fort Loyal. Do you have any better suggestions?" The gray-haired leader turned to him with a mild expression. It wasn't a challenge, only a question.

The man looked at him a moment, then shook his head again slowly.

"There's a place up ahead called Arch Station where we can leave the horses. It's just a small checkpoint, really, a stable where companies can exchange horses for boats. From there out, we go by raft," Peabody instructed. "There are rapids for the next ninety miles or so to Fort Loyal, where the Black River joins the Henderson, and then it's easier traveling down to Bellefontaine."

Rachel's soul brightened. Bellefontaine! She was nearly there. Her father would be so amazed to see her. She almost laughed aloud, picturing the surprise on his face. She wondered if he had grown a great gray beard and wore patched canvas trousers and a floppy-brimmed hat. Well, of course he would; he was a miner now, wasn't he? It was difficult to picture, though, since at home he had always worn a respectable suit and hat befitting a factory owner.

Arch Station did indeed prove to be nothing more than a stable with an elderly man ensconced there to watch over the animals. Rachel marveled that someone would choose such a life, rarely seeing other people, living off of the fish he caught in the river. But he seemed a cheerful old man and lavished affection on the horses in his care. She never did learn his name.

The rafts were in a state of semidisrepair, however, and it took three days to make them river worthy. The largest was fitted with rails around the sides, like a floating corral, for the cows. Rachel couldn't imagine how they would be able to convince the beasts to board it, but they were docile enough as the men drove them onto the raft, never suspecting what lay ahead of them.

Rachel herself couldn't summon much enthusiasm for the river trip. If she had only known when she had set out from Toronto so optimistically what lay in store, she would never have attempted this stupid, stupid adventure. But there was no turning back now and no way to retrace her steps. There was no way but forward.

The company was ready to set out. All goods were strapped in place and, at Jonas Peabody's insistence, the children lashed to the rafts by long lengths of rope. "I don't want anyone going overboard and being carried away by the current," he explained. "It can get rough on this part of the river."

Lizzie's family, Rachel, Peter, and Frank were assigned to a large raft, along with four other men, two of them with a lot of experience running the Henderson River. They took their places at the poles that would guide the raft down the river and away from the rocks. When all possible preparations had been made, Lizzie pulled her boys together for a prayer, asking in a tremulous voice that God help them in this next dangerous leg of their journey. Rachel, who had been feeling more and more queasy, caught the fear in Lizzie's voice and began to feel truly sick to her stomach. But there wasn't time to get cold feet because in what seemed like no time at all, they were pushing off into the river and the raft was caught in the current.

Lizzie knelt with her arms around her boys in the center of the raft, her eyes tightly closed and her face white, but Rachel couldn't close her eyes. They seemed frozen open so she could hardly blink. She had never felt so terrified. The rocking feeling of the raft was nothing like their small boat on the Amiskwayan. The up-and-down plunging unnerved her, and once, the raft spun around and started going backward downstream until the men could get it turned and into the original position again. Not that Rachel thought it mattered much which side of the square raft went first, but apparently it did matter because of the way the freight was tied down.

Peter was on the right side of the raft, holding one of the poles, helping to push away from the rocks they passed. She saw his lips moving but didn't hear what he was saying. From the look on his face, she thought perhaps it was better that she couldn't hear him. He didn't look any more pleased about their mode of transportation than she was.

She couldn't sustain such terror for long though. In exhaustion, she let her teeth unclench and resigned herself to the rough ride. After all, keeping her eyes on the white water wouldn't stop the raft from smashing into the boulders if it had a mind to, and her grip on the ropes wouldn't guide the raft to safety. It was completely out of her control. There was nothing she could do but let the river carry her. And she could marvel that her father had surely come this way too. She couldn't imagine her brother or Philip doing this, not at all. And just imagine! She had set out on this ridiculous journey with a domestic *cat*! What had she been thinking?

She allowed herself to turn a little so she faced Peter. The look on his face had changed to an excited grin. He had mastered the rhythm of the water, and she could see that his consternation had changed to glee. He shot her a look that reminded her of a little boy at a carnival and let out a shout as the raft tipped down the side of a swell of water and righted itself at the last possible moment. "Like riding a bronco!" he shouted.

Rachel wasn't sure what he meant, but Frank and the other men laughed loudly.

Even Harry seemed to enjoy the thrilling ride, yipping and wagging his tail as he stood, feet braced apart and head flung back in the spray. Walter called the dog to him and kept a protective arm around his neck, but Harry only wriggled with impatience, not understanding why the boy didn't seem as pleased with this new adventure as he was. Rachel wished she could be as focused on the experience instead of the terror.

At one point the rapids became too swift and dangerous, and the men directed the rafts to the riverbank, where they laboriously took all their supplies off. When Rachel stepped ashore with trembling legs, she wondered if she was going to vomit. The ground seemed to swell and drop beneath her feet, and she staggered for a moment until she grew accustomed again to solid earth.

Three men with ropes jogged along the bank to guide each raft, now riderless, down that stretch of the river, while the others all carted their belongings through the rocks and trees, walking back and forth several times along the bank to shuttle everything to the point where they could reboard the rafts. The cows, which had been bawling and snorting since their floating corral left the bank, seemed no happier at being driven along the narrow path between rock and water. When it came time to load them onto the raft again, several of them panicked and balked, knowing what to expect this time. A few bolted, and precious time was spent having to recapture them. By the time they were back on the raft, the men were sweating and desperately tired, but they took up their poles and set out again. There was nowhere broad enough in the gulch to make camp if they'd wanted to. As the rafts spun out into the current once more, the cows rolled their eyes and bellowed. This drama played out several times along the river, portage after portage, until Rachel stopped counting and fell into an exhausted stupor.

They finally made camp on a narrow stretch of land beside the river at the base of a jutting stone cliff, and the sound of the rushing water filled Rachel's dreams that night. The next day was a repeat of the first, only this time she was too tired to feel the sharpest edges of her terror, and even Lizzie had ceased her constant muttered praying.

Just before noon, they rounded a bend and came upon a particularly bad stretch of rapids with no time to pull for the bank and portage. Rachel gripped the ropes tightly but could still feel herself sliding across the surface of the raft as it bucked and dove down into a trough. Then they were charging upward again, and she would have been flung off the raft entirely if it hadn't been for her hold on the ropes. She felt like a flag whipping on a flagpole. She heard Lizzie scream, and Walter shouted as he was thrown backward. Rachel saw him tumble across the length of the raft, unable to find purchase on the heaving surface beneath him. Harry sprawled on his belly and barked frantically.

Just as she feared Walter would somersault overboard, Frank lurched from his post and thrust his long pole forward. Walter grabbed at it and managed to catch it. As Lizzie sobbed, Peter and Frank hauled the boy back from the edge to safety. Harry inched along on his stomach until he reached Walter and then bathed the boy with kisses. Walter clung to the dog's neck and tried to hide the fear on his face.

There was no time to draw breath before there was a smashing, shuddering sound behind them. Rachel pushed her wet hair out of her eyes and craned to look. The raft just behind theirs had not negotiated the turn correctly, and one side of it was lifted up onto bare boulders out of the river. The other side dipped under the water. As Rachel watched in helpless horror, everything on the raft began to slide down the sloping logs into the water and wash away. She saw human figures tumble down and disappear into white froth. Then the logs themselves came apart from their lashings and plunged into the current. Instantly they became battering rams, splintering and heaving against the boulders, and Peter and the other men fought desperately to keep the swiftly moving logs from striking their raft as they shot past.

There was another terrific sound as the next raft, carrying the cows, rounded the bend and plunged forward into a trough. The combined weight of the cattle being flung forward proved too much for the railings. The fence smashed, and several cows tumbled into the waves. Some went under while the raft popped upright and floated over their heads.

Rachel heard shouts and saw several people's heads bobbing in the water, gliding over the rocks in the wash of white water, and an arm flailing above the current. And then she couldn't see them anymore. Lizzie's son David Jr. buried his face in his mother's shoulder, and she clung to him, tears streaming down her face. Rachel forced herself to her feet and staggered toward Peter, clinging to the safety rope stretched across the raft.

"There! There!" she cried, pointing as a man's head rose above the water five feet from their raft. Peter moved quickly, thrusting his pole out. He managed to maneuver it in front of the man just in time for him to grab it, and together he and Rachel dragged the man in like a fish to lie gasping on the logs. Peter pulled him away from the edge and turned back to his work, and Rachel knelt beside the man and rolled him onto his side so he could cough up water. There was a bloody gash on his forehead, but other than that he appeared to be unharmed. Rachel realized it was Mr. Glade. She turned back to scan the water quickly, looking for his wife and children.

The current diminished a hundred yards down the river, and the group of rafts made for shore. As soon as they were on land, all the men who could be spared went searching down the riverbank for survivors and what goods they could retrieve from the wrecked raft. The few cows that had fallen in managed to swim to shore, where they stood shaking and blowing and disoriented. Walter and David Jr. went to round them up, assisted by Harry, who looked none the worse for the ride, but it took a lot of coaxing to urge the stunned animals back to their jittery companions.

The men returned from their search half an hour later bearing one of the Glade children, who had been tossed by the current into a jutting tree branch and saved from drowning. They also had the body of one of the other men from the raft. Mr. Glade, his head wrapped in a bandage, held his arms out to hold his little boy, murmuring reassurances while he wept.

The men had rescued a canvas tent that had become entangled in the same tree and a floating box of food, but everything else from the wreck had been swept away.

Peter, who had gone with the search party, returned to camp soaked and shivering. He had been the one to wade into the river to pull out the snagged body of the drowned man, and his lips were blue as Rachel ran to put a blanket around his shoulders and draw him close to the fire. Her hand touched his, and she found his skin deathly cold.

Seven people had been lost, including Mrs. Glade and her other three children. There was only the one body to bury, and they laid the man to rest with great solemnity in a little hollow. Rachel stood looking down at the grave piled with stones and listened to Jonas Peabody's hoarse voice as he read a passage from the Bible. Rachel thought she would go mad with the awfulness of it. Her heart railed against the injustice, that such innocent lives could be lost so easily. She hadn't felt any great affection for the Glades, but she still mourned them. She had known this journey was not to be undertaken lightly, but somehow she had not truly believed there was danger in it, that she really could die trying to join her father.

Beside her, Lizzie dabbed at her eyes and scowled ferociously in her effort to hold back her tears. Peter, on Rachel's other side, was stone-faced, but as the assembled company turned to go back to camp, he reached out and took Rachel's hand tightly in his. His touch was still cold. She walked with him back to the fire, but after a while, she couldn't hold the tears back anymore. She pulled her hand from his, rushed into the trees outside of camp, and had a private howl. She half expected Peter to follow her to comfort her, but he didn't come. She wrapped her arms around herself, wishing they were his, and rocked back and forth. She'd never felt so alone.

When Rachel had composed herself again, she walked back toward camp through the gathering dusk. The company had lit several fires to prepare supper, and firelight danced on the surrounding rocks. The river sounded hollow as it slid past. Stars began to come out overhead. Rachel sat down beside Lizzie, who was scraping halfheartedly at supper in a frying pan over the flames. Lizzie glanced at her and looked away again politely, and Rachel knew her face must be a mess from her crying.

Peter came over, the blanket still around his shoulders, and Rachel scrubbed at her eyes with the sleeve of her dress, trying to repair the damage. Peter began to speak, but Lizzie waved him away. "Not right now, William. Women don't like to be seen crying, not by the men they love. We're vain that way."

Peter looked startled, looking from Lizzie to Rachel. "The men they . . ."

"Go on, give her a moment. We're all of us upset right now," Lizzie instructed. So Peter moved away again, and Rachel gave Lizzie a grateful look. Lizzie placed some of the food on a tin plate and handed it to Rachel.

"Get that inside you. It isn't much, but the warmth will steady you."

"Thank you," Rachel murmured. But she didn't feel like eating. She pushed the beans around her plate without interest.

Finally she set it aside and turned to her new friend. "How can you keep going?" she whispered.

Lizzie turned her head and looked at Rachel.

"What do you mean, Mary?"

"I mean how can you stand to get up every morning and keep going, one foot in front of the other? So many hard things have happened to you: your family turning against you, having to move from place to place, your husband gone for months at a time . . . and now Mrs. Glade and those children today. I would want to curl up on the ground and just lie there until I died."

Lizzie put one arm around Rachel's shoulders. "You would not. You're not the type to give up when things are difficult; I can tell. You have what my husband calls grit."

Rachel muttered, wiping at her eyes, which didn't seem to want to stop watering. "No, I haven't. Look at me; I'm hopeless. You're here cooking dinner while I'm out bawling in the wilderness."

Lizzie laughed. "I'm cooking dinner because people are hungry. It's something to do when you don't know what to do. When you *can't* do anything to fix things. And don't think I haven't salted the beans with a few tears of my own."

"I'm not as strong as you."

"Don't be so hard on yourself. You're doing fine. I used to think the first Mormon pioneers were able to withstand the persecution and cross the plains because they were strong." Lizzie sighed. "I had it backward though. I learned it was the persecution and the crossing that made them that way." She picked up the plate Rachel had set down and handed it to her again. "You keep going because it's the only thing to do. You deal with the bad and the good as they come to you, and you learn from both. You grow stronger with each challenge. As long as the sun still gets up every morning, there's still a reason for you to, too."

"But what is at the end of it? What is there to look forward to if we're all going to die someday anyway?"

"Freedom. Safety. A home of our own where no one will harm us. Those are worth the journey, don't you think?"

Rachel looked up at the darkening sky, wondering. A home of her own . . . She didn't have one, not really.

Chapter Twenty

The next morning Peter awoke with a sore throat and a slight fever. He tried to act as if it was nothing, but Rachel watched him closely and could tell he wasn't feeling good. By noon the fever was raging, and he couldn't hide it anymore. He could hardly help with poling the raft, his chin slumped on his chest, and Rachel feared he would lose his hold and fall in the water.

When the company stopped for supper in a shallow valley, Rachel insisted Peter lie down on his bedroll. He went, protesting, but by evening he was semiconscious and made no sound as she forced cold water between his lips and bathed his forehead. Lizzie had Julia, the company's midwife, examine him. She pursed her lips and shook her graying head, but she went to work, stripping off his shirt and peeling back the top of his union suit to expose his chest. In the light of dusk, his torso looked unhealthily pale. Rachel thought there was something awful about seeing that broad, muscular frame stretched out helpless on the ground. Julia packed cold, wet towels under his arms and behind his neck and gave him a dose of some vile-smelling liquid.

"That should break the fever," she said, putting a gentle hand on Rachel's arm. "Your husband will be all right in a few days, I think. I know it's difficult, but you should try to keep him lying down and dry. You must make him rest."

Rachel had no idea how she would accomplish this since they would be back on the rafts again in the morning, but she thanked Julia and went to sit beside Peter. She knew she should help Lizzie set up camp for the night, but she couldn't bring herself to leave his side. Lizzie was silent, letting her sit in stillness, and kept the boys away so Peter could get what rest he could.

Rachel's thoughts were in turmoil. What would she do if Peter died? How could she go on without him? She didn't *want* to go on without him. Somehow, without realizing it, the object of her journey had faded in the importance of the journey itself. She was on the river, in the last stage of the trip, and was headed for her father . . . yet she didn't want to arrive without Peter. Somehow in the last few weeks, she had not let herself imagine what would happen once she arrived in Bellefontaine. It didn't seem possible that she could just say good-bye to Peter and each go their own way.

She reached out and lightly drew her fingers along Peter's whiskered jaw. He wouldn't die; she wouldn't let him. That much she knew. The future would take whatever course it took, but right now, she would not let him go. Rachel took his hot hand between both of hers and gazed intently into Peter's face. He shifted uncomfortably, but his eyes didn't open.

Rachel looked up at the darkening sky, the stars coming out in the gap of sky between the mountain ridges on both sides of the river. Her aunt had been religious and had dragged Rachel to church with her each week, but the prayers Rachel had dutifully recited had never come from her heart. Now she fervently sent the thoughts of her heart upward, seeking the God Lizzie seemed to know so well and have such confidence in, projecting her petition like a silent song into the sky and hoping it found its mark in a listening and compassionate ear.

There wasn't much else she could do, then, but sit with Peter's head cushioned in her lap and smooth his hair from his forehead, letting her eyes linger on his fine-cut features, his curving muscles now lax.

Her father had told her stories of how he had crossed the Atlantic from his native Scotland, subsisting for two months on nothing but potato soup, of how he had built his business from nothing through sheer hard work and determination. Peter reminded her of her father: strong, even invincible. It would take a lot to kill him, even as she knew it would be no easy thing to defeat Hamish Hamilton.

Lizzie and the boys took the larger tent and left the smaller tent to Rachel and Peter, while Frank declared himself satisfied with just his bedroll by the fire. The air was cold in the mountains, and the extra blanket Lizzie had put around Rachel's shoulders before retiring for the night did little to fend off the chill. Rachel bent her head down and rested her cheek on Peter's forehead. He was so hot it burned her.

She must have dozed off. She was awakened by violent shivers coursing through Peter's body. The fire was banked low outside the door of the tent, casting little light or heat. Rachel put a hand on Peter's cheek. His skin was dry and hot like a baked stone. The shivers wracked him, and he tossed uncomfortably, moaning, "So cold. So cold."

Her fingers shaking with anxiety, Rachel lay down full length on the ground beside him and pulled the blanket over them both. Wrapping her arms around him, she pressed against him and tried consciously to transfer her own heat to him. His tremors shook them both until she couldn't tell if they came from him or from her. She pushed her face into the soft joining of his neck and shoulders and breathed hard against his skin with her warm breath.

It seemed like ages before his chills lessened and he grew limp. As the shivering subsided, he fell into a deep sleep, his breath low but not raspy. Sweat stood out on his face, and Rachel smoothed it away with a corner of the blanket. She lightly, slowly pressed kisses all over his face, his eyes, his forehead. He was unconscious;

he'd never know, and at the moment, she was in as much need of comfort as he.

The next morning, Julia came again. Rachel had risen early and then fallen asleep again with her head at an awkward angle. She woke with a start when Julia touched her shoulder, then looked immediately to Peter. His face was glazed with sweat in the early morning glow of the sunrise coming through the canvas of the tent, but he seemed to be resting peacefully.

"The fever has broken," Julia announced, smiling. "The worst is past."

"Yes, I think it did in the middle of the night. Is he all right?" Rachel looked at Peter doubtfully. The bronzed skin of his face was sallow under his tan, more than the golden glow of the sunrise could account for. His hair was plastered darkly to his forehead and temples. His chest rose and fell in even breaths.

"His lungs sound clear. It won't turn into pneumonia. He'll be fine in no time now that the fever's down," Julia assured her. "Go get something to eat and wash up and brush your hair. You want to be a pretty sight for him to open his eyes to."

Rachel made a face at her but knew she was right; she'd feel better too if she followed the advice.

The men carried Peter to the raft that morning and tied him to the logs with rope as if he was part of the cargo. Rachel sat beside him, her feet tucked beneath her, leaning against a box of tools and watching him carefully. Harry pressed himself against Peter's other side like a conscientious nursemaid. Peter was only half-awake, but he seemed in no distress as the raft pitched and spun. Rachel wished they could have waited one more day before moving on, but she knew it wasn't reasonable to ask the entire company to wait. There was no choice but to go with them.

Impossibly, Rachel fell asleep sometime around noon, into the deepest sleep she had allowed herself in a while. She dreamt she was in a Red River cart, rocking back and forth rhythmically as the wheels lurched over juts and bumps in the dirt road. She had no idea where she was traveling to, nor did she care. She awoke when the rocking motion stopped.

She lay slumped against the box, blinking disorientedly in the slanting sunshine, and tried to remember where she was. The raft had been drawn to the bank of the river, and people were setting about lighting fires to cook fish for supper. The light had that brassy look that came right before dusk, and she knew somewhere the sun was setting, but she couldn't see it because of the cliffs on either side of the river.

Rachel remembered, then, and turned to look at Peter. His eyes were open and focused on her. He gave a feeble smile.

"Lot of help I've been," he murmured.

"You've been ill, but you're all right now," Rachel told him in relief. She smoothed his forehead with a hand that trembled with pent-up anxiety. She didn't stop to think what he would make of the tender gesture.

"I feel like I've been dragged behind a horse," Peter said.

"I don't doubt it. You'll feel fine in a day or two." Rachel stretched her aching back and felt the rough cloth of her dress stick to her sweaty skin. She needed a bath and a hot meal and a soft bed. But Peter was all right. He would be well. That was all that mattered. She smiled down at him.

Peter lifted a hand and touched a strand of her hair that had fallen from her braid. He curled it lightly around his finger. "Who was the lady with the nasty-tasting stuff?"

"Julia Barker. She's not a physician, but she midwifes."

"I thought she was a witch from my nightmare."

Rachel punched his shoulder lightly. "That old witch probably saved your life, William Mitchell. Show proper gratitude."

"Yes, ma'am," he said meekly. His face broke into a weak grin, a shadow of his usual self returning. His hand moved to the back of her head, pulling her gently down toward him. His lips brushed lightly against hers but pulled away too soon. "Now be a good wife and help me find my shirt."

"You're not to get up yet," she protested. Her cheeks were pink, and she glanced around to make sure no one had seen the kiss. Everyone seemed occupied with their own tasks, and, she reasoned, none of them would have thought anything of it even if they had noticed. After all, they all thought she and Peter were husband and wife.

"I'm well enough to come sit by the fire," Peter said firmly. "And I'm not going to do it in my union suit. So fetch my shirt, and don't argue."

Rachel rolled her eyes at him and climbed stiffly to her feet. Lizzie and Frank were building a fire on the narrow bank beside the river, and the two boys were seeing to the fish. Lizzie looked up as Rachel approached.

"He's awake and insisting on coming to sit by the fire," Rachel reported.

Lizzie's face relaxed into a smile. "That's good news, Mary. I'm glad he's better. Boys, roll that log over here for Mr. Mitchell to sit on."

Rachel located Peter's shirt and boots, helped him dress (stopping short of buttoning the buttons for him), and helped him to the fire. He walked slowly, as if not sure of his feet, and sat on the log without protest. He watched the others fix dinner while the sky darkened from bronze to salmon to a gathering gray over the top of the cliffs.

While they were eating, the company captain approached. "Good to see you up and going," he greeted Peter.

"Good to be," Peter replied.

"I wanted to let you know there's a three-day portage at Ponosay Canyon up ahead, but we other men can help you so you don't have to carry so much weight. I want you to take it carefully there and not overdo it." As Peter began to protest, Peabody raised his hand. "Listen to me, son. I know it's difficult, but sometimes you have to let other people help you. Otherwise it's plain foolishness. That's the purpose of a company, really, isn't it? You're not going down this river alone."

Peter frowned. Peabody nodded. "That's settled, then. Once the river gets past that point, it should be smoother going. We'll be in Fort Loyal within ten days."

"Just in time," Lizzie remarked. "We're running low on flour."

Rachel felt her smile spread across her face. She beamed at Peter. "We're almost there. We've nearly made it. The worst is over."

"Don't speak too soon," he said. "We've made it through the mountains, but there's still the stretch of river from Fort Loyal to Bellefontaine."

"And you said you were meeting your father there, is that right?" Lizzie asked, lifting a sizzling fish from the fire and putting it on a tin plate.

"Yes," Rachel told her happily. "He went out to mine. He owns the Happy Scot Mine on Washed-Out Creek. I believe it's quite prosperous." After all, she told herself, hadn't he sent her all that money with his last letter? It *could* be true.

"Does he know you're coming?" Lizzie asked.

"No, I didn't write. I thought I'd surprise him," Rachel said vaguely. Beside her, Peter stiffened and gave her a funny look.

Lizzie handed a plate to Peter. "I was kind of hoping I could convince you to go to Briarton with us. I . . . I like you both very much. It would be fun to be neighbors, wouldn't it?"

Rachel was caught off guard by this sudden suggestion. She glanced at Peter. "Yes, it would. I'd like that very much. But William isn't a farmer. There wouldn't be anything for us to do in Briarton."

Lizzie blinked at Peter. "I just assumed . . . What do you do, William?"

Peter took a mouthful of biscuit, chewed it carefully, and swallowed before saying, "I'm a teacher."

"Are you? But that's wonderful! We could certainly use a teacher on the frontier," Lizzie exclaimed. "The only one we had was Mrs. Glade, and . . . well. I realize you have other plans, of course, and you want to see your father, but consider coming to join us one day."

Rachel felt an odd tightening in her throat at the earnest appeal on Lizzie's face. She found herself nodding stupidly. "We'll certainly consider it," she heard herself say. "You and your family have been more than kind to us."

When they had finished eating, Peter confessed he was exhausted and started to move to return to his bedroll. He took Rachel's hand and made as if he was leaning on her for support, but his grip was tight, and he towed her along without giving her any choice in the matter. His jaw was clenched, and his eyebrows were lowered. Once out of earshot of Lizzie and her sons, he hauled Rachel around to face him. "What do you mean, we'll consider it?" he hissed in a low voice. "Why did you say that to her? You'll only get her hopes up."

"I didn't know what else to say," Rachel said. "She was so sincere and so kind . . ."

"All the more reason not to lie to her," he replied sharply. "You and I both know there's no possibility of our coming back to join them in Briarton."

"I know," Rachel said and suddenly felt the fighting spirit go out of her. She dropped onto the crumpled blankets and hugged her drawn-up knees to her chest, tucking her skirt over her feet. "I know," she repeated glumly. "But for just a minute there, it sounded rather nice to be neighbors . . . to stop . . ."

He stood looking down at her a moment, then shook his head and knelt beside her. "Are you saying you *want* to stop? And not go on to meet your father when we're so close?"

Rachel thought of the grueling months behind her and the distance yet before her. She could scarcely remember a time when she'd been clean and comfortable and well fed, when her poor hands hadn't been rough and dry and her clothes not tattered and dirty. She remembered soft slippers and oriental carpets, cool, clean bed sheets, and white china chamber pots as if from a childhood dream. She'd given up that comfort and security to find her father. She couldn't very well stop now when she was so close. She owed it to her father and to herself.

Besides, she and Peter couldn't take up residence in Briarton. They were only pretending to be married so they could travel together. She would go find her father, and Peter would go do whatever it was he was going to do.

At last she raised her eyes to his. "No, of course I need to keep going. As you say, we're almost there. I just thought it sounded nice, that's all."

His face relaxed. "Yes, it did."

Rachel played with the worn toe of her shoe, poking her finger in a little hole over her big toe. She wondered how long the shoes would last, how long the thin fabric of her dress would withstand mending.

Beside her, Peter stretched out on his back with a deep sigh and put his hands behind his head. "This feels better than being tossed around on that infernal raft," he said.

"I wish we could linger here a few days and let you get your strength fully back," Rachel told him. "I wish we had a wagon to pull you in instead of tying you to that raft like a sack of potatoes."

Peter chuckled. His smile caused deep creases in his tanned face, and Rachel noted how tightly the skin was stretched over his cheekbones, the lines of weariness etched into his face. The lines seemed to deepen more each day.

"Peter . . . I mean, William . . . if you don't want to go on to Bellefontaine, it's all right. I'm with the company now, and it's just a matter of staying on the Henderson River, right? I can't really get lost at this point. So . . ."

"What? You're tired of my company? Is that what you're saying?" he murmured, closing his eyes.

"Of course not. But you've been so kind to me already. I was silly and selfish to even ask it of you in the first place. You've gotten me this far. I've put you out of your way enough. I can't ask more of you. Maybe you should stay at Fort Loyal and regain your strength." She stopped. She wasn't able to say what she really felt, that the longer she spent time with him, the harder it would be to let him go in the end. And if accompanying her across the country cost him his health or even his life, she would never be able to deal with it.

Peter opened his eyes again and stared at her with a peculiar expression.

"What is it?" she asked.

"I know it will sound daft," he said mildly, "but somehow I never really thought about what it will be like when we do eventually part ways. Somehow it feels like we'll just keep going on like this forever."

"I know it must seem like an eternity to you," she said with a smile.

He grinned back. "Sometimes."

"And I've been a burden."

"Once in a while."

"And aggravating," Rachel added sadly.

"At first. Not so much lately."

"I've become stronger and more capable; you've said so yourself."

"That you have."

"Mr. Peabody can get me to Bellefontaine from here. I just have to hang on to the raft, and we'll get there eventually."

"True."

She took a shaky breath. "So I'm releasing you from your agreement," she said.

He raised himself onto one elbow, looking seriously into her face. "No one coerced me into this," he said darkly. "I don't feel bound, and I don't need anyone to tell me when I can come or go."

"That isn't what I meant."

"And if I said all right, I'm turning back, just how do you propose I get up the river and back through Sugarloaf Pass on my own?"

"Oh." She hadn't thought of that. There really was no way to make the trip back alone. "It's just that if something happened to you and it was my fault I got you into this—"

"Then what?"

She shrugged awkwardly. "I'd feel awful, that's all."

"I don't know all that lies ahead," he said firmly, "but I do know this journey isn't over yet."

She was locked into his gaze. "Why?" she murmured. "Why are you putting yourself through this?"

"I have my reasons."

"Give me one."

He eyed her a moment, as if debating, then glanced toward the fire where the others were engrossed in their own activities. Then he reached up, cupped the back of Rachel's head in his palm, and pulled her down toward him until her lips met his. She thought he tasted of sun-baked rock and campfire smoke and something indefinably *him*. His few days' growth of whiskers was rough on her skin, but Rachel closed her eyes and let herself respond, leaning into him. His fingers moved to tangle in her hair. The kiss lasted longer than their first, and for a moment, she forgot to breathe. At last he released her and studied her with narrowed eyes.

"Reason one," he murmured.

She felt a goofy smile creep over her face. "And reason two?"

His eyes widened. With a sharp laugh, he pushed her away. "You're going to be the death of me, Rachel Hamilton. Go on, get out of here, and let an invalid get some rest."

Laughing, she went back to the fire.

Chapter Twenty-One

Lizzie looked up at the sight of Rachel's flushed face and disheveled hair.

"I take it your husband is fully recovered?" she said peacefully.

"Well on the way to it," Rachel said. The fire felt hot on her face, and she brushed her hands on her faded skirt. Frank's eyes were steady on hers across the fire.

"I'll . . . be back," she said and strode quickly away.

She went some distance downriver from the camp into the scrub pine that bristled from the valley walls, under the pretense of visiting the prairie dogs. She needed to get away from everyone, from Lizzie's friendly but too-perceptive eyes, from Frank's knowing smile, from Peter. Most especially from Peter.

Her face burned her palms when she touched it. What on earth had possessed her? From what she'd gathered over the years from various aunts and female friends, if a man did such a thing to a woman, she was supposed to slap his face. Or burst into tears and have hysterics. She had done neither of those things. She had kissed him back. She'd *wanted* him to kiss her. Oh, yes, she had, and what was more, she'd wanted him to keep doing it for a very long time. She'd practically dared him to do it again. She should feel ashamed of herself, but she didn't.

Something had awakened within her that she wasn't sure she was ready for, but there was no denying how she felt about Peter. William, rather. Or Jacob. She laughed aloud, and her voice echoed off the rugged rock walls around her. Fancy that. She hardly knew who she was in love with. Because she knew that was what she was feeling. There was no other possible name for it.

"What a fine fix to get yourself into," she exclaimed aloud. "You're in love with your supposed husband." She knew nothing could come of it, and yet she wondered. What would Peter do once they reached Bellefontaine? He'd mentioned that perhaps it was time for him to return to civilization. Had he meant it? Would he return to teaching in the east as if nothing had happened? Carry on to Victoria? And once she'd found Washed-Out Creek and proven to Richard that their father was still alive, what was to happen to her then? Would she return to Toronto? To what? Philip Wycott's mild, characterless face flashed into her mind, and she frowned. Certainly not that. Whereas she'd been hesitant before, she was sure now. Nothing Richard did or said could make her love Philip, and she knew without a doubt that she couldn't marry someone she didn't love. Not now that she'd felt what it could be like. She would be firm. She would stand up to him. She would be very brave.

Rachel stopped walking suddenly and looked about her. It was nearly dark. There was an unfamiliar dry, scratchy sound she couldn't place, and it took her a moment to notice the brown and gold snake coiled neatly on the gray stone at her feet, its diamond-shaped head flattened and poised, its tail delicately vibrating. She'd nearly stepped on it in the gloom.

Immediately she gathered her skirts and ran back toward camp, cold sweat breaking out between her shoulder blades. Oh, yes, she was very brave. Brave indeed, she snorted. She was gasping for air by the time she reached the camp but more from laughter at herself than from her sprint.

That night she slept in the smaller tent with Lizzie again, rolled in her blanket against the cold night air, and Peter returned to the larger tent with Frank and the two boys. Rachel listened to Harry settle himself across the tent door and slept without dreams. When she woke the next morning, Peter had already risen and started the fire, and the healthy color had returned to his cheeks.

That morning they reached Ponosay Canyon and began another portage, and Rachel felt she had been endlessly lugging belongings back and forth along the river for weeks rather than hours. The low brush along the riverbank snagged her skirts and tripped her feet. The air was mercifully too cold for mosquitoes, but gnats hovered around her face, and boggy spots sucked at her broken shoes and soaked her feet. For three days, they hauled their belongings and supplies and drove the cows overland while some of the men towed the rafts with ropes, fighting the rapids that sounded like galloping herds of horses to Rachel. The sheer sight of the plunging white water took her breath away and filled her dreams with terror.

Then the river mellowed and widened, and they were able to take to their rafts again. All hands were kept busy with the work, and the days flew by faster and faster until before she was ready for it, Rachel saw Fort Loyal around the bend.

The fort was built where the two great rivers met, the Black and the Henderson, and consisted of a collection of steep-roofed wooden buildings with rail-fenced paddocks around them. There was an iron forge, a stores house, a carpenter, a butcher, and numerous other amenities available, and Rachel found it less of a shock this time, being in civilization once more. She had grown accustomed to traveling with the company now, and the sound of voices didn't shatter her ears the way it had when she'd first come off the prairie.

There was another company at the fort heading the opposite direction, fifteen men laden with supplies who were coming from Bellefontaine. There was an eager exchange of information between the two parties and much talk of the weather. The meeting was made all the more joyful in that one of the men turned out to be a close friend of the son of one of the men in Peabody's company,

Nathan Findlay. His son had preceded him west and lived in Bellefontaine. The friend brought the good news that Findlay was a grandfather, for his son's wife had just given birth to a boy before the company had left Bellefontaine. Nathan Findlay wept with joy at the news.

Fresh food was available for purchase—flour and corn, fruit, beans, and bacon. Peabody declared it a holiday, and there was a dance and dinner that night for the whole camp. Someone had a fiddle, and someone else pulled out a battered guitar, and Lizzie somehow contrived to produce apple pudding baked in dutch ovens over the fires.

Listening to the music, her mouth filled with hot apples and cinnamon, and with Peter sitting beside her, Rachel felt completely and deeply happy. She liked these people who worked hard when they worked and played hard when they played. The music jigged up toward the black sky, setting the very stars to dancing. They were nearing the end of the trail for most of them, some turning west toward the Dunant Mountains to try their luck at gold mining, others going on to the farming communities springing up in the interior of the colony.

Rachel glanced up and saw Peter watching her. The firelight glimmered in his eyes and smoothed the lean planes of his face. He had removed his hat, and his hair was sticking up on one side. Without thinking, she reached to smooth it down.

Peter caught her hand in his. "Dance with me," he said and pulled her to her feet.

Rachel went with him. The fiddle was scraping out a waltz, and Peter held her daringly close as they danced. She moved with him, enjoying the feel of his hand light on her back and hardly hearing the music. She ignored the crush of people around them and allowed herself, for just a moment, to lose herself in the music. Peter's breath stirred the wisps of hair on her forehead. She closed her eyes and tipped toward him until her forehead rested against his chin. His hand was rough and warm, enclosing hers against his chest. She felt somehow anchored and freed all at the same time.

Then all too soon the tune ended and the musicians broke into a reel. She and Peter were swept apart as the lines formed for the dance. It took her a few disoriented moments to fall into step, and then a man she didn't know caught her hands and swung her around. Her hair, always unruly, came free from its knot in a yellow cascade. She laughed, her mouth wide, and Lizzie, dancing beside Rachel with her oldest son, laughed with her.

Only a few more days, Rachel thought, and Lizzie would be in her new home with her husband and her boys. She felt a sharp pang of envy but pushed it away. Lizzie may have a home, but she had the stalwart Davey Myers to share it with, not Peter. No, Rachel wouldn't trade places with Lizzie for all the comfort and security in the world. She turned her attention to the reel. Frank was sitting to one side, watching with an indulgent expression as if he thought these people rather silly, though she saw his foot tapping to the music in spite of himself. She could see Peter gallantly trying to keep step farther down the line, and his look of serious concentration made her laugh again. But try as she might to maneuver it, she didn't end up his partner again for the rest of the dance.

They walked back to the camp in the dark with Frank, Lizzie, and her sons. Lizzie rattled on about how jolly it would be to settle down and how happy she would be to have a real oven again. The new apples were very good after eating last year's tough dried apples the whole trip. She was looking forward to having time to do more knitting. No doubt the harvest was already in. She wondered how harsh the winters would be.

Rachel listened with a vague smile, not really hearing anything the good woman said. Her thoughts were too full of images—the firelight, the stamping fiddler, the stars, Peter's awkward dancing. She laughed and looked up to find Peter scowling.

"What is it?" she whispered, but before he could reply, Lizzie had realized they were trailing a little behind and had turned back to link her arm through Rachel's.

"It will be good to sit down. My poor feet aren't up to dancing anymore," Lizzie continued to chatter happily. "Walter, mind your step. There's uneven ground along here. Don't forget your prayers, boys." She gave Rachel's arm a little squeeze. "I'm so excited at the thought of seeing the house Davey's built for us. I feel I won't sleep a wink tonight."

Rachel cast a look at Peter, who rolled his eyes and gave a wry smile. There was no chance to talk, no chance to be alone. The fire was banked for the night, and Lizzie began bustling around caring for the tents and bedrolls, getting her boys settled.

Peter cleared his throat and finally spoke. "I was talking to some of the men from the fort tonight," he said. "The river will carry us sixty miles through Henderson Canyon to Bellefontaine, then it meanders south through arable land and large floodplains, through Dubois and Fort Duncan, and ultimately to Briarton. But our destination is closer than that."

"Yes?" Rachel asked quickly.

"One fellow said he had heard of Washed-Out Creek. It's only a few miles past Bellefontaine."

"That's wonderful news!" Rachel cried, wondering why Peter looked so gloomy about it.

"He also said there's a winter storm brewing south of here. He said we've left it too late in the season, and he advised us to stay at Fort Loyal until spring before moving on."

"I can't possibly," Lizzie declared, straightening with a tent peg in her hand. "I'm so close to my husband now. I can't dither here until *spring*."

"Me neither," Rachel agreed. "You said it's only sixty miles away. Surely the weather won't turn too bad by then."

"Some of these men have spent most of their lives in this area. I think we should listen to them."

"Frank, you've been this way more than a few times," Rachel said. "Have you ever heard of a snow storm in this area in late October?"

"Yes," Frank said firmly.

"Oh." This set her back a bit, but she added, chin up, "But the river won't freeze, will it?"

"No, not this early."

"Then we can still travel on it."

"Maybe so," Peter said. "But you don't want to be caught in a blizzard in these mountains."

"Is Jonas Peabody intending to press on with his company?" Lizzie asked.

"Yes, last I heard. Though we will doubtless discuss it again before deciding."

"Well, we will see what he decides to do," Rachel said. "But my vote is to keep going. We're so close."

"Even if the company decides to stop, I'm not going to," Lizzie said. "Even if I have to swipe a canoe from a Native and paddle it south myself!" She glanced apologetically at Frank, who smiled back.

"What do you think?" Rachel asked Frank. "You know this area better than the rest of us do. Would you recommend staying or continuing on?"

Frank frowned, looking from one to the other. Then he said something in Blackfoot that made Peter laugh.

"What did he say?" Lizzie pressed.

"He said if he had to stay at Fort Loyal all winter with this gaggle of honking geese, he would go crazy. He's for pressing on."

The others laughed, and Lizzie nodded firmly. "There, you see? Decision made."

"We'll talk more about it in the morning," Peter said. He squeezed Rachel's hand. "Good night, Mary."

"Good night, William." She reluctantly slipped her fingers from his and ducked into her tent.

The night was still but for the rush of the river. Despite her excitement, Lizzie fell sleep. From the other tent came the low buzz of Frank snoring softly. Rachel lay looking up at the dark ceiling of her tent and fancied she could hear Peter's breath too across the glowing embers of the fire. She thought about the short journey left ahead of her. Soon, she thought. Soon she would be in Bellefontaine. What would she find? And more importantly, what would she do once she found it?

* * *

The company decided to press on as fast as possible to try to reach their various destinations before winter set in with a vengeance. Rachel was torn, wanting to stretch out her time with Peter but anxious to be at the end of her journey. It was with a new sense of urgency that the company took to their rafts two days later, supplies replenished. Mr. Glade and his remaining son had decided to stay at the fort; the man had lost the purpose of the trip and needed time to recover from his loss. But the others were up early and away before dawn.

The river was wider and not as rough now, but it was swollen with the autumn rains, and the current bore them swiftly along. Portages were less frequent, and they made good time. Rachel wore her blanket like a shawl against the icy spray and kept one eye on the low gray clouds. The cold rose at night, but the snow held off other than a few light flurries that disappeared as quickly as they came. Finally one afternoon Mr. Peabody announced Bellefontaine was approaching just around the river bend.

Rachel knelt on the raft, clinging to a rope with one hand and holding her hair out of her eyes with the other. A sharp wind that day loosened her braid and brought red into her cheeks. Excitement flashed in her eyes as the goal of the last few months came into view.

It wasn't much to see—slightly more impressive than Fort Loyal, it was still nothing like she had imagined and a far cry from Toronto. There was an extensive landing built on the river, for sternwheelers came along the Henderson to the town, though Rachel didn't see any there now. It consisted of a few hastily built buildings and houses laid out in a grid pattern between the hills and the Henderson, with a flat stretch of farmland reaching to a hazy blue smudge of trees in the distance—that was all. But here she was at last. The rafts pulled ashore, and she stepped off onto hard-frozen earth.

"This is where we part company," Peter announced. Rachel jerked in surprise and spun to face him but saw that he was looking at Lizzie and her sons. And it hit her with a heavy thump in her chest that reaching Bellefontaine meant the end of the line for her, but Lizzie was going on to Briarton farther south. She would likely never see Lizzie again. Of all the women she had met in her travels, she would miss cheerful, friendly Lizzie the most.

"So soon?" Lizzie's eyes glittered with tears, and she came to hug Rachel tightly. "I knew this was coming, but I still hate to see you go."

"This journey seems to be about me coming to love people only to lose them again," Rachel said sadly.

"Isn't that what *life* is about?" Peter asked, a bitter edge to his voice.

"No," Lizzie said, looking surprised. "Life is about finding people to love and forging eternal bonds with them. You might be separated for a time, but you don't have to lose them forever."

"Is that what the Mormons teach?" Rachel asked.

"Yes."

"You must find that belief very comforting. I wish I were as sure of that as you."

"You boys stay safe, now, and help your mother," Peter said, adding, "Not that you need telling. You're good boys, both of you, and I hope you enjoy your new home."

David Jr. and Walter gave him shy looks as he shook their hands, and Lizzie stuck out her hand to give Peter a formal handshake.

"Think about what I said," Lizzie told him, tipping her head back to look up seriously into his face. "Come join us in Briarton if you've a mind to. Or at least come to visit one day."

"We'll certainly try," Peter replied and carefully avoided looking at Rachel.

"You're a good man, William. Take care of Mary for me."

"I . . . I will. Say hello to Davey Myers for me, and tell him I'm sorry I couldn't meet him, but he's got a great couple of boys and a fine wife."

Lizzie laughed. "That I will."

Rachel knelt to give Harry a final hug and turned away to hide her own tears. This parting felt too sudden, but what else had she expected? The company was staying overnight at Bellefontaine, but Peter had been told Washed-Out Creek was only a couple of miles away overland from here, and there was still half a day of daylight to travel in. They could reach it by nightfall.

"I'll say my good-byes here too," Frank piped up. "I'm going to sign on with a sternwheeler down to Victoria for the winter."

Rachel blinked, caught off guard. She had known he would leave them eventually, but she wasn't quite ready for him to go yet either. "Are you sure?"

"Yes. I still have family there. I've been away too long."

"Well, I can certainly understand that." She held out a hand, and he shook it.

"Thank you," she said, looking him in the eyes. "We wouldn't have made it without you. I'm pleased to have you for a friend."

Frank gave Rachel's hand a strong squeeze and nodded at her, smiling. "Watch for bears," he said, then turned and took up his bedroll and walked away.

"Did you already pay him?" Rachel asked Peter in a whisper.

"Yes, when I hired him."

She mulled this over. To pay Frank up front and then receive his services . . . She understood now how deeply Peter had trusted him. She realized she had trusted him too. And he had proven himself worthy of that trust. She smiled to herself, thinking how much her attitude had changed. She looked up to see Peter watching her with a curious expression. "Let's get our things and take our leave of Mr. Peabody," she said.

CHAPTER TWENTY-TWO

RACHEL AND PETER STOPPED AT the dry goods store to pick up a few more supplies before heading out. Rachel allowed herself a few minutes to linger over the fabrics and sewing notions, unable to stop herself from comparing the bright calicos and cottons to her faded and travel-ruined dress. What a sight she must be! She'd lost her sunbonnet ages ago, her skin was dark and freckled, her hair was like corn silk, all fly-away, and her nails were broken and blackened with dirt she couldn't seem to scrub away. Her toes poked fully out of the tip of her left shoe. She felt ashamed to be seen on the street.

Peter was watching her from across the store, and after a while he called, "Rachel, why don't you buy some of those ribbons you're fingering?"

She snorted and dropped the silky strands.

"I have some money," he added in a quieter voice, but she shook her head.

"What's the use of the cherry without the ice cream sundae to go with it?" she replied, trying to sound cheerful. "I guess Miss Rachel Hamilton can survive a while longer without silks and satins."

The man behind the counter lifted his head and studied her with interest. He was a portly man in his late fifties, with balding hair and a florid tone to his cheeks that hinted at a fondness for the drink.

"Did you say Rachel Hamilton?" he asked.

Looking at him in surprise, Rachel felt a sudden sinking in her stomach. She had completely forgotten.

"I'm sorry, no," she stuttered. "I'm Rachel Cameron."

"You said Hamilton just now. There's a bulletin out about a runaway. Came some weeks ago. Same name and fits your description. Where did I put it?" He began patting his pockets and looking around the counter as if expecting the document to be at hand.

Rachel shook her head, but before she could speak again, Peter was at her elbow.

"You've got the wrong Rachel, mister. This is my wife. Rachel . . . Cameron. I'm Peter Cameron. We've been married some two years now."

Rachel sent him a silent look of gratitude as the man coughed and apologized.

"Guess I heard wrong. Sorry."

"Rachel Cameron?" a voice said.

Rachel turned in astonishment to find Lucas—Lucy—standing in the next aisle. She held a jar of molasses in her hand, forgotten, as she stared at Rachel.

"Rachel!" she cried. Lucy became aware of the jar in her hand, set it down hastily, and rushed forward to take Rachel's hand in hers.

"Luca—Lucy!" Rachel could hardly speak. The person before her was no longer dressed in shapeless men's clothing and hat but in a bonnet and trim yellow dress spread out over her crinoline like an umbrella. Her hands were soft and lotioned. From lace collar to button shoes, she was dainty and feminine. And Rachel felt more like flotsam washed up on a beach than ever. "I hardly recognize you," she stammered.

"I'm a woman again," Lucy said with a casual shrug, and Peter's and the man's eyes widened.

"What are you doing here?" Rachel asked. She thought it wonderful to run into her old acquaintance again, but her mind was skittering away at the same time, wondering where Marshall was. Was he here in town?

"I dropped out of the company when it got here, and I've opened my own bakery. I'm a businesswoman now. But whatever happened to you, Rachel? You simply disappeared, and I didn't know what to think."

The man behind the counter gave a cough. "You know this woman too?"

"Yes, she's my friend. We met on the trail," Lucy said.

Rachel gritted her teeth and hoped it looked like a smile. "Lucy, this is my husband Peter *Cameron*," she said. "Peter, this is Lucy . . . um."

Lucy blinked at Rachel for half a beat and then smiled and briskly offered Peter her hand. "Jones. Lucy Jones. Friend of Rachel's. Ah . . . I'm glad to meet you at last, Mr. Cameron. Rachel's told me so much about you." She smiled brightly at the man behind the counter. "Well, isn't this nice for old friends to meet like this?"

"Let's find a place to sit and catch up with each other's news," Rachel suggested, linking arms with Lucy, and together they swept from the store, Peter following bemusedly. Once well out of earshot, Rachel turned to Lucy with a smile. "You're quick on the uptake," she said admiringly.

"I've been known to indulge in a little subterfuge myself," Lucy replied. "I could tell right away you didn't want that storekeeper to know your name. Though why, I can't imagine." She looked cheerfully from Rachel to Peter. "So are you going to tell me the real story, or do I have to guess? Did you throw me over for him? Wasn't I a good enough husband to you?" She shouted with laughter.

Peter looked confusedly at Rachel, who shook her head. "Let's go down to the river and sit for a while. This story will take some time."

It took about an hour, in fact. Peter was slightly scandalized at the idea that Lucy had crossed the country disguised as a man, but Rachel explained the necessity of it. When she told Lucy what Marshall had done and how she had accidentally become separated from the company, Lucy nodded grimly. "I wondered if it was something like that. Adam Marshall came to my tent that night, yelling and drunk, looking for you. He frightened me. You see, I used to be married to a man like that. A terrible temper. That was why I was running west in the first place and why my cousin Thomas—Mr. McMicking is my cousin—agreed to help me, however reluctantly. It seemed the best way to get away from my husband where he'd never follow. When Adam Marshall came round shouting and banging, I . . . I betrayed myself for the hysterical, crying female I was. The secret was out."

"Oh no!" Rachel cried. "What happened?"

"He went into a rage. Said all women were deceiving sinners. Tore everything apart, brought his friends back, and they knocked down my tent and busted up everything I owned, as well as your trunk. Thomas intervened as soon as he became aware of it, but it was too late. They didn't ruin the stove though. There's only so much you can do to cast iron."

"Oh, Lucy! I'm so sorry."

"There wasn't much I could do after that. There was no hiding the fact I was a female. The rest of the journey wasn't very pleasant, I can tell you. The men in the company weren't pleased at being deceived, and Thomas had to pretend he'd had no inkling of it. I took all the blame and said I'd deceived him. Otherwise he would have lost the confidence of the men, you see. Anyway, I couldn't get away from the company fast enough as soon as we got here."

"I'm sorry that happened," Rachel said earnestly. "I wish I could pay you back for what you lost. It was all my fault. But I don't have a penny to my name. Maybe when I meet up with my father . . ."

"Not to worry. I've since more than made up for anything I lost. They got your money, though, when they busted everything up. Oh, and your poor cat—"

Rachel swallowed. "I know. I was following on the trail behind the company. I found him."

Lucy put her hand on Rachel's arm. "I'm sorry. I tried to stop him."

"I see now that it was completely ludicrous to try to bring Geordie along in the first place. I had no idea what I was getting into." Rachel wiped at her eyes. "I know he was just a cat, but he was the only friend I had. Until I met others." She reached out and grasped Lucy's hand and gave her a watery smile.

Lucy cast her eyes toward Peter, waiting patiently. "A handsome new friend too, I might add. And you say he's your husband?"

"Same as you were," Rachel confided. "It's just safer that way on the trail."

"Well, this is becoming quite a habit for you, Miss Rachel. Picking up and discarding husbands right and left! Though, if I were you, I might consider making this one genuine." Lucy laughed.

Rachel glanced at Peter; he was listening with a half-smile, his eyes lowered as if something on the ground had captured his interest.

"Anyway, I traveled on with the McMicking company, and then a few days after you disappeared, a woman named Catherine Schubert joined the company with her husband and three children and another one on the way. So I wasn't entirely alone with all those men," Lucy said. "I teamed up with the Schuberts and was able to be of use to her. Marshall didn't bother me after that, though the men gave me plenty of teasing."

"I imagine. Is Marshall here in Bellefontaine?" Rachel asked worriedly.

"No, he left the company when we got to Fort Loyal. Said he was going to go up to the Dunant Mountains to hunt gold. I don't think we'll hear from him anymore."

"So you're being yourself now?" Rachel asked. "You're back to being Lucy Cameron."

"I am. Well, Lucy Everett. That's my real name." Lucy glanced at Peter's shuttered face. Her tone turned slightly defensive as she said, "Lots of women have disguised themselves as men and gone to settle the west, you know. I'm not the only one. There are historical precedents too. I mean, Joan of Arc dressed as a man for her own protection."

"Yes, and she was put to death for heresy, was she not?" Peter replied, lips twitching.

"Well, then there was James Gray of the Royal Marines," Lucy persisted. "She fought in battle and even received a military pension after she revealed her real name was Hannah Snell."

"Just so she could go to war?" Rachel gasped.

"So you mustn't think too harshly of me," Lucy said to Peter. "Necessity can make you do some pretty unconventional things."

Rachel glanced at Peter and thought about the way she had been living and deceiving people for months now. She looked away.

"Anyway," Lucy said, "I'm just as glad to be plain old me now. I'm doing all right with my bakery too. Whether or not they strike it rich, the men have to eat. That's where I come in."

"That's wise," Rachel said. "You'll make more money doing that than panning for gold, I'm willing to bet."

"That's the plan, anyway. When I left my husband, I vowed I'd never depend on a man again to support me, and it looks as if I'll be able to keep that vow."

"I wish you all the luck in the world," Rachel told her sincerely. "And thank you again for trying to help me, Lucy. You were a fine husband."

As both women burst into peals of laughter, Peter shook his head and pulled his hat down over his eyes.

* * *

The trail to the south followed the edge of the river, clear and easy to find, being well traveled by those passing through on their way to the gold fields of the Dunant District. The terrain was boggy in places and stony in others, and the cliffs crowded in to overhang the river so closely in some spots that Rachel and Peter had to walk single file between rock and water. The wind rushing down the river was freezing against her face, but Rachel welcomed the sensation. It kept her mind off of Lizzie and the boys and the heavy pack on her back. She imagined Lizzie moving on south through British Columbia, reaching her destination, finding Davey Myers, and settling onto their new farm. She hoped Lizzie would find everything she had hoped for. She thought of Lucy Everett running her own successful business in Bellefontaine and couldn't help smiling. What a funny old world this was!

It seemed strangely silent now, with the noise and clatter of the company far behind them and nothing but the hum of the river to keep them company. The quiet was almost unnerving, she'd grown so used to Lizzie's cheerful gabbing. Rachel imagined herself on a horse, swaying from side to side. Or perhaps a camel—that was better. She imagined herself swathed in flowing gossamer veils and decorated with chains of beads and little metal discs, her skin lotioned and perfumed, her tired feet in cool leather sandals instead of damp and broken boots . . . As a child, she had once seen a picture in a book about Egypt, and it had made a great impression on her. But the fanciful daydream grew thin and fell away after a while.

It was nearing dusk when they reached a narrow stream running out of the rocks into the Henderson. It was narrow enough that it could be easily forded in two strides, and the water, when she tasted it, was fresh and cold enough to make her head ache.

"Washed-Out Creek, as far as I can tell," Peter announced. "It looks like it runs down out of that little valley up there. Do you know how far upstream your father's mine is?"

"I'm not sure. Do you think we should camp here for th—" She broke off in a squeal as a quail burst out of the brush at her feet and flapped away in an explosion of sound. Peter chuckled.

"Just a bird," he said. "And, yes, let's make camp here. I don't want to be trekking up some unfamiliar mountain in the dark."

They built a cheerful fire against the curve of a large protective boulder and sat close to it, warming their hands and faces. Rachel wished there was a way to warm both front and back at the same time. With the sun going down, the cold was bitter.

The flames snapped, and the river wooshed, but it was still too quiet. No shouting back and forth, no Lizzie laughing, no cattle or horses or friendly Harry. Just the vast, darkening expanse beyond the ring of their little fire. She wondered if there were wolves out there in the twilight.

She sat with drawn-up knees, feeling very small, and watched the pork sizzle and jump in the frying pan. She smiled at herself, remembering how she'd longed for solitude, to be alone with Peter on the open road. Now here she was missing Lizzie's comforting chatter and the movement of people around her. Tomorrow she would probably reach her father's mine, and she and Peter wouldn't be alone again.

"What are you thinking about?" Peter asked from across the fire. The shadows bunched under the brim of his hat, and she couldn't see his face.

"I was just thinking how glad I am that I'm not out here alone," she said. "This seems ten times more desolate than the prairie."

He moved around the fire to sit beside her and put an arm lightly around her blanketed shoulders, pulling her gently against his side. "I'm with you," he murmured. "And I won't let anything happen to you."

Warmed by his words, she rested her head on his shoulder. They sat motionless and gazed at the snapping flames, listening to the spitting pork and the crackling, fragrant sage as the fire devoured it. The cold penetrated to Rachel's bones, and she snuggled her blanket closer. The moon rose, and Peter moved away to serve their dinner. The hot food warmed her and dispelled some of her somber mood.

When they had finished eating, Rachel wriggled down to lie on her side so she could keep her back close to the fire and watch the light paint Peter's face as he sat staring into the flames. She could see only half of his face, but he appeared to be far away in his thoughts, and she didn't want to disturb him by striking up a conversation. She fell asleep with the flames flickering behind her eyelids.

She awoke in darkness. The fire had died out, and she had no idea what time it was. She squirmed to find a more comfortable position, but the ground was packed hard, and the blanket around her shoulders smelled strongly of horse. She missed the cozy hush of the Hunsakers' hayloft.

"Can't sleep?" Peter's voice was muffled.

"I'm freezing," Rachel admitted. "And I'm too excited to sleep. It feels like Christmas Eve."

She heard a rustling sound and the strike of flint, and then a faint spark began to glow. Peter leaned over it, cupping it as he breathed softly to fan the tiny flicker. Patiently he fed it with twigs, then larger sticks. When he had a good flame going, he crawled over and draped his own blanket over Rachel. The shadows jumped and wavered over his face. He had removed his hat, and she saw his hair sticking up again in the same spot it usually did.

"You'll be warmer in a minute," he said. He tucked the blanket around her as if she was a child.

"I am already, thank you. You're very thoughtful," she said, and without even thinking about it, she caught his hand in hers and kissed the backs of his fingers. He paused, and she couldn't read his expression in the dancing light. Slowly he moved one finger to stroke her cheek, outlining her profile as he had once before in the golden glow of the loft.

"Rachel," he whispered thickly. "I've been alone so long. A year, but it seems so long."

"I know."

"There are times I miss my wife so much I think I'll never be happy again. And yet, there have been times along the trail this past while that I think I've never been happier. It's confusing. It feels like a betrayal."

She didn't know what to say to this and remained silent. She hadn't heard a man confess to weakness before, and it unnerved her a little. Peter ran his fingers through his shaggy hair, making it stand out even worse.

"Do you think—" he began, then stopped.

She slid her arm further out of the enveloping blanket and put her hand on his arm. "Do I think what?"

"Do you think my wife . . . Do you think Angelina would mind so very much if I decide to go on living? Without her?"

Rachel felt tears start in her throat and swallowed hard. "No," she said firmly. "I'm sure that's what she would want for you. I'm sure she would want you to be happy."

He let out a long breath, looking away into the flames that spit and snapped as they reached a pocket of pitch in the wood. "I'm not sure what will make me happy at this point. But I hope I figure it out soon." He turned to look at her, forcing his voice to be light. "What will make you happy, Rachel Mary? Reaching your father, I suppose."

Rachel nearly said, *You.* She cleared her throat to stop the traitorous word and said instead, "Yes, I guess so."

"What sort of man is your father?" he asked. "Is he the gentle, white-haired, grandfatherly type?"

"Not at all." She smiled at the thought. "He's more like me, I suppose. Impulsive, stubborn, not always wise, well-meaning, but prone to be impatient."

"Ah. Then he's probably the type to go after a man with a shotgun for despoiling his daughter."

Rachel burst out laughing, and the intimate mood was shattered. She sat up, wrapped the blankets tightly around her, and wiped her nose with the back of her hand.

"I'm afraid he is the shotgun type, yes," she told him. "He has a great bristling beard and a voice like the trumpet of Gabriel when he's angry."

"I was afraid he might be." Peter sighed and lay back in the dry grass with his hands under his head. "Just my luck."

Rachel wasn't sure how to reply to this either. She felt suddenly thrown into unfamiliar territory, and she wasn't sure if he was serious or jesting with her. She felt terribly young and inexperienced.

"You love him. I can hear it in your voice when you speak of him," Peter observed.

"Yes," she said, "and he loves me."

"Funny way of showing it, leaving you behind. How long has it been since you last saw him?"

"Five years," Rachel said. "But he wrote—"

Peter made a sputtering sound. "Five years? You haven't seen him in all that time?"

"Father thought the best way to show his love for his family was to provide well for them," Rachel said a touch defensively. "He thought gold was the best way to do that. The factory was doing all right, of course, but he is an adventurer, and he thought gold mining—"

"Factory? Wait a minute." Peter sat upright again, jaw slack. "Hamilton. You aren't one of *the* Hamiltons of Acton Manufacturing, are you?"

"Yes. My father founded Acton. Have you heard of it?"

"The entire eastern seaboard has heard of it," he said. "He's one of the richest men in all of Upper Canada. Good grief, I've been sharing my blanket with a blooming heiress. I should have known it, with your white, perfect hands and your snooty airs."

"Snooty!"

"As if you expected a maid to pop along at any moment to drawn your bath."

"Well, yes, it *has* been difficult getting used to doing without Dorothy," Rachel admitted.

Peter groaned, then laughed. "You've made a good go of it, I'll have to say. I admit you've surprised me, sticking it out the way you have. The first time I saw you, I wouldn't have bet you'd make it this far. I thought you'd turn around and scamper back to Toronto."

"To a patronizing, overbearing brother like Richard? No, thank you. I'd be dubbed the family lunatic and kept under lock and key."

"You should be, giving up a life like that for a life like this," Peter declared. "If that's not loony, I don't know what is."

"I just want to see my father."

"Are you going to stay and mine for gold too?" He chuckled. "I can see you now with a pan in your hands and dirt all over your face."

"You've seen me look worse," she replied.

"True."

"You needn't agree so readily." She flounced back in her cocoon of blankets. She had felt guilty for taking his blanket, but not anymore. "Besides, the Happy Scot isn't a placer mine. It's . . . you know, a regular hole-in-the-side-of-the-mountain type of mine. I don't remember what he called it in his letter."

"Ah. I see. So instead of a pan in your hands, you'd have a candle in your hat."

"Anyway, I think I'd like to stay here in British Columbia," Rachel said. "Maybe I'll go to Victoria and train as a nurse. There's nothing for me back in Toronto. I don't have a reason to go back there, and it all seems very far away now. Besides, I can't imagine making this trek again but in reverse!" She squirmed onto her side to face him. "What about you, Peter? What will you do when this journey is over?"

He lay down again, arms tucked under his head. She was unable to see his face in the dark again. "I don't know," he said.

"Do you have any ideas?"

"Maybe," he said vaguely. "I'll let you know when I know."

* * *

A mile upstream the next morning, they came to a sheltered valley between two granite cliffs where a mining camp of some size had been thrown together. It was surprisingly large, filling the five or six acres of the valley floor—shanties and lean-tos, a poled corral holding several sway-backed mares, and even a surveyor's office with glass windows. It wasn't exactly the romantic image of the western frontier Rachel had imagined. She had somehow pictured her father working in isolation on his lonely claim, but there had to be thirty or forty men here, and there was a sense of bustle and industry. They passed an outhouse, which stank, and the smell of tobacco was ripe in the air. The men Rachel saw looked to be more hair and dirt than flesh and bone and looked as disheveled as she and Peter did after months of travel.

"Um . . ." Rachel said.

"Stay close to me."

"You should set up shop as a barber," Rachel observed as they made their way through the scattered wooden buildings. "You'd make a fortune here." There didn't seem to be any sort of planning or organization that she could discern. The various shacks sprawled and sprouted higgledy-piggledy all over the little vale. It was a dramatic contrast to the clean, organized settlement of Bellefontaine.

"Where do you suppose my father is?" she asked, looking around in growing disgust. "I didn't think it would be like this."

"It's the beginnings of a town," Peter said. "No birth is very pretty. Give it some years, and it will be like Bellefontaine."

"I need a bath just looking at it."

He grinned. "Into the creek with you, then."

Just then Rachel noticed a long, low, log building with a semblance of a front porch, and in the paper-covered windows a crookedly lettered sign said *Rooms to Let*. "A hotel?" she asked incredulously. "*Here?*"

"I'm not sure I'd want to sleep in whatever passes for a bed in that place," Peter said doubtfully. "We're better off saving our money and keeping to our own camp."

"But where there's a hotel, there might be at least a hip bath," Rachel reasoned. "A *bath*, Peter! With hot water! Wouldn't that be wonderful? I don't want my father to see me like this."

Before he could stop her, she'd hiked up the bedraggled hem of her skirt and climbed the rickety steps. There was a table inside the front door, and a blanket hung over a doorway leading to the kitchen, from the smell of it. No one seemed to be around, but Rachel cleared her throat and called, "Anyone there?"

There was a clatter of pans in the kitchen, and then a greatly mustachioed man with a balding head peered out from behind the blanket. His face brightened, and he came out wiping his hands on his trousers. He wasn't much taller than Rachel and looked perhaps thirty, but he was hefty, which made her think his cooking was probably good. Her hopes rose a little.

"Welcome!" he greeted her. "John Tepperman."

"Mary Mitchell. My husband and I just arrived off the trail," Rachel told him. It was funny how easily that lie fell from her tongue. After weeks of pretending, she half believed it herself. "We don't need a room, but I wondered if you have a bath available."

"We have a tin hip bath," the man replied, nodding vigorously. "And the finest French-milled soap"—this Rachel doubted—"but it goes with the room. A dollar a night."

"That seems very high," Rachel said. "And as I told you, we don't need the room. We have all we require. I'm only interested in the bath."

Tepperman looked from her to Peter, who leaned against the doorway behind her. "Well, now, I'd be charging you a dollar for the bath anyhow. It takes a lot of work to heat up the water on the stove, you know."

"If it's a dollar for a room and a bath, then the bath without the room shouldn't cost the same," Rachel argued. She was beginning to feel ludicrous and felt Peter's eyes burning the back of her head. "I'll give you . . ." She looked at Peter, suddenly wondering how much money he had.

"Twenty-five cents," he said.

"The bath comes with the room," Tepperman insisted. "A dollar for both. I'm the only hotel in the place, so if you don't like the price, you can go bathe in the creek. Mighty cold this time of year."

"Just what I was telling her," Peter said.

Rachel shook her head remorsefully. "Thank you anyway."

She turned to leave, but Peter straightened and uncrossed his arms. "All right, a dollar," he said. "But you throw in dinner."

When Tepperman began to object, Peter added, "Since we're paying for more than we wanted."

"Agreed," Tepperman said, subsiding. "This way."

The room he led them to was little more than a woodshed tacked to the side of the building, with a sagging mattress on the bed frame and a cracked china bowl and pitcher on a washstand. There was a window cut into the back wall, and the oiled paper had been torn in one spot, giving them a view of a muddy rear yard and the privy. But at least the blankets and towel appeared to be clean, the floor was swept, and the tantalizing smell of beef stew permeated the place.

Rachel nodded. "This will do nicely, thank you. The hip bath, please?"

Peter went first, because, he explained, he would take half the time Rachel would. She waited in the corridor outside, listening to the splashing and humming behind the door with amusement. When he came out, he'd trimmed his hair, shaved his jaw until it was smooth as polished maple, and had somehow managed to rid his clothes of dust. He was easily the most handsome man she had ever seen, and his satisfied smile warmed her, but she said only, "Took you long enough," and hurried past him into the room.

Tepperman fetched clean water and another towel, and Rachel shut the door in Peter's face and eagerly peeled off her poor dress. The bath water proved to be lukewarm, and the French soap a common lump of homemade lye soap so strong it made her skin burn, but it was still a delicious change from cold river water. Rachel scrubbed her hair ruthlessly and soaked her poor neglected skin, then toweled herself off with energy and combed her hair out with her fingers until it felt like gold silk. She was tanned and freckled beyond repair, but at least her skin was soft and clean once again. She was mortified about wearing such disreputable clothes when she saw her father again, but she could do nothing about them. This was the only dress she had, and the worn fabric wouldn't withstand another washing. And she doubted she could find a pair of women's shoes for sale within a hundred miles anyway.

When she emerged at last, Peter was waiting for her in the twenty-foot-square room that served as a dining room. There was one long table for all, and Rachel saw that several other men were waiting on the benches for their dinner as well. They all looked worn and weary, and they kept their hats on even indoors, but they looked up with interest as she entered and made her way over to sit beside Peter.

Peter held a brown paper package on his lap. As he rose to meet her, he held the package out to her. There was a glint in his eyes.

"Go back to the room and open this and then come back," he instructed.

"What is it?"

"Go find out."

Curious, she took the package back to their room, laid it on the aged mattress, and pulled open the string that tied it. The paper fell back to reveal pink fabric, mounds of it, slick and soft between her fingers. With a cry of delight she lifted it up and shook it out. It was a shawl, store bought and so clean the cloth squeaked. It was big enough that she could put it around her shoulders and throw it across her front, warm and lovely. It seemed to her elegance-starved eyes to be the most beautiful thing she'd seen in a long time. And it did an effective job of hiding the worst of the stains on her dress.

Peter was marvelous. He was perfect. What other man would have thought of it? And where on earth in this miserable settlement had he found it? No one was more kind or compassionate. Her heart sang with it.

Chapter Twenty-Three

When Rachel returned to the dining room, she had to hold herself in check to keep from running. He was waiting at the table, and he made no effort to hide his grin. She twirled before him, letting the shawl fly out in a pink arc.

"Like it?" Peter asked casually.

"I love it. I love you," she said, and there in front of the whole table she threw her arms around his neck and gave him a resounding kiss. The other men erupted in laughter, and she watched with delight as a deep red blush climbed Peter's neck into his face.

"Sit down. You're making a spectacle of us both," he hissed, but he was smiling.

"Wherever did you find it? Surely not *here*." Her gesture took in the whole muddy, ramshackle settlement.

"I got it in Bellefontaine," Peter confessed. "I was waiting for the right moment to give it to you."

"It's perfect," Rachel told him. "And so soft and warm!"

"I'm glad you like it."

Rachel slotted herself onto the bench and looked down the communal table. There were ten other men seated along it now, like crows on a fence rail. Twenty eyes quickly turned back to their bowls, but she caught sight of plenty of smiles in their beards. She felt an expansive good will toward them all.

Tepperman brought out a steaming tureen of beef stew that happily tasted as good as it smelled. Rachel couldn't say much for his manner, but the man indeed could cook. She whispered this to Peter, who replied, "For a dollar, he should be feeding us roasted pheasant." Nonetheless, he spooned up the stew like a starving man.

Keeping her voice low enough that the other men couldn't hear, Rachel said, "I promise I'll repay you just as soon as I locate my father." She hesitated, wondering if she would find him, and if it would be today. Would Hamish Hamilton have money? Was his mine doing well? Well, she could always write to Richard, and he would see that Peter was reimbursed for all his expenses.

Peter waved a hand to dismiss the subject as if he had all the money in the world and reached for the platter of biscuits. "Where does your father live?" he asked, breaking the biscuit in half and dipping it into his stew.

"I'm not certain, but it shouldn't be hard to find. The Happy Scot Mine is somewhere on Washed-Out Creek was all he said in his letter, but I'm sure someone here will be able to tell us exactly where."

The man on her right turned and arched a thick eyebrow. He was a grizzled, burly man in a filthy leather coat, with red cheeks and a beard dotted with biscuit crumbs. He reeked of stale sweat, and he had a pistol poking out of his too-tight belt, as if he had need of such a thing at a dinner table. His teeth were stained the color of old ivory. "Sorry, I couldn't help overhearing," he said politely. "You folks are looking for the Happy Scot?"

"Why, yes. Have you heard of it?" Rachel asked, pleased. This would be simpler than she'd thought.

"Can't say I have," the stranger said cheerily. "And I've been in these parts since 1855, when gold was first discovered on the Henderson. If I haven't heard of it, it isn't here."

"Certainly it's here," Rachel said, waving a dismissive hand as Peter had done a moment before. "It's on Washed-Out Creek. Isn't that what this is?"

"Yes, ma'am, that's what they call this place."

"Then it's here somewhere."

"I've been all up and down this creek and the Henderson too," the man insisted. "I know every tributary. And there's no claim I know of named the Happy Scot."

"It's a mine. A proper one, not just panning for gold in the river but digging underground," Rachel explained.

The man gave a barking laugh. "A proper one," he shouted, hitting the table. "Digging underground!" The men around him laughed too.

"What's so funny?" Rachel frowned. "It *is* underground."

The man wiped his eyes on his dirty sleeve. "Sorry, missus. Um . . . Happy Scot . . . a good name, that. I would remember it because my mother was Scottish, you see."

Rachel didn't see, and the man was annoying her. "Just because you aren't familiar with it doesn't mean it doesn't exist."

"Well, now, Mary," Peter drawled, taking on the friendly stranger's drawn-out manner of speaking, "don't argue with the gentleman. If he's been here this long—"

"Since '55," the man said, nodding. He pushed away his empty bowl and leaned across Rachel to shake Peter's hand. "Jack Wylie."

"William Mitchell," Peter said with a smile, wincing as Jack's hand crushed his.

"Pleased to meet you. You're from back east, sounds like."

"Toronto. Just arrived today."

Rachel didn't know why Peter was being so friendly with Jack Wylie. She thought him slightly repulsive and irritating.

"You and the little missus are looking for this particular mine for a reason?" He rubbed his nose with the back of his hand.

"We're looking for her father, Hamish Hamilton. He owns the Happy Scot."

"Ah. Um." Jack considered this, his elbows planted on the table and his thick fingers boring into his temples. "Name doesn't ring a bell with me either. Hey, Ev!"

A gaunt, gray-haired man farther down the table leaned forward, dragging the strings of his stained hat into his soup bowl.

"Ever heard of a fellow named Hamish Hamilton? Owns the Happy Scot Mine? *Underground?*"

"The Happy Who?"

The name was passed down the noisy table from person to person, and the answer returned good-naturedly the same way. Jack shook his head.

"If Ev Kimball hasn't heard of it, there's no such place, and if he's never heard of Hamish Hamilton, there's no such man."

"This is ridiculous," Rachel exploded, rising to her feet. "Of course there's such a man; he's my father. And the Happy Scot Mine is around here somewhere. It was producing gold three years ago. I have proof of it. Er—I did. Anyway, maybe it isn't being worked anymore, for whatever reason, but it's here somewhere, and I aim to find it and him."

She tried to make a dignified exit, but it was difficult to climb over the bench in her skirt. She nearly tipped over, and Jack caught her elbow to steady her. She gave him an icy thank you.

"Didn't mean to upset you, ma'am," he murmured as she marched toward the door.

"Never mind. I have to apologize for her," she heard Peter say behind her. "She's just tired, no doubt. It's been a long journey."

She was halfway down the corridor when Peter came stomping after her. He caught her outside the bedroom, gripping her arm so she was forced to stop and face him.

"That was very rude," he said, his voice level but his eyebrows lowered. "Jack Wylie was attempting to assist us."

"I don't need his assistance."

"Oh, no? Then how do you propose to find what you're looking for? Send your butler out to make inquiries? This isn't Toronto, where you can flick a finger and things are done for you. Here people help their friends and shoot their enemies, so you'd best mind who you make your enemy."

"Mr. Wylie doesn't frighten me."

"He should. He appears to be someone to reckon with around here." Peter rubbed a hand over his face. "Just watch your step, all right? We don't know these people. We're new here. It won't do to start ruffling feathers the wrong way. You need these people on your side if you're going to get any information at all."

She ground her teeth together. "Point taken," she snapped. "May I go now?"

Peter let his breath out in a hard stream through his teeth and released her arm. "I'm going back to the dining room to chat with the men," he said. "I'll see if I can smooth things over and learn anything useful."

"Fine."

"Just tell me one thing first," Peter said. "You said you knew the mine was producing gold three years ago. How do you know?"

"Because my father sent me money from the proceeds. Two hundred dollars in silver coin. The last of it was stolen from my trunk by that Marshall person. But it proves that the mine was producing."

Peter stared at her hard for a moment, and when he spoke next, his voice was dangerously quiet. "When was this? Three years ago?"

"That's what I said."

"Has he sent you any money since?"

"No."

"Has he told you why not?"

"No."

"So you don't know if the mine is still operating?"

"No."

Peter closed his eyes briefly.

"When did you last hear from your father?" He spoke through clenched teeth.

Rachel hesitated, but Peter saw the truth in her face and rolled his eyes.

"Oh, great. This is just great. You told me he wrote to you."

"He did, for the first two years. I . . . I haven't heard from him in the last three years."

"Not at all?"

"We've had no word," Rachel admitted. "That's why—"

"You mean this has all been a wild goose chase? You don't even know if he's alive or not, do you?"

"That's why I had to come," Rachel explained, throwing her arms wide. "I had to try to find him, Peter. Can't you understand that? My brother wants to have him declared legally dead so he can fully take over Father's factory. It has been in the hands of a board of trustees since Father left five years ago, but Richard is determined to take charge. I know he's going to change everything, to do business with the Americans. He's going to ruin Father's business and reputation. I can't let him do that if there's the slightest chance my father is still alive. And he could be. For all we know, he's right here in this town somewhere." Her voice trailed off, and she spread her hands as if she'd just had him there in her grasp a minute ago. "He has to be," she said softly.

"You couldn't mention this little uncertainty to me, this remote possibility that your father might not be here waiting for you? That we might be on a trip to nowhere?"

"Would you have brought me if I had?"

"You dragged me all this way knowing full well your father is likely dead. Even your brother believes so! What kind of person crosses a continent through months of misery knowing there's no hope?"

"There's always hope! There has to be!" The tears rose in her throat.

"You should have warned me that it might be a goose chase."

"Why should I have?" she retorted.

Peter leaned down, his face an inch from hers, glaring into her startled eyes. "Because, little girl, if we can't find him, what am I supposed to do with you? Just leave you here by yourself? Or do you expect me to escort you back across the continent again for another six months? 'Oh, sorry to inconvenience you, but you don't have a life of your own anyway, do you?'"

Rachel felt the heat crawling up her neck into her cheeks. She gripped her shawl with both hands to keep them from shaking. She had been an idiot, she realized with awful clarity. She hadn't thought things through. And she'd allowed herself to think Peter might regret parting ways in British Columbia. That he might care for her a little. Now she could see that he still considered her just a burden, a bundle to be delivered. He was only too eager to be rid of her. And she didn't blame him. "You can write to my brother, Richard . . . I'll give you the address . . . and tell him you've got me. You'll get five hundred dollars reward money for your pains."

"I ought to!"

Rachel felt her mouth sag in dismay, feeling the betrayal rise up in her chest to choke her, and she couldn't think of another word to say. She spun away and fled into the bedroom, slamming the flimsy door behind her.

Chapter Twenty-Four

Tepperman rubbed the end of his voluminous mustache between his fingers, thinking. "Your best bet is to check with Mattie Albright," he said. Rachel had sought him out first thing after breakfast and explained her search. The man told her he too had been in the area since the first whiff of gold had been found, and he hadn't heard of Hamish Hamilton either. "But if anyone knows the people in this area, it's Mattie."

"Who?"

He jerked his thumb toward the west. "About fifty yards down, with the red door. Nothing happens in this place without Mattie knowing about it. Talk to her."

Rachel thanked him and stepped outside the hotel, drawing her shawl close against the chill air. Her back ached from the lumpy mattress, and she tried to stretch out the kinks as she walked. Peter hadn't come back after their argument last night, and she had no idea where he'd spent the night. He'd probably pitched camp somewhere outside of town by the creek. She hoped his back was hurting him as much as hers.

She hoped he wasn't already on his way back to Bellefontaine without her . . .

This last thought sent fear scrambling like a chipmunk up from her stomach into her throat, making her cough. He wouldn't really leave her here alone, would he? She was penniless and friendless and had no idea what she would do if he abandoned her. The thought of never seeing him again took the air out of her lungs. Angrily she gave herself a shake. "You don't know that he's gone," she scolded herself sternly aloud. "Peter wouldn't do such a callous thing. You're being stupid. Stop flying into a panic until you know for certain."

She walked on, fists at her sides, unaware of the scowl on her face as she fought her feelings back under control. The few men in the road that morning watched her striding along with thunder on her face and gave her wide berth. By the time she reached her destination fifty yards from the hotel, she had managed to regain her composure, though her cheeks were flushed and her fingers seemed unable to uncurl from their fists.

She stopped before a dilapidated building with a door painted a surprising shade of red. It contrasted with the dingy brown street like a cherry. A bucket of geraniums bloomed on each side of the door. She decided Mattie must be a positive sort of person to attempt to cheer up her doorway in such a way. She imagined bringing beauty and color into such a place as this would be an exceptional challenge.

She pushed inside and stood in the entry, blinking as her eyes adjusted after the bright sunlight outside. There was a brightly colored rag carpet under her feet, homemade but lovely, and she could smell roses and heavy perfume on the air. She stepped into the front room, expecting a front desk or office of some sort, but found it was a parlor decorated in heavy red brocade and dark furniture, with a gilt mirror hanging on the wall above an iron wood stove. In spite of the daylight coming through the gaps in the warped wall boards, it was an astonishingly civilized-looking room.

"Can I help you, my dear?"

Rachel spun around, stammering with embarrassment.

"I'm sorry, I thought this was a business of some sort. I didn't mean to walk right into your home. The man at the hotel said to come see you . . ."

The woman in the doorway of the kitchen waved a hand, chuckling. She was a very large woman, round as a pumpkin, with impossibly blonde hair piled in a tower on her head. She wore a dressing gown, even though it was midmorning, and chunky green glass drops at her ears.

"Don't fret, dearie. This is my home *and* my business," she said and laughed loudly as if she'd said something very funny. "I'm Mattie Albright. Can I do something for you?"

"I hope so," Rachel said with some relief. "My name is Rachel Hamilton. I'm trying to locate information about my father, and the man at the hotel directed me to you. He said you know everything that happens in this place."

"And right he is," Mattie agreed, lowering herself into a horsehair chair and waving Rachel onto the wooden, cushion-piled bench that served as a sofa. Her robe gaped at the neck, revealing an astonishing amount of quivery pale flesh. Unconcerned, she stretched out slippered feet and flexed her thick ankles with a sigh. "We'll have to keep our voices down. I'm letting the girls have a bit of a lie-in. A late night last night," she said, and giggled again. "Now, you said your father . . . ?"

"Yes," Rachel said, wondering what sort of mother let her daughters lie in bed until nearly ten. "Hamish Hamilton, from Toronto. He came here about four years ago. He was on the Henderson River for a year before that. Anyway, he came to Washed-Out Creek to mine—"

"The Happy Scot," the woman said peacefully.

"You know it, then?" Rachel cried, forgetting to keep her voice down.

"I knew it," the woman corrected. "It's no longer active, of course." She reached to ring a tiny silver bell on a table, and at once a frowsy-haired woman poked her head into the room.

"Tea, please, Elsie."

"For two, ma'am?"

"Of course only for two. It's not even eleven yet."

The woman disappeared, and Rachel sank further into the cushions on the bench, relishing the idea of being served. The heavy fragrance in the air, the soft fabrics of the cushions, and the hushed comfort took her back to her home in Toronto. She admired Mattie for bringing such elegance to such a harsh town. All of this finery had to have come by sternwheeler to Bellefontaine and then been packed overland to Washed-Out Creek, quite a feat.

"If you know of the Happy Scot, you must know my father."

Mattie gave her a bemused look. "I knew him well. I considered him more than a client. He was my friend. A real gentleman, I thought him."

Rachel felt a cold wave slide over her scalp and down her spine. "Was?"

Mattie opened her mouth, hesitated, and tipped her head to one side. Her blue eyes narrowed. "Of course. He's gone, child. Surely you know that. What, did you think he was still in Washed-Out Creek?"

"I thought—Well, yes. That was what he said."

"When did he say this?"

Rachel looked away. "He wrote to me steadily until three years ago. He told me about leaving the Henderson River and coming here. He seemed very happy. And then . . . then I didn't hear anything after that, not a word in the last three years. So I came to find out what's become of him."

"Oh, you poor child." Mattie's face had paled beneath the powder. She pushed herself out of her chair, tightened the belt of her dressing gown, and came to sit on the sofa beside Rachel. She patted her own hair distractedly as if wondering what she had on her head.

"Hamish came here maybe three and a half or four years ago, yes. He staked his claim about two miles up the ridge, not on the creek where everyone else was. Everyone thought he was foolish to try to mine instead of panning for gold, but he was sure he'd have luck there. He said he was a lucky man. And he did have success for a time. He said he found the right kind of dirt, and he was sure there would be a vein. The Happy Scot, he called it." She touched Rachel's hand softly. "He rarely came into town—well, if you can call this a town—but he did come down here to see me sometimes. I hope that doesn't shock you. I was led to believe he was a widower."

"Yes, he is," Rachel said. The thought that her father might have courted someone did not bother her as much as she'd thought it might. He had been alone for many years since Rachel's mother's death, and if he had managed to find happiness with this woman seated beside her, then she was glad for him. Mattie seemed kind.

"He was a fun old fellow, very jolly, spoke like a gentleman, always talking about his mine and the gold he would uncover there. Very confident. He seemed to do all right at first too. Never a big vein but enough small stuff to line his pockets. He always had plenty to spend here, if you know what I mean." She nudged Rachel familiarly in the ribs and chuckled.

"And then?" Rachel prompted.

"He went away," Mattie said simply. "About three years ago. I never saw him again."

"Just like that? He abandoned his claim without a word?"

Mattie chewed her lower lip, spoiling the red lipstick there. "I remember thinking it odd. He was always talking about the wealth he'd get from that mine. He talked about it as if it was a person, almost as if he loved it like a woman. He kept saying he was about to become a very rich man, and then he'd say, 'Well, richer,' and laugh, like he had a great secret that amused him."

"Well, my father was already a very wealthy man," Rachel said, then worried that that sounded like crass boasting. But Mattie only nodded.

"I wondered, from the educated way he talked and the way he carried himself . . . He wasn't like the others you find here.

I liked him. But why would he come hunt for a fortune if he already had one?"

"A sense of adventure, perhaps," Rachel said. She suspected she had a touch of that herself as well. "He wanted to provide for his family, but he also wanted to do it in an unconventional and exciting way. I was quite young when he left, only fourteen, but I sensed sometimes that he was . . . well, a bit bored, maybe, in his work. He certainly enjoyed taking time away from it." Rachel stopped, afraid she was on the verge of tears at the memory of her father. Where could he have gone? "You say he just left the area?"

"Without a word to anyone," Mattie said. "Of course, that left his claim open, and others moved in quick enough. Some rough-looking fellows from San Francisco took over the Happy Scot and changed its name to Magnolia or some such silly thing. But they never did very well from it, I heard, and then a year or so ago it flooded, and the mine was abandoned. No one works it anymore. It wasn't producing enough to bother pumping it out. The fellows moved on to a mine called the Cracker Jack."

She released Rachel's hand as Elsie brought the tea tray in and set it in front of them. Mattie poured out, glancing at Rachel from under penciled brows.

"I hope something I've told you is beneficial to your search. I'm surprised he didn't tell his own family where he was going. I . . . I'm afraid I didn't know he had children; we didn't speak about our personal lives very much, of course. But it seems he would have sent you word. But, perhaps, after all, he couldn't." The thought seemed to come to her suddenly, and she set the pot down with a thump.

Rachel's cup froze midair. "Do you think he came to harm?" Her throat was so constricted she could hardly talk.

"What other explanation is there?" Mattie asked sadly. "I wondered at the time why he would abandon a mine he thought was going to be prosperous and walk away from it just like that. I figured he must have better prospects somewhere else. No

miners hang around forever, after all. For most of them, it isn't
the find so much as the thrill of the chase, you see, so a lot of
people come and go around here. Mining is a hard life. I . . . I
wasn't surprised he didn't tell me good-bye. But if he didn't tell
his *family*, and you haven't had word in all this time . . . well, I'm
sure if he could have sent you word, he would have. I'm sorry
how that sounds."

Rachel set her cup down with trembling fingers. It was one
thing to think the fearful words in her head, push them away,
ignore them—and she had always resisted them when Richard
spoke them—but to hear this gentle lady, who had obviously
cared for her father, say them . . . Rachel put her hand to her lips.

"I'm sorry," Mattie said again, her shoulders sagging. She
set down her tea cup as well and stared dully at it. "I did think
it strange . . . I should have thought."

Rachel remembered the letter she had saved over the years,
the last letter from her father, treasured and now lost along
with all her other possessions in her trunk. He'd declared that
the Happy Scot was producing gold and he expected it to just
get better and better. He'd expected to send for her shortly. She
considered what else the letter had said.

"What are you thinking?" Mattie was watching her closely.

"In my father's last letter, he said he would be meeting with
some important investors the next week and that he would
send me news afterward. He never did. Did he ever mention to
you what investors he was meeting?"

Mattie frowned and patted her hair again thoughtfully.
"Not that I recall. Perhaps he was going to take on a partner."

Rachel picked up her cup again but couldn't bring herself to
drink it. Her throat felt too constricted. She set it down again
and stood up.

"Thank you for your help, Mrs. Albright. I appreciate your
taking the time to talk to me."

"Of course, child. But I'm concerned for you, coming all
this way. Are you here alone?"

"I have a friend with me." She wondered if that was still true, remembering Peter's anger the night before. Had he abandoned her? Was he going to come back? What if she never saw him again? He had been so frightfully angry last night, more than she'd ever seen him before. She ran her fingers over the fringe of her new shawl, then gripped her hands together and forced herself to smile, pushing away the frightening thoughts ricocheting through her head. She couldn't break down in front of this woman.

"That's good, then." Mattie laid her hand briefly on Rachel's cheek. The cloying sweetness of her perfume was overpowering, but Rachel thought it would be pleasant in smaller doses, like lilac.

"I wish you luck, my dear," Mattie said. "If you ever need a place to stay or a friend to help you, please call on me."

"I will, thank you. You're very kind."

"You'll send me word if you find out about Hamish?"

Rachel looked into the woman's anxious face and felt a sudden rush of affection for her. Her father had clearly liked this person. And who knew? Maybe under other circumstances, she would have become Rachel's stepmother. She thought she would have liked that. And if Mattie had daughters, Rachel would have had sisters, something she had always wanted. She felt a sharp pang of the loss of something she had never had and now probably never would. "Of course I will," she said quietly.

"What will be your next step?" Mattie asked as they walked to the door.

Rachel considered. "First," she said resolutely, "I will find these rough fellows from San Francisco."

When she stepped out onto the porch and the door closed behind her, she blinked momentarily in the bright sunlight. There were people moving amongst the ramshackle buildings, men smoking as they leaned in doorways, men saddling horses, the clang somewhere of a hammer against metal. She could smell bacon frying. The air was cold enough to make her nostrils ache, and she pulled the shawl up around her ears. She didn't see Peter coming until his hand clamped down on her elbow and towed her away from the red door.

"What on earth are you doing here?" he demanded.

Relief at seeing him flooded through her.

"Mr. Tepperman told me to come see someone—" Rachel began to explain, but Peter was plowing down the road, pulling her behind him so quickly she could hardly catch her breath. Only a moment ago, Rachel had been afraid she might never see him again. Now, ten feet along the road, she planted her feet and yanked free of his grip in irritation. "Let go of me!"

He rounded on her.

"You're crazy, you know that?" he barked. "You're the craziest person I've ever met. What were you thinking, going in that place? What was Tepperman thinking to send you there? I'll have a word with him, see if I don't!"

"What place? Mattie Albright's, you mean? Mrs. Albright knew my father."

Peter snorted like a horse. "I'm sure she did, but it's a delicate topic for a well-brought-up girl to discuss. Especially standing on the road in broad daylight."

"You chose the setting," Rachel retorted, then paused and scowled at him. "What do you mean, it's a delicate topic?"

Peter rolled his eyes and resumed walking toward the hotel. Rachel ran after him.

"If you're going to lecture me, at least have the decency to tell me what I've done," she demanded.

"Spare me from naïve girls from Toronto," he replied, not slowing his stride. "You don't have a clue what I'm talking about, do you? Do you even know what place you were just in? Or did it go right over your head?"

Rachel felt foolish running after him like a puppy. She stopped short, and as she'd predicted, he stopped too.

"Mattie Albright was my father's friend. She told me some very helpful information. She gave me tea, and she also very kindly inquired if I was alone and if I needed a place to stay."

"A place to stay? There? You couldn't stay there, and if she really was a friend of your father's, she wouldn't suggest such a thing! Don't you care at all about your reputation?"

She thought this a very silly statement coming from the man she'd traveled with for the past several months.

"She was trying to help me. I could use a *friend* in this place," she said pointedly.

Peter clapped his hands on his head, struggling to regain his composure. He straightened with a sigh. "It's a brothel," he said in a quieter voice. "You just had tea in a brothel. You just got invited to stay with the prostitutes."

Rachel blinked stupidly at him, assimilating this information. Mattie? Surely not! Rachel's *father*? Never! Good heavens!

She realized Peter was still standing there watching her. She thrust her chin in the air. "Of course I knew that," she said loftily. "But unlike *some* people, I know not to pass judgment on others. I, for one, am able to look beyond the exterior and see that Mattie is a perfectly kind woman." She spun on her heel, prepared to march away in offended dignity.

He snorted again. "This from the woman who turned up her nose at the Natives."

Rachel felt her cheeks go as hot as if he had struck them. She spun back to face him, ready to deny this, but then her heart sank and the air went out of her. "Fair enough," she said. "But I trust I'm not that person anymore." And she stamped into the hotel, humiliated beyond endurance. But even beneath the turmoil flooding her brain, a little part of her took time to notice that he had finally called her a woman, not a little girl.

Chapter Twenty-Five

Jack Wylie was just coming into the dining room, and Rachel was glad to see him. "Oh, Mr. Wylie!" she hailed him. "I wanted to apologize for my rude behavior at dinner last night. The strain of the journey and everything . . ." she added vaguely.

"Not at all, Mrs. Mitchell. I quite understand. You weren't rude; you were just charming, I'm sure." He hitched his straining belt further up his stomach. He still wore the pearl-handled pistol conspicuously at his hip.

Rachel cut across his effusive talk. "Could you tell me if you've ever heard of a mine about two miles up the ridge called the Magnolia or some such thing? I believe some men from San Francisco worked it."

Jack's face cleared. "Sure. You must mean the place below Dunbar Ridge. It used to be called the Magnolia."

"It isn't called that now?"

"No, it isn't in operation anymore. It flooded a year ago, as I recall, and no one wanted to trouble themselves with it. Could have told them it was a foolish place to dig, anyway, being at the base of the mountain like that. Sure to flood."

It confirmed what Mattie had told her. "That was known as the Happy Scot a few years ago, before it became the Magnolia."

"Oh!" He looked a bit muddled as he assimilated this.

"Do you know the men who owned the Magnolia, Mr. Wylie?"

"The Harringer brothers. They're out at the Cracker Jack now. They don't go for placer mines, the Harringers don't. This one is a shaft as well, like the Happy Scot, but cut deeper. Bought out old Phil Gerhardt. He was a German feller getting a bit old for the mining life. Moved to live with his daughter in Victoria. I tell you, I know 'em all," he said, regaining his pride.

"Can you tell me how to get to this Cracker Jack mine?"

Jack Wylie looked doubtful. "I don't know what a decent lady like you would want with that trash. You're not planning to go out there, are you, ma'am? Those Harringers are kind of ornery folks. Not real sociable. Not the kind I'd want my wife going out there to see, if you understand me."

"I understand, and thank you for your concern. Of course I'm not going alone. I'll be accompanied by my husband. Can you tell me how to find them?" Rachel persisted.

Jack debated with himself, then nodded. "I can draw you a map if you like. It's not on Washed-Out Creek; it's a tributary of the Henderson called Ezekiel Creek."

"Thank you. I'd very much appreciate a map."

Jack spread his hands as if to say, *What can a fellow do? I warned you.* "All right, ma'am. I'll show you how to get there."

"And I'll need to know where I can hire a horse. Um . . . I mean two horses, of course. For myself and my husband."

* * *

Rachel's grip on the reins was so tight the mare was unsure whether to move forward or back up. Rachel was determined to see this thing through, but she was more afraid than she'd admit, and she was mad as a wet cat that after all they'd gone through together, Peter wasn't with her now. She didn't even know where he was this afternoon, even if she'd felt like asking him to accompany her. He had stormed off in one direction, and she had stormed in the other, and she was not about to go searching for him. He'd treated her like a willful child, as if she'd dragged him across the continent on a lark. He had no idea of the turmoil she was in. If all went well and she didn't get lost but found this mine and the fellows working it, she would know about her father. She could hardly believe the uncertainty was almost over. But there was a growing knot in the pit of her stomach, a voice in the back of her mind that whispered, *You know the answer already.*

She tried to push the voice away as she had so many times before, but it was growing more insistent. *Face the truth*, it said. From Mattie's account, it sounded as if her father's letters had stopped at the same time he had abruptly left Washed-Out Creek, leaving his mine and Mattie without a word or explanation. While Rachel realized miners moved from place to place looking for the object of their desires, she didn't think her father would have done so without telling *someone*. After all, when he had moved from the Henderson to Washed-Out Creek, he had written to tell her so. But if he hadn't sent word to her and hadn't so much as said good-bye to Mattie . . . Rachel feared she was not going to find a happy ending.

She tried to ease her grip on the reins and relax her shoulders. The air was cold with the nip of snow coming, a different sort of taste than she'd experienced back east. There was the oily scent of the pines, and the rocky scenery around her was lovely but remote, and she felt no interest in it. She felt very alone and far from home. She took deep breaths of the chilled air and let the rhythmic rocking of the horse beneath her lull her gradually into a less anxious mood. She thought about what Lizzie Myers would have done in her situation. She wouldn't retreat or resort to tears; she would go determinedly on and face whatever lay ahead. And she would pray.

Rachel still wasn't sure about the God Lizzie prayed to, but she knew Lizzie believed, so Rachel sent a prayer skyward, hoping He would hear her for Lizzie's friendship's sake. She had expected to plead that God would lead her to her father and that she would find him whole and healthy. But instead she was surprised to hear the words that came out of her mouth. "Make me strong enough to cope with whatever I find."

After what seemed like hours, when she was starting to worry she had missed the landmarks Jack Wylie had outlined for her, she saw a streak of darkness on the hillside, a dirty black scar in the earth. A narrow track was beaten up to it, zigzagging across the face of the hill. Heaps of crumbled rock and soil were piled aside, and a funny thing that looked like a child's wooden slide was erected beside them, running down the hill. The sluice, Mr. Wylie had called it, and she knew she was in the right place at last. She could hear the distant thrum of motion and noise far away, the trickle of water, and with a feeling of self-congratulation, she rode closer.

As she watched, two figures came out of the little wooden shanty built over the mouth of the mine. They were pushing a metal cart heaped with dirt. One man balanced a pick over his shoulder; the other straightened and stood with hands on hips, watching her approach. They were filthy and bearded, taller even than Peter, and Rachel felt a vague foreboding. She reined in the horse but made no attempt to dismount.

"Good afternoon," she called. "Am I right in thinking this is the Cracker Jack?"

The man with the pick spat on the ground. "That's right."

"Are you the Harringer brothers?"

They exchanged glances, and the second one said, "Two of 'em."

"Are you the same gentlemen who operated the Magnolia?" She pointed back the way she had come.

A third man came out of the mine, scruffier-looking than the first two and taller. He spat too. "Why?"

"If you are, I want to talk to you." She took a deep breath and dismounted as gracefully as she could, thanking her stars that her skirt didn't ride up as she slid off. She shook out her skirt and approached, leading the horse behind her. The three men came down the path to meet her, and the first man set down his pick and seized the mare's bridle.

"I wouldn't mind talking to you," he drawled and laughed.

The third man jabbed him in the ribs to silence him. Rachel decided he was the leader.

"Maybe we are, and maybe we aren't," he said. "What do you want to talk about?"

Rachel glanced around the empty valley, the bare rock ridges, the looming dark pines. The sun would set soon. There was no one else for miles, and she knew she had made a serious mistake in coming alone. There was nothing for it though. Peter had left her with no alternative. She raised her chin.

"The Magnolia, the one that flooded."

"What about it?" the leader said.

"It used to be called the Happy Scot."

Pickaxe shrugged. The others didn't move.

"You acquired it about three years ago," Rachel went on doggedly.

The leader spat again. "Don't remember," he said. His tobacco juice lay in a glistening glob in the dirt, and Rachel felt her throat closing in.

"The man you got it from . . ." she said, but her voice was hoarse, and she had to stop to clear her throat.

"City feller, I recall," the second man said. "All talk and no action."

The leader grinned to reveal yellow teeth like a horse's. "What you come out here for, asking questions, honey? You're a long way from town."

Rachel stepped backward. "I am looking for the man who owned the Happy Scot. I want to know where he went."

"Oh, he's long gone," the leader said, grinning. He reached out and smoothed his hand along the mare's neck.

"Gone?" Rachel said. Something in her chest flipped over. "Where did—"

"Left town."

"Le—?"

Pickaxe looked surprised, glanced at the leader, and then stammered, "Uh, yeah. That's right."

"Shut up. She was talking to me," the leader said.

"I saw her first," Pickaxe muttered, scowling now. "You was still inside when she come."

"Was not," the second man said. "He was right behind me."

The leader pushed past the other two men and took Rachel's wrist in a tight hold. His fingers were rough and dirty, and she couldn't help pulling away with a squeal. Her mare tossed her head at the sound and tugged against Pickaxe's grip on the bridle. He yanked the horse down with a curse.

"That will do."

The voice rang out behind them. All four turned to see Peter astride a lathered mare, rifle poised across his thighs. A few feet behind him, Jack Wylie sat on his own horse, his pistol in his hand.

"I'll thank you to let go of that young lady and her horse," Peter said evenly.

The leader grinned, releasing Rachel and spreading his hands wide.

"Now, mister, no harm done. We thought this little lady was alone out here in the mountains, and we was just helping her along."

Pickaxe hadn't let go of the bridle. His face flushed red above his beard. "What's she to you?" he demanded.

Peter glanced at Rachel, expressionless. "Nothing," he said, "but I don't like to see a woman mishandled. Or a horse."

Jack Wylie looked a little surprised but kept his mouth shut.

Rachel's fear switched instantly to fury. She was nothing to him, was she? How dare he? She resented being seen as a female who couldn't carry out her own business by herself. She resented having been followed. And most of all, she resented the relief that coursed through her at seeing Peter. "I can manage this," she called.

"I can see you can," Peter replied wryly. "I just came out to ask some questions of these gentlemen, and then I'll leave you to them. Are you the men who operated the Magnolia?"

"I said I—" Rachel began, but a sharp look from him stilled her tongue. Jack Wylie had obviously told him everything. Peter must have a course of action he was pursuing, and he wouldn't appreciate her interference in it, that much was plain.

"Who's asking?" the leader demanded.

"Name's William Mitchell. I might be interested in buying it off you."

The looks on the three men's faces changed visibly. Number two wiped his palms on his filthy pants and nudged Pickaxe.

"You do still own it, don't you?" Peter added.

"Yeah."

"Might be we can do some business, then."

The three brothers gave each other considering looks.

"I know you, don't I?" the leader asked Jack.

"Jack Wylie. Most people 'round here know me," Jack replied.

"You know this feller?"

"Can't say that I do," Jack said honestly. "He just come into town the other day, staying at the hotel. He's from back east somewhere. Offered me five dollars to show him how to get to the Cracker Jack. That's my only interest in all this."

The leader transferred his suspicious gaze back to Peter. "You say this lady's nothing to you, but you both come out here at the same time asking about the Magnolia?" he said.

Rachel glanced from Peter to the brothers, sensing their doubt and skepticism, their withdrawal, and quickly she interjected, "Don't listen to him. *I'm* here to buy the Magnolia from you. I was here first; you have to deal with me."

"Don't have to deal with either one of you," the leader said. But she saw the interest perking in his eyes. Two potential buyers might start a bidding war. She could see him sizing up the opportunity to make significant money. "Why are you interested?" He directed the question to Peter.

"It's just a flooded shaft," Pickaxe said.

The leader shot him a nasty look and hissed between his teeth, and Rachel tried to hide her smile. Yes, he was definitely keen.

"I heard," Peter said, waving a hand vaguely. "Can it be salvaged?"

Another wordless communication was exchanged between the brothers.

"Could be. Anything is possible for the right price," the leader drawled. "We just never had the capital to pump it out."

"Were you the first to stake the claim?" Peter asked mildly.

"Second. Feller before us got a bit of a start made, but we're the ones who extended the tunnel half a mile back and put in air shafts. Put in iron rails too, but it's all under water now. Cost us a pretty penny to do it. But there's gold down there," he added quickly. "We know it."

"Maybe I can get back your investment for you," Peter said.

"Maybe." The Harringers exchanged grins.

Peter framed his next questions carefully, with an uncaring air, not looking at Rachel. "What happened to the first fellow? The one who owned it before you? Any particular reason he didn't stick it out?"

"He was a city feller from back east, didn't know what he was getting into. All grand talk about how he was going to find a big vein and strike it rich." The leader spat again.

"Man didn't know when to keep his mouth shut," Pickaxe said.

The others laughed.

"We listened to all his boasting and thought maybe he was onto something though. Some promising-looking dirt. So we bought the place off him."

"You bought it?"

"Well, in a manner of speaking. He signed it over to us right before he died," the leader said with a curl of his lip.

"Might say it was lucky timing," the second man added with a chuckle.

"We worked it for a couple of years and didn't get a—" He caught himself. This was a potential buyer he was addressing. He abruptly changed tune. "'Course the old man died before he could tell us just which direction to tunnel in, so it ain't nobody's fault we didn't locate the big vein. Oh, plenty of smaller ones, sure. No problem there. But the mother lode is still down there waiting, and I guess only that old feller knew where. Who knows? Just because we didn't find it doesn't mean you won't."

"Of course. I understand it's a gamble," Peter said smoothly. He ignored Rachel, who stood silent, swaying slightly.

"No reason to think it was empty talk, no, sir," the leader assured him. "He was certain there was a fortune in that mine, and as I said, before it flooded, we did find some promising color."

"I did think he always dressed awful well," Pickaxe added. "Always had plenty of money to stand drinks."

"That's true. Did seem an honest old man."

Rachel took one step forward. There was a rushing sound in her ears, and she couldn't seem to focus her vision. Peter touched his heels to his horse and moved casually alongside her, blocking her from moving toward the men. She gave a low whimper that only he could have heard. Sweat started to form on his upper lip as he nodded at the men.

"I certainly think we can talk business," he said. "I can put up the capital to pump the mine out. I'm proposing a partnership with you gentlemen. I don't know much about mining"—he saw the brothers exchange pleased looks—"but I'm sure you can handle the practical end, and I'll handle the financial end. We'll make a good team. You interested?"

The leader eyed Rachel. "Well, now, seems she was here first. Seems only fair to hear her out if she's interested in making an offer."

Rachel shook her head mutely, and Peter leaned forward intently in his saddle, keeping his eyes on the man's so as to keep his attention off of Rachel.

"I'm pretty confident she won't have the kind of capital I can raise," he said. "Don't know that you'd prefer a young lady as a partner anyway, telling you how to do your business, would you? Like I said, I'll leave the decision-making and mining work to you and won't interfere. I just want a cut of the proceeds."

They didn't even have to consult each other. They all agreed.

Peter turned to Rachel and tipped his hat. "Thank you for being gracious about this, ma'am. I don't like to cut out a competitor as pretty as you, but you know it's only business, not personal."

Rachel shook her head again, unable to trust her voice.

Jack Wylie cleared his throat. "It's a cold day to be out," he said, his drawl casual. "Can I escort you back to town, miss?"

Peter turned back to the leader. "What say we all meet at the hotel in Washed-Out Creek tomorrow night for supper and talk it over?"

"All right, man, you can be sure we'll be there."

Peter reached down and took Rachel's horse's bridle from Harringer. "Climb on," he said quietly, firmly, and Rachel did so with some effort.

"See you tomorrow, boys."

They rode off, leaving three grinning men spitting on the ground and congratulating each other.

"Of all the idiotic things to do, girl," Peter muttered when they were out of earshot.

"As I said, it's my fault for telling her where the Cracker Jack was," Jack said. "She said—I honestly didn't think she'd go running out here by herself without you."

Rachel didn't respond. The horses got only as far as the other side of the next knoll before she pulled her mare to a stop. "I have to get down."

They halted, and she slid to the ground, where she fell to her knees and was immediately and violently sick. She felt she would bring up her whole insides. Over and over in her head, she heard, *The old man died before he could tell us* . . . She saw the leering grins, the flying spittle, and retched again. She'd come so far; she'd been so close. Richard had been right. Their father was gone, and there was nothing more she could do.

Peter dismounted, and when at last Rachel had exhausted herself, he helped her sit under a nearby tree, her back against it.

"Sorry," she whispered, laying her head back with her eyes closed. "I seem to get sick whenever I'm upset . . . It's something I never knew about myself before this trip."

"You likely didn't have much to be upset over before this trip." Peter squatted before her, peering anxiously into her face. "I'm so sorry, Rachel."

"He's dead."

"Yes." His voice was gentle.

"He's been dead for three years."

"I know." His fingers brushed the hair from her cheek in a tender gesture. The animosity that had flared between them was gone. He slipped his hand behind her neck, massaging gently.

"I really thought I'd find him. I thought my brother suspected he was still alive and I'd find him."

"I know."

"I came all this way!" she wailed.

Jack Wylie dismounted and came to crouch heavily beside them. "I'm not sure what all is going on," he said, "or why your name is suddenly Rachel instead of Mary, but I can see you've lost someone, and I'm mightily sorry."

"Thank you," Rachel said. "My . . . my father."

"Ah. The one who owned the Magnolia . . . the Happy Scot."

"Yes." She put her hand on his wrist. Through her tears and exhaustion, she saw the compassion in his face and felt a rush of gratitude toward him. "Thank you for bringing Peter—I mean William . . ."

Jack and Peter looked at each other. Jack rubbed his nose. "I'm not going to ask."

Rachel turned to Peter, wiping at the tears on her cheeks. "Do you think they really bought the Happy Scot?"

"They said so," he said slowly.

"More likely they killed him and took the mine," Rachel cried, drained. "Father never could keep quiet when he was excited about something. We always knew what our Christmas presents were a week beforehand. If he really thought there was gold in that mine, he would have talked too much about it."

"It's their own bad luck they jumped the gun and didn't get the details before . . . Well, it serves them right," Peter said.

"Do you think there's really gold down there?" Her hands were trembling in her lap.

Peter covered them with his hands and held them still. "I don't know. It doesn't matter. Those three couldn't find it anyway if there was."

"Something must have gotten my father's hopes up."

"As they said . . . the right color dirt, a smaller vein maybe. It doesn't mean there's a payload. We'll never know. I'm certainly not going to take up mining, and I don't have the money to pump the mine out if I were."

"I'm glad the place flooded before they could profit from it," Rachel said.

"Wait," Jack said, trying to catch up with the conversation. "You aren't planning to invest in their mine?"

"Of course not. I just wanted information from them about her father."

"But they're expecting to meet you at the hotel tomorrow night."

"You can bet by tomorrow night we'll be as far from Washed-Out Creek as we can get."

There was a cold wind coming from the direction of the river, pushing the gathering black clouds, and the air tasted of the coming snow. Rachel tipped her head back, looking up at the sky, letting the wind slap her cheeks pink.

"Storm coming in," Jack pronounced, looking up as well. "Look at them clouds."

"They're going to go free," Rachel said angrily. "Justice won't ever be done."

Peter bit his lips together at the flatness of her voice. He leaned forward, staring hard into her eyes, forcing her to look at him.

"You have no proof of what they did, no matter how sure you may be in your heart."

"They killed my father!"

"Don't start a battle you can't win, Rachel. Take it from me. Railing against the unfairness of life gets you nowhere but lost."

Seeing the pain in his eyes, she knew he spoke the truth. He knew from experience the futility of it. Bitterness would bring her heart only isolation, not comfort. She nodded and took a shaky breath. "I know," she said reluctantly.

"Better?" he asked.

"No. But I will be. Thank you," she whispered.

Without thinking about it, she reached to put her hand softly against his hard jaw. Peter turned his head and brushed her palm with his lips. Then he took her hand to help her up, molding his palm over hers and sealing the spot where his lips had touched.

"Let's go," he said quietly.

He helped her up onto her mare and then surprised her by swinging up behind her. He wrapped his arms around her, leaning her back against his chest, and they moved slowly back toward Washed-Out Creek with Jack leading Peter's horse behind them.

Chapter Twenty-Six

THE NEXT MORNING, RACHEL AWOKE feeling lead-headed from a night of weeping, but her soul felt somewhat lighter. She had an answered, at least. She could go home knowing her father's fate.

Home. Richard. Philip. The weight returned to her heart. The idea of going back to Toronto brought her no comfort. Even the idea of having her maid back brought only irritation. No, she didn't want to go back there.

Peter had given Tepperman another dollar for the room last night, but he had gone out to his own camp to sleep. She expected to find him in the dining room this morning, but he wasn't there. Dully she ate breakfast without looking up, not tasting the food, not speaking to anyone. The other occupants of the dining room observed her red-rimmed eyes and tactfully avoided her.

All except Jack Wylie. He sidled over, carrying his plate of greasy sausage and flapjacks, and plopped himself down beside her on the bench.

"Morning, Mrs. Mitchell. I'm glad to see you looking better."

She thought it was a kind lie. She knew she looked horrible and puffy-faced. "Good morning, Mr. Wylie."

"Jack," he said.

"Have you seen Pe—William this morning?" She reminded herself to focus. Her weariness and sorrow were making her careless. But then, did their ruse really matter now?

"I reckon he's still out at the Cracker Jack, ma'am. The men are taking it in shifts. I'll be going back out there myself once I've had something to eat and get a fresh horse."

Rachel frowned. Her brain felt like fuzzy wool. "What are you talking about, Mr. Wylie?"

"Well, don't tell me you haven't heard!"

"Heard what?"

"There was a cave-in at the Cracker Jack yesterday evening. Whole central tunnel just collapsed. Happened not two hours after we left there."

Rachel froze. "What?" Her voice came out as a squawk.

"Old Ev was passing by and brought the news. You must have been asleep and missed all the excitement. Rescue team has been working all night, your husband with them, but it's sure as shootin' no one's coming out of that tunnel alive. Nobody knows what caused it. Misset fuse, most likely. The Harringers always were fools with explosives . . . and I wouldn't be surprised if they'd been drinking after we left, in celebration. Anticipating getting money out of your husband, I mean. Not a wise combination, rot-gut and dynamite."

She didn't know what to say. Mr. Wylie leaned close, spraying bits of flapjack as he whispered, "I'd have felt bad if you'd been out there when it happened. It was quite a coincidence, the tunnel collapsing like that when it did."

"Yes. I—Thank you." Rachel jumped to her feet and fled back to her room, leaving her breakfast half finished. Her head swam in confusion, and her heart felt as if it would pound its way out of her chest. In her mind, she kept seeing the three Harringer brothers, their crooked teeth, their filthy faces.

She was lying on the narrow bed, staring out the window at nothing, when a tap sounded at the door. Peter poked his head in. His lean face was drawn, his eyes red-rimmed and serious. His skin was pink as if he'd scrubbed it too hard. "May I come in?"

She sat up, and he closed the door behind him and sat on the edge of the bed. She just looked at him.

"Are you all right?" His voice was gentle.

"I'll get better with time." She paused. "Are you?"

He gave a lopsided shrug. "I've been better. You heard what happened?"

"Mr. Wylie told me this morning."

"I didn't want to wake you to tell you last night."

"Peter, what about what you said to me yesterday? All that about railing against the unfairness of life? Letting go?"

He let out a long breath. "Sometimes life has a way of leveling things out." He studied her a moment as if he'd just noticed something in her face, and then he leaned forward and said firmly, "I didn't set the explosives, Rachel, if that's what you're thinking. Is that what you thought?"

"I . . . well, what else can I think? That it's a coincidence? It happened right after we were there talking to them. Right after we found out . . ." She stuttered to a halt.

"I've been trying to dig them out half the night." Peter scowled.

"Of course. Every man is taking a turn," Rachel said. "How would it look if you didn't?"

Peter's face turned a deep scarlet, and he stood. "Is that really what you think of me? You think I'd kill those men?"

She looked up into his face, studying his expression, and felt a deep shame spread over her. She thought of how he had gently cared for the deserter all night, the way he had treated Shorty so kindly. His compassion toward her. Her stomach sank. "No," she said in a low voice. "I know you wouldn't. I'm sorry."

Peter stood a moment, looking down at his feet, hands on his hips, and then he sighed and sat down again. After a moment, Rachel asked quietly, "Do you know if they were in the mine when it collapsed?"

"We're assuming, because no one has seen them since. If they weren't caught in the actual fall, they're behind it, and by the time they move all those tons of dirt and rock, it'll be too late."

Rachel felt a wave of nausea and covered her face. "It's too awful. I can't help admitting I'm glad they're gone. I wanted them to suffer, to go to prison for what they did . . . what I *think* they did. But I didn't want this to happen."

He took her hands in his and gave them a squeeze.

"Doesn't pay to think about it too much," he said. "It's over, and whatever justice needed doing has been done. I'm going to go find something to eat, and then I'm riding back out. I just wanted to see you."

She watched him go, and when he reached the door, she said his name. He looked back at her.

"I'm glad it wasn't you. I'm sorry I thought it was."

"I haven't lived a perfect life, Rachel, but there are some things I wouldn't do, not even for you. Just about anything else, but not that." He went out.

Rachel sat on the edge of the bed with her arms hugging her ribs as she rocked slowly back and forth. She felt as if she'd been dragged behind a horse, every bit of her exhausted and sad. She wished for the comfort of the strong women she had met on her journey, wished Lizzie was there to give her a hug.

Lizzie. She had said something just the other day about how someone might be separated from their loved ones but that it didn't have to be forever. Rachel thought maybe Lizzie had been talking about being together again in heaven. She wasn't sure what she believed on that score, but she knew Lizzie had a deep faith in her belief. Rachel clung to that notion, and she found herself once again whispering a fervent prayer. *Please let Lizzie be right. Please let me see my father again. Even if it means I have to wait a while longer.*

After a time, the sorrow and ache eased a little, and Rachel felt a comforting warmth come over her, almost as if she was getting that hug she desperately wanted from Lizzie. She savored the feeling and started to dare to think that maybe she really would be all right one day. It hurt, but she thought maybe it wasn't an unbearable hurt.

And then she remembered she wasn't the only one hurting. Rachel stood, washed her face in the cracked china wash basin, and pulled herself together. She had a visit to make. There was someone who deserved to know the truth about Hamish Hamilton.

* * *

This time she knocked on the red door. A slender girl in a blue silk dress, who looked just older than Rachel, opened it. For a moment, Rachel was so astonished to see the bright, clean color of the fabric before her, so incongruous in its drab surroundings, that she forgot why she was there.

"Yes?" the girl prompted.

"Oh! Sorry. Is Mattie Albright in, please?"

The girl showed Rachel into the parlor, and a few minutes later, Mattie entered. She wore a steel gray dress today, formidably circumspect with a tight collar and no lace or frills. When she saw Rachel, she seemed to hesitate in the doorway. Her shoulders slumped in defeat, and she went to a sideboard and poured herself a brandy. She swallowed it in one slug before she turned back to Rachel.

"That didn't take long," she said dully. "Is the militia right behind you?"

Rachel stared at her, mouth frozen half open to speak. She noted Mattie's pale cheeks, the trembling in her rouged lips, and slowly, unbelievably, the truth dawned on her. Mattie poured another drink and dropped into a chair. Rachel lowered herself slowly onto the sofa opposite. "You?" She finally found her voice. "It was *you*?"

Mattie stared at her. Horror passed over her face, leaving it white. "You mean that's not why you came? You didn't know . . ."

Rachel quickly leaned forward to take Mattie's hand. "No. I was only going to tell you what I'd learned. I—it *was* you?"

Mattie gave her a wry smile. "I've lived in mining towns most of my life. You get to know a thing or two about explosives." She held her cool drink against her forehead and closed her eyes. "After you left yesterday, I thought and thought about it.

And I knew it had to be those San Francisco men who were responsible for Hamish disappearing. All these years I thought he'd just moved on without a thought for me. Woman like me, I should be used to men not saying good-bye. But then when you said he hadn't been in touch with his own family either . . ."

Rachel shook her head mutely, her throat too tight to speak. She squeezed Mattie's hands.

"It's not as if we ever have real relationships; I know that," Mattie went on. "But Hamish, he was different. He was something special. He treated me like I was a person." She opened her eyes. "Like you do." Tears began to spill down her cheeks, forming tracks in the heavy powder on her face. "He didn't leave without saying good-bye, did he?"

"No, he didn't." Rachel knelt on the floor and put her arms around the older woman. For a long time, they cried together.

"You *are* a person, Mrs. Albright," Rachel said finally. "And I'm glad my father had you for a friend."

"Call me Mattie," Mattie said, swiping at her cheeks with the back of her fingers.

"Mattie," Rachel said warmly, smiling. One more thing Richard wouldn't have approved of. She kissed Mattie on the cheek. "But what are we going to do?"

Mattie rubbed her eyes, smudging them. "I don't know. No one in this town liked those Harringers. And I doubt there's a marshal within a hundred miles of here. If you don't say anything . . ."

"But, Mattie, how can I not?" Rachel cried. "You've confessed it. It was murder."

Mattie pulled away from her and, standing, went to look out the window at the street. "I confessed to blowing the place up. I could say I didn't know there were people inside at the time. It was late evening. Most people are at the saloon or at supper by then."

"Do you think a jury would believe you?"

Mattie spun to look at Rachel, her eyes wide and her face even paler, if that was possible. "A jury? Are you turning me in?"

"I don't know what to do," Rachel wailed. "I understand why you did it, and I'm ashamed to say I can't even truthfully be sorry you did, but—No, that's not true." She realized that at some point during her night of tears, she had let go of the wish for revenge. She took a shaky breath, feeling her soul lighten even more at that realization. "I *do* wish you hadn't done it, especially since you can't know for certain that they were guilty. It was wrong."

Mattie stood staring a minute, then turned back to the window and put her hands to her face.

"It's not as if I'm famous in this town for doing *right*!" she muttered in a strangled voice.

"You need to turn yourself in."

Mattie gave a barking laugh. "What world are you from, honey? That is not going to happen."

Rachel rubbed her own cheeks, trying hard to convince herself that she needn't act. She had wanted justice for the Harringers. Now she didn't want it for Mattie. Mattie would go to prison, maybe even hang. But Rachel couldn't deny what she knew. Was it enough to tell the truth only if asked? Or did she have to speak first? She was afraid she knew the answer to that.

Mattie seemed to sense this because she turned to face her then and said quietly, "I could stop you from telling anyone, you know."

"I know you could," Rachel said simply, surprised to find she wasn't afraid. "But you won't. There are the girls upstairs, for one thing. They would be witnesses. Would you silence them too? Where would it all end, Mattie?"

"I did it for Hamish. Doesn't that mean anything to you?"

"Then you wouldn't turn around and hurt his daughter, would you? Not if you loved him the way I think you did."

Mattie shook her head, drawing herself up and blinking back the tears. "I did love him. Enough to see that his killers got justice. They never would have gotten it otherwise, not in this place."

"I think you didn't do it for justice for my father." Rachel sighed. "You did it for yourself because you were hurting. You took the law into your own hands."

"And 'vengeance is mine . . . saith the Lord.' Is that it?" Mattie said scornfully.

"Something like that," Rachel said sadly.

"How can you forgive them for what they did?" Mattie protested.

"I can't, at least not yet. It's too much to ask and too soon. I don't know if I'll ever be able to really let go of that, but I hope one day I can," Rachel said quietly. "I don't want to live with hate in my heart. And I hope you don't either."

"I'll hate you if you say anything!" Mattie cried. As Rachel turned toward the door, she added desperately, "At least give me a head start."

Rachel looked back at her, feeling her heart breaking. "I'm sorry," she said.

* * *

Mattie had been right; there were no marshals within a hundred miles of Washed-Out Creek. But Jack Wylie was as close to law as the town had, so, astonished and dismayed, he took Mattie Albright into custody, and John Tepperman offered one of his hotel rooms as a holding cell until such time as the proper authority could be located.

Rachel didn't want to see Mattie being taken in, so she borrowed a horse again from the man who had lent her one the day before and rode out to the Cracker Jack. It was after noon, and she met a few men riding back from the mine who brought the worrisome report that there had been a secondary collapse. Rachel didn't know what she would do if anything happened to Peter. She spurred her horse into a canter.

The place had been transformed overnight, and there was no risk of overlooking the location this time. The long grass had been trampled to mud, the heaps of rock and dirt had been moved farther from the mine entrance and added to, and men and horses milled around the site in organized chaos. Everywhere, there were men with buckets, pickaxes, and shovels. These were miners, hard-bitten and overworked and most of them down on their luck, but the disaster had united them in the desperate attempt to save their fellow miners. Rachel didn't have to ask if there had been any success; their defeat and weariness were plain on their bleak faces.

The sun had reached its zenith and was slipping down the sky, and a bitterly cold wind came down the canyon with the sound of a freight train, bringing with it the first few flakes of the snow that had held off this long. Rachel huddled within her inadequate but lovely shawl and crept as close to the mine entrance as she dared without getting in the way of the working men.

As she watched, several men came staggering out of the tunnel and sank to the ground on their hands and knees, coughing. As the other men hurried toward them, they shook their heads, and she heard one of them say, "That does it. There's no sense going on after that last rock fall. There's nothing left of them by now."

"The mine isn't worth salvaging," someone else said. "They never did get more than a few dollars a month out of it."

"Them Harringers never did have no luck," the first man added. "And nobody'll care if they get a decent burial or not."

"Shouldn't say such a thing, Dan."

"It's true. We're all thinking it. I'm just saying what we're all thinking."

The crowd shifted, and Rachel saw with a lurch in her chest that Peter was one of the men kneeling on the ground. He was gray with dust, and she watched him spit mud from his mouth. He rolled onto his back on the crushed grass and looked up at the harsh white sky, making no attempt to brush away the light flakes of snow that landed on his upturned face. Rachel pushed her way toward him through the mass of men and dropped to her knees beside him.

"Breathe," she told him.

Peter turned his head to look at her in surprise, and then he sank back and closed his eyes in exhaustion. "What are you doing here?"

"I guess I came to take you home," she said.

"Home." He half smiled. "Where is that, exactly?"

She nearly said, *With me.* Instead she pulled his arm and helped him sit up.

"There's no point in digging," he said. "We all know it, but no one wants to be the first to give up."

Rachel hadn't known if she would feel relieved or sad, but now, looking at the exhausted men and the gaping entrance of the mine, she felt only sorrow. "Mattie Albright has been arrested for setting off the charges," she said.

Peter started and looked at her in astonishment.

"The—I mean, from the brothel? She blew the tunnel on purpose?"

"Yes. She loved my father."

Peter wiped his hands over his face. "I know you said your father liked her."

"I liked her too. She confessed it to me. I . . . I turned her in."

He looked at her a moment in stillness, then put a dirty hand on hers. "I'm sorry. That must have been a difficult choice."

"I couldn't do anything else," she said quietly.

Peter stood and trudged to his horse, where it waited patiently with a knot of others. Wordlessly he untied it and mounted. The other men glanced at him, turned away, then avoided each other's eyes as they began to move toward their own mounts. Rachel retrieved her mare and fell in beside Peter, heading back toward Washed-Out Creek. The snow thickened, already softening the unevenness of the trail.

"So that ends that," Peter said after a long silence.

"Yes."

"You're only given so much of this fragile life to live, and if it runs out like water through a sieve before you're done with it, well, that's that. There's no calling it back."

"No."

He rubbed his sleeve across his face. "I feel like I've been buried alive myself."

"You can have another bath when we get back to the hotel." Rachel tried not to think about Mattie sitting alone in one of the hotel rooms, awaiting whatever lay ahead of her. "We still have the room for the rest of today."

"That sounds so good," he agreed. He glanced down at himself. "My poor clothes will never be the same."

Rachel looked down at her own tattered state and didn't speak, only pulled the shawl tighter under her chin.

* * *

Rachel went to sit in the dining room while Peter scrubbed in the tin hip bath. Mr. Tepperman had stoked the iron stove high against the descending cold, but the winter air still seeped through the gaps in the wallboards and up through the floor. Her feet were cold, and she thought about having another bath herself just to warm up.

Peter entered the room, then, and she forgot all about being cold. His hair was slicked down, his clean skin was aglow with warmth, and he'd beaten the worst of the dirt from his clothes. His eyes found hers, and he came to sit beside her. There were other men beginning to gather for supper, but they were at the far end of the long table, talking in a low murmur, and she and Peter had a little privacy.

Peter concentrated on trying to remove some dirt he'd missed under his fingernails for a few minutes, and then abruptly he said, "What I said earlier, about not being able to hold on to life . . ."

"Yes?" Rachel prompted.

"Well, any intelligent being would make the most of what he had left every day."

"Yes, that's reasonable."

He paused, and then he asked abruptly, "What will you do now?"

Rachel was watching the kitchen doorway. "Well, have supper, I suppose. Isn't that why we're—"

"You know that's not what I meant. I didn't mean right *now*. I mean after this. Do you want to go back to Toronto?"

"No," Rachel said flatly. "There's nothing for me there. And as I said, I sincerely can't imagine turning around and traveling all that distance back again."

"Do you want to train as a nurse?"

"Maybe. I don't really know. I think it would be a wonderful thing to do, but I don't think I have the stomach for it, to be honest."

Peter looked away out the window. The sun was sinking behind the saloon across the way, obscured by thick flying snow. They were in for a blizzard. They could hear horses in the road going past quickly as people sought shelter. Somewhere two men were shouting at each other. A door slammed, and there was a crash of pots and pans in the kitchen. Then quiet.

"I've been thinking all day while I was in that mine," Peter said, turning back to her. "I wondered how you'd fancy going to Briarton."

"Briarton!" It wasn't what she'd expected him to say.

"I'm sure Lizzie'd still like you for a neighbor."

The idea roused Rachel's interest. It *was* a possibility. Surely there was some need for her there in that young, growing community. She could teach children or . . . well, she was experienced in a dairy, if nothing else. Maybe she could even get a few cows of her own and become a cheesemaker.

"I think I like that idea," Rachel said, plucking at a thread unraveling from her cuff. She made her mouth form the next words, hating the betraying wistfulness in her voice and the way her heart was pounding. "And you? What will you do?"

"I think it's time for me to teach again. I think about standing up in front of a class, the smell of chalk and books, and I like it. It's still in my blood." He shrugged and gave a crooked smile. "Maybe they can put me to good use."

Rachel frowned, puzzled. "Who?"

"The town. The people in Briarton."

"You're coming?" Rachel felt her breath grow still at the thought. He was coming with her. She'd see him . . .

Peter's lips twitched with amusement held in check. The wrinkles at the corners of his eyes deepened. "Someone has to keep an eye on you. You're useless on your own, remember? Mary and William Mitchell made a good team."

Something sank inside her. Rachel shook her head. "I can't be Mary again. I don't want to keep lying to Lizzie. I want to be Rachel Hamilton."

He leaned close, a hand braced on the table.

"No," he murmured. "You'll be Rachel Sinclair. And I'll be Jacob again."

Rachel stared at him, her mouth falling open. Her head felt suddenly foggy, and she struggled to find a coherent reply.

"What do you think of the idea?" he asked quietly. His voice was even and nonchalant, but his eyes sparked with blue fire.

"Do you mean it?" she breathed.

He broke into a grin. "I knew you were a mistake from the first moment I saw you with your head bowed to the ground on that prairie. I should have ridden right on by and left you there. But somehow you've wormed your way into my heart, Rachel Mary Hamilton Cameron Mitchell. I don't want to think about a life without you."

A wonderful glow began deep inside her chest, expanding outward, dispelling the gloom, shining from her eyes. "Oh, Peter—William—Jacob!"

And she threw herself joyfully into his arms, heedless of the staring men around them.

EPILOGUE

DEAR RICHARD—

I am writing to inform you I am all right, and I am making cheese from the milk of my own small herd of dairy cows in a frontier town in the Colony of British Columbia. I am sorry for leaving without a word, but I knew you would not let me go if I told you of my plans. I am sorry to report that I have learned, as you feared, our father died three years ago at the hands of three other miners who are now also deceased. However, I have the pleasure of telling you that before he died, Father drew up a will and left it in the care of a lawyer in Victoria, a Mr. Charles Danforth, who will be contacting you shortly. Apparently Father left his business concerns jointly to both of us to be administered by the board in perpetuity because he knew neither of us had any business sense. The claim to the Happy Scot mine is also filed in Victoria and has been left to me. It is not currently in operation, but if Jacob and I ever decide to mine it, I will be happy to share the proceeds with you of anything we find. We have not been the best of friends, you and I, as siblings ought to be, but neither do I regard you as an enemy. I do wish you well in your life, Richard, and hope you will do the same for me.

Which leads me to the last part of my news. I have married. His name is Jacob Sinclair, and he is a professor of languages, though right now he is teaching children at the local grammar school. Please express my polite regrets to Mr. Wycott, if indeed he even remembers me. He can soften any disappointment with the knowledge that I am happy and most content.

If you need to reach me, you may write to me in care of Mr. Danforth.

Best wishes from your sister,
Rachel Sinclair

About the Author

Kristen Garner McKendry began writing in her teens, and her work has been published in both Canada and the U.S. She received a Mississauga Arts Council MARTY Award in Established Literary Arts in 2012, and her book *Garden Plot* was nominated in 2011 for a Whitney Award for excellence in LDS literature.

Kristen received a bachelor's degree in linguistics from Brigham Young University and has always been a voracious reader. She has a strong interest in urban agriculture and environmental issues. She enjoys playing the bagpipes, learning obscure languages, growing wheat in the backyard, and making cheese. A native of Utah and mother of three, she now resides with her family in Canada. The idea for this story came while she was reading about adventurers in the Yukon and British Columbia and wishing she could go join them.

For more information about Kristen and her books, check out her website at www.kristenmckendry.webs.com, where you will also find a link to her blog, *My Daily Slog Blog*.